NETWORK OF KILLERS

D. B. REYNOLDS

This book is a work of fiction. The names, characters, places, and incidents are the results of the author's sole imagination or are used fictitiously. Any resemblance to actual events, locales, or persons, living or dead, is purely coincidental.

Copyright © 2011 by D. B. Reynolds

All rights reserved. Except as permitted under the U.S. Copyright act of 1976, no part of this publication may be reproduced, distributed, or transmitted in any form or by any means, or stored in a database or retrieval system, without the prior written permission of the author or publisher.

For more information on this book, visit the Web site at: www.d.b.reynolds.com, or at www.amazon.com and www.createspace.com

First edition: August 2011

Library of Congress Cataloging-in-Publication Data

Reynolds, D. B.

"An FBI agent knew little. A criminal dynasty knew enough. But, the witnesses knew too much". _____Provided by the Author.

ISBN-13: 978-1463780609

ISBN-10: 1463780605

For Anthony Civella

Acknowledgements

Many thanks to the select few who stayed in the race with me. The journey in arriving at this point was long and tedious, but I wouldn't have traded it for anything. A sincere thanks to Mr. William Ouseley for his expertise and insight into the history of organized crime in Kansas City.

A Note from the Author

While growing up in Kansas City, Missouri as a youngster, I recall the times when my two foster brothers and I would sneak away from our disenfranchised foster home. The three of us ended up at the north end of the city, in a section of town called the *River Quay*. A group of Italian and Sicilian men would hire us to unload several fruit and vegetable trucks. We would sometimes work 10 hours, often getting paid $10.00 dollars. Boy, we were happy to get that $10.00 dollars! But, what my foster brothers and I weren't aware of, is that a serious Mafia war would soon escalate in the *River Quay*.

We reported the following week to our pending work assignment, only to see a series of buildings that were practically blown to confetti. Rival Mafiosos had blown away the businesses of one another in the *River Quay*. Well, that ended our secretive money-making venture, in which our foster mother never knew where we'd go for many hours on the weekends. To this day, I look back and find it amazing how we had worked in the shadow of powerful organized crime figures. It's been said that everyone has a story to tell. I decided to pull a chapter out Kansas City history and tell a story about the legendary *River Quay*, a story about the Mafia, the FBI, and the Teamsters Union. The elements of love, sex, betrayal, corruption, and murder have been incorporated to make the story flavorfully spicy.

Chapter 1

FOUR STICKS OF DYNAMITE fizzled underneath a solid building structure. The force of an atrocious blast sent Carlo "The Beast" Binaggio crashing through a thick glass window of his adult movie theater. Severe wounds covering his body left him without an ounce of fluid. A pair of his own detached testicles were blown under a sign advertising feature porno movies. His blood made a splatter on the sidewalk near the demolished X-rated theater. Sinister Mafia plots were hatched throughout Kansas City, Missouri. The year was 1977. A bloodbath ensued within the wake of the city's deep dark inner sanctums. Control for sacred turf ran rapid through the veins of vicious men like raging nitro fuel.

Nineteen Seventy-Seven also became a year when Kansas City Mafia families spoiled for the bloodiest wars in the city's history. Angelo "The Animal" Galluccio wanted the entire River Quay section of the city all for his Mafia family. For sixty-eight years old, Angelo wasn't a bad looking man. He was medium in height, lean in body shape, and fierce in character. He claimed the Kansas City organized crime crown belonged to him. No one could snatch it away from him, not unless they wanted a gruesome war on their hands. The message of terror was quite clear. The *River Quay Wars* were in full effect.

"When the Galluccios spit, the other families drown," Galluccio once bragged to his closest Mafia contemporaries.

With the approval and protection of the Chicago Mafia family, he helped control the multi-billion-dollar Health and Welfare Pension Funds for the Teamsters Union. The Teamsters was their very bloodline.

The bars, strip clubs, restaurants, and vendors, Galluccio wanted every dime made in the River Quay section for himself. Every business paid tribute to his Mafia family. A breezy late Fall night in Kansas City proved to be one of the most violent nights the city had ever experienced. Thugs sent by Galluccio were just getting warmed up. They were in place to plant more dynamite in or around the businesses of disgusting punks who thought they had the juice to challenge the Galluccio Mafia family. None of them would sign their businesses up with the Teamsters Union. Galluccio once boasted, "I own the Teamsters and all of Kansas City, Missouri."

The night first rocked with an explosion of Binaggio's sleazy porn theater. The drunks, whores, tricks, and druggies, they had the time of their lives inside the many bars and strip clubs in the heart of River Quay.

Monty "Dirty Face" Pirelli, a frightening soldier in the Galluccio family with a heavily-scarred face and bullneck, led his group of thugs to a dark side street behind the host of buildings overlooking the *Mighty* Missouri River.

There were a total of six brutal executioners. Each of them had sticks of unlit dynamite curled in their hands. They were ready, willing, and able to do some massive damage. Mass destruction surely followed in their wake.

"Listen up good, men," Pirelli hawked to the other five Mafia killers. "These joints ran by Boriello, Agnello, Marinelli and Rosetti, they're to be blown all over this River Quay area. Since they don't wanna sign up with the Teamsters, then their businesses won't be a part of nothing. Angie gave us the orders to blow these fucking places up until they're nothing but piles of junk. Am I understood, men?"

Displaying great loyalty, the five Mafiosos nodded their heads with approval. When Pirelli spoke, they listened with impunity.

Pirelli sunk his upper teeth into his bottom lip with force. A nasty grimace plastered the meaning of producing fear to his unattractive face. "We've already blown Binaggio and his porno palace to high hell. Too bad the prick decided to stick around after business hours. The fun is just starting, men."

The band of vicious rogues looked to the west end of River Quay. The monstrous blazes ate away at the one-time adult theater.

"Vito, I want you to give Boriello's bar a couple'a sticks," Pirelli instructed. "Understand?"

"Understood, Monty," Vito complied.

"Binaggio was just target practice for us."

"Sort'a like a teaser."

"Tony, I want you to give Agnello's strip joint a couple'a sticks," Pirelli barked in a dictorial fashion. "Understood?"

"Definitely understood, Monty."

"Sal, I want you to give Marinelli's restaurant at least four sticks," Pirelli guided. "That place is humongous, like the size of a tiny football field. It'll take four sticks to bring that joint to the ground. You understand?"

"Definitely, Monty."

"Nino and Pete, I want you two to give Rosetti's strip joints two sticks a piece. You two guys understand?"

"Sure do, Monty," Nino said.

"Certainly, Monty," Pete said.

"After tonight, all these pukebags here in River Quay will know that Angie means business. As for me, four more sticks are going under the car of Leonetti. Angie gave me the orders to blow that sonofabitch straight to fucking hell."

"Got all the wiring you'll need, Monty?" asked Tony.

"I'm the wiring expert. Remember?"

"How can any of us forget?" Vito said.

"If I had my way, I'd shove one of these dynamite sticks up Leonetti's ass, and then watch his bowels shower every inch of this River Quay area."

"Or watch his rectum being blown straight through his goddam throat," Pete added, an even nastier look on his roguish face. "Have'em shitting right out of his mouth."

"The FBI nor the KCPD will know who did what. They won't know what they did it for after they do their pussyfied investigation. And believe me, they will come here in River Quay asking people questions."

"Shutting up those who talk too much. Isn't that what we do best, Monty?"

"Like Angie always told us, when you've got no witnesses, you've got no goddam case."

"We're with ya on that tip, Monty," Nino agreed.

"Alright men, let's move out."

The six Mafia killers wasted no time following the orders of Angelo Galluccio. The bars, strip clubs, restaurants and street vendors had closed for the night. Patrons drifted away from the River Quay area at a gradual tempo. Drunk fools lingered around the parking lot.

Eventually, they cruised onto Main or Broadway streets. Payback for the Kansas City Mafiosos who defied Angelo became pure hell. The six maddog *goombahs* working under Galluccio were ready to make their move. The pungent aroma of Italian sausage and barbecue saturated the air. The smell teased their willing tastebuds.

Cousin Johnny's, a bar ran exclusively by Joseph Boriello, had closed for business until Monday evening. Vito, a loyal soldier of Galluccio, planted two sticks of lit dynamite under the leveled foundation of the building. With quickness, he ran faster than a thief towards an open bank vault.

"So long, Cousin Johnny's!" Vito howled, his voice rather cryptic.

Cotton Eyed Joe's, a strip joint owned and operated by Gino Agnello, displayed nothing but darkness inside since business was closed until Monday afternoon. Tony Angelini, another dedicated soldier of Galluccio, shoved two sticks of lit dynamite in the very back of the building, right under an opening with space. Using common sense, he sprinted away from the soon-to-be catastrophic scene, not stupid to look back.

"No more Cotton Eyed Joe's!" Tony rumbled, already halfway around the corner.

Sal Fazzino, another soldier who'd been with Galluccio almost from the very start, crept on the side of *Mama Maria's*. The very spacious restaurant was under the control of Tony Marinelli. Having the veteran skills of an explosive expert, Sal broke two windows on the side of the building and tossed four sticks of sizzling dynamite inside.

"Been fun having ya around, Mama Maria's!" Sal giggled, running quite fast.

Nino Cambiano and Pete Grosso, two vicious killers in every sense of the word, were thrilled to put an end to the profitable River Quay strip club businesses ran by Charlie Rosetti. First, Nino wanted to make a statement by slinging two sticks of sizzling dynamite through the window of *The Pink Garter* strip club. Second, Pete had a message of his own to send to other insubordinate rivals. Forcefully, he made sure two sticks of sparkling dynamite went flying through a window inside *The Goldmine* strip club.

"Final call for all the tricks who loved The Pink Garter!" Nino mocked, racing faster than he'd ever done.

"For all the drunks and tricks and druggies, this is your last chance to see The Goldmine in one piece!" Pete ostracized, his adrenalin pumped to the maximum.

He ran several feet behind Nino before both men disappeared into a sheet of darkness.

Last, Monty "Dirty Face" Pirelli tiptoed towards the silverish Cadillac owned by Dino Leonetti. The fancy car remained parked on the side of his highly-profitable business known as *The Godfather Lounge*. Galluccio had nursed a hatred for Leonetti every since he tried to backstab his way to the very top of the Kansas City Mafia throne.

Leonetti encroached upon his territory with no remorse whatsoever. The ignorant prick even went as far as badmouthing Galluccio to close friends. Pirelli looked around to make sure none of the River Quay nosy asses were in the vicinity. The coast couldn't've been clearer. The timing was perfect for him to make his move.

"This'll teach a scumsucking sonofabitch like Leonetti a good lesson," Pirelli whispered with pure vengeance to himself. "After tonight, this punk is gonna be minus a pair of balls and an arm and a leg, just like Binaggio over at his burning skin flick joint."

Darkness engulfed the entire perimeter where the car was parked. He slid halfway under the Cadillac with four sticks of dynamite and some wire. His principle intention was to wire a boobytrap bomb to the car. Pirelli wrapped the wire around the dynamite in the tightest fashion. More wire went spiraling around the fuel tank, carbeurator, and transmission. Being an expert in explosives, he slid from under the car and disappeared within a flash.

In a matter of minutes, a series of simultaneous explosions erupted. The explosions rocked River Quay, downtown Kansas City, the west side and points beyond. Strips of wood, shards of glass, chunks of plaster, sections of tile and marble, they all shot into the air like building materials raining from the sky. A bright light illuminated the once dark skies over River Quay.

Fire and smoke raced across the atmosphere. The toxic fumes spread for several blocks. Residents nearby were frightened by the earth-shattering rumble. Craters formed three and four feet deep around *Mama Maria's* and *Cousin Johnny's*. Concrete around the buildings were blasted away with great authority.

Dino Leonetti, a man of mid-height with a trim figure, deep-set eyes, and thinning brown hair, dashed for his car and slammed the door. A low-ranking Mafioso, Leonetti feared he might've been marked for death. After a hard jerk of the ignition, he learned his Cadillac wouldn't crank up.

"C'mon and start up, goddammit!" Leonetti grizzled. "This car's in tip-top shape."

He jerked the ignition with the key once more. A commanding explosion blew him and the car to pieces. In the midst of the angry blaze, his mangled body was eaten by fire. Smoking body parts were stretched across the bloody concrete. And just like "Dirty Face" Pirelli predicted, a pair of Leonetti's bloody family jewels were blasted off his body. The disturbing noise from the series of explosions reached Wayne Miner, a nearby housing project located only a mile east of River Quay and downtown Kansas City.

"Good Lord!" cried a black woman sitting outside smoking a joint.

"Look like it came from over there," pointed another black woman, sipping on a bottle of chilled Wild Irish Rose.

"Where?"

"Somewhere near downtown."

"What, River Quay?"

"Could be."

"Doesn't surprise me a bit."

"Why not?"

"River Quay's ran by those Italians."

"Mafia men?"

"Whaddaya think happened over there?"

"Sounded like a bunch of bombs going off."

"As long as they don't come over here in Wayne Miner blowing shit up."

"They stay in their part of town, we stay in our part of town."

"Those goddam dagos are dangerous."

"Fuck around with them, you'll end up with your throat cut wearing a pair of cement shoes."

"We'll be seeing it on the news tomorrow."

"And the next day."

"And the next day after that."

Pirelli and his squad of rogues left nothing but piles of junk behind. Eventually, Angelo "The Animal" Galluccio gained control of River Quay. Under his rule, new businesses flourished. To ensure they wouldn't suffer the same fate as others, business owners wasted no time signing up with the Teamsters Union. Those who operated in the River Quay area exacted a tribute to Galluccio. The KCPD and the FBI had a general idea who was behind the building explosions and the deaths of Dino Leonetti and Carlo Binaggio. No one, not even the bravest of souls, were willing to talk.

Taking complete control over River Quay wasn't enough for Galluccio. Greed was his blood type. Treachery was his constitution. He wanted it all for his crime family. He stopped at nothing to achieve his criminalistic goals. The chaos Galluccio orchestrated in Kansas City's River Quay section determined the fate of the Teamsters Union and his mob family for decades to come.

Chapter 2

KANSAS CITY'S POWERFUL GALLUCCIO Mafia family muscled in on food manufacturing, automobile sales, the steel industry, dairy businesses, breweries, and liquor sales and distribution. Galluccio tied big money into banks, restaurants, nightclubs, real estate, coin machines, garbage collection, trucking, insurance, parking lots, and construction. Very few businesses and industries avoided the wrath of the Galluccio crime family's investments within substantial segments of the economy. Leaders of the family still controlled top Teamsters Unions. Only through extortion, bribery, and violence did Galluccio maintain a monopoly over many operations.

For those who rejected opportunities to be a part of the Teamsters Union, Galluccio, a master of extortion and manipulation, sent reminders to the stubborn ones. With the great power he derived, basically through the Mafia bosses in Chicago, he rendered anyone from making a living. Fair or not, it became his routine way of doing business. So many idiots had to be made examples out of. A secretive meeting took place in the basement of the North Kansas City home owned by Galluccio and his wife. "Dirty Face" Pirelli and the five other *goombahs* circled around their boss, waiting for their next set of orders.

Galluccio stood under a lamp in the middle of the room. The soft, bright light beamed down on top of his pure white hair. A fierce wisdom was etched across his aging face. More plots were being hatched against their rivals.

He spoke and his league of goons offered their full attention. "Joe LaRocca owns R and J Meat Company. This joint's located at the deep north end of Kansas City. The truckers who supply the meat to his company, he doesn't wanna sign them up with the Teamsters, claims it saves his company big money."

The six men made into his beloved Mafia family stared deep into his eyes as though he'd been crowned *King of the Universe*. They'd become accustomed to worshipping him. Pirelli would be the first soldier to receive his orders.

"Monty, can you get access to the refrigeration system inside R and J Meats?" Galluccio asked his most vicious thug, a true asset to his powerful Mafia organization.

"Angie, I can learn the ins and outs of that meat company," Pirelli assured Galluccio, the scars of battle shown clearly across his rough face from the beaming light above.

"Look, I want you to shut off the freezer system where all that meat's stored," Galluccio plotted.

"No problem, Angie."

"I want every piece of beef, pork, poultry, and lamb spoiled rotten."

"Angie, your wish is my command."

"When we're through with R and J Meats, they won't be able to sell one piece of fresh meat."

"Not a single piece of meat."

"If those health department officials can prove LaRocca sells any kind of spoiled meat, they'll shut him down right away."

"And that's when the family can take over his meat company, Angie."

"If you need extra help, then take another guy with you."

"I've got the perfect guy for the job."

"Alright, Monty, you've got your orders."

Galluccio now turned his attention to a soldier who'd been just as loyal and ruthless as Pirelli. Vito stared with ferocity into the eyes of his boss. He itched for his next set of orders.

"Vito, you think we've got the juice to shut Caldrone down?" Angelo questioned Vito.

"Angie, Caldrone's a cowboy, for chrissake," Vito shot back, also yearning to please his Mafia commander.

"Think we can run the prick out of business?"

"Why not? Last week, he sent some of his rogues into another bar over in North Kansas City to rob the owner of cigarettes and soda."

"Just like LaRocca, the truckers who supply the sodas and cigarettes to his joint aren't signed up with the Teamsters."

"A puke like Caldrone's suppressing the competition."

"Shouldn't that be enough to shut him down?"

"Enough to have fire shooting from his ass," Vito giggled. "Pulling the right strings, we can add fuel to the fire. We can have prosecutors over at Jackson County ready to run him straight out'a business."

"The sooner you help run him out of business, the sooner the Galluccio family can take over his joint."

"I'm on the case, Angie."

"Good."

The next soldier to receive his set of orders happened to be Sal Fazzino. Sal did everything in his power to prove to Galluccio he'd die and go to hell and back for him.

Galluccio looked deep into the piercing eyes of Sal. "Sal, I know that Charlie DeVito owns and runs I-70 Drive In. Word got back to me that he's allowing kids to just walk through and watch skin flicks. That's one of the very reasons why Binaggio got blown straight to hell. Like dope, porno needs to be kept away from children."

Sal jerked his head and created a wave of anger. "DeVito's doing enough to be put in jail for exploiting children. Where the hell's the KCPD when ya need them? The feds should be up in his ass like a stuck turd."

"DeVito's doing his part by fucking kids minds up," Galluccio hissed. "A sleazeball in every sense of the word."

"Kids are gonna learn about sex sooner or later."

"But that perverted prick's giving them a headstart."

"He certainly is."

"Didn't take me long to find out that the guys who truck in his concession goods and supplies aren't signed up with the Teamsters. That scum wants to cut costs by not having any of those truckers unionized. We're going to fix this problem nice and easy."

"So, Angie, how're we gonna shut this lowlife pukebag down?"

"Easy."

"Think K.C.'s finest will take the money under the table?"

"Why not?" Galluccio reasoned. "Those guys on the force are always looking to get their palms greased."

"Consider it done, Angie."

The next two Galluccio loyalists waiting to hear their orders were Nino Cambiano and Pete Grosso. The pair of vicious rogues stood on opposite sides of their supreme boss.

Galluccio thrusted an erect finger at both men. "Jimmy Strada's got big money tied in with Auto Grand Salvage. People have been complaining that he's selling bad engines and car parts. Now, that's considered ripping his customers off, the same people who put those parts on their cars. The truckers who haul in all that junk to his salvage yard, they aren't signed up with the Teamsters. It irks the living fuck out of me when these sonofabitches try and cut costs and undermine the competition. Nino and Pete, this is where you two guys come in."

"Anything, Angie, anything," Nino vowed with respect.

"Just say the word, Angie," Pete followed.

"I want every tire on every car sitting in that junkyard sliced up. I want every wire connected to every engine around that whole lot disconnected. Bust out every window of every car. Dent in every door and hood and trunk on every car. Strada's gotta learn what being a stubborn, bullheaded puke will cost him."

"We're looking to run Strada straight out'a business," Nino schemed, the glowing light highlighting his menacing features.

"You've given the orders."

"Nino and Pete, this should be second nature since you guys know the inside and outside of cars better than anyone."

Nino nodded his head with profound assurance. "Angie, my old man was a mechanic. He taught me how to take an engine apart and put it back together blindfolded. I learned the inside of a car like Hefner knows the inside of a broad's pussy."

"Same here, Angie," Pete added. "I've worked on cars the majority of my life."

Yes, Galluccio wanted his men to create a total disaster.

"Consider it done, Angie," said Nino.

"Should be a piece of cake," said Pete.

"Once Strada goes into the poorhouse, that's when we'll make our move on his junkyard."

"He'll be penniless when we're done."

"And holding his *cajones*."

The last soldier to receive his orders was Tony. The other five Mafia hounds backed away as Galluccio threw his hand over his shoulder. He spoke to him in a voice laced with wise sentiments. "Tony, you know that Eddie Brocato owns the Missouri Coin Company. Some of my inside people looked at the books for that company. And let me tell you, Brocato's making money hand-over-first."

"Pulling in grand larceny."

"Not for too much longer," Galluccio promised Tony. "A Senate Investigation Committee believes that Brocato's an alleged syndicate leader here in Kansas City. We don't have to believe anything, we already know he's connected."

"Politicians and policemen already know that Brocato's coin company is just a front operation," Tony recited to Galluccio.

"Missouri politicians are no dummies. At this point, they're hot on Brocato's ass."

"Whaddaya think they can pinch him for?"

"Money laundering and tax fraud."

"Really?"

"Brocato's men have rigged machines around Kansas City for years," Galluccio mentioned. "People have lost big bucks at a lot of those carwashes and laundry houses where he supplies the machines with change. But his fun's about to come to an end."

"There's big money tied into coin companies. There're guys out there raking in crazy bucks."

"I want the Galluccio family to cash in some of the chips."

"What'cha have in mind, Angie?" Tony asked.

"I want to make a move on the Missouri Coin Company. I want you, Tony, to go to some of those carwashes and bust up the machines where people washing their cars get change. I want you to go inside some of those laundry houses and just demolish those machines that people get change from. The Galluccio family should be the ones who shell out change to those people who can't get enough of washing their dirty cars and dirty laundry."

"Sounds like a brilliant idea."

"The guys who truck in those coin machines have skipped around being signed up with the Teamsters long enough. Believe me when I tell you, all these non-union punks who have avoided being a part of the unions, they'll change their tune once we're done dealing with them."

"Your wish is my pleasure."

The group of six thuggish henchmen all exchanged intense eye contact with Galluccio. The stares translated into a band of seven men all being able to sense familiar vibes. The series of schemes hatched were just the opposite of River Quay. None of the rivals they plotted against would suffer the fate of having their businesses blown to tiny pieces. None of the men would be murdered or tortured in any fashion.

Galluccio coughed as a noticeable gesture. His men knew he had something quite serious to say. "Listen up, men. And please, listen up real good. The mess made in River Quay might've been the biggest mistake we've ever made. Sure, a lot of those jerkoffs didn't wanna be signed up with the Teamsters, which had me scratching my balls at night. It insults my intelligence and screws with my ego when guys who should be unionized with the Teamsters just flat out ignore my requests and suggestions made to them. And speaking of balls, we had to blow off the balls of two cocksuckers who forgot the rules of the game. Yes, I'm talking about Binaggio and Leonetti. One wanted to be a dopehead and peddle porno to children, while the other wanted muscle in on another made guy's territory, not to mention how he badmouthed me all over town."

"Dirty Face" Pirelli stepped closer and patted Galluccio across the chest. "Now that River Quay's a whole new part of town, Angie, whaddaya think the future will be for that part of town?"

"I'll leave that to my nephew Tommy to figure out when he takes over this family."

"We followed through with the orders you gave us."

"You men did a beautiful piece of work. But I still maintain that things could've been handled a lot more systematically."

"No time for regrets, Angie."

Galluccio stared down at his watch. Exactly 1:30 a.m. was displayed across the face of his Timex. "Alright men, it's time to make your move. By morning, I want all these scums we plan to move in on crying big tears out of their asses."

Another meeting had been adjourned by Galluccio. The assembly of six men scattered and were on to their assigned destinations.

Chapter 3

MONTY "DIRTY FACE" Pirelli and an expert locksmith and master of shutting off electrical systems, arrived at R and J Meat Company at precisely 2:00 a.m. The helper, Dennis DeMarco, a tall, tan-skinned and thin-built man, had been hired to do the job on short notice. Thin sheets of light surrounded the perimeter of the building. Having no fences or dogs around the complex worked in their favor.

"Okay DeMarco, let's see how good you are," Pirelli challenged, anxious to get in and out to get the job done.

"I've been doing this almost since the day I learned to walk," DeMarco responded in confidence.

"When we open that door to this place, let's go right to work."

"No problem."

Pirelli scanned the nearby block to make sure none of the snoopy neighbors watched them break into R and J Meats. Not a soul walked the dark streets. DeMarco jammed one of his specialized tools into the lock. A few jerks here and there and the deadbolt lock slid away from the connecting slot.

The same was done for another lock underneath the first one. Pirelli and DeMarco crept into the dark building where they were met by thick frost. The bonechilling temperature wasted no time letting them know that frost bit at their fingers and faces.

"Jeez DeMarco!" Pirelli shivered. "It's colder than an Eskimo pussy in here. We better get in and out of here before we become blocks of ice."

"My hands are already starting to feel like cold pieces of stone."

"I don't want to leave here with frozen balls."

"Neither do I."

"Then we'd better move fast."

Pirelli and DeMarco traveled further into the building. Soon, they were met by slabs of meat hanging from large hooks. Chains suspended to the ceiling were lined in a symmetrical order. Cows, pigs, lambs, chickens and even turkeys, hung like racks of clothing in a department store. Both men were equipped with the tools necessary to do the job.

A fully equipped utility belt hung around their waists. Pirelli and DeMarco reached for their flashlights for better orientation. The further they traveled into the building, the colder the temperature became. A purplish red formed at the fingertips of Pirelli's hands. A violet red spread across the face of DeMarco. Without notice, both men heard a familiar squealing noise.

"DeMarco, did you hear that?" Pirelli asked, shining his flashlight every which direction.

"Sure did," DeMarco noticed, bobbing his flashlight from the floor to the ceiling. "And I've heard that sound before."

"Whaddaya think it could be?"

"Your guess is as good as mine's."

"Whatever it is, I hope it's got a life insurance policy."

"This meat house is starting to give me the creeps."

"That piece of work Angie gave me in River Quay was easier than this."

The squealing sound seeped further into their ears. Pirelli scooted along a wooden table used for chopping meat. DeMarco stood at least two feet in front of him. The creature which'd been squealing looked into the brightness of their flashlights. A supersized rat stood on its hind legs and bolstered the large teeth sticking out of its mouth.

Acting on impulse, Pirelli snatched a meat cleaver off the table. The razor sharp blade went slicing through the mid-section of the rat. Bloody organs went flying over the table and onto the floor. The frightening excitement hadn't begun. Another rat jumped from the side of the table. Using the survival skills he'd been accustomed to, Pirelli whacked away at the second rodent. Blood covered every inch of the cleaver blade.

"Dammit DeMarco!" Pirelli huffed and puffed out in strong spurts. "Where'd those rats come from? Those things looked like a couple'a huge possums."

"Who knows where they came from?" DeMarco nodded, quite shook up himself. "Question is, how many more of those sonofabitches are in here?"

"I'd better keep this meat cleaver in my hand just in case more of them jump out of nowhere."

"If enough of those rats get to us, they'll find us as dead meat among all this other dead meat."

"Got that right, buddy. Like I said, that River Quay job was a lot easier. All we had to do was just throw dynamite and run. Here in this place, we almost get attacked by a couple'a rats big enough to get inside a wrestling ring."

"How can they stay alive in this blistering cold?"

"Rats can survive in any conditions."

"We better get moving, Monty."

"We've got to find the fuse box."

"We don't have all night."

Layers of excruciating frostbite caused more torture to their hands and face. They kept their bodies in motion to create warmth. Silence turned into intensity. Pirelli rubbed his palms and locked his fingers to ward off more frostbite. He held onto the meat cleaver like a paranoid soldier. DeMarco twisted the muscles in his face just to be able to talk.

"Why'd they have to keep it so cold in here?" Pirelli asked.

"All this meat hanging around has to be kept frozen solid," DeMarco answered back.

"It'd take all this meat a week to thaw out."

"A lot lesser time than that."

DeMarco positioned his flashlight towards a corner of the building. He struck gold right away. A large fuse box sat at the middle of the wall. Pirelli stampeded in front of DeMarco. Both thugs reached into the fuse box and ripped out one fuse after another. They reached for the side of their utility belts and fished up wire cutters. Wire after wire along the adjacent walls got clipped. Sparks shot into the air.

Smoke from the sparks blended in with the smoke from the frost. R and J Meats had not an ounce of power. The refrigeration system shut down with not a single generator moving.

"Notice how fast it's getting warm in here?" Pirelli asked DeMarco, blowing thinner frost from his mouth.

"My face has warmed with the quickness," DeMarco smiled.

"My hands have warmed up, too."

"Think all this meat in here will be spoiled by the time they get here in the morning?"

"Good question, DeMarco."

"It'll be a shame to see all of our hard work go down the drain."

"Anyway, let's get the hell out of here."

Pirelli and DeMarco disappeared from R and J Meats with hopes every slab of meat inside spoiled rotten.

Nino Cambiano and Pete Grosso arrived at Auto Grand Salvage at exactly 2:30 a.m. The pair of eager rogues were equipped with everything needed to complete their assignment. Two .38 calibre pistols rested in holsters on their left sides. Utility belts with hammers and wire cutters and long sharp knives hung around their waists.

Nino held a pan with four well cooked beef steaks inside. Impregnated into the juicy steaks were the most potent concentration of cyanide poisoning. The succulent juices made the steaks look irresistible.

"Alright Pete, you know what to do when we get over that fence?" Nino inquired to his partner.

"Yes I do," Pete subjected to Nino.

"Let's hear it."

"Get to bashing in and cutting up everything in sight."

"Strada's junkyard is gonna be junkier than it already is."

"And you know it, Nino."

"We're gonna turn into demolition men."

"That we are."

Nino rattled the fence enclosing the salvage yard with aggression. Two strong Dobermans with shiny black coats and impressive muscle tones rushed to the fence. The dogs barked at Nino and Pete with long sharp teeth. Nino unfolded back the foil to the pan and slung all four steaks over the fence. Patience was the key. The Dobermans sunk their teeth into the meat like there would been no tomorrow.

The destructive pair of men waited for the results. And the results were quite pleasing. Within five minutes, the dogs slumbered onto their sides. The potency of the cyanide poisoning ripped away at their stomachs. Foamy saliva shot from their mouths. Cries of pain and death wavered beyond the salvage yard. Both Dobermans were dead and now the henchmen could put their plans into action. Nino and Pete scaled the eight foot fence like professionals.

Once on the other side, they snatched up their hammers and wire cutters and knives.

Windows on almost every car were bashed in. Glass shot into the air like big chunks of raindrops. Tires were sliced. Doors and hoods and trunks were bashed in. They went under the hoods of nearly every car and cut wires like doctors cutting umbilical chords. Seats within the interior were ripped apart. The damage they'd created wasn't pretty. Junk inside Auto Grand Salvage just got junkier.

"We've worked up a sweat demolishing these cars," Pete said, taking a quick breather.

Nino brushed off a patch of sweat from his face. "I'd have to say that slinging dynamite under buildings in River Quay had to be a lot easier than fucking cars up."

"We can't expect every piece of work Angie gives us to be easy."

"That's true, Pete. Bashing up these cars was actually good exercise."

"River Quay was just something to get us warmed up for this job."

"That is was."

"Let's get out'a here before somebody sees us."

Nino and Pete climbed back to the other side and disappeared.

Tony arrived at one of K.C.'s most profitable laundry cleaning facilities like clockwork. The time on his watch read 2:50 a.m. Also an expert at picking locks, he manipulated the deadbolt until it surrendered from the slot. Staring at him inside the dark facility were rows and rows of washing machines and dryers. Empty boxes of laundry detergent were scattered across the floor. The doors to the place opened at 5:00 a.m. He knew he had to move fast. His destructive tool of choice? A large sledgehammer.

Tony went right to work on his assignment. And like a railroad worker hammering down on iron railroad tracks, he bashed in the washing machines and dryers with intense force. Not a single machine would be operational when the attendants were due to arrive. The frames of the machines were wharped out of shape. Coin slots spilled out quarters onto the floor. Part of his work was completed. The damge had been done. He rushed out the building and on to his next assignment.

Tony showed up at one of the biggest and most thriving car washes in K.C. With the sledgehammer he'd used to destroy the washing machines and dryers, he went right to work on the change machines built into the concrete walls of the carwash. The damage of the hammer caused quarters to spit out of the machine one after another.

One might ask: *Why didn't he pocket some of the money from the laundry facility and the carwash?* The answer couldn't've been easier. Galluccio wanted to send a message, make a clear statement. Leaving the money behind let the silly assholes know that Galluccio meant business. Maybe street bums or drunks would be lucky enough to stumble upon the money to further their unconventional lifestyles.

The six men sent out by Galluccio performed the tasks their supreme boss assigned to them. The messages came in crystal clear. Sign up with the Teamsters and prosper. Avoid the Teamsters and suffer. Galluccio successfully moved in on the businesses of every rival he plotted against. Watching the coffers of his Mafia family swell out of control brought him the greatest sense of pleasure.

Chapter 4

THE YEAR 1985 ARRIVED quicker than Galluccio could've ever imagined. Several hours passed at Saint Joseph Medical Center on Kansas City's south side and Galluccio had only moments to live. Being on his deathbed gave him time to reminisce about his colorful criminal career. Standing at his bedside was his beloved nephew, Thomas "Tommy The Caveman" Galluccio, a fiercely loyal relative. Tommy stood mid-height, possessed a proud lean figure, and bolstered manly good looks. He'd taken care of himself over the years. Relatively good health could account for it.

Angelo spoke to Tommy in a sickly, gravel voice. "Tommy, I'm naming you the new boss of the Galluccio family. I spent over thirty years building this family into what it is today. The mess that I made in the River Quay back in the seventies, Tommy, I don't want you making the same mess. It costed the family too much money, not to mention the heat we got from the coppers and the G-men. I let that bad fucking temper of mine get in the way of being a rational man with a real mind for business. You and I both know, the less violence we deal with, the less trouble we have to deal with. Don't go around blowing guys's balls off just because they won't sign up with the Teamsters."

Tommy cracked a wise smile. "Are you speaking of Leonetti and Binaggio?"

"You remember, huh?"

"Like it was yesterday. But the family still believes that Leonetti and Binaggio definitely had it coming."

"They deserved all of it."

"Uncle Angie, it's a real honor to have you crown me the new boss. I promise you that I'll move our Kansas City family in the right direction. I promise you that I won't demolish a guy's business like those *River Quay Wars*."

With Tommy being the future of the Galluccio family, Angelo sensed things looked brighter than ever.

"Tommy, you'll get the backing from the bosses out of Chicago," Angelo enlightened his favorite nephew. "Carmine and Mikey Bernazzoli will be watching your back every step of the way."

"We're a blood brotherhood, Uncle Angie. I won't let no one take that away from us."

"No one, Tommy."

"This *thing of our's* is now and forever."

Angelo grabbed the hand of Tommy and held it tight. "Tommy, promise me before I take my last breath that you'll guard the Teamsters Union with your very life. Me and the other bosses, we dedicated our whole lives to building the unions into an unstoppable force. Promise me that you'll keep the *codes of omerta* when it comes to this *thing of our's*. Son, you'll have to learn that the government's gonna try and force you out with all that legal, federal bullshit."

"The Teamsters is the heart and soul that ticks in this *thing of ours*. Being the new boss, I will live, eat, breathe, drink, fart, fuck, and sleep the Teamsters."

"Tommy, this *thing of our's* is forever and ever."

"Forever and a day, Uncle Angie."

The hospital room converted to a sentimental silence.

Angelo could've been minutes away from death. Tommy stared down at his beloved uncle with tears welled up in his eyes.

"You know Hoffa would be proud to hear you speak those words."

"And the bosses, too."

Angelo held a tighter grip around the hand of Tommy. "You'll have a lot of muscle to work with now that you're the new boss. You've got ten state representatives and eight state senators in Missouri who are dues-paying members of Local 45. You know that's a lot of political clout."

"Is that one senator still on the payroll of the Galluccio family?"

"What senator?"

"The jewish guy from down there near St. Louis."

"Joey Weinberg?"

"Yes, that's who I'm talking about."

"Joey's not going anywhere. His old man and I have a lot of history. And good history at that."

"What about any coppers?"

"What about them?"

"Do we have any left on our payroll?"

"There's your cousin Carlo Ruggiero. He runs the whole narcotics division inside the KCPD. If you need more coppers, then just grease their palms real good, they'll take the money under the table."

"I'll be meeting with Carmine and Mikey in the future to iron out some fresh details about Local 45."

"We brought up Hoffa a minute ago in this conversation. Like myself, Hoffa let steam shoot out of his ass and ordered guys to blow up businesses all over the place. Please hear me when I tell you that that's not the way to go. The G-men and the coppers will tolerate certain things for so long, but there comes a time when even they've had enough."

"Sometimes money isn't a good enough reason for them to look the other way."

"You've caught on, nephew."

Tommy stared deep into the eyes of his dying uncle. "I've always had a master teacher, Uncle Angie."

Angelo might've been only breaths away from death. "Before I close my eyes, I want to leave you with some solid advice. Monty, Vito, Tony, Sal, and Nino and Pete are all gone now. I thought I'd always be the one who checked out before them. All six of those guys stayed loyal to me in the end. Sure, they got pinched by the government, and half of them ended up dying in the can. Tommy, you will never receive loyalty or respect by being one of those nice soft guys. Punks get screwed right up the ass. Nice guys always run in second, third, and fourth place. People shit on them all the time. Remember that fear and money makes unbelievable power. If you have enough money, you can make your men fear you. They'll show you the utmost respect and loyalty. Fear keeps people in line. Do you think the six guys who did my legwork liked me, whether some of the time or part of the time? Had I been some softie, my men would've stuck it in from sixteen different directions. One way or another, you've got to keep your men in line. Have them to fear you, and they'll respect you, and show you loyalty to the end."

"Does that include our International President, too."

"Yes, that includes Mason Shellenberger, too."

"Shell has stuck to you like paint on a wall."

"He's shown complete loyalty the last twenty something years."

"Local Forty Five and some of the other unions have grown and grown over the years."

"And that came with power, strength, organization, and respect."

"You're a brilliant man, Uncle Angie. Just look what you and the other bosses did for the Teamsters and Las Vegas. It's amazing how you men could walk into a company and tell them that you wanted to organize."

"They'd sometimes ask who we were."

"What would you tell them?"

"We'd tell them we were the Teamsters and they'd be kissing every inch of our asses."

"Everytime I think of Las Vegas, I'll think of you. It's genius how you and the bosses helped turn a dry desert town into bright lights, beautiful broads, good food, the best booze, fine entertainment, and the best hotel-casinos."

"We had it all back then."

"And lots more."

Angelo started breathing in heavy spurts. An aura of death blanketed his flushed face. Tommy grabbed him across his shoulders.

"Are you alright, Uncle Angie?"

He lifted both arms and locked hands with his nephew. "Tommy, it's all about to end. But before I check out, I just wanted to tell you that being the new boss of the Galluccio family is not going to be easy. You'll be paying for the sins of your fathers. You'll be going up against men who've had a real past and identity problems with our family. The *River Quay Wars* never really ended. The G-men still want to put the people responsible for blowing those buildings away in the can. They still wanted to know who clipped Binaggio and Leonetti. Only problem, all of us will be dead by the time they figure it out. The feds are going to put you under the miscroscope since you're the new boss. Don't be surprised if the government brings the family under investigation and tries to rip apart our *borgata*."

"Everything you've said is true," Tommy aligned with Angelo. "The feds got cameras to see how we move about here and there. The G-men, they plant bugs all over the place to hear everything we're talking about. But, I've got my own resources to keep them from seeing and hearing what we're doing. I believe I will catch hell for what happened in River Quay. Everything they bring my way, I'll just send it right back their way."

"Hear me good on this one. We'll never be in the clear with this River Quay thing. Those demons will always come back to haunt us. Don't be surprised if the G-men start a witch hunt in the years to come."

Angelo thrusted his chest forward. Heavy breaths shot out in strong spurts. Hospital staff rushed into the room. Nurses checked his pulse and heartrate. He stopped breathing as a visible mist seeped from his mouth. Tommy stared down at the bed and knew his uncle had died. He crossed himself while tears spilled from his eyes and down his face. The last rites were given to Angelo "The Animal" Galluccio.

Tommy "The Caveman" Galluccio became leader of the Kansas City crime family whose uncle's name it came to bear. He developed an extraordinary mind for business and rapidly connived to build an economic dynasty which would probably far out live him. Galluccio knew the future for the family was far up in the air. With Angelo's untimely death, a void was left at the head of the legendary Kansas City crime family.

The International Brotherhood of Teamsters for years had been scarred by allegations of ties to organized crime families throughout the country. Federal authorities linked Kansas City based Teamster boss Mason Shellenberger to Tommy Galluccio and some powerful Chicago mob leaders. Shellenberger had been indicted three times by federal grand juries and was never convicted. He was a powerful international president who also ran an eight-hundred thousand member Central Conference of Teamsters.

He headed the union team which negotiated national freight-hauling contracts. Tommy Galluccio had much to worry about since his lawyer informed him an indictment would be coming down against Shellenberger from an ambitious Federal Grand Jury. The newly-sanctioned Kansas City Mafia boss played a high stakes game. Galluccio had to call an urgent meeting.

Chapter 5

THE YEAR 1994 HAD arrived. The place was Kansas City, Missouri. The International Brotherhood of the Teamsters Union was still dominated by the Galluccio Mafia family. Tommy Galluccio, the balding and baggy-eyed Mafia chieftain with puppy dog cheeks, was given the baton by his deceased uncle. He'd been handed exclusive control over rackets in Kansas City and points beyond. He allowed his housekeeper, the beautiful and elegant Angela Claybrook, to host his most trusted associates and family members in his beautiful mansion in the quiet and exclusively wealthy section of Ward Parkway.

Angela represented the epitome of beauty. She stood at a comanding five-foot-eight inches. A dangerously beautiful face she had, with a chiseled body to match. A witty personality and suspenseful intellect were her endearing qualities. Galluccio desired beautiful blondes to no apparent end. Blondes with blue eyes and hard bodies were like goddesses to him. Bringing Angela into his house to serve as his housekeeper was an answered prayer. Ever since his indefinite separation from his wife Phyllis, Galluccio actually hired Angela to be his cook, maid, errand girl, and best of all, his constant lover. Some men seemed to just have all the luck.

How could she resist? He paid her top dollars. He treated her better than any man had ever done. She even got higher preferential treatment than his own wife.

"Tommy, can I ask you a question?" Angela said, intrigued with the power and charisma her boss possessed.

"Anything, Angela," Galluccio replied, staring at Angela like he wanted to rip her clothes off for some serious sex.

"Why are the real interesting men always married?"

Galluccio smiled and tucked in his bottom lip. "Honey, there are plenty of single men who are interesting."

"Doesn't seem that way," Angela rejected.

"Before I got married, I was quite interesting myself."

"Had I met you when you were still single, I probably wouldn't've found you interesting."

"Maybe that's it," Galluccio said. "Women don't find men interesting unless they're married or got a girlfriend. You women always want something you can't have."

Being a humble woman with the face of a Euro-centric queen and the body of a Greek goddess, made Galluccio a *sucker* for her kind. Maybe Galluccio would've divorced Phyllis and married Angela had it not been for him corrupting family values. He existed in a culture which believed in keeping honor within the family. Maybe he would've married a black woman, a Sicilian man with an appetite for those brown sugars, a voracious appetite yet to be filled.

On the contrary, he viciously hated black men. They were less than nothing to him. He only used them to do his dirty work whenever needed. They weren't allowed in his house or around his family members. He kept them around as *yard apes* and *fence monkeys* to run his many neighborhood liquor stores and cheap restaurants.

"Question," Angela said, her sparkling blue eyes hypnotic.

"Talk to me, babe," Galluccio smiled.

"If you divorce your wife, do you think you'll ever get married again?"

"That's hard to say at this point," Galluccio thought.

"Men like you are a rarity."

"That's a nice thing to say."

"It's the truth, Tommy."

"Alright, let me get ready for this meeting."

Galluccio planned an important meeting for five o'clock p.m. He wanted to meet with some of his most trusted men, matters which involved crucial family business. Angela entered the kitchen with a snow-white, terry towel clutched in her hand. The musical doorbell rung with softness. She answered the door with a seductive greeting and warm smile. The Mafiosos studiously took their seats at the enormous conference table. Angela went into the kitchen to make two large pots of coffee while they waited for Galluccio to make his presence known. Large buckets of ice were prepared for the men who wanted to guzzle down their favorite cocktails.

Wine glasses and coffee mugs were brought out of the cabinets. Angela had been trained to serve the men of Galluccio quite well. Seated at the east end of the table was the very man who federal authorities labeled as the fiery-tempered Teamster leader of Kansas City, Missouri, Mason Shellenberger. As a Jewish Ivy Leaguer, a man who clawed his way to the top of being the undisputed leader of the International Brotherhood of Teamsters there in the Midwest, he used bribery, intimidation, and even murder to assume his position. His presence at the meeting was incisive.

Summoned also to the meeting was Francisco "Frankie Bonecutter" Provenzano, a tall, slender-built, and conservatively handsome Mafioso. He gained the reputation of being a rough, tough, and brutal murderer with quickness. Representing interest for Chicago's powerful Bernazzoli Brothers was Gino "The Bulldog" Vazzano, a short, chubby, and inadequately insensitive man with a round, bulldoggish face. Fat suspended around his body that could've never been friendly to the well being of his health.

Vazzano fought a serious weight problem for years, but didn't help the problem by eating everything in sight. Provenzano remained a high-ranking member of the Galluccio crime family for several years. Indeed, a brutal man, Galluccio used him to violently enforce his authority. He earned the nickname *Frankie Bonecutter* from his proficiency with a chainsaw. It became the tool used in the capacity of sawing apart the bodies of tortured murder victims. His graphic nature became legendary in Kansas City and throughout the Midwest. He'd been known to have chainsawed apart the bodies in abandoned warehouses. The dismembered body parts of their enemies were rumored to have been put in trashbags and scattered in dumpsters around the city.

Gino Vazzano was officially a made member of the Chicago Mafia Outfit. Galluccio and the Bernazzoli Brothers sanctioned him to strongarm the growing number of strip clubs around the Kansas City, St. Louis, Wichita, Omaha, Des Moines, and Chicago areas. Vazzano muscled his way into a variety of interests in the booming porno business. He'd been commissioned to run several porno shops in most areas of the Midwest. The Galluccio family was still under considerable domination by the Chicago Outfit, in which the Bernazzoli Brothers exerted important influence over Tommy Galluccio. There remained one strict rule laid down by most Chicago Mafia leaders.

The dons from the old school, as well as the modern day bosses, sanctioned there would be no drug dealing, under penalty of an immediate death. There was so much money to be made in drugs until most Mafiosos bent the rules with a nudge and a wink. A native Chicagoan named Mickey Castucci attended the important meeting Galluccio arranged hours in advance. Castucci, a stout man with broad shoulders and cauliflower ears, helped finance a vast narcotics ring which stretched throughout America.

Under the stewardship of Carmine and Michael Bernazzoli, the burgeoning drug business earned big dollars for the midwestern crime families. His connections branched as far away as the cocaine cartels in Cartegena and Medellin. The narcotics business got bigger all the time. The money poured in at record numbers.

Angela reached over the men at the table before the meeting got underway. Silver platters of meats, crackers, dips, chips, fruits, vegetables, and pastries were lined along the table. She pampered them by placing cups of coffee and glasses of ice in front of their chairs. She exchanged smiles with Provenzano, then said in a pleasant tone, "Good afternoon, Frankie. How are you doing today, sir?"

"Can't complain, Angela," Provenzano replied with casualty. He felt as special as his boss after being greeted in such a manner. Often, Provenzano wondered where a man could meet an American woman like Angela, a woman who treated her man as good as she treated Galluccio and those associated with him. "How are you doing on this lovely afternoon?"

"Couldn't be better, sir."

"You're looking lovely as ever."

"Thank you, sir."

"How's your family?"

"Everyone's doing great."

"Superb."

Angela poured coffee into their cups. She returned later with cream and sugar. Other associates poured their favorite cocktails into the sparkling glasses. With respect for her boss, Angela disappeared when Galluccio walked into the enormous dining room. Blessed with taste for fashion, he wore his black smoker's jacket with a pair of matching silk slacks.

A dazzling stare grew on the faces of the cadre of men. An aura of respect engulfed the room. Galluccio pulled out his chair and took a seat. Warm greetings took place among the men before the meeting started. Handshakes were exchanged from across the table. The Mafiosos appeared to be in high spirits. Cigarettes and cigars were fired up. This brought immediate clouds of smoke into the air. The Pendergast Mansion remained the perfect place for Galluccio to conduct his secretive Mafia meetings.

Galluccio motioned for Angela to keep the coffee mugs and cocktail glasses full at all times. She knew to keep herself scarce when the secretive meeting was in effect. She went to the head of the table and poured him a straight shot of brandy. He patted her firm ass for performing such hospitable deeds. Angela smiled and faded away. Galluccio opened his crucial meeting by thanking the important men and the less important associates for being in attendance. The undisputed Kansas City Mafia boss fired up a fat cigar. He was now ready to preside over a meeting which involved Midwestern criminal dignitaries. His eyes averted over to Mason Shellenberger.

"Shell," Galluccio mildly spoke. "My Uncle Angie pulled a lot of strings to put you in that top Teamster's boss spot. He's long gone and now we've got to find a way to get you out of another one of these fucking federal indictments."

"Goddammit, Tommy, the law keeps on coming!" Shellenberger consorted out of raw anger. "Three times in the last five years the Grand Jury indicted me."

"And three times in the last five years you haven't been convicted," Galluccio confirmed.

"How long will our luck last? We've slipped away time and time again." Shellenberger had borne a share of the federal spotlight and he was dead tired of it.

"We'll just put together a few thousand and pay off one of the jurors."

"Let's hope one of the jurors is for sell."

"How many times do I have'ta tell you, doesn't everybody have a price?"

"We've got to find out when jury selection begins."

"In due time, we'll find out who'll be on that jury panel."

"It's good that you've always got a plan, Tommy."

"What are the feds trying to come at you with now?"

"Embezzlement."

"How much?"

"A hundred grand."

"So what."

"They're charging that I payed myself a bonus without proper authorization from the union."

"Those government scumbags in Washington! Those selfish Fortune 500 pricks in Corporate America! Do they get authorizations to take out fat bonuses for themselves?"

"Not'a one of those conniving thieves."

"Tell me, what's in the works now?"

"We're negotiating a huge national freight-hauling contract," Shellenberger explained for intent business purposes. "This time, we're looking at some really big bucks coming into the union."

Galluccio helped mastermind a scheme to steal union funds by inflating expenses. The alleged misuse of worker's money in the past pressured Shellenberger and other union officials into resigning as trustees of the giant Central States Pension Fund and the Central States Health and Welfare Fund. But, they came back even stronger. A clever move on the part of The Department of Labor, since the Justice Department was ready to kick mob goons out of the Teamsters Union once and for all.

Galluccio spoke with all reason. "Give me some more information about this bum you're dealing with out in California."

"He's a Chicago insurance hotshot named David Bakewell. They gave him a new contract to administer the Central States insurance claims."

"Do you trust this prick?" Galluccio asked, precautionary. He kept outside associates under tight scrutiny.

"With my life, Tommy."

"Didn't he screw things up for the bosses in Chicago?" Galluccio examined. He raised questions of suspicion since he shared the spoils of mobster revenues with Chicago, Cleveland, and Milwaukee.

"He accepted 200 grand from a Beverly Hills insurance swindler who pleaded guilty to stealing millions from the Teamster's premiums."

"Let's hope your men won't screw up like this prick."

"My men are loyal to the end. I've got them in key positions."

"We're on a roll, Shell."

"But the feds are gonna keep coming after us."

"We'll be on easy street after this federal trial."

"Every step that we take could be monitored or bugged," Shellenberger feared. "There could be infiltration by informants."

Shellenberger developed an extreme bunker mentality. He also knew the war between the feds and the Teamsters Union never really ended. A winner emerged over the years. The winner happened to be the law. If Galluccio could convince Shellenberger he had little trouble buying off police and political protection, then maybe there could be a comfort level between both men.

"If the feds send me up on this case, then we could lose everything we've worked for, Tommy," Shellenberger noted in detail. "This go round, the government's trying to stick it where it hurts the most."

"No goddam way!" Galluccio yelled, ferociousness in his voice. The hard pounding of his fist sent scary vibes around the room. "Nobody's going to take the Teamsters away from us. My Uncle Angie grinded his balls into the dirt to help build the Teamsters into what it is today. He fronted the money for those goddam casinos out in Las Vegas, not to mention that he helped make those gambling establishments into what they are today. We can thank some incompetent fuckhead who screwed things up, just like that Bakewell prick screwed things up for us out in California. Uncle Angie's parents, my beloved grandparents, they came to America with barely two nickels to rub together. They died poor and left my old man and his brothers and sisters with nothing.

I'll take a bullet to the forehead before the feds come along and snatch the Teamsters away from us."

"The way I see it, Tommy, we'll all take a bullet to the forehead before we let the government jerk the Teamsters from under us," Shellenberger entailed with strong conviction.

"I promised my Uncle Angie on his deathbed that I wouldn't go back to the cowboy days of the *River Quay Wars*. I promised him that I wouldn't go around blowing up everything in sight, just because a bunch'a fuckheads wouldn't sign their businesses up with the Teamsters. I swore an oath to my uncle, and I'm damn sure going to keep it."

"And we'll have'ta keep that promise to Angie."

"Uncle Angie also told me on his deathbed that the feds were gonna start up another one of their witch hunts, long after the mess that was made in River Quay."

Galluccio meant every word of what he told all the men present at the informal Mafia meeting. Not a soul living or breathing on the Earth was going to snatch the Teamsters Union from his legendary Kansas City crime family. The dining room, which was used solely for conference purposes, shifted to a creepy silence. Galluccio threw his head back and drifted into a world of void. Briefly, he reminisced about how a jerkoff named Sal Rizzitello fucked everything up for the rest of the crime family. This only raised his blood pressure to unnecessary heights.

Millions of dollars per year skimmed from the Las Vegas casinos were sucked down the drain. How could Rizzitello have been so stupid, so goddamned careless? But still, Galluccio refused to allow the federal government to snatch away the money and power his Uncle Angelo Galluccio had built from the ground up. He remained determined to keep an iron grip on the Teamsters Union, specifically in the Midwestern region, which he had direct access to, and the contracts that Mason Shellenberger negotiated.

"See what happens when you get too relaxed?" Galluccio explained to Shellenberger. Redness formed at the tip of his nose. A lethal dose of anger filled his mind.

"What's going on, Tommy?" Shellenberger asked, noticing the rise in Galluccio's flaring Sicilian temper.

"Fuckups like *Rizzo* made my Uncle Angie lose out on millions of dollars."

"Sal Rizzitello?"

"That stupid cocksucking-motherfucking-sonofabitch kept his private notes out in the open!" Galluccio exploded. "My Uncle Angie told this prick to keep the cash and notes in a safe in his basement. When the feds kicked into his house, they found everything they needed to put all the bosses in the fucking can."

"Didn't they find detailed records of receipts from the casinos out in Vegas?"

"Receipts along with a lot of other stuff."

"So Tommy, what do you want me to do until my trial comes up?"

"Keep doing what you've always been doing. We'll get access to the jury foreman and you'll beat that case with a breeze."

"How're we going to do that?"

"How else, Shell? Elections are coming up real soon. My political contacts around Kansas City need their palms greased. Their girlfriends are just as needy as them. You know, those kinda broads who think money washes up on beaches."

"Sometimes, I wish I could give those goddamn feds a piece of my mind."

"Be careful, cause speaking your mind can get you into a lot of trouble."

"How?"

"Capone once spoke his mind and it got him a slash right across the face."

"Yeah, yeah, I've heard that story before."

"Told some guy's sister that she had a beautiful ass. Before he could turn around, a sharp blade came whisking across his jaw."

"Guess that's how he got the nickname *Scarface*."

"My Uncle Angie met Capone when he became a made Kansas City guy."

Galluccio now averted his attention over to Gino "The Bulldog" Vazzano. There were a growing number of strip joints around the greater Metropolitan-Kansas City area. The problems grew to the point of total frustration.

This raised concerns for a weary Galluccio. City Hall never stopped putting restrictions on the skin clubs around the city. You played by their rules or you didn't operate a skin business. Local politicians didn't want any of the jerkoffs touching the girls during lap dances. None of the young and pimple-faced teenagers under eighteen were admitted in the clubs.

Total nudity meant non-alcoholic drinks. The strippers had to be eighteen and older. If sexual acts were performed, they were carried on outside the clubs with the horny tricks in hotels or in the privacy of someone's home.

Galluccio felt he pumped life into their meeting. Finally, he got around to the subject of child pornography. Vazzano sensed the vibes wavering off Galluccio. Judging from his body language and facial expression, he'd become very upset.

"Nobody's going to put our families in jeopardy over shoving kids in porno movies and magazines," Galluccio spoke with authority. He steered his eyes of fury over at Vazzano. "I've said it before, and I'll say it a million more times, kids are innocent and they don't hurt nobody. They should all be taught well by their parents. They should be given a chance at life by finishing school, going to college or the military afterwards, then doing right by their family and friends, and the people in their neighborhoods."

Vazzano penetrated the blatant expression across the face of the wily Kansas City Mafia boss. Demons of guilt nagged at him. "Is there a problem here, Tommy?"

"Sure, Gino, there's something I'm having problems with," Galluccio interjected. "What's going on with these teen girls you're hiring in our strip clubs?"

"It's only a few of them who work for me at *Glitter Girl's*."

"Word got back to me that these girls are only fifteen and sixteen."

"Well—."

"Gino, please tell me that it's not true," Galluccio expressed with disappointment.

"Yes, Tommy, but—."

"Word also got back to me that you're going to allow one of your porno buddies out in California to use young girls in some of his skin flicks," Galluccio revealed to Vazzano.

The titanic temper of Galluccio was on the rise.

"Their legal ages were changed to eighteen on their birth certificates."

"Who'd you have'ta pay under the table?"

"Some of my political contacts here in Kansas City."

"What political contacts?"

"Some city and county political guys who're friendly with Carmine and Mikey."

"Changing their legal ages shouldn't've mattered in the first place, Gino. That's child pornography and you're inviting the FBI to come after us."

"My orders come from the bosses out of Chicago, Tommy."

Galluccio blasted straight at Vazzano. He whisked his finger right in his face. "You're dead motherfucking wrong, Gino! Your orders come straight out of both Kansas City and Chicago. You've got bosses in Chicago and Kansas City who hands down your orders."

"The bosses in Kansas City have always taken their orders from the bosses in Chicago," Vazzano argued with impunity.

Vazzano didn't mind shooting off sparks of belligerency at Galluccio.

"Have you lost the better part of your fucking mind?"

"No, I haven't."

"Since when did you stop doing what your bosses have assigned you to do?"

"Tommy, I've never been insubordinate with any of the bosses."

"I can't tell."

"Maybe we should speak with Carmine and Mikey about this issue."

"On an issue like this, we don't have'ta speak with Carmine and Mikey Bernazzoli," Galluccio proudly boasted. "Is that understood?"

"Yes, it's understood," Vazzano replied, his voice cluttered with resentment. "I've understood every word you've spoken at this meeting."

Galluccio shot up from his seat. His dark Sicilian eyes burned with fury. "When my Uncle Angie was the boss of the *Kansas City Outfit*, he dealt with some punk who let kids come through his drive-in theatre and watch porno movies. He dealt with another shitbag who peddled porno to kids and snorted the powder. One ended up losing his drive-in without a penny to his name, while the other ended up getting his theatre burned down and his balls blown off. Myself and the bosses in Chicago take this child porno shit real serious. The guys made into our families take it real serious, too."

"I take it serious, too," Vazzano substantiated.

"The legal age for those young girls dancing in our strip clubs, and the ones going off into skin flicks out there in California, is eighteen years old. No younger than that age, Gino."

"Whatever you say, Tommy."

"Don't ever let me have'ta repeat it again."

As a veteran in the adult entertainment industry, Vazzano already knew federal laws prohibited strippers and adult film stars under the age of eighteen. If only he knew the uncomfortable position he'd put the Midwestern crime families in, Vazzano would've willingly submitted. His two interests remained the same, which was money and more money.

"Gino, I've told you a million times to slow things down," Galluccio complained. "You've got your palms wrapped around all the porno operations in Kansas City, St. Louis, and Chicago. I understand that you've got some things working in Wichita, Oklahoma City, Des Moines, and Omaha, not to mention the strip joints that're making a killing in some of those smaller hick towns. You're running the bookstores and video stores, the adult film warehouses and distribution networks, all with your buddy out in California. When is the Galluccio family going to get their cut of this goldmine?"

"Don't worry, Tommy, your family will get a piece of the action."

"When?"

"Times have changed," Vazzano enlightened Galluccio. His rattling voice was laced with elusiveness. "Those city council pricks are always trying to get zoning ordinances passed. They're trying to keep us from operating within 500 feet of schools and daycare centers and churches."

"Here in Kansas City?" Galluccio asked.

"Yes, right in this city."

"But Chicago's not much different from Kansas City."

"The action is much hotter there. You've got more big spenders in Chicago."

"Money talks, Gino. Bullshit limps around on crutches."

"The way I see it, all the crimes are committed up there on Capitol Hill."

"Talking about those scumbag politicians again?"

"Of course," Vazzano purred. "If the right side of the government went up there on Capitol Hill and did serious background checks, half those politicians would be in jail."

"Do you want to see some real crooks?" Galluccio giggled. "Take a good fucking look at the same city council sonofabitches up there at city hall. They call us gangsters and racketeers because we're supposedly breaking the law. They're the most disgusting kind of thieves within the law. Those cocksuckers steal from our tax dollars and spend the money like it's running water. They pay for all of their personal expenses. They buy expensive presents for their families; hotshot shit like fancy sports cars, fur coats, and gold and diamond jewelry for their wives and girlfriends. They're nothing but legal gangsters, anyway. So, fuck the city council pricks and those other politicians, too. Sometimes you have'ta fight their asses all the way up to the Supreme Court."

Galluccio viewed politicians as nothing but sweat, piss, shit, vomit, and spit, the same human filth all mixed in together. His now deceased uncle, legendary Kansas City Mafioso, Angelo "The Animal" Galluccio, taught him that if you didn't fuck the system, then the system eventually fucked you first. Imagine the concrete balls the government had threatening to kick organized crime out of the Teamsters Union.

Imagine them trying to shut down some of their profitable strip club operations. Angela re-entered the dining room in a gracious manner. Submissively, she poured Galluccio another glass of scotch until the glass almost overflowed. She disappeared with the quickness.

"Don't worry, Tommy, everything's going to work out okay," Vazzano appeased Galluccio with great confidence. "We've got plans to iron out all of our problems and concerns."

"What are these plans?"

"While out in California, my business partner, Arthur Whitley, he and I discussed plans of moving into phone sex and adult cable programming. Hell, maybe even computer internet porn. Those businesses are producing big bucks these days, Tommy."

"Exactly, who is this Arthur Whitley character?"

"The *Godfather of the Porno Industry.*"

"Question is, can you men generate bigger revenues for the Kansas City and Chicago families?"

"Cash beyond your wildest dreams."

"Alright, bring it to the table," Galluccio ordered, sipping lightly on his scotch.

"Look at it this way," Vazzano propositioned. "If major corporations can get some of the gravy, then why can't we?"

"Which major corporations?"

"Hotel chains and major media outlets. Money's pouring out of their asses from skin flicks being shown in their hotel rooms. Cash is spilling out of their ears, eyes, and noses from exclusive rights and distributorship of the porn merchandise."

"How much initial investment are we talking about putting up?"

"Just a few thousands."

"Which'll do what for us?"

"Convert those thousands into millions," Vazzano spoke convincingly.

"Can't argue with that."

"Tommy, porn's a multi-billion dollar a year industry. It's getting bigger all the time. There're bums out there cleaning up. We're talking about an industry that pulls in more than Major League Baseball, the National Basketball Association, and the National Football League, all combined."

"Wow, that's serious!" Galluccio fizzled with interest.

"There's no reason why we can't muscle in and cream off some of the millions that're waiting for us."

"Alright, sounds like a plan I'm willing to roll with," Galluccio approved. "But before we make any key moves with any further porn operations, we've got to get the approval and protection from the bosses in Chicago. It sounds like a strong business plan that Carmine and Mikey will fall in love with. Remember, keep those underage girls out of the strip club and porno businesses. With Shell's trial coming up, we don't need any more heat from the law than we're already getting."

"The rules do apply to everyone," Vazzano smiled.

"Shell's already got the feds breathing their hot smelly breath up his ass."

Galluccio covered every important topic. He decided to adjourn the meeting and retire for the day.

Chapter 6

GALLUCCIO CARRIED CRUCIAL matters over into the next day. He felt he had complete control of another important meeting. Finally, he landed on the subject of drugs. This really made everyone sit up. Galluccio was aware of how all the men present looked back and forth at one another. Their rolling eyes went from across the table and from opposite ends. Ever since the 1920s and 30s, and on into the 1990s, there'd been repeated condemnations of drug dealing. Like many of the Mafiosos in Kansas City and elsewhere, Galluccio decided to bend the rules. There was far too much money to be made from the sale of drugs.

He knew this from having kept his eye on a group of inexperienced hoods who sold drugs out of one of his liquor stores on Independence Avenue. Angelo Galluccio always reasoned, *"You can get involved in drugs, just don't get caught dealing in drugs."* The Galluccio crime family made a small fortune from dealing in heroin and cocaine. A changing of the guard had taken place. Many years were spent trafficking heroin from Sicily into the United States. The family's main connection was to the Colombians who found a way to process their own heroin. The good news for the midwestern crime families was how heroin had made a comeback well into the early 90s. Whether shooting it into their veins or snorting it up their noses, the demand for the white powder remained serious. The man who Galluccio and the Chicago bosses enlisted to control narcotics within their Midwest families was a muscle named Mickey Castucci. He possessed a powerful build with cauliflower ears and brown wavy hair. A man of fine taste, he dressed in tailor-designed Italian suits and sampled the best Italian food at legendary Kansas City restaurants like *Jaspers* and *Italian Gardens*.

Galluccio jerked his head back to take a long swig of scotch. The assiduous men knew he prepared to discuss the most important subject of all, judging from the inquisitive expression outlined on his face. The spacious dining room became very quiet.

The puffy red eyes of Galluccio circled the table and he spoke. "For a lot of years, we've taken our cut of the drug money that's been made out on the streets. Mickey has handled the shit for our family here in Kansas City and for the bosses in Chicago. The spics over in Colombia have always been good at supplying Mickey with all the coke he's needed. With a big supply of coke, crack-cocaine can be made and distributed around to the dealers and junkies. The cops and politicians are taking money under the table like never before, while the product is still being spread out on the streets. The judges will take their payoffs, too, especially if the money is big enough. That way, everybody's protected, from the highest to the lowest liasions. I personally know several men in politics, right here in Kansas City, but it wouldn't do no goddam good if we didn't handle this drug business systematically. When I was only 17 years old, I had trouble with drugs myself. And let me tell you men something, the shit sent me into a frenzy. I'm a business man, just like my Uncle Angie was. He always told me to give people what they wanted in such a way that it didn't hurt other people. People wanted to gamble and we helped them gamble; they wanted liquor, cigarettes, gas, and meat around the wartime, and my Uncle Angie's family took care of all that."

Castucci spoke in an advisory tone. "We won't have to worry about the law if we don't take care of our problem that's happening down in Colombia."

Galluccio shot Castucci one serious stare.

"Problem?" Galluccio asked. "What problem are you talking about?"

The attentive Mafiosos twisted and turned in their seats. None had a single clue as to what Castucci was talking about.

"The spics are down in Colombia helping the DEA wipe out the coca plant crops," Castucci explained to his colleagues. "The bastards are flying over the plants with those fucking crop-dusting planes, then dropping fumigation chemicals to wipe out everything on the fields."

"That will gravely cut down on our supply of coke," Galluccio feared.

"No doubt, Tommy."

"So, those pricks think they've got the *cajones*!" Galluccio gristled. He slammed his glass down on the hard oak table. Then, he ejected a grumbling noise into the air.

"But the good news is that the Campesinos are shooting up at those planes with their M-60s. They'll probably back out sooner or later when they find out that it's not worth the risk and expense."

Castucci rationalized his point quite well. He swayed his head repeatedly at Galluccio.

"Are your men ready to make their move to Miami?" Galluccio inquired, his tone consultative. He blew thick cigar smoke in the direction of Castucci.

"Hector Victorio and Tricky Sam have got everything they need to make the run."

"Don't let the nigger and the spic screw things up. We've got too much at stake for them to be making any costly mistakes."

Galluccio, being the veteran Mafioso he'd been groomed to be, knew heat from drug trafficking burned hotter than a mad furnace.

"The shipment is coming into Puerto Rico from Colombia in about a week," Castucci detailed. "They've got everything under control as far as I can see."

"You won't have no problems getting the shipment out of Puerto Rico and into Miami?"

"None, not as far as I can see."

"Question is, Mick, do you really have everything under control?"

"Absolutely, Tommy."

"Look, Mick, make sure everything's set up positively right."

"Everything'll come together like clockwork."

"The feds nowadays are breathing down our fucking necks. Their breath is just like a hot blowtorch melting away cast iron."

"We'll keep the feds at bay while getting the goods to the Midwest."

Galluccio never wanted to sound like some paranoid space cadet. He only looked out for the best interest of his crime family. He knew very well how the U.S. Government had plenty of radars and boats and planes which were used for busting drug smugglers. Over a ton of cocaine was due to arrive in Miami to feed the multi-billion dollar drug market in the United States. Like Galluccio mentioned, no screwups were permitted. He closed the meeting by expressing his sincere thanks to everyone in attendance.

Chapter 7

FEW WERE LEFT to wear the crown of *"King of Kansas City Organized Crime"*. The late Angelo "The Animal" Galluccio, the old man who'd been regarded as the *Godfather of the Kansas City Mafia*, had been let out of a Springfield, Missouri prison just to die. With delight, he passed the torch on to his handpicked successor, his brutal and equally notorious nephew, Tommy "The Caveman" Galluccio. Law enforcement officials knew organized crime in Kansas City wasn't dead, though it'd been crippled over the years. FBI Agents might've chopped off the head of the Galluccio crime family, but the arms and legs were still functional.

The war between organized crime and the law never ended. The winner who'd emerged over the years was still the law. Tommy Galluccio didn't ignore the fact that every step of known Midwestern mobsters were being monitored and bugged by FBI Agents hungry to put them away. The nightmare of infiltration by an informant caused Galluccio and other upper-rank figures to develop an extreme bunker mentality. Word got around how some of Galluccio's Chicago crime colleagues traveled to meetings in the trunks of cars to avoid detection.

Some were paranoid to the point of avoiding opportunities for promotion within their own crime families. Mason Shellenberger found himself back in the hot seat once again. Galluccio enlisted the services of his most trusted attorney, Michael Curren. He'd become the power attorney whose family background had defended three generations of the Galluccio faction. Michael recently ran for the coveted position of Jackson County Prosecutor, but critics within the political arena argued he was nothing more than a defense lawyer who had spent his career keeping criminals out of jail.

They reasoned how Michael used his skills to keep people like Angelo Galluccio and other mob-related folks out of prison. They felt more comfortable having someone serving in the capacity of having prosecutorial experience. Those bureaucratic assholes needed to stop kidding themselves. Whether they were the prosecution or the defense, they all had something crooked up their sleeves, either party playing both sides of the fence.

On the other hand, political leaders in Kansas City wanted to move a former U.S. Attorney into the top spot. They saw this conservative prick as someone uniquely qualified to redirect and mold the Jackson County Prosecutor's Office into the innovative and strong office he was capable of doing. They viewed him as being an aggressive and level-headed prosecutor with a proven track record of putting away and fighting to keep criminals in jail. Michael Curren never cared what sort of scrutiny he came under. Everytime he defended someone bearing the last name of *Galluccio* or an associate, his paycheck always flashed big dollar signs.

If given the opportunity, some of the same people who criticized him would defend the same crooks. The end result was always money. Everyone was out to grab their share of it. Mason Shellenberger entered the courtroom wearing one of his many tailor-made Italian suits. Michael Curren followed behind him with his large black briefcase swinging down by his legs. Both men sat with commanding poses over at the defense table. The prosecutors and witnesses sat with patience.

The jury box filled up with their twelve members. A small portion of Shellenberger supporters came into the courtroom and sat quietly. Yet another one of those boring preliminary hearings. The Honorable Alfred McNeal emerged from his chambers to speak with the parties involved in the trial. The fireworks had ignited in the upcoming case of the United States of America versus Mason Shellenberger. It would be the first case on the docket ready to explode. The United States was represented by Brian Woddell and Shelton Bailey, two special attorneys with The Department of Justice. The preliminary proceedings got underway and Woddell questioned Shellenberger.

"Are you Mason Shellenberger?" Woddell asked his adversary.

"Yes sir," Shellenberger answered, quite mild-mannered.

"Are you here represented by your retained counsel, Mr. Michael Curren?"

"Yes sir."

Brian Woddell turned to the Honorable Alfred McNeal and said, "Sir, we are here for arraignment."

"Very well, Mr. Woddell," the Honorable McNeal gestured. "Will you read the indictment in order that we may enter the plea?"

"Yes, your honor."

"Mr. Clerk, get me Title 37, will you, please? Mr. Shellenberger, you have heard the indictment. What is your plea?"

"Not guilty, your honor," Shellenberger blurted out with supreme confidence.

"Plea of not guilty will be entered," Honorable McNeal purred. "The court finds that on page 18 of the omnibus, hear that the defendant anticipates the filing of a number of motions, including production of Grand Jury transcripts. Apparently, the government has no objection to production, if ordered by the court; also to dismiss the indictment for failure to state an offense, and to dismiss the indictment on constitutional grounds. There may be other motions."

Sets of mysterious and curious eyes watched every breath Shellenberger took.

Honorable McNeal picked up where he left off. "Mr. Curren, may I make an inquiry as to how long you would like to prepare, serve, and file all motions which you anticipate filing in this case?"

"Your honor, I have a case before Judge Hollister that is going to go to trial on April 29th in Jefferson City, Missouri."

Michael cleared his throat and continued. "I would request that the court, and I have already told the government that I would make this request, that I get until we have filed all of our motions, and I expect to have them by then."

"Well, I would like to get the motions in before then, because this case will probably be on the trial docket to be tried. Ordinarily, I permit at least ten days for filing. If you need a bit longer, I would give consideration to doing that. What I would anticipate doing in this case is to set up a briefing schedule, and then set the case under Rule 15.4 for a pre-trial at which any and all the underbrush be cleared out. If your motion is well taken, I will grant your motion. That will be the end of it. If your motions are not well taken, you have an appropriate record on appeal. Will 20 days be enough, and 10 days for the government to answer, Mr. Curren?"

Michael rushed to answer your Honor McNeal's question. "I am still working on motions, your Honor. Would you extend me five more days?"

"Yes, I would."

"Great, your Honor."

The Honorable McNeal turned to speak to Brian Woddell and Shelton Bailey. "Prosecution, I'll need you to prepare, serve, and file all motions within 20 days. How long do you want, Mr. Bailey, to respond? Ten days?"

"Ten days is sufficient, Your Honor."

"The government is to file suggestions, in which I would assume opposition."

"Yes, Your Honor," Woddell said, clearly picturing the legal war between his team and Shellenberger.

"Now, what is the situation as far as the Grand Jury transcript is concerned? I notice that the offense involved in this indictment allegedly occurred and related to offenses back in 1982 and 1983. Is there any reason why the government will not turn over promptly to Mr. Curren for his examination, and by examination of his client, but not to be released further without order of court the transcript of the Grand Jury testimony?"

"No objection, Your Honor," Shelton Bailey prompted. "We stated this in the omnibus hearing."

"Are there any preliminary matters that would be necessary for the defense to be able to prepare the motions? I would think that with the Grand Jury transcript, that would be all you would need under the circumstances."

This was the part of the preliminary hearing which got real juicy. Woddell wanted more than anything to entrap Shellenberger. Fully, he knew Shellenberger was connected to the Galluccio crime family, the same Kansas City crime family who controlled the Midwest Teamsters Unions and the billion-dollar pension funds for several decades. To put an end to their absolute control over the labor unions, which remained under the iron grip of the Galluccios and the Bernazzolis, would be a badge of honor for federal prosecutors. Something had to be done about a group of hoods dipping in and out of the Teamsters pension funds for their own personal needs.

"Your Honor, we do have a problem," Michael replied, cocky-voiced. "This case arises out of a civil case that was tried before Judge Davidson in January of 1983. The government's major witness, and probably the only witness that will bear on the merits of the case, was the recording secretary named Richard Delaney. Mr. Delaney testified against Mr. Shellenberger in the last trial, in which he was acquitted. He testified before Judge Davidson that the minutes were true, they were correct, they were made at the time, and accurately of the transactions that were recorded."

"Was the transcript ever written up?"

"Well, Your Honor, I assume it was because I think it is required under federal rules to be filed. We have the other three transcripts, but we don't have any transcripts of the major witness who testified to the contrary."

"Where did you get those transcripts?"

Michael and Shellenberger turned to lock eyes. A sudden feeling of apprehensiveness gripped both of them.

"I got them from the union, Your Honor, as best I remember."

Shellenberger intervened by saying, "They sent them out to us, which we asked for them from the court reporter."

"Let me see one of the transcripts."

"That would be Anne Baker, Your Honor."

"I have concluded that after the court states the additional questions, which have arisen, that the hearing on the pending motions should be continued until nine o'clock on Monday morning."

Shellenberger continued to slip away time and time again. The government never made a successful prosecution against him. Of course, those were the fringe benefits of being connected to organized crime families in Kansas City and Chicago. The muscle of Galluccio had been called upon. He'd been a man with lots of policemen, politicians, and judges in his hip pocket. Michael Curren and Mason Shellenberger walked down the federal courtroom steps in downtown Kansas City with their arms interlocked. Both men shared similar sentiments about politicians.

"Mike, politicians are greedy," Shellenberger connotated.

"They can be easily paid off," Michael added, followed by a disgruntled smile.

"And you can practically get away with anything."

"Angelo Galluccio proved that when he was still alive."

"Tom Pendergast proved it, too."

"Think we'll beat this case?" Shellenberger inquired.

"Hands down, we'll beat it."

Shellenberger realized he was under tremendous target by the federal government. Government officials knew corruption still existed within the Teamsters Union, even since the early days of Jimmy Hoffa. Now, they had to prove their case in court once again.

Chapter 8

THE BIG DAY FOR the trial of the United States of America versus Mason Lowenstein Shellenberger arrived. Their main target had been indicted three times before the current trial. Shellenberger willfully and knowingly made false and fictitious entries for labor organizations and secretly increased union dues for thousands of union members. The International President of the Over-the-Road and City Transfer Drivers, Helpers, Dockmen and Warehousemen, for Local Union Number 45, sat with confidence over at the defense table. He bolstered one of his favorite tailor-made Italian suits. Supporters of Shellenberger occupied the whole left side of the spacious courtroom.

Prosecuting attorney Brian Woddell and defense attorney Michael Curren gave impressive opening statements. Woddell stood at the witness stand, ready to cross-examine their first witness. The secretary for the powerful Local Union Number 45, Richard Delaney, had been called as a key witness before the Federal Grand Jury. Richard displayed a nervous demeanor. He'd been duly sworn before giving his crucial testimony. Woddell glided towards the witness stand and the questioning began.

"Will you state your name for the record, please, sir?" Woddell requested.

"Richard Delaney," Richard bounced back.

"And how are you presently employed, Mr. Delaney?"

"Secretary for the Mid-American Truck Lines."

"Okay. Are you presently a full member of the Local 45, The Teamsters Union?"

"Yes."

"How long have you been a member of Local 45?"

"Since 1975."

"Are you presently an officer of Local 45?"

"No."

"Are you presently a candidate for office?"

"Yes."

"Which office is that?"

"Treasurer," Richard cited.

He took a moment to exchange serious stares with Shellenberger.

"Are you running on a slate with candidates of other offices for Local 45?"

"Yes."

"And who's running for president on that slate?"

"I believe a gentleman by the name of Joel Price."

"Okay," Woddell paused. His sharp eyes rolled around the tense courtroom. "Now, Mr. Delaney, have you ever held an office in Local 45?"

"Yes."

"And which office was that?"

"Recording Secretary."

"And when did you assume that position?"

"Starting in 1982."

"And for how long did you serve as recording secretary?"

"Until April or May of last year."

"Was that after the indictment in this case?"

"Yes."

"How did you learn of your duties as recording secretary?"

"Through a gentleman named Robert Hudson, the previous recording secretary."

"And what was your understanding of what your duties were as a recording secretary?"

"Taking down the minutes of the important things and resolutions that went on in the membership meetings."

"Were you also to attend executive board meetings and take down the minutes?"

"Yes."

"Did that understanding of your duties ever change while you were recording secretary?"

Discreetly, Richard glanced out at Shellenberger again. Only those two men knew he'd been paid to lie up on the witness stand. The hefty cash paid to Richard, which had been authorized by Galluccio, was generous enough to even make the Pope tell lies.

"No."

"Did you in fact take down the minutes at board meetings?"

"Yes."

"Did you take down minutes at meetings of the membership during those years?"

"Yes."

"During those meetings, when you took down minutes as recording secretary, did you do your best to include all the matters passed by the board or membership?"

"Yes."

"Did you ever intentionally leave anything out of your handwritten minutes?"

Once again, the weary-glossy eyes of Richard motioned out to where Shellenberger sat as cool as an iceberg.

The intimidating eyes of Shellenberger reminded Richard how he'd been paid to fabricate his testimony. Richard knew the dreaded consequences if he didn't twist his story around.

"No."

"What did you do, Mr. Delaney, with the handwritten minutes at the conclusion of the meetings?"

"I'd leave them on John Knoll's desk."

"What was Mr. Knoll's position?"

"Vice-President."

"Did you sign your handwritten minutes?"

"No sir, I didn't."

"Who'd sign them, Mr. Delaney?"

"John Knoll signed them."

"Weren't these handwritten minutes typed by someone?"

"Yes."

"Who usually typed them?"

"A woman named Carol Wright."

"Wasn't she the bookkeeper for Local 45? Isn't that correct, Mr. Delaney?"

"Yes."

"Didn't you later sign her handwritten minutes?"

It wasn't always easy to tell lies. When the piercing eyes of many watched you from around the courtroom, you'd become nervous. Richard couldn't slip up and get caught in one of his own tales.

"No."

"Who signed them?"

"John Knoll signed them."

"Well, explain that for us, please."

"After John became Vice-President, he carefully read over the minutes and they were approved."

"Did Mr. Knoll chair some of the meetings?"

"Yes."

"Who else chaired meetings in those years for the membership?"

"Only John Knoll."

Brian Woddell pictured the word "lie" scribbled all over the sunken face of Richard Delaney. He suspected something rather strange about the manner in which he answered the questions. Somehow, he just couldn't place a glove on it.

"At any of the meetings, would you sign your typewritten minutes of the board meetings?"

"No."

"I don't believe you're telling us the truth about the meetings you were at, Mr. Delaney."

Woddell took a short breath and continued. He had a wealth of arsenal to fire away at Richard. "Mr. Delaney, isn't it true that you looked the other way while Mr. Shellenberger and other union officials misappropriated union funds?"

"No, that's not true," Richard denied.

The arsenal in Woddell's questioning grew more intense.

"Mr. Delaney, isn't it true that you were fully aware that Mr. Shellenberger and other union officials dipped into the Teamsters Union pension for their own personal needs?"

"No, sir, that's not true."

Shellenberger seemed to have had a hypnotic effect on Richard. It's almost like he fed him the exact lies to tell.

"Weren't you aware of a $100,000 payment that Mr. Shellenberger authorized to himself?"

"I wasn't aware of such a payment."

"How about Mr. Shellenberger's gangster cronies?"

"What gangster cronies?"

"Mafioso characters out of Kansas City and Chicago who've controlled the International Brotherhood of Midwestern Teamsters Unions for several decades."

"Sir, I'm not aware of such Mafioso characters."

Woddell continued to blast away with damaging questions.

"You're not aware, Mr. Delaney, of these Mafia cronies because you turned a deaf ear and a blind eye whenever important union meetings took place."

"Sir, I don't know what you're talking about."

"Do you recall the *River Quay Mafia Wars* of the 1970s?"

"Yes, I do."

"The long destructive wars which perpetrated violence by the Galluccio Mafia family? The same vicious wars which involved business owners and their disassociation with the Teamsters Union? Do you recall any of this, Mr. Delaney?"

"Vaguely."

Michael Curren hopped up from his seat and cried, "Your Honor, if the prosecution is going to ask questions of the witness about these meetings, I would like him to ascertain whether he has any independent memory of whether he is testifying under the doctrine of past recollections recorded from the actual minutes in these meetings."

"Sustained," the Honorable Alfred McNeal said.

"There'll be no further questions."

Michael Curren approached the witness stand straightening his tie. He shot straight into his cross-examination of Richard Delaney. "Mr. Delaney, you don't have any independent memory of what took place at any of those meetings, do you?"

"No."

"I guess that qualifies no past recollection," Michael suavely mentioned. "None of them were made at the time that you were at any of the meetings?"

"No, they weren't."

"Wasn't there a token of appreciation for the work, time, and energy expended by my client, Mr. Mason Shellenberger, on behalf of Local Union 45?"

"Yes, there was," Delaney jarred, having concealed his timidness.

"To the best of your knowledge, did Mason Shellenberger authorize a $100,000 bonus for himself?"

"No."

"Did the highly-esteemed President, Mr. Mason Shellenberger, on behalf of Local Union 45, recommend to delegates a resolution authorizing a payment of $100,000 to be paid for the compensation for vacations that he had not used in the past ten years or so?"

"No, that's not true at all."

"Are you testifying under oath that you have no independent memory, Mr. Delaney?"

"Yes, I am."

"Do you ever recall Mr. Shellenberger misappropriating union funds?"

"No, I don't."

"Do you ever recall Mr. Shellenberger having liasions or conducting business with so-called Mafioso characters?"

"Never."

"Hasn't Mr. Shellenberger always kept the International Brotherhood of the Midwestern Teamsters Union an honest and clean union?"

"Definitely."

"How would you personally describe the overall character of Mason Shellenberger?"

From over at the defense table, Shellenberger cut a slight grin. He fixed his tie and sat in the most erect stance.

"Mr. Shellenberger's an honest, hardworking, fair, standup, and intelligent man."

"I'll have no further questions, your Honor."

Woddell and Michael executed masterful closing arguments. Once again, the verdict turned out to be "not guilty" on all charges. Mason Lowenstein Shellenberger became victorious over the U.S. government.

No one could've been happier than Galluccio. He positioned Shellenberger as his supreme flunky. No one, absolutely not a soul, was going to snatch the International Brotherhood of Teamsters away from the Galluccio and Bernazzoli crime families. Their livelihood depended upon them keeping a chokehold on the powerful unions.

The *Kansas City Times* and *Chicago Tribune* newspapers never stopped printing headline articles such as: **Teamster Official Still Linked With Chicago and Kansas City Mobsters.**

Was Mason Shellenberger out of the FBI's crosshairs? Only time would tell if the spotlight would come shining his direction again.

Chapter 9

WORKING AT THE Internal Revenue Service for Randy Rivera turned out to be a nice place of employment. Randy possessed handsome-manchild looks which were quite eye-catching. He stood mid-height, kept himself well-groomed, and dressed in the latest contemporary fashions. Sure, working a seasonal government job didn't carry any benefits, but it certainly presented him with the grand opportunity to seduce as many women as possible. The number of single, lonely, and desperate women walking around the IRS complex were quite amazing. The number of divorced women with children was even greater.

While passing the Code and Editing Department, the loveliest sight struck Randy like electricity. Another IRS worker with a desirable face and hard-toned body walked towards one of the canteens. She knew how to swivel her sinful body parts. This might've been an invitation for Randy to make his presence known. He followed the beauty into the canteen and stood beside her at one of the vending machines. She swung her head sideways. With surprise, she stared right into Randy's handsome face. The attraction between the two seemed to click.

Now the mold had been broken. Both parties were tongue-tied, not knowing how to start off with a conversation.

"I'm.....I'm.....speechless," Randy juggled with his words.

Usually, he was a seasoned womanizer when it came to flirting with women. The young lady with superb model looks might've been the challenge he desired.

"Why?" she replied, a gleaming smile like a toothpaste ad.

"You look so good."

"You're quite handsome yourself."

"So I've been told."

"What's your name?" she asked, seeming quite interested.

"Randy Rivera. And yours?"

"Tracey Jones."

"I see you work in Code and Editing here at the IRS."

"So much work we've got in there. What unit do you work in?"

"Data Conversion."

"I saw you at the all-employee meeting in the cafeteria."

"The Rules and Conduct Meeting?"

"That's the one."

"Wanted to fall asleep in that boring meeting."

"You were conversing with some girl."

"Thick sideburns on her face?" Randy described, the details quite insulting. "Thick hair all on her arms and legs?"

"That's not nice," Tracey defended.

She cracked a smile while covering her mouth.

"Jeeeezzzz!" Randy shivered. "Her name is Lucy Green. She's uglier than homemade sin. She looks just like a mad pitbull in the face."

"You're cruel."

"I only call it the way I see it."

"I see."

Randy looked down at one of the tables in the canteen. He noticed the front page headline of the *Kansas City Times*. He picked it up to read an interesting article.

"Anything exciting on the front of the newspaper?" Tracey asked.

"Just an article about some Teamsters Union President guy here in Kansas City."

"So, is the write up talking about anything interesting?"

"Says that this Teamsters Union guy might still be connected with Mafia men here in Kansas City and Chicago."

"Mafia guys?"

"Yeah."

"What's his name?"

"Mason Shellenberger."

"You can't get no more Jewish than a name like *Shellenberger*."

"Got that right."

"From my understanding, Jews and Italians have always been tight with one another."

"When my uncle worked for a local dairy company, he was a member of the Teamsters Union."

"Growing up as a kid here in Kansas City, I remember bombs blowing up buildings down in the River Quay area."

"You remember, too? If my memory serves me right, the River Quay Wars were about the Teamsters and the Mafia."

"You're right."

"Back in the day, it wasn't nothing down in River Quay but strips clubs and adult porno theatres."

"Don't forget the city market."

"How can I? Fruits, vegetables, chickens, and Italian sausages were at your disposal."

Randy glanced down at his watch and told Tracey, "Look, I have to get back to my work station. The white boss lady in Data Conversion is one of the biggest racists in the whole world. Catch my drift, sweetheart?"

"Around here, anybody of color would catch your drift."

"Glad to know that I'm not alone about issues like that."

"Around here, you can smell racism in the air."

"Boy, ain't that the truth," Randy accepted.

"Let me give you my telephone number," Tracey smiled, reaching for a pen and paper.

This shocked Randy into a brief daze. Tracey volunteered to give up her phone number? Maybe there were still some women who weren't uptight and were attractive at the same time.

"So, this is your number?" Randy asked with delight.

"Yes, and please use it," Tracey offered with more delight.

"I'll give you a call."

"See you later."

"Okay."

Tracey Jones walked back to the Code and Editing unit. The art of her shapely body captured the vivid imagination of Randy. Nosy workers from her area stuck their heads out from their cubicles. They slid their chairs near the aisles. The nosy asses wanted to see what was going on. They weren't much different than most of the jerkoffs from around the IRS building. A possible love connection had been made.

Chapter 10

THE FEARS OF GALLUCCIO, Shellenberger, and Chicago's powerful Bernazzoli Brothers were abruptly rekindled. They learned how the Washington, D.C. based Organized Crime section of the FBI had assigned a Special Agent to come to Kansas City, Missouri. An anonymous agent had been assigned to gather information from local FBI files on the International Brotherhood of the Teamsters Union members who allegedly had an unholy alliance with organized crime. Shellenberger had been acquitted over and over. The federal government decided to come back at him full force.

The thought of government officials snatching his iron grip off the Teamsters Union brought tears to the eyes of Galluccio. Taking the powerful union away from his notorious crime family would've been worse than taking the Superbowl and the World Series away from diehard football and baseball fans worldwide. Now more than ever, the FBI had its eyes on Shellenberger and the organized crime underlings he was tied in with. Galluccio reflected back to when *Time* magazine had mentioned his Uncle Angelo being part of an exclusive article as a *Kansas City Mafia Don* who directed killings from the Federal Penitentiary in Springfield, Missouri.

Prison bars couldn't crush the empire that Angelo "The Animal" Galluccio built with impunity. Fear, intimidation, murder, and bribery were the elements his nephew used to keep the empire going strong. Galluccio, in the meantime, didn't worry much about any future indictments handed down by the U.S. Attorney's Office.

Hundreds of people poured into the enormous Pendergast Mansion in the heavy traffic and non-stop busy section of Ward Parkway. Galluccio and his wife Phyllis had experienced marital problems. They'd gone through trial separations. He loved her dearly and would lay his life down for her. The oldtime Sicilians believed in it until death. She complained about many things, but it was just part of being a woman.

NETWORK OF KILLERS

He didn't spend much time with his four children since he was busy overseeing his criminal empire. For many men, a wife was nothing but a permanent live-in whore, a whore men grew to love unconditionally or to hate eternally. There lied in the difference of why so many men remained single and usually paid for sex. Angelo handed down some valuable advice to his nephew Tommy about women.

"It's beautiful to have a woman by your side," Angelo once told his young teenage nephew. *"But remember that women can be like a piece of property, you have to spend money on them to keep them up. You stop spending money, and their value will depreciate, just like an old building or car that hasn't had any upkeep."*

"Uncle Angie, are all women like that?" Tommy asked his favorite uncle.

"Most women won't admit it, but they love receiving the finer things in life."

"So, you're saying that all women come at a price?"

"Absolutely."

"Why's that?"

"Read your Bible sometimes, nephew. Eve came at a price. Delilah came at a price. Bathsheba came at a price. Even Jezebel had her evil price."

"I just don't understand, Uncle Angie."

"When you get a little older, you'll understand, nephew."

Phyllis required the finer things in life. She had to maintain a certain lifestyle. Galluccio didn't have a problem showering her with the finest cars and jewelry and clothing. Their children attended topnotch private schools in North Kansas City. Anything to keep her mouth from running off to some greedy divorce lawyer was well worth it. Today was their thirty-fifth wedding anniversary. Elite people from all areas of Kansas City, Chicago, and St. Louis came to join in on the celebration. A bursting sun shot rays of light across the clear Kansas City skies. The temperature cooperated for their wedding anniversary. A mild 70 degrees tingled with a light breeze out of the east.

Judges and special prosecutors, top corporate executives and CEO's, wealthy lawyers and doctors with their own private practices, professional athletes, and local entertainers filled every inch of space on the first level of the enormous mansion. A large painted portrait of *"Kansas City Political Machine"* Tom Pendergast hung gracefully near the front corridor. The portrait attracted bystanders like hungry lions drawn to an African buffalo. Pendergast became one of the most famous Kansas Citians ever. He once owned the very mansion in which the guests occupied. He was also the godfather of Tommy Galluccio, and one of the closest friends his Uncle Angelo Galluccio ever knew.

The beautiful maid-housekeeper, Angela Claybrook, traveled to every room with platters of food and cocktails. Rudely, guests snatched drinks off the platters, then faded away with no remorse. Some figured out how she'd become the temporary whore Galluccio kept on his payroll for both work and play. The rotating eyes of several men followed her around the room. Their wives were right beside them, but it didn't taint their lustful spirits. Her alluring beauty possessed an irresistable charm. She'd been used for the sexual disposal of Galluccio.

"Look at the juicy juggs on that broad," commented a senator from the Eastern District of Missouri. He stood still holding a glass of bourbon on the rocks.

"Can't miss those set of tits," replied a Missouri State Representative, standing shoulder-to-shoulder with the senator. His mouth hung wide open as he lusted for Angela.

"Tommy's got the good life."

"Any guy'd love to be him."

"Women, money, power, what more could a guy ask for?"

"Think he's sticking it to that broad?"

"I'd say he was."

"Understand she works for him here at the *Pendergast Mansion*."

"Nothing like having a gorgeous live-in piece of ass."

"Especially with a beautiful face and body to match."

"I'll toast to that."

The two Missouri politicians tapped glasses and belted down shots of their cocktails. They were the biggest whores in the world, which was to say the least. Other caterers kept drinks in the hands of thirsty guests and food in their hungry mouths. A live band hired exclusively by Shellenberger played jazz and light rock music for everyone's listening entertainment pleasures. Galluccio summoned for all of his guests to crowd into the huge living room. All glasses were filled while the band cut off the music.

"Listen up, everyone!" Galluccio happily yelled before the group of people. "I'd like to propose a toast to my beautiful and supportive wife of 35 years."

Phyllis held her glass up before all of the people and said, "And I'd like to propose a toast to my wonderful and handsome husband of 35 years."

"Phyllis," Galluccio said softspoken. "You're a very special woman, and you've always made my life complete."

"Tommy," Phyllis said, her voice heartfelt. "You've always been good to me for these 35 wonderful years. There's not a man more special on this Earth than you."

"When I first set eyes on you, Phyllis, I knew you were that special one. My whole life had changed the day that I met you."

"I'm looking forward to another 35 wonderful years with you."

"So am I."

The striking couple kissed and hugged. Lovingly, they dazed into one another's eyes. The guests erupted into applauses and whistles and laughter. The band played the mega-hit pop and r&b tune entitled *Biggest Part of Me*. The crowd parted while Phyllis and Tommy were given enough space to dance and serenade one another. Other couples came forward to dance. The wedding anniversary celebration ran smooth, and it was now time for Galluccio to get to the real order of business.

Chapter 11

HEAT FROM THE Federal Government, which was due to come down on Galluccio and the others at any given time, spit out flames hotter than any furnace. On short notice, Galluccio called an important meeting at the *Pendergast Mansion* two days following his 35th wedding anniversary. The meeting was so important that the top bosses from Chicago were flown in. Carmine and Michael Bernazzoli, the supreme bosses who controlled all the territories west of Chicago, including Cleveland, Kansas City, Milwaukee, Denver, Las Vegas, Reno, Los Angeles, and San Diego, had to step out of their territory to preside with Galluccio.

One of the men who attended the secretive meeting was Carlo Ruggiero. He was a corrupt narcotics detective who'd been employed by the KCPD for more than 25 years. Galluccio summoned Ruggiero, his cousin and trusted confidant, because he mastered the executing tactics of bribery and gaining special information. Shellenberger rushed in on short notice. He kept his profile low until given the signal to meet with other members of the Mafia family. After going through the trial of a lifetime, he wanted to take a break from all the hoopla.

Senator Joseph Weinberg, an absolute corrupt Missouri politician who represented Jackson County, accepted Galluccio's invitation to be in attendance. Weinberg, a true veteran of dirty politics, was mid-height, handsome, well-dressed, and full of vitality. He did the same thing so many other wicked politicians did. He took the money now and asked questions later. When Galluccio discovered he'd still been for sale, he jumped at the opportunity to put him on his payroll. To his advantage, Galluccio still followed the advice of his beloved Uncle Angelo. Politicians were greedy. They could be paid off. You could practically get away with anything. If left up to Weinberg, Galluccio and the Bernazzoli Brothers would get away with just about any crime.

Francisco "Frankie Bonecutter" Provenzano and another Galluccio soldier, Robert "Bobby Crusher" Randazzo, zoomed in when their bosses barked out his requests for them to be in attendance. Randazzo, a short, stout, and brutal man with limited intellectual stature, worked hand-in-hand with Provenzano when it came down to committing murders or roughing up a few tough guys who got out of line. Soldiers from Carmine and Michael Bernazzoli's Chicago street crews took the first plane out of Chicago and into Kansas City when they first heard their orders.

Angela had everything set up for the Midwestern Mafiosos hours before the meeting began. An assortment of silver platters with food lined the polished oak conference table. Liquor bottles sat before all the attendees. Sparkling glasses with smoking ice cubes melted away. Once everyone had taken their seats and gotten comfortable around the huge conference table, Galluccio turned to glance into the eyes of his concerned criminal contemporaries.

"Men, we are honored to be in the presence of two men who are a man's man," Galluccio expressed out of great respect. Opening the meeting with genuine compliments for his two bosses was commonplace. "When I say this, I speak for myself and everyone else in this room. It is a great privilege as well as a pleasure, to have Carmine and Mikey Bernazzoli to be in attendance at this important meeting."

Carmine Bernazzoli nodded with respect. "Everyone should be gracious to Tommy Galluccio for arranging this meeting. Tommy's also a man's man, someone we've come to trust and respect."

Michael Bernazzoli laced his voice with honor. "Men, everyone should be honored to be guests here in the *Pendergast Mansion*. We are thankful to Tommy Galluccio for putting this meeting together. Tommy's a man of honor, and we have come to appreciate that greatly."

To hear his Mafia superiors shell out such compliments, made Galluccio feel an aura of invincibility.

"Men, it's time to get this problem out in the open," Galluccio said. "We've got bigger problems that I'm sure you already know about."

"The FBI Agent coming to Kansas City?" Shellenberger mentioned before everyone. Intense worry rung out through his voice.

"Yes, the goddamn FBI agent on his way to Kansas City!" Galluccio thundered.

"Washington's sending him down here to Kansas City," Shellenberger revealed.

"Yeah, yeah, Carlo already told me."

"What are we going to do, Tommy?"

"Recently, Carlo introduced me to an older broad who works in the Jackson County Prosecutor's Office, with ties that cross over into the FBI and U.S. Attorney's Offices."

"How's she going to help us?"

"Easily," Galluccio yielded, speaking light-winded.

Cleverly, Galluccio thought of a powerful masterplan.

"How?"

"This broad has access to files in the FBI's office."

"The Kansas City field office?" Shellenberger quizzed Galluccio.

"Where else, Shell?"

"You're shitting me!" Shellenberger responded with amazement.

"No, I'm not," Galluccio added. "In fact, she can get this agent's name who's coming down from Washington. She can tell us exactly where he'll be staying once he gets here to Kansas City."

"Shiiiiiittttttt!" Shellenberger fizzled, his chest pumped far out.

"Men, the pressure's gonna come from all sides."

"The U.S. Attorney's Office is ready to drop a ton of boulders down on us."

"This broad actually supervises the division of the prosecutor's office that handles complaints about those selfish pricks who aren't making their child support payments."

Carmine interjected with a commanding hand signal. "When will this agent be in town?"

"Next week, Carmine," Galluccio unveiled.

"Is there a name, Tommy?" Michael asked.

"Not yet, Mikey," Galluccio said. "Understand he's some Puerto Rican guy."

"They're sending a spic down to Kansas City to investigate us?" Carmine giggled.

Galluccio lashed out with some harsh racial insults. "Some taco-burrito-menudo-eating-greaseball-spicaroo!"

"I'd like to know, what the fuck's going on with the government?" Michael inquired.

"They just don't quit!" Galluccio snarled. "They just won't go away. They're still pissed off about Shell beating that last embezzlement case."

"And their way of retaliating is to sick one of their federal pitbulls on us."

"Shell beating that case, they look at it as a spit right in the face."

"Tell us more about this broad," Carmine requested.

"When Uncle Angie was still alive, she helped him with some tax collector's property tax receipts that he needed for getting some license plates and property lease documents."

"Do you trust her, Tommy?" Michael inquired, his voice tainted with suspicion.

"Sure, I trust her," Galluccio nodded. "She'll give us the information that we need, and that's all that counts at this point."

"So far, so good."

"She'd come over to Uncle Angie's house to do up his wife's hair. Aunt Florence loved this woman to death."

"What exactly will we have to do for her?" Carmine asked.

"Grease her palms with a few thousand bucks. We can send her on an all-expense paid trip to somewhere like Vegas or the Bahamas. Nothing more, Carmine."

"Her name?"

"Sally McNeil."

"Guess that's the name of a woman you can trust."

Before the highly secretive meeting proceeded, Galluccio turned his attention over to Senator Joseph Weinberg. "Joey, you're gonna have'ta help us out on this one."

Senator Weinberg ejected a tender smile back at Galluccio. "Tommy, you've been good to me over the last few years. Your Uncle Angelo was always good to me. You've made substantial contributions to my political campaigns over the years. You've been good to all of the staff in my office, not to mention all the other special favors you've given."

"And that's why we'd like to ask this special favor of you," Galluccio reciprocated.

"Just name it, Tommy."

"This Sally McNeil gaining access to those private FBI files won't be easy. With you being a senator strongly representing Jackson County, can you use your contacts to help us infiltrate that FBI office?"

"Shouldn't be a problem," Senator Weinberg spoke with confidence. "Senate hearings occur all the time. Some of those same hearings require information from FBI sources who usually hand over documents from their field office."

Corruption at the highest level took place inside the *Pendergast Mansion*.

The criminal element knew no boundaries, whether in politics or law enforcement.

"You see, Joey, when we send Sally in the FBI's field office, we're going to need agents and other workers in that very office to look the other way. We don't need no shit like *Watergate* happening here in Kansas City. It's not good for business, and they could end up doing a clean sweep of all of us."

"Hoffa would roll over in his grave several times if he knew something like that took place with the Teamsters," Carmine respectfully intervened.

"I personally know several agents who work out of the K.C. office. I can arrange for the right agents to disappear while she's getting the information you're needing. All you have to do is let me know the exact time she'll be present in their offices."

"Joey, don't know what we'd do without you."

Senator Weinberg shot Galluccio a discerned look. "For the record, Tommy, with the federal government cracking down on organized crime and the Teamsters all over the country, everybody's going to eventually feel the pinch."

"Everybody?" Galluccio shrugged. "Whaddaya mean, everybody?"

"Before long, the feds up there in Washington, they're going to be on everyone's backs."

"Not you guys. But, why?"

"Officials with the Department of Labor are coming down hard on everybody. Questions about politicians on the city, state, county, and federal levels not monitoring unions in the fashion that pleases them have become part of their agendas."

From inside the dining room, Galluccio uncovered a 60 widescreen television. After slipping a recent tape into the VCR, he pressed the play button to the remote. For all intent purposes, he wanted every attendee to know why they had reason to be worried.

A top anchorman with NBC News in New York reported before many viewers how the nation's largest trade union got hit by a truck today.

"The Justice Department moved to wipe the mob out of the Teamsters once and for all," the NBC reporter told millions of American viewers.

"We all might be in deep shit," Carmine feared.

"This is serious shit," Michael baffled.

"Guys, the government's playing for keeps," Weinberg contested.

"That's to say the least," Galluccio confirmed.

The NBC reporter picked up where he left off. "Armed with over 200 criminal convictions of Teamsters officials and mob members within the last 20 years, the Justice Department is suing to have the top national union officials thrown out of office."

"That could very well be you, Shell," Galluccio enlightened Shellenberger.

"Let's hope not," Shellenberger detested.

Edward McNaughton, a top New York U.S. attorney for the Eastern District of New York, flashed his serious face across the widescreen television and said, "Today, the United States Government is bringing a major lawsuit to attack and reverse, once and for all, a major American scandal, organized crime's alliance with the Teamsters."

Galluccio pressed the stop button. He glanced at Shellenberger with exclusivity. "They're putting heat on Teamsters officials all over the fucking country!"

"Just when we thought we'd gotten those cocksuckers off our backs."

"Exactly!" Galluccio huffed.

"This go round, the government's serious," Carmine said.

"Either we move fast, or we're all dead meat," Michael said.

"Like I told ya earlier, they're pissed-the-fuck-off that Shell beat that last case."

"Sounds like it's become a personal vendetta."

"What are we going to do about this FBI Agent when he gets to Kansas City?" Shellenberger asked, just as worried as his criminal superiors.

Galluccio turned to lock eyes with Carmine and Michael. Carmine, being the master schemer from the old school, must've had a million ideas bouncing inside his head. For them, time wasn't forever.

The federal government made plans to move against them. As a last desperate measure, they had to move against the federal government. Somebody had to act first. Far too much was at stake for the *good old boys*.

"I say he's gotta be hit," Galluccio barked, his voice Napoleonic. "Carmine and Mikey, with your permission and your blessings, I say we take out this agent once he gets here to Kansas City."

"My permission and blessings you have, Tommy," Carmine approved.

"Like my brother, Tommy, you also have my permission and blessings," Michael added, no remorse to follow.

The Chicago bosses spoke, and in the world they co-existed in, their word was law.

"Say what!" Shellenberger gestured with a bodily wiggle in his chair.

"Something wrong, Shell?" Carmine asked.

"Talk about heat, Carmine," Shellenberger feared with intensity. "We bump this G-man off, the feds will come at us with everything they've got."

"Not if the hit's executed the right way," Michael disputed. "It's never what you do, Shell, it's how you do it."

"Are you sure, Mikey? Now's not the time for the feds to be sticking blowtorches up our asses. All these indictments I've come up against are starting to sting."

Carmine signaled with a hiss. A shot of brandy gurgled in his mouth. "Shell, do you know what we're up against? Do you realize what we stand to lose? Wasn't it you who told us what this agent's matter of business was? Wasn't it you who told us that if this agent finishes his matter of business here in Kansas City, that all of us will be crippled to our knees?"

"Sure, Carmine, I said all of that," Shellenberger admitted. "If he collects all of his data from the local FBI files, and takes all of that information back to Washington, the

U.S. Attorney's Office can build a strong case against us and the Teamsters. If solid indictments and convictions come down, then we're all finished."

"My point, exactly," Carmine said. "Normally, we don't clip G-men or coppers or politicians unless we do special favors for them, and then they turn around and fuck us royally. But in this case, this agent's gotta be hit."

Galluccio interjected by saying, "Shell, this time around, the government's playing for keeps. Their trains are on the tracks, and they're gonna come after all of us full speed ahead. They're gonna run over everything in its path. Uncle Angie guaranteed me that the government would start up another one of their witch hunts. Well, we're going up against another one of their witch hunts. Sure, I promised him on his deathbed that I'd never go back to the destructive days of the *River Quay Wars*."

"The *River Quay Wars* were quite counterproductive," Shellenberger reminded his constituents. "Bumping off this agent might also prove to be counterproductive."

"Carmine and Tommy's right," Michael confirmed. "Every since Capone and Giancana's days, coppers and sheriffs and G-men were usually left alone, but we're dealing with some real serious shit here. Keep in mind, the bosses from the old days were the ones who built this Teamsters empire into what it is today. Ask yourselves, do you really want to jeopardize one of our biggest operations going today?"

"The contract for this agent's head has already been given to Frankie Bonecutter and Bobby Crusher," Galluccio unveiled before his criminal colleagues.

Galluccio, being the one brave soul he was, especially when it came down to taking out the highest of government officials, didn't mind playing another game of high stakes. Dollar signs blinded him when there were issues of morality and pious innuendos. The Bernazzoli Brothers didn't give a shit about murdering an FBI agent. If the Mafia could assasinate the President of the United States, then why couldn't they eliminate a relatively unknown FBI agent? If they could bribe judges and politicians and police officers into allowing them to operate their corrupt businesses, then why couldn't they move someone out of their way who posed as a serious threat to a billion dollar criminal enterprise?

All sets of eyes landed over to the seat of Carmine Bernazzoli. The dining room converted to a respectful silence.

"As we all know, a hit like this can't be carried out without us covering up our tracks," Carmine warned everyone in his presence. "Tommy, you can brief Frankie Bonecutter and Bobby Crusher on the ins and outs of this hit. Mikey and I can ship some backup guys into Kansas City from Chicago."

"A little extra manpower for this job wouldn't hurt things," Michael compounded.

"Either we clip this G-man now, or all of us are headed straight to the poorhouse, maybe even the jailhouse," Galluccio envisioned for all involved parties.

The main topic being the plot to assassinate an FBI Special Agent was due to make a 90-degree turn.

Galluccio bolted his arm to the middle of the table and said, "Like I told some of you men before, I'd do anything to keep from going back to the cowboy days of River Quay."

Carlo Ruggiero broke his long silence. He weaved into the intense discussion. "Sally McNeil couldn't give us any present information about where the agent will be staying. I'm sure we can get access to the information about which hotel he'll be staying at."

"How?" Galluccio asked his cousin.

"He'll be on the lists at one of these Kansas City hotels."

"And you've got access to those lists?"

"At my disposal."

"How about access to names on hotel rosters?"

"Every one of them around the city."

"Are you sure, Carlo?"

"I'm the law," Ruggiero bragged, displaying raw arrogance. "When matters involve the law, I'm above it, I'm around it, I'm between it, and I'm certainly not below it. The convention bureau will give up any information that I request."

"Finding out his whereabouts when he gets to Kansas City will be a big help before we carry out this hit."

"Indeed, Tommy."

Galluccio suddenly turned beet red in the face. He threw out a bold hand signal. "Like I told Shell the other day, I promised Uncle Angie that I wouldn't go back to those crazy, fucked up days of River Quay. Blowing up the places of business for those muthafuckas who wouldn't sign up with the Teamsters, isn't going to solve a goddamn thing."

"Angie'd be proud of what we've accomplished here in the 90s," Shellenberger said.

"Pukes like Binaggio and Leonetti deserved to have gotten their balls blown off."

The ruthless Sicilian blood of Ruggiero ran rapid through his veins. Corruption was business-as-usual for the notorious narcotics detective who remained on the payroll of his treacherous cousin. Galluccio washed the back of Ruggiero. In return, Ruggiero washed the back of Galluccio. The Bernazzoli Brothers turned to Galluccio with a set of vehement eyes.

"Tommy, once Carlo passes the information on to you, get the information passed on to Frankie and Bobby," Carmine ordered Galluccio.

"Will do, Carmine," Galluccio bowed.

"I do mean PDQ."

"And it will be pretty dam quick."

Did holding on to the Teamsters Union mean that much to the crime bosses of the Midwest? Enough was enough and a war between the casualties hadn't started. While other union officials around America were quitting, retiring, dying, or in the process of stepping down, Shellenberger was just getting warmed up. The Midwestern bosses refused to let him leave his high position. No one could take the place of their top man, a man who Angelo Galluccio entrusted all the way up to his deathbed.

"They're squeezing the NPWU guys there in Chicago," Carmine asserted. "The government's trying to bump all the Chicago guys right out of Local 207."

"They're appealing it, too," Michael said.

"The government's witch hunt done made its way into Chicago."

Galluccio passed around major newspaper publications from New York City and Chicago and Los Angeles, as well as other major cities in between. Flashing before the mysterious eyes of everyone, were a recent wave of headlines which talked about the turmoil within the Teamsters Union. Allegations ranging from from Mafia links to embezzlement, from extortion to intimidation, and from bribery to murder, were like words growing legs and jumping off the page.

"Carmine, how much does Local 207 pull in a year?" Galluccio asked.

"Ten million, at least," Carmine calculated.

"Betcha holding multiple union jobs together in Chi-town ain't easy."

"It's like trying to keep a soft dick while jerking off."

The biggest challenge the Midwest Mafia bosses faced was the government's war on organized crime and their alliance with the Teamsters Union. For the time being, they had to sit, wait, listen, and seize the opportune time to make their move on an unsuspected FBI agent.

Chapter 12

DAYS FOLLOWING THEIR meeting with Carmine and Michael Bernazzoli, Galluccio summoned Provenzano and Randazzo to another secretive meeting at the *Pendergast Mansion*. The two feared executioners entered the dining room and fell into one of the seats around the huge conference table. As he promised, Carmine shipped two backup shooters in from Chicago. The maddog killers from their Chicago street crew drove into Kansas City earlier during the day. Judging from the looks etched on their faces and in their strong posture, fear appeared to waver off them.

Galluccio learned from his Uncle Angelo how contract murders had to be entrusted to made men in their own families. Made men had the incentive to get the job done. They carried out contract murders down to the minute detail. Galluccio and Ruggiero devised a plan which placed an identity on the FBI special agent due to arrive in Kansas City in a few days. Everything was outlined of how the agent was going to be murdered. The four vicious killers sat like men of nobility. The room converted to a silence so intense until the only sounds made were the beating hearts of the five men present. An FBI Agent's life was in their hands. The floor was turned over to Galluccio.

"Listen up closely, men," Galluccio signaled to the foursome. "Myself and the bosses in Chicago couldn't be more happier. The woman Carlo gave us access to, she got inside the FBI's Field Office here in Kansas City. With the help of Joey Weinberg, she got access to the information that we'd been dying to get. We have everything we need to know about this agent on his way to Kansas City."

"His name?" Provenzano asked his boss.

"Wilfredo Feliciano," Galluccio answered with a smile.

"A spic?"

"Yeah, a Puerto Rican guy originally from New York."

"The hotel? Where will he be staying?"

"The Holiday Inn in Westport."

"On Westport Road?"

"Yes, that's the exact location."

"What day will he be here?"

"Monday."

"Next week?" Provenzano inquired.

"Yes, on the 24th."

"Of October, huh?"

"Yes."

"That's my mother's birthday."

"Happy birthday to your moms, Frankie Bonecutter."

"Thanks, Tommy. Any description of this agent?"

Galluccio reached down into a large brown envelope. He produced an eight-by-ten glossy photocopy of the same FBI special agent due to arrive in Kansas City in just a few days. The vivid photo was passed over to Provenzano. He studied the features of the good-looking Puerto Rican man for the moment. After brief scrutiny, the photo was passed over to Randazzo.

"How'd this Sally McNeil broad get this photo out of the FBI's office?" Provenzano questioned Galluccio.

"Photocopied it and slipped it in her purse," Galluccio explained.

"Now that's clever, Tommy. So, this is the spic that we'll be looking for?"

Galluccio sucked in a strong breath. "That's him."

"Carlo moves pretty fast. Didn't take him long getting access to those hotel rosters."

"Not long at all."

"This body of work should be a piece of cake."

"Are your instructions clear?" Galluccio asked Provenzano.

Galluccio sent intense vibes into the air. He penetrated the dark eyes of his most trusted killer.

"We understand, Tommy," Provenzano said in full compliance.

"Do you understand how this hit's supposed to be carried out?"

"Yeah, every single detail."

"You men are going to be equipped with guns, walkie talkies, scanners, binoculars, and a getaway car with a skilled driver."

"And we'll need all of that to finish the job."

"Also, we want you to be dressed for the occasion," Galluccio guided his cold-blooded killers.

"Whaddaya mean dressed for the occasion?"

"Remember what we talked about at the meeting the other day?"

"Yeah, I do."

"When Carmine said that we'd have to cover up our tracks?"

"I remember."

"We don't want no witnesses identifying any of you guys."

"That'd defeat our whole fucking purpose."

"The right clothes were picked out for you men from one of these surplus stores."

"I was once in the military," Provenzano mentioned. "The right clothes would have to be a black shirt, black khaki pants, black gloves, a black skull cap, and black boots."

"Black's always the best disguising color when you're carrying out a hit."

"So far, the plan sounds good."

Galluccio jerked around in his seat. For identification purposes, he pointed at the two men who'd been quiet during the secretive meeting. "Frankie and Bobby, this is Louie Calabrese and Bart Gagliano. They're from Carmine and Mikey's Chicago street crew. They handle the loansharking, gambling, extortion, and other strongarm work on Chicago's South Side. If the need be, we're going to use them as backup shooters."

"Who's going to be driving the getaway car?" Provenzano wondered.

"Carmine picked out another one of his Chicago guys to be behind the wheel."

"Does he know the Kansas City area well?"

"It'll be your job to show him the route to take after the job's finished."

"No problem," Randazzo said.

"The job should go smoothly," Provenzano promised his Mafia superior. "I can assure you of that."

"Frankie, I don't want no goddamn screwups!" Galluccio jolted, mild-manneredly. He wanted the sophisticated murder to go as planned. "Carmine and Mikey wanted to send a hit team in from Chicago to do the job. Since this agent's coming on Kansas City turf, then I asked them to let me use my own men and handle most of the arrangements."

"There won't be any fuckups, Tommy. I can promise you that."

"Alright, let's go over the details again."

Provenzano gathered his thoughts together before detailing the pre-meditated murder. "First, we slip into the right clothes, which'll be all black. Our heads and part of our faces will be covered with the black skull caps. Second, we're going to make sure that all of our equipment is fully operational."

"You're doing good so far," Galluccio praised.

"Then, it'll be our job to watch this agent like a hawk. When the time's right, that's when we'll make the hit."

"Make sure there're few people as possible around when you do the hit."

"Absolutely."

"You're not shooting to hurt him, you're shooting to kill him. Is that understood?"

"Shoot to kill, Tommy. Those are our orders."

"If you and Bobby have'ta empty both of your pistols in this G-man, then do whatever's necessary."

"When we're finished, he'll be dead from lead poisoning."

"Pump as many shots as possible into this FBI prick and run for your fucking lives."

"He's as good as dead, Tommy."

Like the sands running through an hourglass, time remained a major factor for the Galluccio and Bernazzoli Mafia families. There'd been strict rules laid down by Mafia bosses from the old days. The rules stated how the killing of honest lawmen were prohibited. Death sentences were usually imposed on those who took out honest policemen and FBI agents and Federal Marshals. As for Galluccio and the Bernazzoli Brothers, they ignored the rules and established some rules of their own.

Galluccio and his organization didn't take lightly that they plotted the murder of an FBI special agent. Wiping him out would probably get the government off their backs. Their problems were much bigger. As of the present, his killing would be the biggest risk they'd been willing to take. Now was not the time to worry about the government sicking their hounds on a criminal organization as powerful as their's. In the meantime, Shellenberger remained the anointed Midwestern Teamsters Union boss. Along the way, he abused his power by dipping into the pension funds and skimming huge profits from phony and legitimate documents. All of it was to benefit himself and the crime families he represented.

The meeting between Galluccio and the four extreme executioners was adjourned. The only two people left in the *Pendergast Mansion* were Galluccio and Angela Claybrook. Both parties met down at his olympic size swimming pool in the lower section of the enormous mansion. Their eyes narrowed at one another. It'd been weeks since he made love to Angela.

"Angela, you are just one beautiful creature," Galluccio marveled to his housekeeper.

"Compliments from you, Tommy, is like money in the bank," Angela marveled back.

"You have that magnetic effect on men."

"Whaddaya mean?"

"Guys walk past you and their dicks get hard."

"Oh, stop it," Angela chuckled.

A charasmatic energy filled the pool area. Angela dropped her terry towel robe to the ground. In the total nude, she jumped inside the pool and swam four laps. She floated to the edge and Galluccio pulled her out of the water. Beads of water dripped from her sculptured body. She dropped to her knees and unzipped his pants. A raw piece of meat met up close to her lips.

"No! No! No!" Galluccio rejected, drawing Angela back up to where their eyes met. "I don't want you giving me a blowjob yet."

"Something wrong, Tommy?" Angela asked, eager to unleash her freakish talents on him.

"I don't always like having my dick sucked before this lovemaking crap."

"Why not?"

"It's something that my Uncle Angie always told me."

"What's that?"

"Get this," Galluccio said, then firing up a fat cigar. "A guy getting his dick sucked means that he's in bad shape."

"Not true, Tommy."

"If a guy can get it up naturally, then he can fuck 20 times as hard. If a woman's gotta do these crazy tricks with her mouth to get it up, then there's something weak about a guy."

Getting a blowjob from Angela wasn't such a tragedy. She had a velvet mouth. She sucked men off until they came like a nuclear explosion.

The kisses exchanged between Angela and Galluccio were potent. Their closeness earned him an instant erection. No other woman satisfied him the way Angela did.

"You look like you're ready to explode," Angela laughed.

"Can you blame me? Look at this body of your's!"

"Wanna suck a tittie?"

"Hey, Angela, my brand's two-percent skim," Galluccio joked.

He dropped his pants and boxing shorts to the wet floor while she ripped his shirt off.

Angela tilted her head and grabbed the hardness of Galluccio. "My, my, Tommy, I didn't know that this gun of your's was loaded."

"This is a hold up! Now drop down and spread'em."

"Oh yeah, stick me up with that hard dick, baby."

Galluccio and Angela entered the warm pool in the nude. Their bodies met with a sensual slap of tender flesh. He entered her willing moistness. She bent forward for him to clamp her needle-sharp nipples with his pliable lips. Her sharp nails sunk into his back. Up and down, Angela initiated the greatest sex to Galluccio. He worked facial muscles he thought he never had.

"Oh, Angela, it's going to happen, baby!" Galluccio moaned.

"C'mon, Tommy, you can do it!" Angela moaned back.

"Angela, you're gonna make me—!"

"Go ahead and come, baby!

"Oh, here it comes!"

A powerful orgasm exploded inside of Angela, certainly a relief for Galluccio.

Chapter 13

GALLUCCIO AND SHELLENBERGER decided to act out airtight alibis just in case local law enforcement agents came asking questions. What better place to go than to Chicago? The bosses in the "Windy City" had no problem with them coming on such short notice. One of the trusted bodyguards and chauffeurs of Galluccio loaded the shiny black Lincoln Towncar with their luggage. He escorted them out to the running car. The traffic out on Ward Parkway slowed up considerably while the Lincoln rolled out of the driveway. Their brief journey to Chicago began.

A brief meeting between Provenzano, Randazzo, Louie Calabrese, and Bart Gagliano took place in an abandoned warehouse in the West Bottoms of Kansas City, which sat near a set of old railroad tracks. Expertly, they cleaned their guns. They checked to make sure their walkie talkies were in perfect working order. The foursome had been fitted for their all-black clothing. In repeated fashions, they rehearsed how the murder of the FBI special agent would be carried out.

"Alright men," Provenzano began. "Again, let's go over how this hit's gonna take place. Bobby, do you understand the orders Tommy gave us?"

"Piece by piece, Frankie Bonecutter," Randazzo alertly responded.

"Are you sure?" Provenzano asked, his voice tainted with reinforcement.

"Right down to the wire."

"How many shots?"

"Enough until he's dead," Randazzo recited. "At least try and empty my gun into this spicaroo."

"What're you going to do after the last shot?"

"Run for my fucking life. Run until we make it to the getaway car."

Provenzano circled around Randazzo inside the dim warehouse. He also had to go over the plans with Bart and Louie, the two backup shooters from Chicago.

"Louie, do you remember all the details?"

"Like a piece of pussy I've been sticking all my life," Calabrese said.

"Bart, do you remember everything?"

"Like the dirty underwear that I change everyday," Gagliano said.

"What are you two guys going to do just in case our guns jam up?" Provenzano inquired to both backup shooters.

"Fall in right behind you guys and start blasting away," Calabrese outlined.

"Assist you guys in taking out this agent," Gagliano added.

"What happens after you guys fire your shots?"

"Run like hell to the getaway car."

"Run as fast as we can and don't look back."

"Bobby, are the walkie talkies in perfect working order?"

Randazzo checked to make sure all five walkie talkies were fully operational. "Ready to go, Frankie."

"The pistols?"

He looked inside the chambers of the guns to make sure they were clean. "Mind if I try them out?"

"Go ahead," Provenzano okayed.

Randazzo set up a makeshift firing range inside the old warehouse. At the other end of the room was a 20-by-30 poster with a full body drawn in the middle of the paper. He mounted a thick piece of wood to the poster. At different intervals, he fired all four pistols at least twice. The soundproof room masked any disturbing noises.

"We're good to go," Randazzo assured everyone.

"Perfect!" Provenzano cheered. "Like Tommy told us, there absolutely can't be no fuckups. This agent's gotta be taken out as quickly and cleanly as possible. Is that understood, men?"

"Understood," Randazzo complied.

"Same here," Calabrese said.

"Definitely," Gagliano said.

Provenzano turned his attention over to the man behind the wheel, the driver of the getaway car. "Driver, are you clear on your instructions?"

"Clear as Visine," the driver said.

"Okay, what are they?"

"Stay parked at the south end of Westport."

"What else?"

"Keep the car running and in park."

"What else?"

"Listen in closely after the job's done."

"What else?"

"Drive like a bat out of hell once you four guys make it back to the car."

"But to also be careful and not get us into a wreck."

"Certainly not."

"Remember this, Westport's a real big party section of Kansas City. Traffic's crazy around those parts, especially on the weekend when all those college kids roll into town."

"Frankie, what about the cops down there?" Randazzo asked his partner.

"What about them?"

"On the weekend, there are cops crawling all over the place."

"That's where Carlo comes in. He's been with the KCPD for about 25 years. With the muscle he's got, he'll make sure that all of those KCPD boys are paid off when we do the hit."

"But somebody's gotta keep those drunk college kids in order."

"The cops will disappear long enough for us to finish the job."

"What about Westport's security system?"

"Don't worry about the security men down in Westport. Once Carlo passes the word on to the KCPD cops, then they'll pass the word on to Westport's security."

"It's all gonna come together."

"Communication is very a big thing," Provenzano reminded his fellow murderous executioners. "Any mis-communication, and we could fuck this whole thing up."

Before leaving the warehouse, they checked their pistols and walkie talkies once again. The assassination of an FBI special agent wasn't something to be taken lightly.

Chapter 14

FBI SPECIAL AGENT Wilfredo Feliciano arrived at Kansas City International Airport at the beginning of the week from the headquarters in Washington, D.C. He departed from an American Airlines flight and strolled through the K.C. airport carrying a large square briefcase. As ordered, Provenzano and Randazzo were to follow him everywhere. Like a ferocious beast waiting to move in on their prey, they watched Feliciano move over to the baggage carousel. Quite tall, handsome, and well-dressed, he stood around the carousel waiting for his luggage to spring up.

"There's our man," Provenzano whispered to Randazzo.

"That's him, alright," Randazzo whispered back.

"The spic finally made it to Kansas City."

"Too bad he won't be leaving K.C. alive."

"That you can rest assured."

"Let's go get something to eat."

"Yeah, I'm starved."

"Italian Gardens sound good. But we still can't let him out of our sight."

Feliciano grabbed his luggage and made a visit to one of the car rental counters. Provenzano and Randazzo were masters at disguising their true characters. Who was to know they were both maddog killers? Who was to know they were made members of the Galluccio Mafia family of Kansas City? With Feliciano having no clue, they stood aside and watched him give information to the clerk at Avis Rental Car.

"I'd think he would have access to a government vehicle since he's an FBI agent," Provenzano assumed.

"Him being a G-man, I'd think one of his agents working here in Kansas City would've picked him up here at the airport," Randazzo pictured.

"From what Tommy told us, this assignment he's on is strictly confidential."

"Government people picking him up wouldn't be in his best interest."

NETWORK OF KILLERS

"We've gotta watch his every move."

"Let's hope everything goes as planned."

"We just better stay on top of our gameplan."

Feliciano accepted the keys to a rental car and departed from the airport. Provenzano and Randazzo followed in hot pursuit. Since his arrival in K.C., he'd been putting together federal documents to take back with him to the Organized Crime Section of the FBI's Criminal Investigative Division. His tour of duty in Kansas City had been a rather daunting task and the stress he endured only elevated. The FBI office in Kansas City maintained a database of the organized crime criminals who'd been involved with the Teamsters Union over the years.

The familiar names of Angelo Galluccio, Nino Bernazzoli, Jimmy Hoffa, Mason Shellenberger, Richard Delaney, and several others continued to surface. The crimes they'd either been indicted for or convicted of, were bribery, forgery, extortion, labor racketeering, bankruptcy fraud, murder, and the illegal skimming of profits from Las Vegas casinos. Luckily for Tommy Galluccio, no information had come up on the computer database which linked him directly to the Teamsters Union.

He'd fallen into the virgin stages of taking control of the powerful union. He never looked to get his face flashed across a television screen or his name written up in a newspaper article. Behind the private walls of the FBI Field Office, conveniently located in one of the federal courthouses in downtown Kansas City, Feliciano searched the database. He'd learned about the recent trial which involved Mason Shellenberger and Richard Delaney. No, the government hadn't gotten their target. The feds didn't know that Delaney had been paid under the table to fabricate his testimony. Why was Shellenberger and others cunning enough to slip away over and over again?

As Feliciano tapped on the keys of the sophisticated computer database system, the name and face of Angelo Galluccio made an appearance. Information leading to him wouldn't've done no good. The former Mafioso rested under six feet of dirt in one of the most prestigious cemetaries in Kansas City, Missouri. Feliciano searched and searched until he came across information concerning Mason Shellenberger. This might've been the opening he and his FBI colleagues waited so patiently for.

The crucial information lined along the large computer screen indicated Shellenberger and some of his union officials violated companies, corporations, firms, associations, and organizations by extorting in the aid of racketeering, embezzlement of union funds, welfare and pension funds, unauthorized payments by employers to their employees, and to officials of labor organizations.

Shellenberger also engaged in the falsification of reports and maintenance of records by unions and union officials. Shrewdly, he became involved in the deprivation of the rights of union members by force, obstruction of justice, obstruction of criminal investigations, and obstruction of state or local law enforcement. With the great power he derived, he single-handedly cornered travel and transportation in the aid of racketeering, transmission of bets, wagers, and related information by wire communications, perjury, mail fraud, false declarations, interstate transportation of wagering paraphernalia, and the prohibition of illegal gambling businesses.

"My goodness!" Feliciano whiffed, his alert eyes having absorbed all the valuable information stored in the computer database. "What hasn't Shellenberger done corrupt when it come to the Teamsters?"

Dylan Hunter, another one of the FBI special agents based out of the Kansas City Field Office, came across the room to see what had suddenly excited Feliciano. "What is it, Willie F?"

"Shellenberger's done had his hand dipped in everything."

"To say the least, he's quite a remarkable durable guy."

"He's violated most of the RICO statures."

"Some good attorneys and a few breaks will get guys like him off most of the time."

"Think this is enough information to take back to Washington with me?"

"Absolutely."

"The federal prosecutors and ambitious U.S. Attorneys can build a solid case from this information."

Feliciano possessed the gifts of accuracy, honesty, and tenacity when it came to performing his intense FBI investigations.

"And finally send Shellenberger and his Mafia cronies where they belong."

"Wonder if there's political clout behind Shellenberger?" Feliciano inquired.

"Has to be," Dylan said. "Why do you think he's lasted this long?"

"I'd say that he's definitely connected."

"My belief is that a lot of the madness that went on during the *River Quay Wars* back in the 70s is still carrying on?"

"Even into the 90s?" Feliciano asked.

"Of course. The *River Quay Wars* were about the Teamsters and organized crime goons jockeying for money, power, and territory. There's still some aftermath going on."

"Those *River Quay Wars* sure made big headlines back in those days."

"Yes, they did."

"Why do you think Hoover stayed away from the Mafia for so long?"

"Our former, deceased boss, huh? Who knows why he stayed away?"

"A lot of those Mafia guys had judges and politicians and police chiefs right in their hip pockets."

"Yeah, so I've heard."

"But we're honest FBI agents. There's no quitters in our camps."

"Shellenberger's done lived a charmed life for too long."

"His fun's about to come to an end."

Feliciano couldn't wait to gather all the information and rush right out of Kansas City, Missouri. He couldn't wait to hand it over to his superiors in Washington. He knew officials employed by the federal government were less prone to corruption than local law enforcement.

Chapter 15

WILFREDO FELICIANO settled into Kansas City after a few days of working out of the FBI's Field Office. Saturday afternoon arrived and he wanted to take in a movie or even a local nightclub or bar, somewhere which provided excellent food and entertainment. He had a flight due to depart from Kansas City International Airport in the late afternoon hours of Sunday. One of the helpful clerks at the Holiday Inn Hotel Westport Branch stood before the shiny gold *"Holiday Inn"* letters on the wall. On her innocent face, she wore a welcoming smile. She possessed an inviting gesture. She'd been ready to entertain questions for the guests at the hotel.

"Are there any good bars or restaurants around here?" Feliciano asked the supportive front desk clerk.

"You're right in the mecca for bars and restaurants," the clerk informed Feliciano.

She glanced hard and became attracted to his alluring Hispanic features.

"Sounds exciting. I've heard a lot of things about this area."

"Mr. Feliciano, you're in the historic Westport District of Kansas City."

"What would you recommend?"

"Do you like bars or nightclubs that are real hyped?"

"Sure."

"There's Kelly's Westport Inn right up the street."

"Sounds like a really happening place."

"And then there's America's Pub, The Buzzard Beach, or The Hurricane."

"The Hurricane?"

"Probably one of the most exciting clubs here in Westport!" the clerk said, bolted by excitement. "They have live bands mainly on the weekends."

"How's the crowd inside Kelly's?"

"The crowd's really upbeat, usually with lots of college students. There, you've got bigscreen televisions, game rooms, and karaoke."

"What time does all this hoopla start?"

"I'd give it around ten o'clock tonight, Mr. Feliciano."

"Thanks for your help, young lady."

"You're welcome, Mr. Feliciano."

Feliciano left the lobby carrying a leather binder holding the valuable federal information he'd been due to take back to Washington, D.C. Across the street from the Holiday Inn, the cunning eyes of Provenzano and Randazzo penetrated the glass which enclosed the lobby section. Under strict orders, Feliciano wasn't to leave their sight. Standing behind them were Calabrese and Gagliano. The backup shooters were the duo who took their orders from Provenzano and Randazzo.

"There he is, men," Provenzano signaled, talking over the loud traffic which shot through Westport Road. "Just like Carlo told Tommy, he's staying here at The Holiday Inn."

"Won't be long now," Randazzo jolted.

"Tonight, he goes."

"No question about it."

"Now, we have to go and get geared up."

"Who's going to keep an eye on Feliciano?"

"He's not going anywhere."

"But somebody's gotta watch him."

"Feliciano doesn't leave until tomorrow afternoon."

"Let's hope nothing interferes with our plans."

"Either we hit him tonight, or we're all fucked."

"It'll be tonight or never."

"Our orders were for him to leave Kansas City in a pine box. And that's exactly what we're gonna do before tonight's up."

"No better time than the present."

"Alright, let's move out."

The foursome scattered from the Westport District in order to plan for the execution of FBI Special Agent Wilfredo Feliciano.

Chapter 16

A QUICK NAP AND A NICE hot shower did Feliciano just grand. The weather in Kansas City couldn't've been grander. A setting sun still dominated the clear skies. The temperatures were in the high 50s, which wasn't bad for early February in the Midwest. Patrons filled the streets of the Westport area. From Westport Road to Pennsylvania Avenue, and then from Broadway Boulevard to Southwest Trafficway, the hyped crowd took their positions towards the different nightclubs and bars.

Randy Rivera and Tracey Jones drove through an energetic section of the Westport District right at a time when the excitement began. Tracey conveyed an attitude of apprehensiveness. She concluded how Westport was an area of Kansas City where blacks weren't welcome. She wondered how the cops could push black youths along the sidewalk like herds of underprivileged cattle. She reasoned how cops didn't harrass any of the white youths who got just as disorderly as the blacks.

"There's not a lot to choose from," Tracey complained to Randy.

She observed the vast array of people going to and coming from the crowded bars and restaurants.

"What do you mean?" Randy asked, hoping Tracey remained in good spirits.

"We're not wanted anywhere around here."

"True."

"Most young black people try to get in Westport clubs, and they won't let them in unless they're 25 or 30."

"I agree."

"It's really like a no-win situation," Tracey muzzled. "We could've stayed in the part of town where were're welcome."

Many African Americans voiced their concerns about how Kansas City police officers and Westport security officers ushered crowds along, the same ones who kept everyone there in perpetual motion at all times.

"Guess the cops have to keep the sidewalks open for free flowing traffic," Randy opted to say. "I don't want to look at matters in a racial and biased way."

"But the cops don't let you stop for a second to say hello," Tracey said.

"Don't worry about it, Tracey."

"Long after we're gone, there are still plenty of white people standing around on the sidewalks catching up on old times."

"Guess if they see us standing around talking, they think it'll lead to drinking and fighting and shooting."

"To them, black skin means lots of trouble."

"Amen to that."

"Most of the clubs in Westport only play one hip hop song a night," Tracey rationalized.

"And why's that?"

"To minimize the number of blacks who'll come in there."

"Couldn't agree more."

"But, we're still gonna have a good time tonight."

As Randy cruised down Westport Road looking for a parking space, Tracey became silent. Her sweet face lost all expression. She seemed worried, like a vicegrip had squeezed her head out of proportion.

"What's wrong?" Randy asked, her worrying starting to rub off on him.

"An eery feeling has come over me."

"What do you mean?"

"I'm getting vibes that something bad is going to happen down here tonight."

"Don't be ridiculous," Randy smiled. "There are cops crawling all over Westport."

"No, Randy, I'm serious. My instincts are telling me that something bad is going to happen."

"Will you stop worrying?"

"Alright."

Randy found a parking space across the street from the Westport Center. Tracey's worrying had intensified. She didn't possess the gift of psychic powers, but went on her own intuitions about approaching danger. The number of cars cruising along the crowded streets increased. Randy and Tracey walked down Pennsylvania Avenue. They checked out the Manor Square Shopping Mall. They noticed the shiny gold letters above the front entrance. *Kelly's Westport Inn* and *Mill Creek Brewery* were the sites which made the Westport District legendary.

Feliciano stood at the bar inside Kelly's nursing a frosty glass of Miller Genuine Draft. The young men and women from surrounding colleges and universities were in full effect. Hormones bounced around the nightclub like tires at BF Goodrich. Someone looked to score on someone else. Rock music roared through the concert speakers while every sport imaginable flashed across the widescreen televisions. Though he'd been a married man for over 15 years, Feliciano couldn't help scoping in on the young college beauties who wore their jeans with tight fits. For him, firm asses and healthy breasts would've been on the menu.

Silvio Sasso, another Mafia soldier shipped in from Chicago, kept a close eye on Feliciano. From the opposite side of Kelly's, he blended in with the crowd. Courtesy of the Bernazzoli Brothers, Sasso arrived in Kansas City during the early morning hours. He traveled by car with another culprit. Though Sasso was an enforcer who broke the jaws and legs of loanshark and gambling insubordinates, Carmine decided to use him as extra manpower. Sasso excused himself for a trip to the restroom. Between one of the toilet stalls, he slipped out a walkie talkie with powerful range. To make sure none of the other men came inside the restroom, he wedged a trashcan up to the door.

"Frankie Bonecutter, Frankie Bonecutter," Sassso summoned for his fellow Mafioso. "Come in, Frankie Bonecutter."

Sasso waited a few seconds. No response came over his walkie talkie.

"Come in, Frankie Bonecutter."

A crackling noise shot through his walkie talkie.

"This is Frankie Bonecutter. Sasso, am I coming in clear?"

"Yes, Frankie Bonecutter, your response is clear," Sasso confirmed.

"Where are you posted now?" Provenvano chirped into the walkie talkie of Sasso.

Sasso spoke back into his somewhat cluttery radio. "I'm at Kelly's in Westport."

"What's the latest on the G-man?"

"Feliciano's out in the club having a beer."

"How long he's been in there?"

"A little over an hour."

"What time does that bar close?"

Sasso dug into his pocket and flipped open a schedule for Kelly's. "It closes at three o'clock a.m."

"It'll take us at least a half-hour to make it to Westport."

"Where are you guys now?"

"Me, Bobby, Bart, and Louie, we're in the West Bottoms."

"Where in the West Bottoms?"

"In an old warehouse that Tommy owns."

"Look, I'll be posted up in the club until he leaves."

"The second that he steps out of Kelly's, I want you to contact us," Provenzano ordered.

"You've got it, Frankie Bonecutter."

"Stay on schedule, Sasso."

"Will do."

Sasso shut off his walkie talkie and exited the restroom. He returned to the club section. He kept the closest eye possible on Feliciano. Randy and Tracey finished their drinks and chicken fingers. They left Kelly's and moved on to The Hurricane. The Hurricane nightclub had much to offer. After standing in a long line, they got absorbed into the madness. A live band played the latest rap, heavy metal, rock, and R&B music. The popular club became packed with wall-to-wall drunks, people who staggered from one end to the next.

Randy and Tracey raced for the dancefloor. Quickly, their bodies went to work. The closer their bodies met, the more sensual they felt for one another. To release all of their inhibitions was the name of the game, and many came to The Hurricane to relieve much sexual tension.

"Didn't know you could move like that," Randy told Tracey.

"Yeah, I've got a few moves," Tracey hissed over to him.

"The Hurricane is the happening spot in Westport."

"People know how to get loose up in here."

"Sure they do."

"Westport's got some good party spots."

The music roared. The dancefloor pounded. The bodies rocked. The lights flashed everywhere. An inferno of energetic bodies became slaves to the monstrous rhythm.

Chapter 17

DEEP WITHIN THE SINISTER and dark inner sanctums of Kansas City's West Bottoms, Provenzano, Randazzo, Gagliano, and Calabrese, all made final preparations for the assassination-execution of FBI Special Agent Wilfredo Feliciano. Inside the partially-renovated warehouse, they checked their walkie talkies. The trained killers looked down the barrels of their .38 calibre pistols and into the eyes of their binoculars. Dressed in all black, they were ready to pull off one of the biggest murders of their illustrious killing careers.

"Bobby Crusher, how's your walkie talkie working?" Provenzano asked his eager partner.

Randazzo shook his walkie talkie. He pressed the important button, then looked at Provenzano and said, "Working just fine, Frankie."

"Louie, how's your's working?"

"Picks up signals perfectly."

"Bart, how about your's?"

"I can hear everything real clear. Signals go out and come in perfectly."

"Bobby Crusher, check out your pistol," Provenzano instructed his valued fellow executioner.

Randazzo flipped open the chamber of his .38 calibre. He checked to make sure the pistol was clean and fully loaded with bullets.

"Looks okay."

"Good. Bart, check out your pistol."

Gagliano opened his pistol for a thorough inspection. His observation told him he had an operational weapon in his possession.

"You good to go?"

"Yes sir."

"Louie, check to see what you're working with."

Calabrese whipped open his pearl handle .38 calibre like it was his pride and joy. He zoomed in on the chamber to make sure he'd be working with a fully loaded pistol.

"Everything straight?"

"Straighter than an arrow."

Provenzano felt nervous about the killing they were soon to carry out. For all intent and purposes, he kept his composure. "Men, we're about to do something that we've never done since we've all been made guys in the Galluccio and Bernazzoli families. We're going to be taking out an FBI agent. As you know, this is some serious shit, nothing to be taken lightly. Sasso, our watchdog from Chicago, he's posted up right now inside Kelly's. He'll be the key to us staying on schedule when it's time to hit this G-man. Let me go over the instructions one more time. Bobby, the second he steps out of that nightclub, we're going to rush up on him and start blasting away. Remember this, G-men usually keep their service revolvers on them at all times."

"Which is saying that he'll probably have a pistol on him," Randazzo recited back to Provenzano.

The intensity inside the old warehouse became thick enough to cut with a machete.

"Nine times out of ten, yes," Provenzano rectified. "Bobby, you and I are gonna have'ta blast this guy before he can reach for his pistol, way before he can even get one shot off. And for chrissake, we've got to be perfect with our aims. We don't want to accidentally hit none of the innocent bystanders."

"Question is, what if any of those bystanders are shielding Feliciano?"

"The answer being, we'll hit him when he's in the clear. We accidentally pop an innocent bystander, the bosses will be chopping away at our asses forever."

"The streets of Westport are crowded as hell on the weekends."

"Doesn't matter."

"Why not?"

"Once space clears, that's when we'll open up fire on him."

"Got'cha, Frankie."

Provenzano shot his attention over to the two backup shooters. "Bart and Louie, listen to me closely. If either myself or Bobby Crusher can't get our shots off for some crazy reason, that's where you guys come in. I'm suggesting that you two keep a distance of at least a half-block. That way, you can fall in right behind us in just an ample amount of time. Are my instructions clear?"

"Always, Frankie," Gagliano said.

"For sure, Frankie," Calabrese said.

"In case we can't get our shots off, have your pistols drawn and ready to fire. Alright, the driver should be pulling up soon."

The foursome packed their pistols with confidence. They gripped their walkie talkies with the firmest hold. Provenzano and Randazzo held the binoculars in their opposite hand. A potential homicide hung in the balance somewhere around Kansas City, Missouri.

Chapter 18

THE ALREADY THICK CROWD in the *Westport District* of Kansas City got thicker just past midnight. Cars trailed one another from bumper-to-bumper. Wild partygoers sounded their loud horns and yelled obscenities at other drivers and passengers. KCPD cops and Westport Security seemed to have disappeared to areas far off Broadway Boulevard and Pennsylvania Avenue. Why was that? Carlo Ruggiero informed an influential police captain to temporarily use their manpower in areas far away from Westport. Only until a sophisticated murder took place.

Most pedestrians and motorists became unruly. Randy and Tracey dropped in Antonio's Pizza Shop on Pennsylvania for slices of their favorite pizza. The line was moderate and they were able to order within a few minutes. Accidentally, Randy spilled a glob of pizza sauce on his pants.

"Shiiiittttt!" Randy snarled, a real mess he'd made.

"Go to the bathroom and wet some paper towels," Tracey suggested.

"I've got some sanitary wipes in the car."

"Could you get my purse out?"

"Sure can," he grimaced.

"I'll wait here in the pizza shop."

"Give me a few minutes."

"Hurry back."

"I will."

Inside a 1977 Caprice Classic with deep smoked windows, a rusty red car not bearing any license plates, Provenzano, Randazzo, Gagliano, Calabrese and the driver of the getaway car, all cruised down Southwest Trafficway. Cleverly, the driver made a sharp turn onto Westport Road and passed a busy Blockbuster video store. The jammed traffic moved slow, which was to their advantage. Provenzano stared down at his watch. His heart pounded even harder as time closed in. KCPD cops and Westport Security weren't nowhere in sight. After several trips around the block, they were ready to make their move on one of the government's most prized employees.

The driver parked the Caprice Classic on a dark deserted street in the back of the Embassy Suites Hotel. Everyone double-checked to make sure their guns were ready to be fired. For a final time, they checked their walkie talkies. The all-black clothing with matching black skullcaps helped conceal their identities. The haunting voice of Tommy "The Caveman" Galluccio rung inside the paranoid mind of Provenzano. His boss was the voice of dictatorship, and it strictly meant business.

"Remember men," Provenzano ranted once more. "There can't be no fuckups with this FBI agent. Bobby, we rush up on him and get'ta firing away."

For some strange reason, Provenzano couldn't stop going over all the details. The instructions rung inside the ears of his vicious culprits.

"We blast away at him and run like fucking demons out of hell," Randazzo reiterated back to Provenzano.

"We'll empty our pieces into this *spicaroo* and then haul ass like a runaway jet plane."

"Like we discussed down in the warehouse."

"Anything goes wrong, we'll let our backup take care of this G-man."

"Time's ticking away."

Provenzano shifted his attention once again to Calabrese and Gagliano. "Bart and Louie, are you ready?"

"Ready, Frankie," Gagliano said.

"Same here, Frankie," Calabrese complied.

All four men held their guns and walkie talkies with strength.

A crackling noise came over the walkie talkie of Provenzano. "Come in, Frankie Bonecutter. Come in, Frankie Bonecutter."

"Sasso?" Provenzano nervously answered.

"Feliciano's coming out of Kelly's right now."

"How's the crowd in front of the club?"

"Heavy."

"Dammit!"

"You men better make your move now."

Provenzano, holding a tight grip on his pistol and walkie talkie, shouted to the other three killers, "Okay men, let's move out!"

Randazzo held on to his pistol and walkie talkie like they were engaged in holy matrimony. Calabrese and Gagliano rushed behind Provenzano and Randazzo in their pursuit to commit a high-profile killing.

Feliciano decided he'd had enough drinks. He wanted to see other sites around the historical *Westport District*. He stepped onto the crowded sidewalk of Pennsylvania Avenue. He bobbed and weaved around the drunk college students. Covertly, Provenzano and Randazzo rushed from around a smoking hotdog stand and immediately opened fire on Feliciano.

"Oh my God!" Feliciano yelled, the quickest adrenalin rush to his heart and brain.

Angels of Death were in place to take away another living soul on Earth.

His gut instincts told him the footsteps of death had come his way. As Provenzano predicted, Feliciano tried reaching for his service revolver. His timing was way off.

Feliciano jumped forward with a wild spin. Then, he fell back onto one of the iron railings near the wall of Kelly's.

"Ahhhhhhh shiiiiiiiit!" Feliciano screamed once more.

The first shot came from the gun of Provenzano. The angry bullet pierced Feliciano straight into his right hip. He'd been disoriented by now and lunged closer to the sidewalk. His service revolver went slinging down the side of Westport Road. People screamed and dispersed to various locations up and down Westport Road. After having wiped his pants leg with a sanitary wipe, Randy stood frozen solid from across the street. In all of his years on Earth, he'd never witnessed a live murder. He only read about them or saw them happening in Al Pacino or Robert DeNiro gangster movies.

More volleys of shots crashed into the body of Feliciano. His wounded body reeled around the concrete sidewalk. Randazzo stepped up and fired a series of shots into the already wounded FBI Agent. Feliciano fell flat on the sidewalk as the shots kept coming. Literally, Provenzano and Randazzo weren't out to just wound or handicap him, they were out to kill him dead. Three rounds crashed into the front of his skull. Blood and jellyish brain matter splattered all over the sidewalk. Ten bullets total were pumped into Feliciano. All ten bullets hit their target.

One shot crashed into his right hip. Four shots forced their way into both shoulder blades. Two shots ripped apart his stomach and chest with authority. The final three shots sent fine pinkish blood spraying into the air like a miniature fountain. Those were the fatal shots which eventually killed Feliciano.

Randy didn't know whether he should've ran like hell or just stood there frozen like a glacier. While fleeing the brutal murder scene, there appeared to be a brief exchange of eye contact between Provenzano and Randy. The adequately insensitive killer shot Randy the most intimidating stare.

Witnesses couldn't believe the live murder which just took place. Some caught a good glimpse of the murderers. They might've wore all black, but the black didn't totally conceal their faces.

Provenzano yelled into his walkie talkie. "The job's finished! I repeat, the job's finished!"

Randazzo also shouted into his walkie talkie. "Let's get ready to move out! I repeat, let's get ready to move out!"

Running down Pennsylvania Avenue and towards the dark street, Calabrese and Gagliano jetted right behind Provenzano and Randazzo. The four men jumped into the running getaway car.

"Let's get the fuck out of here!" Provenzano screamed to the driver.

The driver jerked the gear into drive and sped over to Broadway Boulevard. Silly teenagers and college students cruised along the congested boulevard. The getaway driver swurved around the other cars in the wildest fashion.

"Get the fuck out of the way!" shouted the driver of the car carrying the assassination team.

A young college student from Kansas University blocked their way near the upcoming intersection. "No, you get the fuck out of the way!"

The driver whipped out a .45 automatic and pointed it at the stupid college student. "Is this enough to make you get out of my goddamn way?"

"It sure is," the student conformed, moving out of their way with quickness.

"Now move, you young dumbfuck!"

The Caprice Classic zoomed down Broadway Boulevard until they reached connecting highways near the West Bottoms of Kansas City.

Chapter 19

THE MURDER OF FBI Special Agent Wilfredo Feliciano began and ended in less than five minutes. Many patrons of the bars and restaurants in the *Westport District* ran up and down the sidewalk on Westport Road to attend to the dead Feliciano. Mass hysteria had been created. A pool of blood which formed six feet wide rolled down the sidewalk. Feliciano could've drowned in his own blood. His lifeless body laid sprawled out on the sidewalk. Women screamed and cried behind the brutal murder.

A whirlwind of commotion caused people throughout the *Westport District* to be in disarray. Tracey ran around the corner to see what had happened. She'd heard the series of gunshots from inside of Antonio's Pizza. From start to finish, Randy witnessed the senseless murder. He was tight-lipped, tongue-tied, and couldn't utter one word.

A woman from in the midst of the hysterical crowd shouted, "Will somebody call a goddamn ambulance for this man!"

People then rushed to pay phones nearby or got on their cell phones to contact nine-one-one.

"Randy! Randy!" Tracey urgently cried. "What happened around here?"

"I......I......don't," Randy stuttered with sheer fright.

Uncontrollably, he shook with the sanitary wipe clutched in his right hand.

"You look like a scared actor from a horror movie."

"Uh.....he.....uh," he mumbled, having been caught in the grip of mild shock.

"Are you going to tell me what happened?"

"Let's get out of here, Tracey."

Tracey looked across the street and noticed a woman cradling the dead Feliciano. She held his head gently in her arms. Blood still leaked from his bullet-punctured body. Randy snatched Tracey by the arm and pulled her up the hill. Men and women coming down the hill on Westport Road recognized the hysteria scribbled across his face. The crowd of people which gathered around the front of *Westport Center* had compressed. By now, two ambulances and three long firetrucks arrived at the scene, and they were ready to go to work on Feliciano.

The roaring sirens of police vehicles also rushed to the scene. Officers jumped out of their squad cars with authority. Detectives from various divisions popped up on short notice. One of the paramedics instantly checked for a pulse. Right then, he confirmed Feliciano was dead. At the corner where Westport Road and Pennsylvania Avenue connected, Tracey allowed Randy a few minutes of recuperation. He'd just witnessed a monolithic murder and the commanding memories raced through his head.

"Randy!" Tracey shouted into the blank face of Randy.

She squeezed him by the arm. She tilted his head so she could make eye contact.

"What happened down the street?" Tracey pressed on.

"Don't wanna talk about it," Randy opposed, ready to deny he ever saw anything.

"Did somebody shoot the Hispanic man lying over there on the ground?"

"Don't know."

"Why won't you talk to me?"

"Let's just get the fuck out of Westport!"

"But—"

"Now!"

"Alright."

Randy and Tracey wasted no time jumping into his car while disappearing from the historical *Westport District*. FBI Special Agent Wilfredo Feliciano only wanted to come to Westport and enjoy himself. Tragically, he got something quite different. Two cold-blooded vicious killers emptied their .38 revolvers into him.

Chapter 20

BRITTANY GOLDBERG, a six-year veteran with the KCPD, weaved her way around the crowd of curious bystanders. She ducked under the police tape which sectioned off the perimeter around Kelly's Inn and *Westport Center*. Most of her colleagues knew her well and there were many questions to be answered. Her awesome beauty alone became a trademark of erotic identification. Often, police officers cited her as a *"Goddess of Law Enforcement"*. Her piercing blue-green eyes, her golden tan, her feathered, strawberry blonde hair, and her chiseled body, they were all a testament to her alluring stature.

News vans carrying hungry reporters from every television station in Kansas City rushed to the scene of the homicide. Surely, it'd become the talk of the town. Police vehicles blocked the perimeter around *Westport Center*. Many bystanders were told to clear the area for investigative purposes. Exasperated impatience filled the air while people were sparked with plenty of fear. What had happened less than 30 minutes ago was an anti-climatic letdown based on prefabricated ideologies. Brittany studied the tired faces of homicide detective Gene Foreman, and his superior, Cyrus Manley.

"What do we have here?" Brittany asked, strong peculiarity in her voice.

"A 187 of an FBI Special Agent," Manley sadly revealed to Brittany.

He scanned the *Westport District* with his attentive eyes for possible evidence.

Cyrus Manley, a barrel-chested man with droopy eyes and dark hair, had seen many murders during his career as a lead homicide detective with the Kansas City, Missouri, Police Department. To know that an FBI special agent had been gunned down in the heart of the *Westport District* on a busy Saturday night, went beyond his comprehensible skills as a servant of the law.

"You're shitting me!" Brittany wooed.

"Wish I was, Goldberg."

"Any positive identification?"

"Been identified as Wilfredo Feliciano. Sent down from Washington to investigate the Teamsters Union alliance with organized crime."

The first and only crime family who came to mind was the Galluccio Mafia family. She'd known them to be the bloodiest assembly of hoodlums that Kansas City had ever known.

"Any recognizable motive, Captain Manley?" Brittany inquired.

"Can't say right now."

"Any witnesses?"

"Several women and some guy coming out of Kelly's claimed to have seen something."

"Kelly's, huh?"

"Yes."

"Why'd someone wanna gun down an FBI Agent in Westport on a Saturday night?"

"That's where the challenge comes in."

"For all of us."

"To say the least."

"My gut instinct tells me that some powerful people are behind this killing."

"Your's and mine both."

Cyrus Manley and Gene Foreman had their suspicions about who could've been behind the tragic murder. This particular murder investigation stretched far beyond their expertise. Just before Kansas City firefighters and medical technicians placed Feliciano inside the ambulance, Brittany unzipped the body bag to glance down at his face.

"What a handsome fella he was," Brittany commented.

"What a waste," Manley added.

"We've lost a valuable law enforcement specialist at such a young age."

The gunshot wounds to his head were visible. Fragments of his skull had been blown away. Brittany zipped the bodybag up for the emergency crew to take him away. Captain Manley and Lieutenant Foreman entertained thoughts of who might've been involved with the bloody homicide. Overtly, skepticism overshadowed their major leads.

"This had to be a professional job," Foreman explained to Manley.

The colorful flashing lights from the police vehicles and fire trucks and ambulances bounced all around the *Westport District*.

"Got the same notion that I've got, Gene?" Manley casted, several suspected people coming to mind.

"Thinking what I'm thinking?"

"The Galluccio Mafia family?"

"Angelo Galluccio died several years ago after they let him out of that Federal Penitentiary down in Springfield, Missouri."

"Somebody had to have taken over his crime family."

"But who?"

"Don't know of any surviving beneficiaries."

"Maybe the goons out of Chicago took over his rackets."

"Kansas City hasn't seen mania like this since the *River Quay Wars*."

"The ghosts of River Quay have come to haunt Kansas City once again."

"And Angelo Galluccio was behind those explosions that blasted away his enemy's businesses down in River Quay."

"That had a lot to do with those guys not signing their businesses up with the Teamsters Union."

"To think, this agent was here in K.C. doing investigation work that involved the Teamsters and some Mafia goons. You think his murder's got anything to do with a throwback to the *River Quay Wars*?"

"We'll find out soon enough."

Manley ordered experts from the KCPD forensic lab to gather any evidence at the crime scene. "Look, if you find any clothing, fingerprints, fibers, hairs, tire, or foot impressions, I want it rushed to the lab right away. I want all reports on my desk bright and early by tomorrow morning."

Chapter 21

BRITTANY GOLDBERG enjoyed her job with the KCPD since she'd become involved with investigative work. Trading her uniform in for plain clothes brought her unspeakable pleasure. Patrolling the streets of Kansas City bored her senselessly. She dealt with a bunch of two-bit knuckleheads and petty criminals. The new challenge of detective work suited her just fine. Several women gathered in front of Kelly's. They were ready to shoot off what they saw during the course of Feliciano's murder. Lieutenant Foreman kicked off the questioning process.

"Your name, ma'am?" Foreman asked.

"Sheila Bridgestone," she smiled.

"I'm Lieutenant Gene Foreman with the Homicide Division of the KCPD."

"Pleased to meet you, Lieutenant Foreman."

"Likewise."

"What do you want to know?" Sheila prompted.

"Ma'am," Foreman said, his smile inviting. "What exactly did you see?"

"Well, my sister and I were coming out of Kelly's and we heard gunshots."

"Approximately, how many?"

"Seven, maybe eight."

"Continue, ma'am."

"Next thing we knew, two men wearing all-black were running across the street."

"Did you get a good description of them?"

"I'd say we did."

"White men? Black men?"

"Both were white."

"How tall would you say they were?"

"I don't know, but they were definitely under six foot."

"Five-one, five-three, maybe five-six, what?"

"Somewhere around 5'6"."

"Okay!" Foreman grilled further. "Did you get a good look at their faces?"

"A very good look."

"Anything stood out?"

"One of them had bushy black eyebrows and a small mole on his right cheek."

"Any other noticeable marks on their faces?"

"Such as?"

"Acne scars, scratches, gashes, cuts, things of that nature."

"No."

"What type of build would you say they had?"

"Both had slender to muscular builds."

"And which direction did they run?"

"Right down Pennsylvania."

"You've been a big help, Miss Bridgestone."

"One more thing, Lieutenant."

"What?"

"They were both yelling into walkie talkies."

"You recall anything they said?"

"They were too far away."

"Thank you, Miss Bridgestone."

"You're welcome."

Sheila Bridgestone told everything she remembered. Did she volunteer too much information? She went downtown to headquarters to give a statement. Lieutenant Foreman took down every piece of information she had submitted. To corroborate her story, he needed her to look at some computer-generated police mugshots.

Standing several feet away, Brittany was interviewing Sheila's sister. Sherry Welch was her name. As a semi-attractive woman, she was medium in height and moderate in build. There had to be leads to help blow the lid off the fresh homicide.

"I want you to tell me everything that happened," Brittany had instructed Sherry.

Sherry spoke with a sense of calmness. "My sister and I were coming out of Kelly's and we heard several gunshots."

"Okay?"

"Someone kept firing their guns off."

"Did you see who they were?"

"They ran so fast down Pennsylvania, until we only caught a quick glimpse of them."

"Out of that quick glimpse, what did you see?"

"Two men dressed in all-black."

"White men or black men?"

"Both were white men."

"Their hair color?"

"They both were wearing black skullcaps."

"Their eye color?"

"Either brown or black."

"Could you guess their height and weight?"

"Both were probably between 5'5" and 5'7"," Sherry recalled. "They probably weighed between 140 and 160 pounds."

"Anything else, Miss Welch?"

"They were shouting into walkie talkies."

"Did you pick up on their conversations?"

"If my memory serves me right, I overheard one of them say that they were finished."

"Finished? Finished with what?"

"That I couldn't tell you, detective."

"And they eventually disappeared further down Pennsylvania Avenue?"

"Yes, they did."

"Miss Welch, you've been a really big help."

Like her sister, she'd volunteered to go downtown to KCPD headquarters and look at some computer-generated police mugshots. A top-notch FBI sketch artist assisted in helping sketch the men they identified.

Sheila Bridgestone and Sherry Welch were two closeknit siblings from the Northeast end of Kansas City. Had they known that they assisted police in identifying two killers made into a powerful Kansas City Mafia family, both women would've kept their mouths shut. Other witnesses, those who turned out to be men and women present when the killing took place, were questioned by authorities and ordered to go downtown to scan through some pictures.

Chapter 22

TO LEARN ABOUT the killing of FBI Special Agent Wilfredo Feliciano brought delight to the ears of Galluccio, Shellenberger, and the Bernazzoli Brothers. After their return from Chicago, Galluccio and Shellenberger didn't take lightly the intrusions of the law into their secret Mafia world. The bosses in Chicago felt more at ease knowing how the investigation of the Teamsters alliance with organized crime in Kansas City and Chicago weren't quite as intense. Blizzards of headlines in the *Kansas City Times* captured the immediate attention of Galluccio.

Inside the *Pendergast Mansion*, he rested on his favorite sofa smoking a fat cigar. Some of the captions headlining the front covers of local newspapers were: **FBI Agent Killed in Westport Area; Agents Not Quitting Until Suspects Are Captured; K.C. Agents and Officers Continue Manhunt; and First FBI Agent Murder in K.C. Since Union Station Massacre.**

The vigilant eyes of Galluccio scanned one of the lengthy articles in the *Kansas City Times*. The six o'clock news emerged onto the 60 inch widescreen television and Galluccio's eyes were attached to the set.

The reddish and patchy-pale face of news anchorman Todd Gwynn looked into the camera. The killing of Feliciano became the headline of the local news for the past three days. Veteran news reporter Nancy Powers stood in front of Kelly's Inn with her camera crew. She walked along the sidewalk and stopped about mid-way.

"Nancy," Todd began from inside the news studio. "Do detectives or police have any leads in the shooting death of FBI Special Agent Wilfredo Feliciano?"

"Todd, local law enforcement agencies have no solid leads, but says they're not letting up on their investigation," Nancy Powers relayed back to Todd from the *Westport District*.

A blanket of cool air circled around her virtuous face.

"Are there any potential suspects in the shooting death?"

"Composite sketches of the two men thought to be responsible for the killing of Agent Feliciano have been posted around the city."

Drawings of both suspected killers flashed in front of the camera. Thousands of Kansas Citians watched in awe. Many tuned in closer than ever to their television sets.

"What is the reward up to?"

"FBI have posted a $50,000 dollar reward for any information leading to the capture of the two assailants."

"We understand that an FBI artist has spent a good part of the week adding greater details to existing sketches based on information from witnesses."

"Yes, Todd, that is correct."

From inside the guest room of the elaborate *Pendergast Mansion*, Galluccio shot from his leather recliner and nearly exploded. Steamy red blood bubbled from under his pliant skin.

"Witnesses!" Galluccio rumbled, throwing the remote across the room. "There weren't supposed to be any goddamned witnesses!"

Witnesses meant that all the cautious plotting of the agent's murder would've gone down the drain, not to mention the money spent on the contracts given to Provenzano, Randazzo, Gagliano, Calabrese and Sasso.

"Goddammit!" Galluccio broiled over. "It fucking can't end like this! Witnesses are worse than parasites and leeches. They feed and feed until everything in their path is muthafucking consumed!"

He calmed down long enough to continue watching the newscast.

"News Channel Seven has learned that police have several witnesses," Todd continued from the anchor desk.

"Again, Todd," Nancy replied. "Several witnesses coming out of Kelly's saw two men carrying weapons, and then fleeing the scene of the murder with walkie talkies."

In an earlier broadcast of News Channel Seven, veteran reporter Diane Spencer interviewed Sheila Bridgestone and her sister Sherry Welch. Had the two siblings known that they squealed on two men associated with the ruthless and powerful Galluccio Mafia family, maybe they would've recoiled from talking to the news media.

"Miss Welch, what exactly did you see?" Diane asked a cooperative Sherry.

Steadily, she held the microphone right at the tip of her loose lips.

"First," Sherry paused. "My sister and I heard gunshots as we were coming out of Kelly's here in Westport. As soon as we walked onto the sidewalk near The Westport Center, we saw two men running across the street wearing all-black with guns and walkie talkies in both hands."

"Did you get a glimpse of the two men?"

"Sure did."

"Which were the composite sketches the FBI released?"

"I believe so."

"And you've been down to the KCPD headquarters looking at computerized police mugshots?"

"Yes, I have."

"Thank you, Sherry."

"My pleasure."

In another segment of an earlier News Channel Seven broadcast, Sherry's sister, the equally cooperative Sheila Bridgestone, stood before another respected reporter named Angela McNichols. Angela became diligent about asking several more questions surrounding Feliciano's untimely murder. Galluccio had his ears and eyes concentrated on the television set.

"Miss Bridgestone, tell us about what happened Saturday night here in Westport," Angela requested, holding the microphone steady.

"My sister and I had just come out of Kelly's when we heard a lot of gunshots," Sheila recited, the memories as clear as glass.

Slight hysteria faltered through her voice.

"How many shots did you hear?" Angela asked.

"Six, seven, maybe about eight of them."

"Did you see the men who fired the shots?"

"Yes, we did," Sheila answered, boldness coating her voice tone. "Every piece of clothing they wore were all-black. They ran down Pennsylvania Avenue holding guns and walkie talkies in both hands."

"You, of course, gave the KCPD and the FBI very good descriptions of the two men?"

"Yes, both me and my sister."

"From the KCPD headquarters, have you made any positive identifications?"

"No, we haven't."

"Thank you, Sherry."

"You're welcome."

Simultaneously, the news cameras switched back and forth between Todd Gwynn and Nancy Powers. From inside KCTZ downtown news studios, and from directly in front of Kelly's Westport Inn, which was the exact location of Feliciano's killing, the story of an FBI's mysterious death rolled on. Galluccio became one unhappy soul. He chomped down on his cigar as though it was one of the witnesses's head.

"Those shithead witnesses are a pain in the fucking ass!" Galluccio fizzled with discontent.

The eager journalists continued with their coverage.

"Nancy, are law enforcement officials rejecting the notion that Agent Feliciano's murder was related to his job?" Todd asked, a hungry journalist in every sense.

He spoke as though he could've cracked the mysterious case himself.

"That's correct, Todd," Nancy answered back to her colleague. "Police and the FBI believe that this was simply a random street robbery. They believe that this homicide had nothing to do with his job, whatsoever."

"News Channel Seven has also learned that Agent Feliciano had been sent down from Washington, D.C. to gather evidence in local FBI files here in Kansas City, all of which was top secret government information to go back with him."

"Agent Feliciano had been appointed to come to Kansas City to gather evidence in helping U.S. Attorneys rid the Teamsters Union of organized crime figures under the civil racketeering statues."

"Nancy Powers reporting from the *Westport District*. Thanks for that story, Nancy."

"You're welcome," Nancy replied, smiling straight into the camera. "Back to you downtown, Todd."

Galluccio took a thorough look at the composite sketches of the two men highlighted on the newscast.

"Those sketches look nothing like Frankie or Bobby," Galluccio growled to himself.

Would Sheila Bridgestone and Sherry Welch continue providing information to the KCPD and the FBI? Would the law collect enough data eventually leading to the capture of the two men so closely associated with Galluccio? Now, he'd been put into a tight spot. There were those detectives assigned to the case who weren't so naive. Most were convinced that the brutal death of Feliciano wasn't merely a random street robbery. Question remained: *Why was his wallet, watch, rings, and even his service revolver, never taken?* Organized crime crossed their minds. What crime family still existed in Kansas City, Missouri?

The only way to keep his rackets purring along smoothly was to eliminate anyone willing to blow the lid off his crime family's secrecy. Unknowing, Sheila and Sherry risked the wrath of the Galluccio Mafia family.

Galluccio summoned for his housekeeper Angela Claybrook to come into the guest room.

"Angela, baby!" Galluccio called, his voice velvet smooth.

"Yes, Tommy?" Angela answered back.

"It's that time, honey."

"Time for what?"

"Time for me to be blown."

"You ready for me, poppy?" Angela chided, her smile brighter than ever.

"I'm ready for you, mommy."

Angela stepped into the room wearing black silk lingerie. Boy did her body look outstanding! Man did her face glow with an effervescent innocence! Galluccio was ready for her to perform a masterful blowjob on him. He smashed out his cigar while she slumbered to her knees. She wrapped her moist lips around his stiff cock. She stroked his cock until he achieved a powerful orgasm.

"Ahhhhhhh shiiiiittttt!" Galluccio screamed, both hands clamped to the side of Angela's head.

Hot loads of white cum shot all over her beautiful face.

"Now, that's the perfect way to end any day," Galluccio exhaled calmly.

"Definitely, Tommy," Angela smiled

"Think I'll retire for the day."

"Wise choice."

After receiving the greatest oral ecstasy, Galluccio had a clear mind to think with again. He had a fresh killing to plot.

Chapter 23

NOT SINCE THE Kansas City Royals disgraced the St. Louis Cardinals in the 1985 World Series, had there been so much hysteria created in Kansas City, Missouri. The FBI worked quite close with the Kansas City Police Department's Homicide Unit. Together, they set up several command posts in the heart of the *Westport District* and in the downtown federal building. More than 60 agents were assigned to the case. The reward for the two killer's capture was beefed up to a whopping $60,000 dollars. Boy! Sixty grand was a great initiative to help find the killers who took out Feliciano.

Owners of bars and restaurants and hotels complained how patrons had feared to frequent the *Westport District* for entertainment since Feliciano's murder became widespread. The energy-charged crowd of college students from surrounding universities gained intense knowledge through all the bad publicity. Many wondered if they had to look over their shoulders. After the prison death of a sick-o who'd been drugging and torturing juvenile male prostitutes around Kansas City, most people watched their backs. A maniac had been on the loose who viciously stuck his victims with unsanitary needles and poured bleach into their eyes to get his kicks.

Sheila Bridgestone sat with homicide detective Brittany Goldberg inside a small room at the KCPD Headquarters once used for conferencing high-ranking police officials. Across a vivid computer screen, photos of criminals who ranged from striking pretty boys to downright ugly ducklings, popped up one after another. Faces scarred from knicks, cuts, acne, and aging flashed across the color screen. Homicide detectives desperately wanted Sheila to identify the two men who were responsible for the killing of Wilfredo Feliciano.

Computer screen after computer screen, Sheila studied the faces of every felon with close detail. The law was at a sole disadvantage. Provenzano had only been charged with a minor traffic violation during his illustrious contract-killing career. Randazzo only spent less than an hour in a courtroom after a domestic dispute with a former girlfriend. Neither men had police mugshots on file. Certainly, it was to their advantage.

"Recognize any of the men yet?" Brittany respectfully interrogated Sheila.

Her service revolver was planted around her waist, a woman quite proud to be a part of homicide detective work. Cracking a case like this would've boosted her career.

Sheila swiveled her head back forth with hopes of coming across a familiar face.

"None of these men look familiar, detective," Sheila said, scanning every mugshot as though her life depended on it.

"Take your time."

"Can't match any of these guys up with the men we saw that night."

"Are you sure, Miss Bridgestone?"

"My sister and I only caught a glimpse of those two men."

"Concentrate, Miss Bridgestone, concentrate," Brittany spoke with reinforcement.

"It happened so fast, Detective Goldberg."

"None of these men's facial features look familiar?"

"No."

"The two creeps who killed the FBI Agent worked rather fast."

Sheila sucked in the strongest breath. She exhaled even stronger. "Mardi Gras in New Orleans isn't coming soon enough."

"Mardi Gras? Whaddaya mean, Miss Bridgestone?"

"I'm flying down to New Orleans for the Mardi Gras festivities."

Brittany snapped her finger. "That's strange, because my boyfriend and I are going down to New Orleans this year for Mardi Gras."

"Do you know where you'll be staying?" Sheila asked with comparison.

"My boyfriend's got a real nice hotel picked out. His father also has business associates down there."

"Sounds great."

"Thanks for your cooperation."

"You're welcome, detective."

The corrupt narcotics detective Carlo Ruggiero happened to be standing in the hallway. His cunning ears dissected every word spoke between Brittany and Sheila. Brittany wasn't expecting to come up empty-handed in her homicide investigation.

Chapter 24

GALLUCCIO BELIEVED IN moving forward, not putting his crime family in a situation where they'd be placed somewhere far in the background. The murder of FBI Special Agent Feliciano proved the Galluccio crime family had been catapulted into a state of progression. A mode of retrogression would've been his worst nightmare. The Justice Department had been called off their backs for the time being. Still, federal prosecutors spoiled for the biggest war in Teamsters Union history. Top union leaders in Kansas City and Chicago, which included Mason Shellenberger, Remo Petrelli, and Jimmy Amato, were left alone for the time being.

Galluccio and the Bernazzoli Brothers conspiring to end the life and career of a FBI special agent helped terminate the Kansas City investigation of the Teamsters. The government's investigation had grounded to a screeching halt. On the contrary, Galluccio and Shellenberger knew federal indictments could surface at any time. A Missouri Democratic Senator stated how Kansas City had always been infested with a small but well organized group of racketeers, men who hired professional killers as casually as someone paid to have their grass cut, leaves raked, or snow shoveled.

The time had arrived to plot another cold-blooded, well-organized, and well-financed killing. The face of Sheila Bridgestone flashed across television screens too many times. Her eyewitness account had been written in the *Kansas City Times* on several occasions. This woman didn't know how those who've crossed the Galluccio Mafia family didn't live long enough to boast of it. Those scheduled to testify against family members suddenly lost their enthusiasm and much of their memory. Witnesses were usually crippled by fear. Had Sheila known that these men were monolithic, she would've recoiled from cooperating and maintained how her safety was a number one priority.

Angela Claybrook received the chief Mafiosos into the *Pendergast Mansion*. The criminal dignitaries were seated in front of platters of food, glasses of water and cocktails, and cups of piping hot coffee. Cigarettes and cigars were fired up. Smoke filled the air quickly. Galluccio made his grand entry and Angela disappeared.

Coming into Kansas City once again on short notice, Carmine and Michael Bernazzoli had rushed in from Chicago. Both brothers were the true "shotcallers" who had to attend the important meeting. Galluccio slipped down into his favorite chair at the head of the huge conference table. He joined his comrades by firing up a juicy cigar. Shellenberger realized how his presence was crucial at the meeting. Galluccio blew a long stream of cigar smoke across the table.

As always, he opened the meetings by thanking everyone present. "Men, we are grateful to Carmine and Mikey Bernazzoli for flying in from Chicago on short notice."

Carmine Bernazzoli broke his brief silence. "We are grateful to Tommy for calling this meeting of urgent business here at the *Pendergast Mansion*. We still know him as a man's man, someone who always keeps his word."

Michael Bernazzoli came in behind his powerful brother. "When we received word from Tommy, we came to Kansas City as soon as possible. I think we all know why we're here. We turn the table back over to Tommy."

Shellenberger couldn't ignore the fact that he still possessed the power to dictate how union member's billions of dollars were to be spent. The billions of dollars in pension and insurance funds were being pumped into a variety of interest.

"Thank you Carmine and Mikey," Galluccio graciously accepted. "Shell, what's the latest news as far as the unions are concerned?"

"We've got problems in the fire department and city administration," Shellenberger disclosed before his colleagues.

He slammed down a big gulp of vodka on the rocks.

"Fire away, Shell," Galluccio ordered.

Shellenberger nodded his head in disgust. "This Felix Harris scumbag, the battalion chief on the west side, he's giving the union major problems."

"Not again!" Galluccio detested.

"Felix moved into that position as president of the fire fighters union local. He got a swole head and a tongue sharper than a triple-edge razor."

"We've been good to that prick," Galluccio chimed. "Why can't he just play ball?"

"Thousands of votes were delivered for that bastard. We stuck our necks out for him. That includes me and Carmine and Mikey."

"What the hell's he trying to prove?" Carmine asked.

"We voted that bastard in," Michael grumbled.

"Felix promised to stop the councilmen from making a public affidavit that wouldn't embarrass us," Shellenberger confirmed.

"Something's got to be done about that sonofabitch!" Galluccio charged with fury. "Nobody goes back on their word when they're dealing with us. Nobody gets special favors from us and then screws us later."

"What do you suggest, Tommy?" Carmine asked.

"We're in the business of selling political influence, Carmine, not a bunch of bullshit, fairytale dreams," Galluccio responded.

Galluccio broadened his scope to legitimate businesses. Traitors like Felix Harris had to be eliminated.

"Felix got bonus after bonus from us, and this is how he shows his appreciation?" Michael charged.

"We'll show our appreciation by punishing this cocksucker," Galluccio threatened.

"Couldn't agree more," Carmine added.

"Imagine the nerves of this sonofabitch," Michael said.

"The Labor Department is still pressuring union bosses everywhere into resigning," Shellenberger presented to his superiors.

Galluccio and the Bernazzoli Brothers believed that the only way to run a successful crime syndicate network, was an atmosphere of violence had to be created. Building an environment of constant fear and intimidation was the only way.

Galluccio gestured with a sudden hand signal. "We'll get back to that in a second, Shell. I thought we were in the clear. But now, we've got some broad who's trying to help these FBI pricks sketch composite drawings of Frankie and Bobby. Carmine and Mikey, I knew you guys wouldn't be too happy once you got the bad news."

Provenzano broke his silence with a vibrant grunt. "It's been the talk of Kansas City. This broad's face pops up on every television screen, and every newspaper in the city is talking about it."

"Why can't that fucking twat just mind her own business?" Galluccio raged.

"And the FBI are beind this broad one-hundred percent," Provenzano recited.

"Shit, they haven't rode us this hard since Hoover was in power," Shellenberger said.

"Hoover was nothing but a fucking fruitcake," Carmine joked. "Hard to believe they'd let a faggot like him stay the FBI director for so long."

"When he wasn't out chasing communists, he was on his knees sucking another faggot's dick," Michael mocked, another one of his harsh insults about the legendary FBI director.

Randazzo motioned with his erect index finger. "Politics kept Hoover the director for so long. It's always about bullshit when it comes to governmental politics."

"What's going to be done about this Sheila Bridgestone broad?" Shellenberger asked.

"Only one thing can be done," Galluccio cited.

"What'd you have in mind, Tommy?" Carmine asked.

"She's got to go."

"Are we going to take this broad out?" Michael asked.

Galluccio turned his estranged eyes back over to the Bernazzoli Brothers. "Carmine and Mikey, with your permission and with your blessings, I'd say that we get rid of this broad as soon as possible. Right now, she poses as the biggest threat."

Never before had the Galluccio and Bernazzoli crime families tried to eliminate innocent blood. Never before had they tried to kill an innocent woman who had absolutely nothing to do with their criminal syndicate. Suddenly, the rules changed. All codes of honor diminished. The 1990s arrived and new sets of rules were enunciated. Galluccio and the Bernazzoli Brothers lost all respect for *La Cosa Nostra*.

Holding positions of special trust and power meant to adhere to the rules. Angelo Galluccio meant for everyone to follow the rules along strict guidelines. The 1990s ceased as the "yuppie generation." Present-day Mafia men were labeled as "yuppie mafiosos," those only interested in themselves above the criminal brotherhood they'd been inducted into. In a tragic sense, it made them especially vulnerable to prosecution by law enforcement.

"We don't want to arouse suspicions with the FBI or the feds up in Washington," Shellenberger warned his constituents.

"We've got to shut this broad up," Galluccio insisted.

"And real fast," Provenzano concluded.

Dictatorship rung through the voice of Michael Bernazzoli. "The FBI got no witnesses, they've got no case."

"I agree with my brother Michael," Carmine gestured before everyone. "Witnesses are pesty motherfuckers! They only shoot off at the mouth to make themselves look good. They only want to win favor with the law. And why? To make others believe that they've performed some public service? They only want their 15 minutes of fame."

"For this chick, it's going to be a lifetime of shame," Michael said.

"Carmine and Mikey have got a good point," Galluccio agreed. "Witnesses are like toxic waste, they pollute everything in their path. They see shit happen and they just have'ta broadcast it to the fucking world."

The only rules Galluccio and the Bernazzoli Brothers entrusted were no rules at all. Not even the innocent blood of Sheila Bridgestone was immune to execution by their vicious organization. No one was going to put Galluccio and the Bernazzoli Brothers in a position where the law constantly looked over their shoulders.

"Have we decided what we're going to do about Felix Harris?" Shellenberger asked.

Galluccio angrily bogarted back into their discussion-at-hand. "We're going to kill that motherfucking-cocksucking-sonofabitch!"

His violent, his vicious, and his vulgar temper shifted into full throttle.

"Can't we settle this feud another way? Can't we give him a warning this time?"

"Shell, this pukebag done crossed us for the last time," Galluccio deflected. "If he was dying of thirst in the desert, I wouldn't piss down his mouth."

"Let's not go back to the violent days of the *River Quay Wars*."

"The *River Quay Wars* are history. Taking out one guy won't cause too big of a mess."

"Tommy's right, Shell," Carmine interposed. "Felix done screwed us for the last time."

"If given the chance, he'll screw us again," Michael said.

"You're the bosses," Shellenberger willingly submitted.

"Frankie Bonecutter's got a street crew who'll get the job done," Galluccio said.

"I want to send in two of my men from Chicago," Carmine plotted.

"Calabrese and Gagliano?" Galluccio asked.

"Yes. They're the best from among our Chicago street crews."

"How soon will Felix go?" Shellenberger asked.

"Right away. I want him hit as soon as possible," Carmine ordered.

"The sooner he's out of the way, the sooner we can vote in a new battalion chief," Michael said.

"Sheila Bridgestone?" Shellenberger asked. "What about her?"

"We'll let that situation simmer a little longer. Frankie and some of Carmine and Mikey's guys will handle it."

"Guess we did give Felix too many chances," Shellenberger determined with reason. "Guess he's got to be taken out."

"We'll go over the final plans with Frankie and his men before they hit Felix," Galluccio said.

The meeting among the important criminal dignitaries was adjourned. Galluccio and Shellenberger, beyond questioning or reasonable doubt, knew if any hits were going to be carried out, they were sanctioned by the powerful Bernazzoli Brothers. Both men were subservient to the bosses in the "Windy City." Angela walked into the meeting room to collect the glasses, platters, and saucers. A fresh killing had been plotted. It meant there'd be one less threat to the Galluccio and Bernazzoli crime families.

Chapter 25

HOMICIDE DETECTIVE Cyrus Manley marched into the Harry S. Truman Medical Center in the midtown section of Kansas City. He made his way straight towards the morgue. Renowned Jackson County Medical Examiner, Dr. Anthony McKinnis, waved for him to enter the autopsy room. The full autopsy had been performed on the body of Wilfredo Feliciano. His family members back in New York City became impatient.

They felt they'd waited long enough and were ready to make funeral arrangements. Feliciano was just another piece of meat inside the cooler of the morgue, waiting to be put six feet under. Lourdes Feliciano complained how the medical center and the FBI were unprofessional about shipping her husband's body back to New York.

"Finished with the autopsy, doc?" Manley asked Dr. McKinnis, just as concerned as the awaiting family back East.

"Just put the finishing touches on it earlier today," Dr. McKinnis assured the detective.

He pulled the drawer open and the ice cool body of Feliciano laid under the white sheet. The toe tag dangled from his left foot. His body took on a pinkish discoloration.

"What the hell's been taking so long?" Manley inquired.

"The FBI warranted further investigation, Detective."

"The KCPD have all the evidence in their case files that they're going to get."

"Yes, they do."

"This guy's got to be flown back to New York."

"If I never see another shot up FBI Agent, it would never be too soon."

"Didn't we get our reports from toxicology?"

"Yes, Detective, we did."

"And reports about the gunshot wounds?"

"Straight to the FBI and the Jackson County Medical Examiner's Office."

Manley moved closer to the body of Feliciano. To himself, he thought, what a shame. There laid an FBI special agent who had a lot of good years left in him as a servant of the law. Morticians back in New York certainly had their work cut out for them. The gunshot wounds to the head remained visible. The slugs created near contact wounds with short flames which burst straight from the barrels of both guns.

"Alright doc, wrap things up for me so we can finish our work at the Headquarters."

"Will do, Detective."

"We've got to turn Feliciano's body over to his family for burial."

"Get to it right away."

Detective Manley exited the autopsy room and left Dr. McKinnis with the duty of sending Feliciano back to New York in the best shape possible. He finished up all the required paperwork before a plane sent Feliciano back to his final resting place. The slugs removed from the body of Feliciano had been taken to an FBI laboratory in Washington, D.C., along with more physical evidence for intense examination. FBI agents and local Kansas City law enforcement officials were determined to crack the case of their murdered comrade.

Chapter 26

THE MASTER PLAN DEVISED to kill Fire Department Battalion Chief Felix Harris had been orchestrated like any other contract killing. There had to be efficiency and expertise in the process. Getting a scumbag like him out of the way, then moving someone else into his position within the Kansas City Fire Department, would've proven beneficial to the Galluccio and Bernazzoli families. Galluccio and others had their way of forcing him out of the Fire Department.

Felix often frequented many strip clubs around Kansas City. The skin clubs became his second home. The dancers and bartenders became his second family. Happily, he lined the deep pockets of every strip club owner in the city. Developing a serious crack-cocaine addiction only worsened with time. Often, he spent over five-hundred dollars a day on his habit.

He'd sometimes tip the waitresses in those sleazy joints $100 dollars a pop. Oftentimes, he propositioned some of the dancers into going to hotels with him for $300 and $400 dollars a round. His undisciplined lifestyle became a hazard to the union boss who he served under the intolerable Mason Shellenberger.

Felix traveled inside Glitter Girls. The upscale gentleman's club sat right on the strip of Grand Boulevard in downtown Kansas City. His droopy and uncharacteristic face was known by every employee inside. Dark circles aligned themselves under his bloodshot eyes. People in the skin club knew his routine down to a science. He grabbed his favorite seat in the same section. He ordered the same cocktails round after every round. He chose the same dancers to come over to his table.

The blonde, the brunette, and the redhead strippers with dangerous curves closed in on him. The rent-a-whores showered him with the phoniest affection possible. There'd be times when two, three, and even four strippers sat on his lap and rubbed all over his chest. Didn't women sure know how to make men feel like they were the *King of the Universe* if they thought he had tons of money? Money to spend on them?

"Hello Felix," regarded a dancer with platinum blonde hair and dark-baked skin.

She had the largest set of boobs which she'd just purchased. Boy, the price tag for those set of tits still hung from her bikini top!

"Miss me, baby?" Felix asked the leggy, shapely stripper.

An intense level of intoxication sounded off in his voice.

"Every minute of the day, sugah," she said arousing.

"Let's do American Inn or Motel 6 tonight."

"Sure, why not."

"You've got me coming back for sloppy seconds."

"Sloppy seconds?" she rejected, pushing him in the chest. "I'm never sloppy seconds."

"Just kidding."

"I'd hope so."

"Bring one of your girlfriends along, too," Felix suggested, a sex-craved addict who just loved those nasty sandwich jobs.

The best part of his escapades with the strippers was that they allowed him to pick his favorite hotels.

"Can you handle two again?" the platinum blonde questioned him.

"What a silly question, girl," Felix giggled.

"We almost fucked you into a cardiac arrest the last time."

"Today's a new day."

"You're feeling energized today."

"Like all the money in the Federal Reserve."

Little did "Miss Blondie" know that the money Felix spent on her and other strippers belonged to part of the Teamsters Union Treasury. It was divine money Felix had no business dipping his dirty hands into. A parasite like him wasn't so naive into believing that he wouldn't pay dearly for such a betrayal.

"The club starts closing down at two-forty-five," the money-hungry blonde told Felix. "Come back at about three o'clock and we'll be ready."

"You've got me cooking like steam in a kitchen," Felix snorkled. "Do you really want me to come back?"

"Yes, I do."

"Do you want me to come?"

"Sure."

"Can you and your girls make me come?"

"Harder than all-night brain surgery."

"Then, I'll see you when the club closes."

"Alright."

Felix agreed to her terms. He'd gotten a few lap dances before leaving the club. He guzzled down a few shots of bourbon and scotch, then left out the door swaying like the pendulum on a clock. His car was parked halfway down the block from Glitter Girls. An old thrift store was next to a dark alley on one of the side streets. Barely able to stand up from being insanely drunk, he fidgeted with his car keys and the lock on the passenger's side.

Light fog crept upon the city. Most headlights from cars driving along Grand Boulevard were swallowed up. The thick fog engulfed the buildings around downtown Kansas City. With no street lights within a two block radius, it became increasingly harder for Felix to get inside his car. Sets of heavy footsteps emerged from the pitch dark alley. Felix listened in rather close. He couldn't spot anyone walking near his car. Gravel from the rocky parking lot juggled around him. Still, no one had been sighted.

"Who's there?" Felix asked, nervously trying to stick his key in the door.

No one answered his question about their presence.

"Who's out there?" he asked again.

Three men wearing all-black clothing with black ski masks appeared from a thick blanket of darkness. Simultaneously, they drew weapons from under their shirts.

"Who in the fuck are you!" Felix yelled, throwing up his arms to try and shield himself from instant death.

"Never mind who we are," one of the gunmen mumbled from under his ski mask.

"No! No! No!" Felix pleaded three times, his loudest voice ever.

"Nightie night, Felix," said another one of the gunman.

"What the—!"

The first gunman placed a .44 magnum at the very back of Felix's head and fired three shots. The powerful shots leveled him straight to the ground. Mists of fine pinkish blood sprayed across the ground and against the passenger's door. Shattered brain matter blew out the entire back of his head. The second gunman raced from around the back of the car and pumped three more bullets into his chest.

To send a message, the first gunman used the tip of his steeltoe construction boot and struck Felix on the side of the face. A noticeable dark print was left behind. The third and final gunman walked from the front of the car and violently discharged two more slugs into the front of his face. Felix Harris died in an instant. He went without much pain. He died a crooked man who refused to follow the orders of a group of *Mafia Pitbulls*.

The gunmen sprinted towards the corner east of Grand Boulevard and jumped into a waiting getaway car. The gunshots were heard by securitymen who stood in front of Glitter Girl's. Along with bouncers, strippers, bartenders, and waitresses, they went in pursuit down the street. One of the securitymen shone a bright flashlight down at the ground. He wavered the flashlight until he found the murdered subject. What they saw on the ground was Felix Harris lying in a pool of his own blood. They saw several bullet holes to his head which leaked gulps of blood. Some noticed where he'd been kicked on the side of the face with the hard boot. A heartless murder in every sense!

"Oh my God!" the platinum blonde stripper cried out. "I knew Felix real well. Who'd want to do something like this to him?"

"Only the people who killed him would know that," replied one of the huge bouncers.

"But Felix never bothered nobody."

"Nobody that we knew of."

"Only someone cold-blooded would've done something like this."

"The world is full cold-blooded people."

Powerful men with lots of muscle who didn't approve of Felix's treachery and back-stabbing would've wanted to murder him execution-style. The blonde exotic dancer, slash whore, slash trick, slash lowlife, only cried because now the money she'd hustle Felix for on the side had been cut off. The bitch had only been thinking about herself. She could've cared less about the man lying on the ground filled with bullet holes. Other strippers joined her with false tears pouring from their eyes. Felix Harris was a big spender at Glitter Girls. The strippers greatly missed him. Those high-class hookers missed the money they'd milk out of him.

Chapter 27

POLICE OFFICERS WITH THE KCPD didn't have far to go after responding to the fresh murder over on Grand Boulevard. KCPD Headquarters was only five blocks away, right in the heart of downtown Kansas City over on Locust Street. Ambulances and fire trucks rushed to the scene after a series of nine-one-one calls. A rainbow of blue, yellow, and red lights bounced off nearby buildings around the downtown area.

Thrill seekers from inside Glitter Girls and regular nightclubs stood closeby to catch a glimpse of the bloody murder scene. Veteran Homicide Detective Jerry Overstreet popped up on the scene after getting a call from one of his detectives over at Headquarters. Overstreet was a tall, lean, robust, and determined detective who kept himself well-groomed and healthy. He ducked under the yellow police tape to be a part of the action.

"Alright, what do we have?" Overstreet asked one of the homicide detectives.

The detective gave Overstreet the straight details. "A 187 of a white male, approximately 50 years old, standing about 5'8", and weighing around a 160 pounds."

"Any positive identification?"

"Felix Harris, Detective Overstreet."

"The fire battalion chief?" Overstreet shrugged with surprise.

The name rung many bells in his head.

"Yes sir."

"That's really strange. I saw Felix coming out of city hall the other day."

"I believe he was involved with Fire Department union affairs."

"The body in the wagon yet?"

"Not yet, sir."

Overstreet walked over to the medical examiner's van. Before the workers put Felix inside, Overstreet unzipped the bodybag to take a good look at the murdered battalion chief.

"About how many times was he shot?" Overstreet asked one of the personnel from the medical examiner's office.

"Anywhere from 15 to 20."

"Jesus Christ!" Overstreet nudged. "They did a real number on him."

"I'd say."

"This was the work of some professionals."

"One of those quickie jobs."

"Sometime this week, I want a full autopsy and toxicology report in my office over at Headquarters. We'll work in conjunction with ballistics and the crime lab."

"Yes, sir."

"Alright, take him away."

Overstreet became a detective who was dedicated to his work. Whenever he worked a homicide case, he wanted real answers and he wanted them expeditiously. Using his professional demeanor, he approached another one of the detectives.

"Any witnesses?" Overstreet asked.

"One of the dancers in the club knew Felix quite well," the detective disclosed.

"Who?"

"The platinum blonde standing over by the door," the officer pointed out.

"Man, that broad's got a rack on her."

"I'd say."

"Sometimes, I feel like I'm getting too old for my job."

Overstreet approached the platinum blonde stripper wearing his best smile. He extended his hand out to her. "I'm Homicide Detective Jerry Overstreet with the Kansas City, Missouri Police Department."

"I'm Debra Schilling," she said with pride.

"Pleased to meet you, Debra," Overstreet obliged, checking out her healthy breasts.

"But all of my friends call me *'Babydoll.'*"

"How well did you know Felix Harris?"

"I knew Felix very well. He came to the club at least four times a week."

"Were you inside the club when he was shot?"

"Yes, I was."

"Was he by himself when he left the club?"

"Yes, I saw him leave by himself."

"Sober or drunk?"

"Drunk out of his everlasting mind."

"Did he ever come to the club with anyone?"

"Never."

"Don't mean to get personal," Overstreet apologized in a premature sense. "But were you involved with Felix in any way at any given time?"

Debra might've not had the most prestigious job, but she believed in being honest. "Felix and I got together a few times outside the club."

"I take it that he was married."

"Yes, he was."

"Did he have any enemies that you knew of?"

"Possibly."

"Whaddaya mean possibly?"

"Felix often talked about Mafia guys that he knew real well," Debra disclosed with bravery. "He often talked about mobsters here in Kansas City and out of Chicago who had gotten pissed off at him."

"Did he ever mention any names?"

"Never."

"Are you sure?"

"I'm positive."

"Give it to me straight, Debra," Overstreet pressed further.

"I'm giving it to you straight. Felix often told me stories about the old *River Quay Wars*."

"River Quay? What'd he say about the *River Quay Wars*?"

"He told me how his father was tied in with some of those Italians who'd gotten their businesses blown away by other jealous Italians. He mentioned something about the Teamsters Union and how some of those Italians were still pissed off at his father."

"So you knew that Felix was involved with the Teamsters?"

"Yes I did."

"He must've trusted you."

"When Felix got drunk, he'd tell me anything."

"Did you know of anyone who might've made threats against Felix?"

"None, whatsoever."

"Are you sure?"

"I'm positive about that, Detective."

"This killing was done execution-style. Somebody with juice wanted him dead."

"Felix could've been involved with some shady people that I didn't know about."

"That's a possibility," Overstreet recognized. "I'm going to need you to come over to Headquarters and give a statement."

"Detective, I don't wanna be putting Felix's business out in the streets. Let's have some respect for the dead. Afterall, he's got a wife and three kids he's done left behind."

"I understand that," Overstreet said. "I assure you that all information that you've given me and the Department will remain strictly confidential."

"None of us are saints here, Detective."

"No, we're not. I promise that you'll remain anonymous."

"But I don't wanna end up shot to death somewhere," Debra feared.

"Are you aware that an investigation is underway involving the Teamsters Union and organized crime here in Kansas City and Chicago?"

"Yes, I've been hearing about it."

"Are you also aware that this same investigation might involve the killing of an FBI Agent?"

"No, Detective, I wasn't aware of that."

"Now, we have to figure out if there's a link between Felix's murder and the FBI agent's murder."

One of the KCPD officers escorted the blonde-haired Debra Schilling over to one of the squad cars. When Overstreet mentioned that someone with juice wanted Felix dead, he wasn't kidding around. The men with the juice he mentioned were the Galluccio and Bernazzoli crime families.

Chapter 28

NO MATTER HOW HARD the law tried, no matter how they persisted, the Mafia in Kansas City and elsewhere seemed to show an uncanny ability to persevere. The government couldn't get rid of the Mafia no matter how hard they tried. Rumor had it how political figures were Mafiosos themselves. Discreetly, they walked on a more legitimate side of the law. Someone had to be the lesser or greater of two evils. There was just entirely too much money to be made. Powerful leaders like Galluccio and the Bernazzoli Brothers wanted it all. Their willingness to promote violence and intimidation to gain their shares of the spoils for their Chicago and Kansas City crime families became mainstream.

Angela Claybrook once again welcomed the most trusted aides and associates of Galluccio into his huge and historical *Pendergast Mansion*. Sitting on one side of the enormous conference table were International Teamsters Union President, Mason Shellenberger, Chicago bosses Carmine and Michael Bernazzoli, corrupt Missouri Senator Joseph Weinberg, chief executioner and extortionist, Francisco "Frankie Bonecutter" Provenzano, and his fellow maddog killer and wack-o friend, Robert "Bobby Crusher" Randazzo.

Sitting on the opposite side of the table were Chicago street crew henchmen Louie Calabrese and Bart Gagliano, narcotics treasurer Mickey "Bareknuckle" Castucci, Midwestern porno kingpin and strip club operator, Gino "The Bulldog" Vazzano, one of his trusted business partners in the porno industry, Daniel "Danny Dago" Pisano, and Galluccio's corrupt cousin and veteran narcotics detective, Carlo Ruggiero.

Angela finished large pots of hot brewed coffee. She prepared cups, saucers, glasses, and large buckets of smoking ice, along with bottles of their favorite drinks. She performed her duties with delight. Galluccio still had her well-trained. She jumped at his every command. The men sitting around the large table in the massive dining room poured themselves cocktails and cups of coffee. They fired up cigarettes and cigars from every end of the table. This caused Angela to hit the switch on the dehumidifier. Keeping the air somewhat clean during the meeting was important.

Galluccio entered the room wearing a paisley smoker's jacket with matching slacks. His usual pose and confident expression commanded attention. Every man present, even the Bernazzoli Brothers, greeted him with respect equal to the President of the United States or The Pope. Before presiding over the meeting with the Bernazzoli Brothers, Angela handed him his favorite brand of cigar and she disappeared within an instant.

"Men," Galluccio hummed, "I thank you once again for being here. I especially thank Carmine and Mikey Bernazzoli for flying in, once again, from Chicago. As you all know, we've got more serious matters of business to discuss concerning our families."

Shellenberger would be the first to bring union business to the table. "I'm worried about this broad whose face keeps popping up on television screens and in the newspapers."

"Are you speaking of that Sheila Bridgestone broad?" Galluccio asked Shellenberger.

"She's getting those FBI pricks closer to figuring out who took out Feliciano," Shellenberger worried senselessly. "It's like she's taking him getting clipped rather personal. I'm starting to believe that she's got her eye on that reward money."

"Who wouldn't have their eyes fixed on that 60 grand?" Galluccio spoke with reason to his criminal colleagues. "Don't worry no more about that broad, Shell. We'll take care of her soon enough."

"Whaddaya have in mind, Tommy?" Shellenberger asked.

Galluccio fixed his lips to speak. He rotated his dark eyes across the enormous conference table. "My cousin Carlo, he got'a hold of some information on this Sheila Bridgestone broad."

"What'd he find out?" Shellenberger said.

Everyone became fearful of Sheila's big mouth and her threat to the future of the International Brotherhood of the Teamsters.

Galluccio jerked his head in the direction of Carlo Ruggiero, a sinister sibling who he trusted with his very life. Ruggiero was quite reliable, an unlawful crook who'd provided Galluccio with vital information.

"I've been keeping tabs on this woman," Ruggiero spoke with insight. "The other day, I overheard her tell one of the homicide detectives down at Headquarters that she'll be taking a trip to Mardi Gras down in New Orleans."

"When will she be leaving?" Shellenberger asked.

"Soon," Ruggiero confirmed.

"What are our plans? We need to zip up this broad's mouth quickly."

Galluccio interjected into the discussion and said, "There's only one thing left to do, Shell."

"We're all listening, Tommy."

"We have'ta take this broad out."

"You want her clipped?" Shellenberger spoke with respectful objection.

"Clipped with quickness."

"You positive about that?"

"More positive than a faggot testing positive for AIDS."

"Didn't you promise your Uncle Angelo that you wouldn't go back to the insanity of the *River Quay Wars*?" Shellenberger quickly reminded Galluccio. "Didn't you promise him that you'd use less force and violence to get your point across?"

"That I did. But still, Shell, this woman's gotta go."

"How?"

"Carmine and Mikey and me came up with a brilliant plan to make her totally disappear," Galluccio explained. "After we're done, there won't be nothing left of her. The KCPD nor the FBI won't have a tiny bit of evidence to go on."

"How, Tommy, how?" Shellenberger asked with urgency.

"We've got strong ties with the Fontanello family down in New Orleans," Galluccio disclosed to Shellenberger. "The New Orleans family have even stronger connections with the unions and airlines down there."

"Could you make yourself a little clearer?"

"The New Orleans family have got union crews that can help us bring the plane down that she'll be boarding on the way back to Kansas City."

"Jesus J. Christ!" Shellenberger bubbled, distaste laced through his voice. "You can't be serious, Tommy?"

"Shell, I'm as serious as a thousand heart attacks."

"What about all those other people getting on that same plane?" Shellenberger questioned his boss. "There could literally be a 100, 200, maybe even 300 innocent people who'll be killed."

"Doesn't matter."

"Can't we find another way to take this broad out?"

"None that I can think of."

"Jesus, Tommy! We could risk everything at this point."

"Time's ticking away, and when time ticks away, money ticks away right along with it. Shell, billions of our union dollars are at stake here."

"You're right about that."

"Look Shell," Galluccio said, his mild blood pressure elevated. "We've got to hurry up and do away with her. She keeps talking to those FBI bums and we're all finished. We own the Teamsters. My Uncle Angie, along with Carmine and Mikey's old man, made the Teamsters what it is today. We can't afford to let the government come along and take something away from us that our people started. We can't afford to let some 'snitching bitch' with loose lips cause all of us to go down."

"But why take out other innocent people?" Shellenberger pleaded.

"I'm the boss, goddammit!" Galluccio violently sneered. "What I say goes."

He slammed both fists down on the hard oak table.

"Okay, Tommy, you're the boss," Shellenberger submitted, his eyes shifting.

Galluccio turned to the Bernazzoli Brothers with eyes begging for their approval. "Carmine and Mikey, with your blessings and your approval, I'd like to follow through with these initial plans."

Carmine produced a smirk across his face. "Tommy, my blessings you have. Someone who stands in our way when it comes to union affairs, they've got to go."

Michael nodded in supreme fashion. "Tommy, you have our permission and our blessings. Like you said, we own the Teamsters. We own it today, we'll own it tomorrow, and we'll own it until the end of time. Billions of dollars are at stake here."

"Shell, this is more serious than you think," Galluccio reasoned. "The boss in New Orleans has agreed to go along with the plan. Afterall, my Uncle Angie, Carmine and Mikey's old man, they shared a big chunk of the unions associated with the Teamsters. They'd turn over in their graves if they knew it all went down the drain."

"Tommy's right, Shell," Carmine added. "For years, they coveted the $2 billion dollar Teamsters Health and Welfare and Pension Funds, which was all headquartered here in Kansas City and out of Chicago. We can't disappoint the bosses of old by letting stoolies threaten our empire."

"My brother's right, Shell," Michael convened. "We're sitting on America's most richest and powerful labor union. The International Brotherhood of Teamsters is our bloodline. We derive the biggest source of power from it. We lose control of it, we lose all sense of our power."

"The craziness from the *River Quay Wars* has got nothing to do with what's going on today," Galluccio chimed in with defense. "Back then, Uncle Angie had to put his foot in a few cocksucker's asses to get his point across."

Galluccio and the Bernazzoli Brothers never lost sight of the fact that it was Teamsters Union money which actually helped build Las Vegas and major corporations. Without visionaries like Angelo Galluccio, Nino Bernazzoli, and other powerful men, there probably wouldn't be a Las Vegas. There wouldn't be an entertainment mecca for veteran sinners to run to.

There wouldn't be a place for men to fuck the most beautiful women in the world, gamble at the highest rolling tables and slot machines, drink the finest liquors, get high on the purest cocaine and heroin, eat the finest cuisine meals right there in the casinos, take their children for family entertainment, and be mesmerized by the some of the world's greatest entertainers.

"We still maintain that Las Vegas became what it is today because of my Uncle Angie and Carmine and Mikey's old man," Galluccio stood firm.

"Tommy's Uncle Angie and our old man were the real godfathers of Las Vegas," Carmine boasted with a barrel chest. "Those casinos can thank the Teamsters, and the Teamsters can thank our old man. That desert town should honor them every year because of their vision and hard work."

"Got that right, brother," Michael asserted. "The high rollers in Vegas should be kissing our asses this very moment. Ask my opinion, I think they should build statues for men like Angelo Galluccio and Nino Bernazzoli."

Shellenberger absorbed every word spoken by his bosses.

What title did Thomas "The Caveman" Galluccio hold other than that of a Kansas City organized crime Mafia boss?

Tommy Galluccio, a killer of innocent babies.

Tommy Galluccio, a killer of innocent children.

Tommy Galluccio, a killer of innocent women.

Tommy Galluccio, a killer of innocent men.

Tommy Galluccio, a cold-blooded killer of families.

Tommy Galluccio, a thug, dope dealer, gangster, womanizer, gambler, loansharker, extortionist, pimp, pornographer, executioner, and maddog killer.

"Can't we catch this broad by herself or wait until she gets back to Kansas City?" Shellenberger asked out of sympathy.

A sad puppy dog look crept across his pudgy Jewish face.

"Shell, my orders are final," Galluccio stood firm. "Carmine and Mikey's orders are final, too."

"You guys are the bosses," Shellenberger sorrowfully submitted.

Galluccio refused to go against the *Codes of Omerta*. Even if it meant sacrificing other innocent human lives. Sheila Bridgestone simply had to be eliminated. The rules of *La Cosa Nostra* had changed drastically from the rules of the old goombah days.

Carlo Ruggiero, the most corrupt of local law enforcement officials, pointed to everyone around the conference table. "But our problems don't stop here."

"My cousin Carlo found out more information that's of great importance to all of us," Galluccio announced to his constituents.

Ruggiero belted down a straight shot of scotch. His eyes shifted around the table. "One of the homicide detectives assigned to the Feliciano case isn't your average chick. She's gung ho about cracking this murder case. She's been bringing in witnesses from all over the place. I've never seen someone as committed as her. If she keeps up her charade, we're all dead meat."

"Who's this broad?" Carmine asked.

"Her name's Brittany Goldberg," Ruggiero unveiled. "She's been working in homicide for the past two years. Talk about a renegade, this broad has helped the KCPD solve a lot of homicides during her law enforcement career."

"So, what're we gonna do about her?" Michael asked.

Ruggiero had a direct answer. "The other day I also overheard her talking about going down to New Orleans for Mardi Gras. She's been having an affair with some rich white guy. She told another one of the detectives that they'll be traveling down there together."

"Think she'll be on the same plane with that Sheila Bridgestone snitch-bitch?" Galluccio penetrated.

"Strong possibility."

"Either way, keep us posted," Carmine instructed Ruggiero. "That way, we can possibly kill two birds with one stone."

"As soon as I hear something, you'll be the first ones to know."

Provenzano sat calmly across the table smoking a cigarette while he sipped on a frosty glass of bourbon. Galluccio tapped his fingers onto the hard table. His piercing eyes were fixed on Provenzano.

"What's the word on Felix Harris?" Galluccio asked his number one contract killer.

"Ha! Ha!" Provenzano laughed. "They're having a homecoming celebration for Felix down in hell."

"Good."

"Felix needs a drink of ice cold water about right now."

"The union is trying to vote in a new battalion chief," Galluccio mentioned.

Shellenberger wedged back into the discussion. "We should let the smoke clear, Tommy."

"What are you talking about, Shell?" Galluccio asked.

"The fire department and city administration are looking deeper into Felix's murder."

"Like I've always said, no witnesses, no evidence, they've got no case."

"They're not going to start voting in a new battalion chief until they get some answers about his killing."

"So what."

"But someone's got to fill that position in the meantime."

"What's the big deal?"

"They're going to start looking at us."

"For what reasons?"

"The unions are connected with the fire department, which are the unions that are connected with us."

"Why do you worry so much, Shell?" Galluccio inquired of his number one flunky. "Don't I always do what I say I'm going to do?"

"Sure you do, Tommy."

"Didn't I help you get acquitted in that embezzling trial?"

"Sure you did."

"Didn't I help you get acquitted in that freight-hauling contract trial?"

"You sure did."

"Didn't I help you get acquitted in that pension and insurance fraud trial?"

"Absolutely, Tommy."

"Then, what the fuck are you worried about?"

Galluccio, being a criminal mastermind, knew how a few breaks and some good attorneys, along with the bribing of corrupt political officials, had the juice to get anyone off and help them escape jail time.

"My word's as good as 90 carat gold."

"You're right, Tommy."

The room converted to silence, which gave everyone time to gather their thoughts.

Chapter 29

OTHER MATTERS OF business were brought to the table. Galluccio and the Bernazzoli Brothers knew they had to move fast. Carmine and Michael thrusted forward in their chairs. Both Chicago bosses pointed over to Provenzano and Randazzo.

"Are the men in position down in New Orleans?" Carmine asked both veteran killers-executioners.

"They're set up near the airport," Provenzano explained to Carmine.

"Somewhere that's accessible," Randazzo relayed to the top boss.

"In one of those transient hotels?" Carmine asked.

"An old place that's not identifiable," Provenzano said.

"Good."

"We've cleared everything with the boss down in New Orleans," Randazzo said.

"We'll owe them a big favor after this," Carmine said.

"Everything's set up perfectly," Provenzano nodded.

"Fontanello's got an excellent crew down there," Michael explained.

"The payoff man is in position inside the New Orleans airport," Galluccio said.

"It's best we get rid of the witness and the detective at the same time," Carmine suggested. "Since we've got those insurance contracts going through the Teamsters guys down in New Orleans, we can't waste a second with a deal as big as this one."

"We'll be meeting with Fontanello and his people here in Kansas City after those two are out of the way," Michael assured everyone present.

Galluccio bolted his eyes over to Shellenberger. Teamsters Union business seemed never-ending. For those who defied Galluccio and the Bernazzoli Brothers, the ones who wanted to operate the union-controlled businesses their way, untamed animals were unleashed to set them straight. Yet another greedy bastard who had big interests in Local Union 45 became a different topic of discussion at their crucial meeting.

"Richard Delaney's gotten way out of control," Shellenberger informed his superiors. Richard turned out to be another big mouth who had the potential to start singing favorable tunes for the federal government.

"The greedy, ungrateful cocksucker!" Galluccio shuddered in a thunderous gesture. He sucked in a thick drag of his cigar.

"Something's got to be done about him and his brother," Shellenberger instigated.

Shellenberger gained knowledge of how Delaney had been trying to solidify a tight grip on the very union controlled by the Galluccio and Bernazzoli crime families.

"Talk about a backstabbing bastard!" Shellenberger charged. "We put up the funds for his brother to start those car businesses in the Northland, and this is how they show their appreciation?"

"Delaney's been stealing big money from Local 45 and doesn't want to share none of the cream with anyone," Michael said, his ability to flush out a thief.

"There's only one thing to do to a thief who steals from the very people who put him where he is!" Galluccio fumed, insulted that a thief might've slipped right past him.

"He's been passing a lot of that same stolen money on to his brother," Shellenberger said.

"Fucking thieves!" Carmine snarled.

"Both of them have gotta be hit," Michael dictated, his Neapolitan blood bubbling under his skin.

"I agree," Galluccio proposed to the criminal council. "After Shell's embezzling trial, I figured that he'd eventually go crying to the feds about crooked union business. Now is the best time to hit that pukebag. That way, we won't have'ta worry about him nor his brother belting out tunes to the feds."

"Then it's official," Carmine sealed. "Delaney and his brother are to be hit."

Galluccio circled his burning red eyes around the table. His eyes landed over to where his personal pitbulls sat. "Frankie and Bobby, we want you two guys to handle this piece of work for us. We want the job done before you guys take off for New Orleans."

"It's done, Tommy," Provenzano said with total submission.

"It'll be an honor, Tommy," Randazzo noted with pride.

Those involved with union affairs had agreed that Richard Delaney and his brother were as good as dead. Galluccio and the Bernazzoli Brothers had to set time aside to speak with Mickey Castucci about a dope shipment coming into Miami in the coming weeks. They had already spoken with Gino Vazzano about critical issues surrounding the strip clubs and porno operations in Kansas City, Chicago, St. Louis, Omaha, and Wichita. Another meeting was officially adjourned.

Chapter 30

BRITTANY GOLDBERG liberated herself after a hard breakup from an old boyfriend. Tyler Kersey was his name, a handsome and ambitious young man who had Brittany's heart on lock and key. She sensed how the infidelities she'd suffered during her courtship with Tyler had diminished. Somewhere in the depths of her heart, she still had crazy love for him. He was the first love of her life. It'd been a part of her which couldn't be denied, no matter how rejection came from her family and friends. Life was about moving towards fresh starts. Like many broken hearts which came before her, in order to move up, one had to move on.

Brittany took a break from her duties as a full-time homicide detective with the Kansas City Police Department to spend time with the new love of her life. Scotty Borthwick was his name. He was a handsome and cleancut white boy, a young man with an aristocratic background and Ivy League education, who was more bareknuckle to her style. Both had grown to like one another. They learned to share love. They learned to be in love with one another, sharing the same values which created an unbreakable bond. Brittany and her significant other decided to frequent Loose Park.

The park was one of those multi-acre landscapes located just south of the upscale Country Club Plaza. Ducks swam and flew around the wide open pond where they walked along the banks holding hands. The sunny and mild late February weather created an aphrodisiac sizzle between the couple. Legend had it how couples often snuck into Loose Park and had sex in the early-early morning hours. Brittany and Scotty stopped at the west end of the pond to sit on a limestone wall.

"I love you, Scotty," Brittany said, her blue-green eyes quite captivating.

A rush of fresh air blew across her beautiful face. She gazed hopelessly into the animated eyes of Scotty.

"Love you more, Britt," Scotty reciprocated, sliding his long arm around her thin waist.

Scotty stared into her alluring gems. For them, there was no greater feeling than to be madly in love.

"This is so romantic being here at Loose Park," Brittany reminded Scotty.

"A place designed for lovers," Scotty smiled, his heart pounding from her presence.

"Know what, Scotty?"

"I'm listening, Britt."

"I've always wanted to start a family."

"Have children?"

"Of course."

"Having children is one of the most exciting things on Earth."

"They bring the greatest joy."

"I'd say so."

"None of us are getting any younger."

"True."

"I mean, no one can wait forever to have children."

"I agree."

"*Mother Nature* has a way of sneaking up on us."

"What are you beating around to?"

"Someday I'd like to have children."

"And you will."

Brittany wanted more than anything to be a loving mother and wife. Being a woman with children, a fulfilling career, and the potential to advance in her work, remained her constant dreams. She locked eyes with Scotty, disappointment etched across her face.

"When are you going to tell your wife?" Brittany genuinely asked Scotty.

The technical movement of her lips, along with the rolling of her aqua blue-green eyes, caught Scotty way off guard.

"What, about us?" Scotty responded, uncertainty molded to his voice.

"Who else?"

"It's hard, Britt."

"Where do we stand, Scotty?"

"I love you, Britt, and you know that."

"Then ask her for a divorce."

"It's not that easy."

"You're going to have to make a choice sooner or later."

"True."

"Why not do it now?"

"You make it sound so simple."

"We can't keep this up forever, Scotty."

"What?"

"Sneaking around."

"I want us to be together forever and you know that."

"I can't keep being second best."

"Seems like we're all caught up in this crazy triangle game."

"It's getting worse by the day."

"There's a lot at stake here."

"My career's going good right now," Brittany intoned to the man that she loved with all her heart. "With us getting married, I'd feel more complete."

"I know."

"Then, why do you keep procrastinating about getting the divorce?"

"What, you want me to run home and just tell my wife that I want a divorce?"

"In so many words, yes."

"You make it sound so simple."

"I'm still assigned to the Feliciano murder case."

"What, the FBI agent being killed in Westport?"

"Yes."

"Thinking about how he got taken out just gives me the creeps."

"Technically, I'm not supposed to leave the city until the case is closed."

"I feel special with you making me an exception."

"Do your parents know about us?"

"Not yet. How about your parents?"

"No."

"We both can do without the shame."

"You running circles around your wife is getting old."

"I'm just as sick of it as you are."

Scotty had developed deep feelings for Brittany. He carried those feelings around like valuable goods. Letting go of her would've been like cutting off his supply of oxygen. Sooner or later, he'd have to make a concrete decision.

"Are you still going with me on that trip?" Scotty asked, his voice tainted with sympathy.

"Where, to New Orleans?" Brittany recalled.

"Yes."

"Exactly when is the trip?" Brittany asked.

"Soon. Mardi Gras is coming up real soon."

"How exciting!" Brittany cheered, a cool blush across her rosy cheeks.

"You'll love it down there, Britt."

"Will I?"

"Mardi Gras is the most exciting event in all the world."

"You know the area pretty well?"

"My father has several business associates all through Louisiana."

"Sounds cool."

"Tour guides are no problem. We'll have the best of everything down there."

Brittany dropped her head in suspense. "What about your wife?"

"Don't worry about her."

"But, I am worried."

"I'll tell her that I'm going to New York on business for my father."

"Think she'll buy that story?"

"My father also has offices in New York and New Jersey."

"And she already knows that?"

"Of course she does."

"Clever, Scotty, real clever."

"I've booked a couple of tickets and hotels for us. Everything's taken care of, darling."

"I love you, Scotty."

"Love you more, Britt."

Brittany and Scotty pressed their bodies together. Their lips met with invitation. They held one another as though there was no tomorrow. Both were happy to be headed to New Orleans for Mardi Gras.

Chapter 31

SHELLENBERGER GAVE Richard Delaney and his brother Mark Delaney several warnings surrounding union business and the direct importance of keeping a low profile. Greed was no good in a business where the feds always looked over one's shoulders. Richard had unceremoniously called an executive board meeting as the recording secretary with Local Union 45. Members with the Over the Road and City Transfer Drivers, Helpers, Dockmen, and Warehousemen, shot straight through the roof after they learned how a dues increase was by way of a referendum ballot. One union member complained how they'd gotten fucked without even getting a kiss.

Only Shellenberger had been given the authority to dictate union affairs. Word got back to Galluccio and the Bernazzoli Brothers how Richard Delaney embezzled union money and laundered the cash over to his brother, strictly for the benefit of his several car lots in the Northland. Provenzano and Randazzo, along with henchmen from Chicago's street crews, were given the contracts to rubout Richard and Mark Delaney. Honor had to be restored within the crime families. Both men were lowlife thieves. The only way to make them pay for their disloyalty was none other than a violent death.

Provenzano and Randazzo split up with the four Chicago executioners shipped in by the Bernazzoli Brothers. Three would finish the job on Richard Delaney while three would do a serious number on Mark Delaney. The casual schedule of both brothers were studied down to a precise science. Inside the glass-cased office of Delaney's Cars and Trucks, Mark Delaney conducted business in his usual notorious fashion.

Preying on the many customers with bad credit, his car businesses flourished through corruption. Many interested car buyers were overcharged with ridiculous monthly car notes and extreme high finance rates. Everyone knew how car dealers were some of the biggest crooks on the planet. They stuck it right in you, not having the common decency to use lubrication.

The Delaney brothers were foolish to believe they'd get away with double-crossing anyone associated with the Galluccio and Bernazzoli families. The bosses scratched their backs whenever it was accessible. They, in turn, stuck knives in their backs. They showed their treachery by thinking it was one big joke.

Mark Delaney locked the door to his office. He shut off all the lights out by the showroom floor and made sure all the alarms were set in motion. The mechanics and salesmen had left hours earlier. A dense patch of darkness engulfed the dealership building. Mark stepped up to his classic Jaguar and heard the clapping of several footsteps approaching him.

"Who's out there?" Mark questioned, wildly jingling his keys down by the door.

No one answered. Not one person was spotted near his car or on the side of the automotive building. Footsteps came in clearer. He struggled to open the door to his Jaguar.

"Who in the hell's coming towards me?" Mark nervously inquired.

He fidgeted with the keys while trying to unlock the door.

"Nightie night, Markie," the husky voice called out.

"What the hell's this?"

Mark Delaney was nothing more than a soft punk who fainted at the sight of blood. An unexpected burst of pandemonium broke out.

Three masked men wearing all-black clothing burst from out of the darkness with weapons drawn. Before Mark uttered another word, a .38 silencer and a .45 automatic was planted at the very back and on the side of his head.

"So, you and your brother wanna be thieves?" said the first gunman.

"So long, Markie," said the second gunman.

The first two bullets discharged from the .38 Smith and Wesson blew part of his brain matter all over the passenger side of the Jaguar. The .45 automatic blew the other side of his brains out. Mists of fine blood stained most of the passenger's side of the car. The third gunman rushed up and pumped four more bullets into the chest and stomach of Mark. The three men moved in close to one another. Distastefully, they stared down at his bullet-riddled body. They worked up their glands until globs of thick saliva gurgled around in their mouths. All three executioners bent forward and spat right into the face of Mark.

"You know, Markie, they say if you'll lie, then you'll steal," mocked the first gunman.

"And they say if you'll steal, then you'll definitely kill," imitated the second gunman.

"Therefore, that makes you a liar, a thief, and a killer," added the third gunman.

The hitman-executioner in the middle kicked Mark on the side of his head. Tiny bits of shattered skull fragments stuck to his steeltoe boot. The next hitman-executioner whipped out a long switchblade and slashed his neck. He stabbed him through the chest and into the lower torso area.

More blood gushed from his lifeless body. *The message of terror was clear!* Cross the wrong the people and your life ended in the blink of an eye. The three killers used a crowbar and jackhammer to pop the trunk of the Jaguar. Mark's brutalized body was stuffed inside a large burlap sack and wrapped tight with string. Blood dripped between the cracks and onto the ground.

"Let this be a lesson for other scums who don't fly straight," commented the first gunman.

"Our work's done here," said the second gunman.

"Alright, let's get out of here," said the third gunman.

"Delaney's history."

The trio fled the murder scene in order to avoid detection. More blood dripped from the trunk of Mark's Jaguar. Before the end of the next business day, someone would have to tell all the employees at Delaney's Cars and Trucks that their boss was dead. Someone would have to tell Mark's wife and children that their husband and father had been brutally murdered in front of his own car dealership. Someone had to be told that Mark ended up being nothing but *trunk music.*

Chapter 32

RICHARD DELANEY PSYCHED himself into believing he could prosper from money stolen out of Local Union 45s treasury. Richard turned the same stolen money over to his brother. *Galluccio and the Bernazzoli Brothers couldn't believe the swollen balls on a cocksucker like him!* To them, Richard had the kind of balls swollen from backed-up come. He had the kind of balls filled with greed, treachery, and thievery. He could've easily given the bosses a piece of his booming action. Greedy scums like him chose to ignore them and selfishly prosper on part of an empire they'd built up with impunity. The Teamsters Union was closest to the fiery hearts of Galluccio and the Bernazzoli Brothers. For those who betrayed their trust, they paid dearly in the most brutal fashion.

Richard drove into his garage after spending a long night at one of the local bars. While sipping on a frosty beer held with one hand, he shut the engine off with the other hand. Before the garage door closed completely, three masked men rushed inside with rope, knives, pistols, and handguns. Just as he took the key out of the ignition, two of the hired assassins simultaneously jerked open both doors. The assassin on the driver's side wrapped a thick bull's rope around Richard's fragile neck.

The assassin on the passenger's side grabbed the other end of the lengthy rope. Both assassins pulled against one another. Violently and aggressively, they played a serious game of tug-of-war. The oxygen-deprived face of Richard had turned a purplish color. A recollected terror filled his eyes. Regurgitated beer shot from his turbulent stomach and sprayed the middle of the windshield. The foamy beer oozed down onto the dashboard. Mucous as thick as paste blasted from both of his nostrils.

"Only dirty motherfuckers steal from their friends!" barked one of the assassins.

"You pushed your luck over the edge, Richie!" bellowed the other assassin, still jerking the rope from the passenger's side.

"You hit us with a low blow, motherfucker!" rumbled the assassin, still on the other end of the rope, pulling harder than ever.

"How does it feel, Richie boy?"

"Yeah, how does it feel?"

"Something wrong? Cat got your tongue?"

"You stinking piece of turd!"

"Nobody steals from us."

"You pitiful pukebag!"

"Nobody dips into union funds without the boss's okay."

Richard tried pulling the rope from around his neck. His efforts were useless. Before all life was squeezed out of him, the third assassin pulled a big hunting knife out of his waistband. Savagely, he sliced Richard's throat and stabbed him multiple times in the chest. An incision the shape of a V had been made across his stomach. Mists of fine pinkish blood sprayed onto the windshield and across the leather seats. Bloody intestinal organs dropped onto the floor near his feet. His bloodshot eyes rolled with fear. His heart pumped closer to death. A bluish discoloration formed around his torso. It was far too late for Richard to think about siphoning off union money for his own needs. It was much too late for him to plead his case about stealing from men who were fair with him.

When they felt all life had left the body of Richard, the two assassins released the rope from their respective ends. To send their own message of terror, the hired executioners used their pistols to blast away at his already lifeless corpse. Shattered glass popped from every direction. Bullets from their weapons punctured his body. One of the assassins planted his pistol into his left eye. Instantly, his eyeball was blown right out of the socket. Both Delaney brothers were now dead from execution-style murders.

The killings happened just the way Galluccio and the Bernazzoli Brothers wanted it. The three hired assassins carried out their duties in a professional and brutal fashion. A messy scene they'd made inside of Richard Delaney's home garage. During the whole execution process, Richard made a mess of his own. Defecation and urine had discharged from his body. His body waste left the smelliest mess behind.

"Whew!" said the assassin at the front of the car.

"Do they always shit and piss?" asked the other assassin behind him.

"Sometimes they piss, sometimes they shit."

"I'd rather him have piss than shit."

"Smells like a rotten fucking sewer in this garage!"

"Guess we weren't lucky this time."

"What the fuck did this scumbag Delaney eat today?"

"God only knows."

"Alright, let's do away with this prick's body."

"Let's strip his clothes off."

"Okay, let's go to work."

Using a large canvas mailbag, the nude corpse of Richard Delaney was stuffed inside. More bull's rope was used to wrap around the canvas bag. All three assassins lifted his body and dumped it into the trunk. And like his brother, Richard Delaney was made into *trunk music*. Honor had once again been restored to the Galluccio and Bernazzoli crime families.

Chapter 33

WORD GOT AROUND fast about the crazy low discounts being offered by travel agencies around Kansas City for the Mardi Gras festivities down in New Orleans. Randy and Tracey were two of the first ones to jump at such an irresistable offer. It took a lot of begging and pleading, but Randy convinced Tracey to travel with him to see all the excitement down in New Orleans. Tracey finally stopped grilling him about what he'd seen that tragic night down in the *Westport District*. She allowed him to deal with his own hidden secrets and exercise those forbidden demons. Their relationship had grown closer. Along with that trust, came confidence and fidelity.

Light rain mixed with snow drizzles blew across the airport windows and built up a thin sheet of ice along the runways. The restlessness of the passengers inside KCI Airport dominated the scene. The hostility of those waiting to board the plane could've transformed into mists of angry steam from their heated bodies. An agent behind one of the ticket counters announced the flight to Chicago. The flight taking passengers on to New Orleans was delayed for another half-hour. People became jittery and fidgeted out of control.

Passengers bumped others in front of them and those behind them. Some used their hands and elbows as signals. Tracey suffered from a bad case of impatience. Often, she cited reasons of high blood pressure and female hormonal disorders. Being in her middle twenties, she had no reason to have high blood pressure. As for the hormonal problems, women couldn't escape it no matter how hard they tried.

"That's why I hate traveling," Tracey complained, her head hung to the side.

She breathed the air of sheer hostility.

"Things'll be alright once we get to New Orleans," Randy spoke in a comforting tone.

He only hoped the thirty minutes would shoot by fast.

"Look at all these people here in KCI."

"I'll bet most are headed to Mardi Gras."

"Guess some will be going to other cities once we get to Chicago."

"Some of these people probably live in Chicago."

Randy experienced a tragic flashback. He suddenly heard gunshots ringing out. He pictured FBI Special Agent Wilfredo Feliciano being pumped with hot slugs. Crowds of people running and screaming crept into his distorted memory. Seeing the two gunmen flee the murder scene became all too clear. Tracey looked over at him. She picked up on his strange behavior.

"Randy?" Tracey called out light-voiced.

Randy gave her no reply, whatsoever.

"What's wrong?" she asked, becoming very concerned.

Still, Randy didn't respond.

She whisked her hand in his face and shouted, "Randy! What're you daydreaming about?"

Randy snapped out of his daze and said, "I've just got a lot of things on my mind."

"You've shut out the whole world?"

"Everything's okay."

"Are you sure?"

"Sure I'm sure."

Brittany and Scotty stood at the very front of the long line. Proudly, they were two wealthy people flying first class. A gleam sparkled from the blue-green eyes of Brittany. A blanket of happiness embraced her whole body.

"Oh Scotty, I'm so happy to be going to New Orleans with you," Brittany vowed.

"I'm happy you decided to come," Scotty said.

"We're going to have the time of our lives," she conceived.

"That you can bet."

Standing towards the middle of the line was Sheila Bridgestone. The FBI and the KCPD's most valuable witness, the woman who cooperated fully in trying to solve the killing of Agent Feliciano, was being watched inside KCI by sets of sinister eyes. Sheila needed time out of Kansas City. After all the phone calls and endless visits by the FBI and the KCPD to her job and residence, she'd become exhausted. Things got to the point where she felt harrassed. The FBI wanted to satisfy a hunger in solving the bizarre murder of their fallen comrade.

Thirty minutes passed quicker than most passengers realized. One of the agents behind the counter had announced that the anticipated flight to Chicago, and then on to New Orleans, was boarding at gate seven. Randy and Tracey snatched their carry-on bags off the ground and moved with the long line. Brittany and Scotty were the first ones to board the plane. Wealth sure had its privileges.

Standing secretly over by a set of pay phones were Provenzano and Randazzo. Galluccio and the Bernazzoli Brothers ordered them to remain posted inside KCI Airport until their potential murder subjects boarded the plane. Dressed rather conservatively, both men wore faded jeans, dingy white T-shirts, dirty worn sneakers, and KC Royals baseball caps. Both sported scraggly goatees coloring their diabolical faces. A look of evil intentions burned through the eyes of Provenzano.

Provenzano eased his hand down into his deep jeans pocket for a fistful of quarters. No one, not even airport security, noticed them standing over by the pay phones.

"I've gotta give Louie and Bart a call in Chicago," Provenzano explained to Randazzo.

"You think they've made it to their post?" Randazzo asked his murderous constituent.

"They should've by now."

"And none of these calls can be traced by the feds?"

"Not'a one of them."

"You sure, Frankie?"

"Positive, Bobby."

"The bosses wanted us to check things out thoroughly."

"Don't worry, Bobby, I've got everything under control."

With crafty eyes zoomed in on Sheila Bridgestone, Randazzo watched her closely, while his partner dropped quarters into the machine. The long line moved rather quickly. Five dollars worth of quarters were fed into the pay phone. Provenzano turned facing away from the busy airport crowd. At close to 500 miles away, the pay phone inside a busy O'Hare International Airport fired off with a noticeable loud ring. Louie Calabrese snatched the phone up like he'd waited for some urgent news.

"Louie, they're leaving Kansas City right now," Provenzano informed his Mafia colleague posted up in Chicago.

"They're on their way to Chicago, right?" asked Calabrese, stationed in the spot he'd been ordered to be at.

"You know what to do when they get to Chicago?"

"Of course."

"Alright, let's hear it."

"Make a call down to New Orleans."

"What else?"

"Don't let them out of our sight until they leave Chicago."

"Okay, what else?" Provenzano grilled further.

"Call you back in Kansas City if there's any change of plans."

"Louie, you keep an eye on the witness. Bart can keep an eye on the detective."

"Every move they make, we'll be watching them."

"And please, for chrissake, stay on schedule."

"Definitely."

"These were the orders from Tommy, Carmine, and Mikey."

"We'll see that those orders are carried out."

"There can't be no fuckups, Louie," Provenzano enunciated in fine detail.

"There won't be any, Frankie."

"Good."

"I'll talk to you soon."

"Okay."

Provenzano placed the phone back on the receiver. Without being noticed, both men walked out of KCI Airport. Passengers had boarded the plane for Chicago.

Randy had more complaints than groups of adolescent women starting their menstrual cycles. Flying was no problem for him. It was having to be seated at the very end of the plane.

"Everytime I fly, I always end up near the restroom," Randy whined to Tracey.

"What's wrong with that?" Tracey asked.

"Do you know what that's like?" he questioned her.

He experienced high levels of discomfort.

"No."

"You don't?"

"Won't you tell me."

"I've flown before, and had to sit right next to the bathroom door."

"Get to the point."

"You can hear people in there farting and dropping loads of turds into the stool," he strongly objected. "You can hear water splashing around the seat and on the floor. And when they open the door afterwards, you can smell the fumes from their shit rushing out of the bathroom. The smell rushes straight up into your nostrils."

"Everybody's shit stinks, Randy," Tracey candidly declared.

"Hey, I know that I don't shit rose petals or peppermint sticks. But some people need to lay off those burritos and chitterlings and navy beans."

"Are you speaking of black people?"

"White people, too."

"It's all a part of nature."

"But, seriously—."

"If you smell something, just cover your nose. You'll survive it, I'm sure."

Randy took his seat in the F section of the Boeing 757 on United Airlines. Tracey didn't mind sitting in the back with a plush pillow resting in her lap. The airline stewardesses rushed up and down the aisle to make sure all overhead luggage were secured. They made sure the passengers were seated properly. Travelers were told to secure their seatbelts in preparation for takeoff.

From the front cabin, one of the pilots picked up the radio and announced, "Flight attendants, prepare for takeoff."

The huge jumbo jet made a u-turn and zoomed down the clear runway. Before long, the plane was lifted off the ground and shot straight for the friendly skies. Randy peeked out his window seat. He looked down at the buildings and residential areas below. The Midwestern city known as *Kansas City* was being left behind for a few days.

"You ready for New Orleans?" Randy asked Tracey.

"Ready as I'll ever be," Tracey answered back.

"Time away from home does everybody good."

"Sure it does," she agreed.

The pilot came over the radio and announced, "Ladies and gentlemen, we are flying at an altitude of 30,000 feet. We will be arriving in Chicago in approximately 40 minutes. By the way, the temperature in Chicago is 15 degrees with light snow drizzles. You are free to move about the cabin. Our flight attendants are here to serve you, and we thank you for flying United Airlines."

Brittany and Scotty enjoyed the royal treatment received in the first class section. The two lovebirds gazed hopelessly into one another's eyes. Brittany had made love to Scotty several times after their initial meeting. She enjoyed their lovemaking to the fullest extent. Her main desire was for him to divorce his wife. Unquestionably, she wanted to marry him since he was the brightest prospect in the looks and financial departments.

Brittany's money-hungry father, the shrew business tyrant, Don Goldberg, somehow heard about Scotty and thought immediate dollar signs. Money usually married money. For the Jewish culture, it became an accepted way of life. For ultimate business purposes, Scotty carried his multi-faceted cell phone around with him. From inside a black leather briefcase, the cell phone rung with soft tones.

"Aren't you going to answer it?" Brittany asked, her suspicions aroused.

Brittany picked up on how Scotty stalled in answering his calls. Business, pleasure, or otherwise, he feared who the caller might've been.

"It's probably not important," Scotty ignored, nervous vibes coming over him.

"Could be an emergency, babe."

"Probably my dad checking up on me."

'At least see who it is.'

"Guess it wouldn't hurt."

Scotty opened the briefcase. Hesitantly, he slid the cell phone out in the open. He stared down at the number and his heart pumped with discontent. His eyes stretched wide open while a patch of light perspiration formed across his face.

"What's wrong, babe?" Brittany asked.

"Can't believe this shit!" he denounced.

Brittany leaned forward to look down at the small window of the cell phone. Her eyes widened with surprise. "Your wife?"

"She's not supposed to be calling me."

"Don't tell me that she found out you're really going to New Orleans."

"She's not supposed to be checking up on me."

"Are you going to answer it?"

"No way!"

"She could be calling you about an emergency."

"I doubt it."

"You never can tell, Scotty."

Whether or not Scotty's wife found out he was headed down to New Orleans, remained a mystery to all parties. Whether or not she suspected he'd been cheating on her remained in question. All women weren't stupid when it came to finding out if their man had other women on the side. The signs were there. The lovemaking wasn't the same anymore. The hugging, caressing, moonlighting, and romantic antics slowly diminished.

"What are you going to do, Scotty?" Brittany asked.

"Just let it ring," Scotty said.

"And what if it doesn't stop ringing?"

"She'll eventually hang up," Scotty insisted.

"Doesn't look good."

"Don't worry about it."

"We didn't go on vacation together to be harassed by unnecessary phone calls."

"Some people just don't give up."

Brittany shot Scotty a look of deprivation and said," Especially if they're your wife."

"Everything will be alright."

"We hope so."

The flight attendants strolled along the aisle handing out snacks and favorite beverages. Sheila Bridgestone sat quietly in the middle row reading the latest edition of the *Kansas City Times* newspaper. She felt she'd served a civic duty by helping the FBI and the KCPD possibly identify the men responsible for the shooting death of Agent Feliciano. They had a lot more questions for her.

More agents sent down from Washington, D.C. wanted to speak with her. Agents who'd become involved with the complicated investigation sought her information. What Sheila didn't realize was how she had become the target of Chicago and Kansas City notorious organized crime families. Galluccio and the Bernazzoli Brothers instructed their men to keep a low profile. No one gave her any indication she was targeted for murder herself.

Chapter 34

THE BOEING 757 carrying passengers from Kansas City landed perfectly on the runway at Chicago's O'Hare Airport. Flight attendants came over the intercom announcing that it was safe for everyone to unfasten their seatbelts. Brittany and Scotty were the first ones to exit the plane once it was aligned with the ramp leading into the airport. Already, they had their carry-on bags tucked under their arms, anxious to loosen up from the brief flight. Randy and Tracey fell in line behind others while they waited for passengers to pull their belongings out of the cargo section. The line moved slowly. People huffed and puffed out of frustration.

Many signaled for the ones with the peanut butter and molasses up their asses to get a move on it. Some appeared to have carried their life's possessions on board. Brittany and Scotty strutted into the enormous O'Hare International Airport with their bags dangling down by their sides. *A "city within a city".* It's exactly what O'Hare International was. Everything to accomodate travelers in between flights was housed inside the colossal airport. Restaurants, giftshops, restrooms, shoe shine stands, leather shops, all of it was at one's disposal. Masses of people moved from one destination to the other.

Brittany and Scotty rushed up to the computerized boards to check arrival and departure times.

"What time does our plane leave for New Orleans?" Brittany asked Scotty.

She pointed to the top of the board with the help of her blue painted nail.

"We'll be here in Chicago for another forty-five minutes," Scotty learned.

He studied the schedule closest to their destination.

"How long is the actual flight to New Orleans?"

"At least a couple'a hours. Maybe it's shorter than that."

"Let's get something to eat," Brittany recommended to Scotty.

A growling echo of hunger had rumbled inside her stomach.

"Where?"

"One of these hotdog restaurants or hamburger places."

"Sounds appetizing to me."

"Let's go eat."

"I'm starved."

Randy and Tracey stepped up to the board while Brittany and Scotty went the other direction. Mixed emotions flared up inside of Tracey like a pimple filled with blood and pus. Long traveling ventures usually got the best of her.

"Can't wait until we get to New Orleans," Tracey proposed to Randy.

She became more irritated by the minute.

"We're only a plane ride away, babe," Randy said in order to console her.

"I can tell you one thing."

"Talk to me."

"I'm ready to taste some of that good old *Cajun-Creole* food down in New Orleans."

"Tracey, don't tempt my tastebuds like that."

"My mouth's watering from just thinking about it."

"Let's find a seat somewhere in this crazy airport."

"Sounds good to me."

"My feet are killing me."

Brittany and Scotty stepped over into the seating area to get off their feet. Sheila Bridgestone traveled along the busy airport looking inside the many shops and restaurants. Traveling alone was nothing new since she was a single woman with no children. Single people sometimes found more excitement than those who traveled in groups. She still had no idea that she'd been marked for death. She had no clue that she'd become the main target of an organized crime network of heartless gangsters. Inside the minds of Galluccio and the Bernazzoli Brothers, she had to be eliminated at all cost. She wasn't to return to Kansas City alive.

Likewise, Brittany had also been marked for death. Being one of the main homicide detectives assigned to the case involving the killing of Agent Feliciano, she'd become a major threat since she dedicated long hours to solving the case. The bosses reasoned: *We can kill two birds with one stone.*

Sheila stepped into a Chinese restaurant towards the south end of O'Hare Airport. The wicked, yet resourceful eyes of Louie Calabrese and Bart Gagliano watched her every move. Dressed in wrinkled faded jeans, long heavy windbreakers, dirty old sneakers, and Chicago Cubs baseball caps, both killers concealed their menacing faces.

Calabrese studied Sheila from over by a set of pay phones. By no means were they to be noticed or identified by suspicious people in the airport. By no means was she to leave their eyesight.

Shrewdly, Calabrese nursed one of the phones into his sweaty hand. Sheila ordered her food and found a seat over by the glass windows. Calabrese quickly dropped five dollars worth of quarters inside the slot. The pay phone inside *The Creole Cafe* down in New Orleans rung with aggressiveness. The thunderous jazz music, along with the shouting and laughing of restaurant patrons, drowned out voices designed for privacy. The steam inside the *Creole* restaurant built up sweat as thick as syrup.

The men contracted by the Galluccio and Bernazzoli crime families served their purposes well. A New Orleans Mafioso made into the Fontanello family tilted his Panama hat sideways to conceal most of his identity.

"She just made it to Chicago," Calabrese relayed to his criminal constituent down in New Orleans.

Fiercely, he watched Shelia with the pay phone planted to his ear.

"Perfect!" cheered the made Mafioso down in New Orleans.

"We're right on schedule," Calabrese expedited.

"We'll know who we're looking for when she gets down here to New Orleans."

"No doubt."

"What's she doing right now?"

"Stuffing her face with some Chinese food."

"How about the homicide detective?"

"What a true beauty!" Calabrese endorsed. "She's sitting over near the terminal with her boyfriend."

"Boyfriend?"

"Yeah, looks like some dorky educated kid with lots of money."

"Hate she's gotta go, too. But those are the orders from the bosses."

"We all hate she's gotta go."

"Anything else?"

"Remember, there can't be no fuckups. If we fuck up, we're gonna get fucked up."

"And there won't be no fuckups."

"Bart and I are gonna meet up with Frankie and Bobby down in New Orleans. We'll be down there soon enough."

"Look forward to seeing you guys down here."

"Likewise."

"Call me the second they start boarding the plane."

"Will do."

"Any changes in their flight schedule, call me right away."

"Won't hesitate."

"Talk to ya later."

"Alright, later."

At brief intervals, both vicious killers hung up. Calabrese and Gagliano stood off to the side reading fresh copies of the *Chicago Tribune*. Sheila Bridgestone wasn't to leave their sight until she actually boarded the plane.

Randy and Tracey found seats closest to the terminal where they were supposed to depart for New Orleans. Nonstop trafficking of people were parading along the walkways. People rampaged in and out of the restaurants and shops. The Mexican and Puerto Rican immigrants emptied trash from the small and large barrels. The hardworking Orientals swept bits of trash from around the seats. Americans sure needed the work ethics they possessed, especially since the average person in the United States was labeled as being "lazy and goaless."

"This is the busiest airport that I've ever been inside," Randy told Tracey.

"Chicago's one of the busiest cities in America," Tracey smiled back at Randy.

"LAX is a busy airport, too."

"That's Los Angeles," Tracey observed. "With the movie stars and all the rich people, I can imagine that city having a busy airport."

Randy drifted into a sudden mode of curiosity. "Tracey, can I ask you something?"

"You sure can."

"Remember when the FBI agent got killed that night in the *Westport District*?"

"How can anyone living in Kansas City forget?"

"Why do you think he was killed?"

"The news and the newspapers said two men were trying to rob him."

"Do you believe that?"

"It's possible," Tracey chirped, her voice rather naive.

"Do you know why he came to Kansas City?" Randy questioned Tracey further.

"The newspaper said to do some investigation work."

"He was investigating the Mafia and the Teamsters," Randy just blurted out.

"Okay, I remember the paper mentioning that."

"We both saw that newspaper in the canteen at the IRS. The article talked about the Mafia and the Teamsters."

"Randy, what exactly are you getting at?"

"Remember when we were kids growing up in Kansas City and remember we'd hear stories about those explosions blowing up buildings in the River Quay area?"

"Who could ever forget?" Tracey noted. "That's all my mother and my father used to talk about. My father knew a lot of Teamsters people from driving trucks over-the-road."

"Those River Quay explosions were about the Mafia and the Teamsters."

Randy shifted into an abrupt mode of silence. Tragically, he heard gunshots ringing out. Agent Feliciano being filled with hot bullets and soaking in his own pool of blood wasn't erased from his memory. People running and screaming along Westport Road and Pennsylvania Avenue haunted him to the fullest extent.

Brittany and Scotty waited with patience for the anticipated announcement for their flight to New Orleans. Every five minutes or so, they looked down at their watches. Scotty flashed a Rolex around his wrist while Brittany showed off her Bulova. Sheila filed in behind other customers while leaving the steamy Chinese restaurant. Her familiar face struck a serious chord with Brittany. How coincidental it was for both of them to be inside Chicago's O'Hare International Airport at the same time. Both of them were destined for the same city.

"Something wrong, Britt?" Scotty asked, studying the many travelers in the airport.

"Jeeeessssh!" Brittany shuddered. "What a strange occurrence, Scotty."

Her sudden strange behavior tickled his senses.

"Did you spot a monster from a creature feature movie?"

"Not exactly, babe."

"What, then?" Scotty wanted to know.

"Remember me telling you about the killing of FBI Special Agent Wilfredo Feliciano back in Kansas City?" Brittany casually reminded Scotty.

"The night you got involved with that homicide case?"

"Precisely, dear."

"Okay?"

"One of the main witnesses, a woman who's been working real close with the FBI and the KCPD in solving that homicide, she's standing right over there."

"Where?"

"Do you really want me to point in her direction?"

"Then make a gesture to where she's standing."

Brittany jerked her head to the left. Cleverly, she humped her shoulders to where Sheila stood. "Right there, Scotty."

"She looks like the typical average Kansas City woman."

"The world's much smaller than I could've ever imagined."

"Life makes people travel in circles."

"She's getting FBI agents from Washington and the KCPD closer to identifying the two men who killed Agent Feliciano."

"Didn't you tell me that he was in K.C. investigating some Mafia men and the Teamsters?"

"Yeah, and he nearly completed his assignment, too."

Scotty couldn't help but blurt out words of true consistencies. "Maybe the Mafia put a contract out on his life."

"Don't be absurd, Scotty."

"Think about it, Britt," Scotty reasoned. "Mafia men can kill anybody they want to."

"These so-called Mafia men didn't know he was in K.C. investigating them."

"Are you sure?"

"Positive," Brittany stood firm. "They don't have access to that type of information."

"You think they don't?"

"I know they don't."

"Didn't the Mafia kill John F. Kennedy?"

"The government still doesn't know."

"They know, alright."

"People can only speculate who assasinated President John F. Kennedy."

"In case you didn't know, darling, the mob knew JFK was on his way to Dallas. They set up shop in Dallas to get him out of the way. I believe they did the same with this FBI agent coming into Kansas City."

"Scotty, that's only poppycock."

"If the mob can take out a president, then they can take out an FBI agent as well."

"I guess."

Scotty angled his head sideways and gestured with his middle finger. "My dad grew up watching gangster movies with Humphrey Bogart, Paul Muni, James Cagney, and Edward G. Robinson in them. I grew up watching gangster movies with Al Pacino, Robert Deniro, Marlon Brando, and Robert Redford in them. Whoever they wanted killed, they'd usually get the job done, or they'd get somebody else to do their dirty work."

"Scotty!" Brittany chuckled. "Hollywood's good at creating those celluloid images."

"Celluloid images created from real life characters," Scotty defended.

"Television does a great job of molding people's minds."

"Have you ever seen *The Godfather*?"

"Only about a thousand times."

"Where do you think the author of that novel got his characters from?"

"Where?"

"From real life gangsters," Scotty intoned. "Do you know anything about the River Quay area?"

"I know a lot about River Quay," Brittany said. "My father had business investors with offices in the River Quay back in the 70s and 80s."

"All through the 70s it was *Mafiaville*. Those Italians ran all the sleazy strip joints and nightclubs. Do you remember the *River Quay Wars* of the 70s?"

"If you're from Kansas City, how could you forget?"

"Those wars were about the Mafia and the Teamsters."

"I'm curious, Scotty, what's your point?"

"It makes you wonder, did the *River Quay Wars* ever end?"

"I think so."

"Then why would the government send an FBI agent to Kansas City to investigate the Mafia and the Teamsters? History makes a point of repeating itself."

"Maybe you should take my job." Brittany joked.

"Maybe I should."

The cell phone stuffed deep into Scotty's travel briefcase rung with authority. Scotty slid his hand down into the case. He only hoped it wasn't his nagging wife checking up on him again. Getting Brittany to believe he left the cell phone active in order to communicate with business associates didn't convince her otherwise.

"Can't believe this shit!" Scotty muttered, his voice low, yet obstructed. "What in Heaven's name does she want?"

"Your wife again?" Brittany queried.

Brittany drowned out all hopes for their bonding relationship.

"Who else?" Scotty said.

First, he noticed the area code of eight-one-six. Next, he scanned the other seven digits. This indicated his wife hadn't given up.

"Something rather strange is going on," Brittany suspected.

"What language are you speaking in?" Scotty asked.

"You're not telling me something, Scotty."

"What secrets would I hide from you, Britt?"

"Something's telling me your wife knows you're going to New Orleans."

"Nancy's wanting to bug the shit out of me. She's got nothing better else to do."

"Nancy wants to bug you, huh?"

"Yes, she does."

"Give it to me straight, Scotty."

"She'll give up once she sees I'm not answering my phone."

"Guess she's got her own suspicions."

"Don't we all."

"Guess she'll have a billion questions for you when you get home."

"Don't worry about her," Scotty assured Brittany. "Let's just forget about home and think about having a good time at Mardi Gras."

"Sure."

An agent behind a TWA ticket counter shoved an intercom up to her active lips and announced that Flight 1634 was boarding at Terminal Two. The flight carrying over 200 passengers on to New Orleans was finally boarding. Brittany and Scotty jerked their belongings off the ground. They were the first ones in line. Back to flying first class for them, a luxury experienced only by the privileged.

Sheila stepped up to an agent and handed over her ticket. Calabrese and Gagliano wanted more than anything to see her board the plane. Their Chicago Cubs caps were cocked downward to cover their sinister faces. Employees and travelers inside O'Hare never noticed the two killers the whole time they stood over by the pay phones. With another load of quarters bulging from his pants pockets, Calabrese reached inside and grabbed a fistful.

The quarters were fed into the activated machine. He waited for a ring at the other end. The pay phone inside the *Café de Broussard* down in New Orleans rung. The made New Orleans Mafioso had switched locations. He waited assiduously for the vital call out of Chicago. He went from a noisy *Creole* restaurant to a busy *Cajun café*. His comrades in Chicago had the number to every New Orleans spot he traveled to.

"She's getting on the plane," Calabrese informed the New Orleans Mafioso.

He observed Sheila closer than a starving pimp watching over his top money-making whore.

"Some of Fontanello's other men are stationed at the airport down here in New Orleans," the New Orleans Mafioso enlightened Calabrese.

"Perfectamundo!" Calabrese exclaimed, speaking in a Spanish vernacular.

"Aren't the bosses to receive word when the contract's finished?"

"Expeditiously."

"Fontanello will get in touch with the bosses in Kansas City and Chicago when the job's done."

"Sure he will."

"Fontanello's men will be watching her until you guys get down here."

"That blabber-mouth broad's gotta go as soon as possible."

"Absolutely."

"Are Frankie and Bobby going to be in position?"

"Yes, they are."

"Louie, are you and Bart ready to be in position?"

"We definitely are."

"Alright, then let all of us stay on schedule."

"We shall stay on schedule."

"Talk to you soon."

"Ten-four, good buddy."

The brief discussion between the Chicago and New Orleans criminal networks ended. Greed filtrated through the innocent lives of those who lived in utter ignorance. Life presented hardcore facts to people who often paid for other people's mistakes. Had Sheila known about the forces working against her, she would've gone back into her mother's womb and start life all over again.

Chapter 35

GALLUCCIO ENJOYED the tranquility of *The Italian Gardens* in the heart of downtown Kansas City. Business conducted inside the *Pendergast Mansion* had certain limitations. Coming to such a world-famous restaurant helped him revisit many memories over the years. With the sole consent of the owner, Galluccio and a Chicago Mafioso named Eddie "The Elephant" Gargotta, an astute business associate of the Bernazzoli Brothers, were granted a special opportunity to have the entire restaurant to themselves. Gargotta was quite an obese character. His double chin flopped everytime he moved his neck. His blubbery belly rested at the edge of his knees everytime he sat down.

Joining them for dinner was Senator Joseph Weinberg, the corrupt Missouri senator who'd been on the Galluccio payroll for many years. Galluccio felt more comfortable being at *The Italian Gardens*. It was the kind of atmosphere which eased all his tension from running a stressful crime family. The chefs and wine servers were tipped off in making themselves scarce during the meeting among Galluccio, Gargotta, and Weinberg. Sufficient amounts of tips kept them back in the kitchen, a place where they had no clue what took place among the men out in the restaurant section.

Galluccio almost worried himself into a nervous breakdown. He tried his best to make sure the unions didn't give Shellenberger any unnecessary trouble. Gargotta shot to Kansas City on short notice after the Chicago bosses summoned him to meet with Galluccio. Weinberg zoomed in from Jefferson City after one of his political liaisons informed him Galluccio wanted to meet. The Bernazzoli Brothers now faced charges a million dollar payoff had been made to them through a phony consulting firm. Part of the same money was funneled into the treasury for the Galluccio crime family. Galluccio couldn't imagine losing a penny of the million dollars to the government.

Before breaking into their crucial meeting, Galluccio scanned the walls of *The Italian Gardens*. His aging puppy dog face beamed with pride. Due to extreme obesity,

Gargotta suffered from a shortness of breath. Stars from all walks of life lined the walls inside the restaurant.

"Classy joint, here," Gargotta jarred, patting his wide chest.

A sip of red wine coated his dry throat. Resuming normal breathing for him wasn't easy.

"A loan for a grand helped get it started," Galluccio explained to Gargotta and Weinberg.

Galluccio took a stab at his plate of veal parmesean while a smile creased his face.

"No kidding?" Gargotta asked, quite amazed.

"My Uncle Angie fronted the cash for his *paisan* named Ross Fazzino."

"You're probably like royalty when you come here."

"Something like that."

"A joint like this must be a goldmine."

"Got a little rough the first few years, but things started taking off after a little while."

The legendary Kansas City restaurant served the city, county, federal, and state, as well as many civic and business organizations, being cited for numerous recognitions.

"Sinatra's been here before!" Gargotta fizzled, his baggy eyes bucked wide open.

"Sat and ate with my Uncle Angie before," Galluccio crowed with pride, his mouth half-stuffed with the delectable veal.

"Goddamn!" Gargotta hummed. "Sinatra's larger-than-life."

"Look around this place, Eddie," Weinberg noticed. "You'll see more stars on the wall than the midnight skies."

Gargotta did exactly as Weinberg suggested. Looking around at the celebrities was more exciting than looking in a journal for "Who's Who in the World."

The wall facing the north end of the restaurant showcased pictures of *Harry S. Truman, Liberace, Elvis Presley, Joe DiMaggio, Bonnie and Clyde, Barbara Streisand, Jimmy Durante, Evil Knievel, Walt Disney, Pretty Boy Floyd, and Lena Horne.*

Covering most of the south wall were framed pictures of *Mickey Mantle, Yogi Berra, Ted Williams, Rocky Marciano, Joe Namath, Len Dawson, Willie Mascone, Wilt Chamberlain, Bill Russell, Jake LaMotta, Rick Flair, and Dusty Rhodes.*

The iconic blue eyes, Frank Sinatra, had a section all to himself.

"See that guy right there?" Galluccio said, pointing directly to the picture of his beloved godfather.

"The sort of chunky guy?" Gargotta asked.

Gargotta casted his eyes towards the spot where his finger pointed. Some nerves he had calling somebody chunky. Roll after roll of sour body fat was wedged between his lap and the table.

"Know who that is?" Galluccio asked Gargotta.

"Have no idea."

"My godfather."

"Face looks real familiar."

"Tom Pendergast."

"The 'Political Machine of Kansas City?'" Gargotta quizzed Galluccio.

"Exactly."

"The guy had some powerful connections," Weinberg researched. "Rubbed shoulders with heavyweights like Luciano and Mangano and Costello out of New York."

"Rubbed shoulders with Capone and Torio and Nitti out of Chicago, too."

"Wow!" Gargotta said in amazement.

"My pops and my Uncle Angie named me after him!" Galluccio cheered with explosive pride.

"Pendergast sure had Kansas City hemmed up at one time," Weinberg recalled.

"Every drop of concrete in this city was courtesy of my godfather," Galluccio specified to his corrupt colleagues.

Galluccio fired up a juicy cigar. Thick rings of smoke circled the table.

"Is that right?" Gargotta marveled.

"City Hall and the Jackson County Courthouse wouldn't be standing without his concrete."

"Now, that's what you call power."

"Pulled a few strings to make Truman president."

Undoubtedly, Harry S. Truman had Tom Pendergast to thank for his unprecedented trip to the White House.

"No question about it."

"Penderast sponsored Truman, just like Giancana sponsored Kennedy," Weinberg noted, a wicked politician who knew the history of politics.

Now came the moment for Gargotta and Weinberg to discuss union business with Galluccio. The trio hoped to alleviate some of the worries the Chicago bosses had. Even more telling, the political crooks in Washington, D.C. had poisoned the minds of the public into believing that honesty and accountability were the new standards of the present-day Teamsters Union. Galluccio and Gargotta and Weinberg couldn't fathom how such vicious liars used poppycock to dissuade people. Weinberg knew better than anyone how corrupt they really were.

"Carmine and Mikey Bernazzoli already told me why you were coming to K.C.," Galluccio chanted to Gargotta.

Casually, he sucked on his sweet and tasty cigar.

Attacking his plate of spaghetti like a drooling mastiff, Gargotta spoke to Galluccio in reasonable terms. "Trustees with Local 690 have filed a suit in Chicago."

"Why can't those selfish morons take the money under the table and keep their fucking mouths closed?" Galluccio complained, irritated to the max.

"Americontinental International Corporation dismissed 50 employees from O'Hare International."

"People get laid off and fired from their jobs everyday. What's so different about letting 50 guys go from O'Hare?"

"Local 690 went bankrupt shortly afterwards."

"How, Eddie?"

"All the funds had been exhausted within the union."

"Couldn't they find these guys other jobs?"

"Those guys were given a week's notice to accept transfers here to Kansas City or to Springfield, Illinois."

"What'd they do?"

"Each one declined."

"Why?"

"Don't know," Gargotta inclined with partiality. "But, I do know that they were dismissed on a whim, and prosecutors claim our union officials violated the collective bargaining agreement by sanctioning the action."

"Let's hear more about these sickening prosecutors."

"Some asslicking federal prosecutor is helping those guys seek civil damages by using the federal Racketeering Influenced Corrupt Organizations Act."

"RICO, huh?" Galluccio disdained.

"Yes, the government's weapon to stick it right up our asses."

Every existing Mafia figure nationwide knew about RICO. The name of RICO had a familiar ring to it, almost like the worn out recording of a hit record.

"Eddie, break off our chunk of the million bucks and we'll all be happy," Galluccio spoke with modesty.

Galluccio hoped to snatch his share of the million dollars before the feds got their greasy palms on it.

"Easier said than done, Tommy," Gargotta said, his tone that of uneasiness. "The Federal District Court in Chicago could have access to that money."

"How in Christ's name could they have access?"

"The money is still sitting in an account."

"Don't tell me, the government's frozen the account?"

"Right you are."

"We're going to lose a million bucks of our own money because of some crybaby jerkoffs who can't learn how to play ball?"

"Sorry, Tommy," Gargotta apologized.

"Wish we had enough manpower to take out all 50 of them union guys."

Once again, Galluccio had a bad case of murder on the brain. For him, it was always kill, kill, kill, kill. Killing was the only way to solve problems for those who stood in his way. This time, he wasn't going to get his way. Americontinental International Corporation had cut back on labor costs by one million dollars a year. The Galluccio and Bernazzoli families now stood to lose even more money.

"Taking out that many guys at one time would be a total disaster," Gargotta objected. "The government would come after us with everything they've got."

"The worst nightmare imaginable," Weinberg warned Galluccio.

"You men might have a very good point," Galluccio agreed.

"We should let things simmer at this point," Gargotta proposed.

Gargotta sliced up portions of his veal like a Samurai warrior chopping up an enemy. Galluccio slurped another strong drag from his cigar. He released the smoke from both thin nostrils. The popping of wine bottle corks signaled they were ready for another round. Galluccio flipped through a recent copy of the local newspaper.

A critical article read: Delaney Brothers Slain Gangland Style.

"Got a brilliant idea, Eddie," Galluccio suggested. "What's the democrat's name from out there in Elgin, Illinois?"

"Dennis McCormick," Gargotta mentioned with the quickness.

"Can't we get him to take the money under the table?"

"I'm not sure."

"Can't we grease his palms in order to get our hands on that millions bucks?"

"It's real risky, Tommy," Gargotta resourcefully rejected.

The whale-like blubber around his stomach wobbled at the edges of the table after hearing the dreadful bribery tactic.

"Everytime those political pricks take money under the table, they're breaking the law," Galluccio protruded to say. "You know that and I know that, Eddie."

"Still, it sounds too risky, Tommy."

"Can't we put McCormick on our payroll?"

"Bribery?"

"What else?"

"We've already got this federal racketeering suit that's about to sting like a hornet," Gargotta concluded. "Let's take care of that first, and then take a shot at McCormick later."

Gargotta expressed a good point. Evading one problem just to immerse into another one wasn't a smart move. There was always a lawman who went days without sleep to put Mafia thugs behind bars for the rest of their lives.

"Know what I say, Eddie?" Galluccio seethed.

"What's that, Tommy?"

"The same thing Capone said before my mother started wiping my snotty nose and cleaning my shitty ass."

"And what would that be?"

"The same thing my godfather Tom Pendergast said before my mother went out on her first date."

"Let me have it, Tommy."

"A thief is simply a thief," Galluccio reasoned. "A crook is still a crook. The guys who front as though they're upkeeping the law, they're the same guys who can rob people at their own authority. The worst type of all these sonofabitches are the politicians. You can't get a second of their time because they're spending lots of time covering up their wrongdoing. No one even knows they're goddamn thieves and liars. Politicians are nothing but legal gangsters."

"Bless Capone and Pendergast for those words of truth," Gargotta said.

"Sometimes, I hate the sight of those pukebags."

Senator Weinberg never took offense since he knew it was the diehard truth.

Galluccio turned in his seat to lock eyes with Senator Weinberg. "Joey, what kind'a pull do you have with those Chicago politicians?"

"I've got big juice with the guys in the Illinois legislative branch," Weinberg revealed.

"Can you help us convince this Senator McCormick in Elgin to release that million bucks?"

Weinberg expedited a clever thought. "If I can't, then some of my colleagues in the legislative branch can. Washington is our meeting place, and I'm sure if we grease some palms, then they'll be convinced to let go of the money."

"We're counting on you, Joey."

"I'll see what I can do."

Gargotta had a notion that Senator Weinberg's political connections crossed over into many different arenas. "Joey, before I can meet with Senator McCormick in Elgin, we're going to need you to act as a sort of mediator. Think you can do that much for us?"

"Sure."

"Good."

The powerful men continued their dinner at the legendary *Italian Gardens*.

Chapter 36

GALLUCCIO, GARGOTTA, and Senator Weinberg decided to meet later on at the *Pendergast Mansion*. A chilled bottle of Bellaggio wine sat next to platters of meats and cheeses and crackers on the conference table. Angela had taken off after her duties were finished. Galluccio and Gargotta exchanged familiar eye contact. Both men knew which gear their discussion had shifted into.

"How're things set up down in New Orleans?" Gargotta quizzed Galluccio.

Gargotta popped the wine bottle with his colossally strong hand. He poured himself a drink.

"Perfectamundo!" Galluccio acclaimed, blowing clusters of smoke above Gargotta's hog-shaped head.

"Everything's been okayed with the boss down in New Orleans?"

"Fontanello's crews are in position down there," Galluccio rectified.

"How about your men?"

"Frankie and Bobby are well in position."

"How about Carmine and Mikey's men?"

"So are they."

"Great!" Gargotta celebrated. "What about the witness working with the FBI, and the KCPD homicide detective assigned to the case?"

"Neither one of those broads will be coming back to K.C. alive."

"What about the other people on the plane?"

"Their families will collect the insurance money," Galluccio spoke in his inadequately insensitive voice.

A vicious atrocity was in the making. For Galluccio and the Bernazzoli Brothers, it was just business-as-usual.

"It'll be no different than any other airplane tragedy."

"No, it won't."

"Brilliant plan, Tommy."

"Either that plane comes crashing down somewhere around New Orleans, or everything we've put into building up the Teamsters comes crashing down on us. And that includes billions of dollars that goes into the unions every year."

"Can't argue with that."

"The Teamsters is our bloodline," Galluccio alluded to say. "The air we breathe is the Teamsters. The food we eat is the Teamsters. The water we drink is the Teamsters. The tears we cry are the Teamsters. I'm not about to let a couple'a dames destroy what my Uncle Angie built up with his own blood, sweat, and tears."

"Jimmy Hoffa would've been proud of you, Tommy."

Galluccio sucked more strong drags from his fat cigar. In repetitious fashions, he thumped the ashes in the crystal ashtray. He slammed down a half-glass of wine and told Gargotta, "But taking out those two broads isn't the end of our problems."

"Could you be more specific?" Gargotta asked.

"The feds, those dirty rotten fuckers, they're not letting up one least bit."

"Things will let up once we get our enemies out of the way."

"Right now, the feds are going around sniffing up everybody's ass here in Kansas City. Shit, they're asking people out on the streets all kinds of questions."

"But there are always more witnesses willing to come forward," Gargotta implied.

"They talk, they die!" Galluccio insisted with fury.

"I agree."

"It's been said a million times that loose lips sink ships."

"I never could stand a snitch."

Posted outside abandoned buildings, stapled to light poles, and pinned to boards inside government offices and businesses was: *Anyone with information in the Agent Feliciano case is asked to call the TIPS Hotline at 471-TIPS, the Ad Hoc Secret Witness line at 931-8000, or the FBI at 221-4000.*

"Those feds, those crooked motherfuckers, they sugarcoat everybody's asses with all these bullshit lies. For chrissake, why can't they just take Feliciano's murder as a loss and move on?"

"No way they'll write his death off so easily," Gargotta exemplified to Galluccio.

"Why, Eddie, why?" Galluccio asked, desperate for true answers.

"The government's got egos bigger than the universe itself."

"Well, somebody needs to punch holes in their egos and bring them down a notch."

"But how many people are willing to stand up to the government?"

"Not many."

"These days, everybody's a follower."

"Makes you wonder what happened to real leaders."

"Like our main man Hoffa."

"Hoffa was quick to tell the government to kiss the rusty side of his ass."

Gargotta reached over the table and shoved mounds of meat and cheese into his moist, hungry mouth. "There's something that does concern me."

"I'm listening."

"It's the FBI and the KCPD."

"What about them?"

"Them being so gung ho about someone taking out one of their own, they're not looking at Feliciano's murder as a throwback to the *River Quay War* days are they?"

Galluccio grinned and puffed on his cigar. "The *River Quay Wars* ended when my Uncle Angie decided to do some restructuring with the Teamsters here in Kansas City. Uncle Angie knew how violence and bloodshed became his biggest expense. Instead of blowing up some guy's business because he bullheadedly refused to sign up with the Teamsters, Uncle Angie simply toted the sonofabitch straight into the poorhouse."

Gargotta gulped down a mouthful of wine before speaking. "When is Fontanello due to come to Kansas City?"

"We're supposed to meet with Fontanello about those government insurance contracts after we get word about the plane crashing around New Orleans."

"And his Teamsters people down there?"

"They'll be coming up, too."

"Sounds perfect."

Thick layers of skin under the chin of Gargotta flapped from much friction. The meeting at the *Pendergast Mansion* ended on a positive note.

Chapter 37

THE SOUTHERN HOSPITALITY in New Orleans turned out to be more than a notion for couples like Randy and Tracey. For lovebirds like Brittany and Scotty, Mardi Gras fever filled the air. Randy was especially blown away by the star treatment they received upon arriving at the airport. The weather was partly sunny with mild breezes blowing out of the Gulf Coast. The temperature was a pleasant 65 degrees.

Hurricanes often swept through The Big Easy, but New Orleans managed to survive the most atrocious attacks from Mother Nature. The trip down to New Orleans caused Randy to build up a ferocious appetite. Echoes of growls created noticeable turbulences inside his stomach. Peanuts and potato chips on the plane only teased his tastebuds.

"I'll tell you one thing," Randy said to Tracey. "I'm ready for some of that Louisiana gumbo."

"I'd like to taste some of that crawfish gumbo," Tracey added.

"We're in the dirty south."

"The land of home cooked meals."

"Food is king in the south."

"People in New Orleans take offense if you don't sit and eat with them."

"How do you know that?" Randy asked.

"Some of my relatives live in Baton Rogue."

"Speaking of food, let's get checked into the hotel and get something to eat."

"Sounds good to me."

Of course, New Orleans became legendary for home cooked meals which filled bellies. Tracey shook off some of the jet lag as she unpacked her belongings. She felt liberated after breathing the muggy New Orleans air. They checked into the elaborate Holiday Inn – Chateau Le Moyne, just one block off world famous Bourbon Street.

How sweet it was to reside inside a breathtaking hotel which were Creole cottages off a tropical courtyard, the rooms furnished with reproductions and antiques. Guests felt right at home with stoves, refrigerators, coffeemakers, hair dryers, irons, and ironing boards. A restaurant, lounge, game room, and pool added more sweetness to the worthwhile trip down South.

"Is this the life or what?" Randy praised, stretching his arms to the sunny New Orleans skies.

"Sure cost enough," Tracey sort of griped.

She followed her sour gripe with a bursting smile.

"You only live once, babe," Randy said, reminding her how life was for the living.

"Guess so."

"I'm starving, babe."

"I can hear the lions roaring inside your stomach," Tracey smiled. "The food on the plane tasted so bland."

"I'm ready for some real down home Southern cooking," Randy pictured, moisture building inside his mouth. "I'm ready for some collard greens, hotwater cornbread, blackeyed peas, neckbones, fried chicken, sweet potatoes, pot roast, banana pudding, and strawberry cheesecake. You know, Tracey, the kind of cooking only the South can do."

"You know country folks can really whip up those home cooked meals."

"Seems as though New Orleans only has real Cajun and Creole dishes."

"Honey, please!" Tracey dejected. "These people wrote the book on real soul food. There are restaurants down here that have all those dishes that you just mentioned."

"Speaking of restaurants, let's find one before I drop dead of starvation."

"Bourbon Street must have a bunch of them."

"Get your credit card ready."

"Yes, I know."

"We're about to eat up some shit."

Randy and Tracey departed the hotel in search of a restaurant close to their style and budget.

Brittany and Scotty never worried about having enough money to pay for anything. With them being aristocrats from wealthy backgrounds, money brought a great sense of comfort into their lives. They decided to spend cash in a royal fashion. For them, money had been thrown around like old paper to be shredded. Scotty had no problem charging a suite for them at the Omni Royal Orleans Hotel right in the heart of the Vieux Carre' of New Orleans.

The couple were swept off their feet the second they walked into the lobby. The sconce-enhanced columns, gilt mirrors, fan windows, and magnificent chandeliers, it blended perfectly with their taste. The scenery created an awesome aura which reigned in New Orleans for more than a century ago. Scotty opened the door to their room and both were taken aback. What appointed the rooms with mesmerizing grace were marble baths and marble-top dressers and tables. Their balcony provided an alluring view of surrounding New Orleans streets.

"Didn't know that New Orleans had hotels as fancy as this one," Scotty had favored.

He stood at the edge of the balcony in his thirsty terry towel robe.

"This marble must've cost a fortune," Brittany said, fascinated with the fixtures.

She glided her soft hands across the smoothness of the breathtaking marble fixtures.

"My dad would freak out over some stuff like this."

"Your dad?" Brittany added. "My dad would probably try and purchase marble like this for his whole house."

"Mr. Goldberg's got that kind of exquisite taste?"

"Like no one else."

"Still can't get over this hotel. You'd probably think kings, queens, presidents, and big time moviestars have come and stayed here."

"Not quite the hotel that me and Tyler once stayed at."

The high-priced suite shifted to a mortal silence. Scotty and Brittany locked eyes with sulky expressions. Why did she have to slip and mention a former boyfriend?

"Who'd you say?" Scotty asked, authoritative echoes ringing through his voice.

"Never mind, Scotty," Brittany denounced.

"No, no, what did you say about Tyler?"

"Drop it, Scotty, okay?"

"No, Britt, I want to talk about it."

"Let it go, honey."

"Why can't you get Tyler out of your system?"

"Jealous?" Brittany instigated.

"We come all the way down to New Orleans, and you've still got that asshole on your mind," Scotty blatantly charged.

"Not true."

"Do you still love that prick?"

"No, I don't."

"You've got me thinking that you've digested Tyler and haven't spit him out."

"Scotty, Tyler is old news."

Scotty just had to press the issue farther.

"Why can't you erase that jerk out of your memory?"

Brittany struck back with her supreme weapon. "Why can't you ask your wife for a fucking divorce?"

Scotty couldn't part his lips in response to her question. His cell phone started ringing again. He snatched it out of the leather traveling bag and peeped down at the number. Was it someone he didn't want to talk to?

"Your wife again?" Brittany inquired.

Her gut feelings told her that their trip to New Orleans might've turned out to be a wasted one.

"Who else?" Scotty bounced back.

"Why don't you turn that damn phone off?"

"Important business associates might be trying to get in touch with me."

"Don't they know you're on vacation?"

"Some do, some don't."

"Is your wife still checking up on you?" Brittany asked, using her own mechanisms of reinforcement.

"No, she's not."

"Maybe you're not telling me everything, Scotty," Brittany suspected.

Her baby blue-green eyes yearned to read the truth buried inside of Scotty.

"What are you insinuating?"

"Do you still love your wife?"

"We don't even sleep in the same bed," Scotty answered in sadness.

"Question remains, do you still love her?"

"Yes, some feelings are still there."

"Am I just a piece of pussy for you to have around at your disposal?"

"Jesus Christ, Britt, that's absurd."

Brittany sure had her way of making Scotty feel as though he didn't appreciate her.

"Am I just a warm piece of meat for you to lay next to when you get sick and tired of your wife?"

"Britt, you're being irrational."

Brittany yelled with the strongest conviction. "Dammit! Answer me, Scotty!"

"Don't put me in a jam like this."

"How much longer are we going to have to play this triangle game?"

"Shiiiiitttttt!" Scotty barked back. "Do you still love Tyler?"

"What's in the past, stays in the past."

"Is that your head talking, or is it your heart talking?"

"Well, we're only human beings," Brittany cracked. "Yes, I still have feelings for Tyler. We were crazy in love at one time. We were one another's world."

"Why did you two fall out of love?" Scotty quizzed Brittany.

"Things happen," Brittany admitted. "People move on after awhile. They grow apart and go their own separate ways."

"Are you gonna move on when you get tired of me?"

"No way!"

The cell phone continued ringing. Had Scotty went ahead and answered it, maybe his wife wouldn't have suspected that he snuck away from Kansas City to have an elaborate rendezvous with a woman he'd been secretly dating for quite some time.

"You're going to have to make a decision sooner or later," Brittany made clear for Scotty.

"You're pushing me off into a tight corner."

"You've pushed yourself into a corner."

Brittany knew she'd have to serve Scotty an ultimatum sooner or later. She got frustrated with all the head games being played. Someone should've warned her early on in life that you didn't fall in love with a married man.

"What are your plans when we get back to Kansas City?" Scotty asked.

"I'm still assigned to the Feliciano murder case. I shouldn't have never come down here to New Orleans with you in the first place."

"Yeah, you told me that when we were in Chicago."

"We're not supposed to leave town in the middle of a homicide case."

"Especially one as high-profile as that one."

"But since I love you, Scotty, I made you an exception."

Scotty suddenly broke out in goose bumps. Beads of sweat popped from his pores. "I believe you're skating on thin ice, Britt."

"Come again?"

"Mafia guys had something to do with killing that FBI agent," Scotty predicted.

The very words he spoke couldn't have been truer-to-life.

"Scotty, you're delusional and have been wrongly informed."

"I don't think so."

"Agent Feliciano was being robbed by a couple of vicious street hoodlums."

"Britt, how can you be so naïve?"

"Scotty, I'm not being naïve."

"Those Mafia guys aren't to be fooled around with."

"Neither are we at the KCPD to be fooled around with."

"Britt, I'm only concerned about your safety," Scotty said, sounding quite worried. "If they had the guts or the balls to take out an FBI agent, what makes you think they won't take out a police officer, or take out a homicide detective like yourself? These people are a bunch of heartless, calculated killers."

"Scotty, you worry more than an old lady with high blood pressure."

"Makes you wonder, did the *River Quay Wars* ever end?"

"Darling, please give it a rest."

"Okay, I'm gonna give it a rest."

"Please do."

Brittany turned around and stepped onto the balcony. She regretted bringing up work-related issues. She and Scotty were both in tight spots. A part of their past and present lingered on. Love sometimes confused the strongest of people. Love caused them to do the dumbest things imaginable. The view from the balcony was simply awesome. The French Quarters was lit up like a nighttime jubilee celebration.

"I'm starved, let's get something to eat," Scotty suggested.

"Anything in mind?" Brittany asked.

"The best Cajun food that New Orleans has to offer."

"Let's see if it's as good as they advertise on television."

Scotty freshened up and got dressed. Brittany killed more time on the balcony. It gave herself time to think about their future together. Practically everything was at their disposal, including an Olympic-size pool, a barbershop and beauty salon, exercise rooms, two lounges, and meetings rooms.

Chapter 38

BRITTANY AND SCOTTY found the perfect dining spot in the heart of the French Quarters. Going inside *Mamma T's Bistro Cafe* near the lively Bourbon Street was a smart move. Frequenting upscale eateries as tourists, they fared better as a wealthy couple. Brittany scanned the establishment with her seductive blue eyes. The gastronomic and celebratory spirit created a charged atmosphere. Scotty played it smart by making their reservations well in advance. Avoiding the mad rush crowd which poured into the restaurants just before the Mardi Gras celebrations saved them a lot of anguish.

The exquisite burnished wood chairs and banquette frames added charm to the sound-absorbing panels which fell just below the 20 foot ceiling. Large cobalt lamps cast a softness of light onto the dishes where the traditional Creole temporary New Orleans style met. The overall atmosphere of the restaurant transcended a notion to Brittany and Scotty about the quality of service which varied from waiter to waiter. A practicality stood out from its Southern appeasement.

"The food smells outstanding," Scotty proclaimed, getting a rush from the aroma.

He studied the menu as though he prepared for an important final exam.

"Builds up an instant appetite from a quick whiff," Brittany said, also scanning the menu.

"Boy!" Scotty cheered. "The fried crawfish tails sound very appetizing."

"The gumbo and roast duck with rice dressing looks so delicious," Brittany praised.

"Check out the deserts."

"Which one do you like?"

"Sweet potato-pecan pie."

"Enough calories to make me as big as a cement truck."

"One slice wouldn't hurt."

"Easy for you to say."

"You guys in law enforcement have free access to gyms and fitness centers. You can exercise any extra calories right off your curvy body."

Scotty couldn't have described the body of Brittany any simpler. She possessed dangerous curves which were eye candy. She toned up the most important areas. She kept her breasts firm as they stood up. Her buttocks were tight and very curvaceous.

"This *Re'moulade* looks too good to be true."

"The menu is making me foam at the mouth."

"The shrimps come with a cold dressing and shredded lettuce, Creole mustard, vinegar, horseradish, paprika, cayenne, celery, and green onion," Brittany named off.

"Stop it, Britt!" Scotty halted. "You're making me want to hijack this restaurant and run out of here with those dishes."

"Let's go ahead and order."

"Good idea."

Brittany and Scotty took a few moments to scan the mouth-watering menus. Both hungry souls found it difficult to pick out dishes which would best suit their appetites. Brittany pulled her menu just below her eyes to where it no longer blocked her view. Sheila Bridgestone walked into the restaurant swinging her red leather purse.

The most cheerful look graced her Midwestern face. She, too, had made reservations well in advance for *Mamma T's Bistro Café*. She'd been ready to dine on some fine cuisine. Dining out became an honored ritual for the tourists of New Orleans. Brittany motioned over to Scotty with a fluctuation of her riveting glossy eyes.

"What's the matter, babe?" Scotty asked, confused as to what he wanted to order.

"Look who just walked in," Brittany gestured, her head swiveling the other direction.

"Who?"

"Look over by the front entrance."

"The same woman from O'Hare Airport in Chicago?" Scotty examined.

"Yes, her."

"So?"

"She did tell me that she'd be coming down here for Mardi Gras when we interviewed her at the Headquarters."

"Let's just hope we'll all have a good time."

"She should've stayed in Kansas City."

"Why?"

"She's closer than ever in helping the FBI and the KCPD find the two men who killed Agent Feliciano."

"You should find that a good thing."

"It is," Brittany acknowledged. "But while the command posts are being set up everywhere, and while the recovered bullets are being examined by forensic experts at the FBI laboratory in Washington, she should've stayed back there to help the sketch artists finish their work."

"Don't you think she deserves some time away?"

"Not when we're trying to find the killers of an FBI agent."

"Couldn't she say the same thing about you?"

"Yes, she could."

"Relax, Britt," Scotty implied. "We're here to get away from all the madness back home."

"Bad vibes are going all through my system."

"The police will eventually catch the bad guys, lock them up for good, and it'll be a happy ending for you and for the rest of the Police Department."

"You make it sound so easy."

"A nice massage and a good soak in the jacuzzi will do you some good."

"Can we change the subject?"

"I'm starved, so let's go ahead and order."

"Now you're talking."

Chapter 39

WITH A MAGNITUDE OF courtesy, one of the waiters seated Sheila in a section where bright red paint set off a yellow captain's chair and wood veneer. The New Orleans Mafioso made into the Fontanello crime family cocked his large Panama brim to the side while he sat alone at a table behind Sheila. During her brief stay in New Orleans, he'd been ordered by Galluccio, the Bernazzoli Brothers, and Fontanello to never let Sheila nor Brittany out of his sight. Watchful piercing eyes followed both women with no clue. Cautiously, he stayed out of their way during their trips around the city.

The fate of the Teamsters Union relied on Sheila not following through as a witness to the killing of FBI Agent Feliciano. Brittany not following through as a gung ho homicide detective working in conjunction with the FBI was equally as important. Mardi Gras hadn't come and gone soon enough for Galluccio and the Bernazzoli Brothers. Other witnesses to the Feliciano killing lurked through the shadowy corridors of the law. Get Sheila and Brittany out of their way, and they still had others cooperating with locals, Washington sent FBI agents, the KCPD, and the Sherriff's Department.

"Ma'am," the waiter said to Sheila. "Are you ready to order now?"

"Yes, I'd like to order the fresh saut'eed fish in cream sauce," Sheila requested.

"Anything else?"

"What about the Fettuccine Alfredo?"

"Probably would go well with the fish."

"Consider me ordering it."

"Would that be all?"

"A glass of water with a frosty glass of lemonade."

"Coming right up."

The New Orleans Mafioso arose from his chair and left the restaurant. Instead of using a pay phone inside the noisy establishment, he decided to take a walk down the block to use a mobile phone. Sheila and Brittany arrived at the prime location where the men wanted them. Time was surely on their side. Their plans moved along like clockwork. In time, they anticipated on sending news back to Kansas City and Chicago to let the big bosses know that their mission had been completed.

"The witness and the detective are inside *Mamma T's* waiting on their orders," the Mafioso informed Provenzano, who happened to be on another side of town.

He reserved his own privacy in one of the alleys off Bourbon Street.

"Don't let them out of your sight for a second," Provenzano ordered the New Orleans Mafioso.

"They'll be in that Cajun joint for awhile."

"Stay in *Mamma T's* until they go back to their hotel or wherever else."

"There's two of them, and there's only one of me."

"I'll send Calabrese and Gagliano to *Mamma T's*."

"It's been hard watching those two broads since they first came to New Orleans."

"Help's on the way."

"The detective came with her husband or boyfriend."

"He's some rich married guy that she's been fucking around with on the side."

"It's been a bitch, but I've been keeping an eye on both of their hotels."

"Tuffy's gonna send more men so you guys can split up. Don't fall asleep on the job."

"So far, I've stayed on schedule."

"Good."

"I've got to get back to *Mamma T's*. Just make sure my relief is there."

"You're covered."

The Fontanello henchman left the alley to return to the Cajun restaurant in the French Quarter.

Chapter 40

OBITUARIES WERE WRITTEN for organized crime all over America. Special prosecutors had put some of the biggest Mafia bosses behind bars for the rest of their natural born lives. It could've been too soon to write those very obituaries. The law couldn't get rid of the Mafia no matter how hard they tried. Always, there was far too much money to be made in vice and corruption. With human nature being what it was, people always paid to sin. Organized crime was plainly a cancerous growth throughout communities in America. Galluccio and the Bernazzoli Brothers often embarrassed and harrassed the competition which surfaced in their cities.

Viciously, they enlisted Irish, Jewish, Dutch, Black, and other Italians to do their dirty work. The three crime bosses often joked about how the U.S. Justice Department's Organized Crime Strike Force had once visited the neighboring Midwestern cities of Kansas City and Chicago to awaken and alert the so-called honest citizenry to the problem of organized crime. What a big fucking joke! Call them leeches, call them parasites, even call them fellow criminal travelers, but they often consorted with one another. Why couldn't the diabolical politicians leave them alone?

"This whole thing with politics just makes me sick," Galluccio once told the Bernazzoli Brothers. "That mayor or senator, or the congressman and his golfing partners at the country club, aren't they the ones who receive the ultimate profit from people hooked on dope and prostitution and gambling and liquor? Don't those same political fuckheads take your money for state sales tax and then fail to turn it over to the state?"

The voices of Angelo Galluccio and Tom Pendergast still cried out from the grave. Their very cries were heard loud and clear by their nephew and godson, Tommy Galluccio.

Homicide Detective Cyrus Manley had been commissioned by FBI agents and KCPD Chief Meyer Kirkpatrick in helping solve the killing of Agent Feliciano. One of his most frustrating assignments was to grill all the bonding companies around Kansas City, both Missouri and Kansas territories. Manley flashed sketches of the two men possibly responsible for the killing before bonding company owners. Kirkpatrick sent him around to the bonding companies to make things look good. He made sure his ass was wiped in case higher authorities came around making routine checks.

The disheartening part of Manley's assignment was that he'd gotten nowhere even after popping in and out of bonding companies all over the city. An all-out campaign had been launched to apprehend Feliciano's killers. Or had it? He walked into Genova's Bonding Company in the heart of downtown Kansas City. Some coffee-guzzling, gum-popping, and cigarette-puffing black woman, sat at her desk shuffling through piles of old papers. She glanced up at Manley and he noticed bags under her eyes puffy enough to sack groceries.

"Can I help you?" the woman asked, her voice scratchy.

She gulped down the last swallow of her black coffee. Then, she took two strong drags off her cigarette. The loud gum-popping continued.

"Need to speak with the owner," Manley said, wishing he could make some strides.

"Made it in just a nick of time."

"Why's that?" Manley asked, rather curious.

"Louie was on his way out the door."

"Could you tell him that it's urgent business?"

She swiveled around in the chair and darted to the back. A short man with an over-lap belly strutted up front with a jacket hung over his shoulders.

"What can I help you with?" he asked Manley.

"Who are you, sir?"

"I'm Louie Genova, the owner."

Guess Louie Genova couldn't be more Italian.

"I'm Detective Cyrus Manley with the KCPD."

"Who did what now?" Louie exhalted.

"I'm sure you've been following the story about an FBI agent killed in Westport."

"That story's been coming out of walls and floors."

Manley slipped FBI composite sketches out of a long folder. The detailed drawings were flashed before Louie. "Have you ever seen any of these two men before?"

Louie took a brief glance at the sketches. "Never seen any of those guys before."

"Are you sure?"

"Positive."

"Look very closely, Mr. Genova."

"I've bonded a lot of guys out of jail in the thirty years I've been in business. I've never seen those guys come in here or seen them out on the streets anywhere."

"Thanks for your cooperation."

"You're welcome, Detective."

Sadly, Manley came up empty-handed once again.

Chapter 41

STEFANO "TUFFY" Fontanello had just as much at stake when it came to his sound investments in the International Brotherhood of Teamsters. The unscrupulous businessman had invested long, hard years into Local Union 45 and the Warehousemen and Helpers of America there in Kansas City and Chicago. Reputedly, he was the supreme Mafia boss of New Orleans. Standing only five-foot-three inches, Fontanello literally stood tall with his deep pockets. He was barrel-chested, bull-necked, and potbellied. How did he earn the nickname *Tuffy*? Easy. Like most successful Mafia bosses, Fontanello's rise to power was grounded in fear.

The extreme power and riches he achieved in New Orleans was grounded in clawing his way out of dire poverty by accumulating vast sums of cash earned from drugs, prostitution, extortion, labor racketeering, hijacking, and political corruption. Fontanello catapulted himself into a position to control powerful labor unions. Buying off political power yielded him considerable influence over most New Orleans communities. Born and raised in New Orleans, Fontanello became a titan throughout the entire Gulf Coast region.

His influential power embraced the Caribbean and parts of South America. Louisiana, Mississippi, Florida, and Texas, all felt the iron grip of Fontanello's immense power. An empire he'd built with impunity was at stake. Final preparations were made to kill off Sheila Bridgestone and Brittany Goldberg. A witness and a homicide detective were the bosses biggest threats.

It was in a soundproof room at the Churchill Farms swampland estate. It was right along the banks of the Mississippi River. Tuffy Fontanello, Provenzano, Randazzo, Calabrese, Gagliano, Fontanello's corrupt Louisiana Teamsters official, Carl Bernstein, and other associates from Kansas City, Chicago and New Orleans, all joined up to finalize their plans. The meeting of criminal minds was in full effect.

The flames of conspiracy had to be quenched before they were sparked into roaring blazes. Out of patriotic indignation, Fontanello joined forces with Galluccio and Bernazzoli's people to clear up the two troublesome blemishes known as Sheila Bridgestone and Brittany Goldberg.

"Men, I thank you for making this special trip down here to my hometown of New Orleans," Fontanello spoke with great modesty. His unique southern Louisiana Sicilian drawl echoed throughout the room. "On the orders and strength of Tommy Galluccio and Carmine and Mikey Bernazzoli, we all agreed that the witness to Feliciano's killing, and the homicide detective handling part of the case, have got to go. Billions of our hard-earned dollars from the Teamsters will go down the tube if they keep working with the FBI and the KCPD there in Kansas City."

"They're already here in New Orleans, and we're just waiting for them to hop on that plane," Provenzano explained to Fontanello with exclusitivity. "Tommy and Carmine and Mikey already gave us the orders to speak with you, Tuffy, about how the plane's going to come down."

"If we stay on schedule," Randazzo included, "then, neither one of them will make it back to Kansas City alive."

"We've been planning this for quite some time," Fontanello strategized. "My men have been watching the witness and the detective around-the-clock. I've given them specific orders to not let them out of their sight, all the way up until they get on that plane going back to Chicago or Kansas City."

"Well, Tuffy, what's your plans on making the plane accidentally drop out of the sky?" Provenzano questioned Fontanello.

"My men and I have definitely got some things in the works," Fontanello promised.

"I'm an expert at a lot of things," Provenzano announced. "After being in the Army and being over in Vietnam, I became an expert in firearms, explosives with emphasis on demolition, and an expert at tactical strategies."

"Frankie, my friend," Fontanello smiled. "We can't go putting no bombs under that plane. We've got to do something to throw the public off, something to throw the government way off. We'll have'ta make it look like a pilot's error or something."

"Once the plane crashes, you know that the FAA and the NTSB will start their investigations," Provenzano reasoned, his Napoleonic intensity having surfaced.

"They won't know what hit them after we're done," Fontanello said.

Provenzano and the others trusted Fontanello to be the central planner of the would-be plane crash. Fontanello acted in an advisory role in helping formulate the plan.

"We're ready to make our move once you okay everything, Tuffy."

Fontanello unveiled a long white paper which was curled up and secured with a thick rubber band. Like a housemaid throwing a freshly washed sheet across a clothesline, he spread the enormous paper across the table for full view. Not all airplanes were constructed alike. Fontanello had a diagram which outlined the Boeing 747s and jumbo jets which flew into and out of New Orleans International Airport. Next, he pulled down a large projector screen facing the opposite wall. Fontanello hit a switch and a sophisticated computerized system lit up.

"How did you get access to this stuff?" Provenzano wondered.

Everyone sitting around the table was totally astonished.

"Pays to know connected people in high places," Fontanello boasted. "Men, right before your very eyes, is how the witness and the detective will become a part of history."

"Along with many other people," Randazzo added, their murderous plans quite evil.

"Precisely."

"We're all ears and eyes, Tuffy," Provenzano said.

Using the mouse connected to the computer, Fontanello moved to various components of the airplane's engine across the big screen. "Most of the jumbo jet 747s that fly into New Orleans International Airport are those wide-bodied commercial jets with four engines that propel the planes."

"I suspect so," Provenzano replied, not quite an expert in aviation.

"Those Boeings have pressurized cabins that enable them to fly in the most fucked up weather conditions."

"Like snow storms and those crazy air turbulences?" Randazzo asked.

"Correct, my friend," Fontanello responded. "They have about four engines that propel the plane, reaching cruising speeds of about five-hundred and fifty miles per hour."

"Wow, Tuffy!" Provenzano optimized. "Did you used to fly planes at one time?"

"No, only know people who are top experts in the field."

"Tell us more."

"Most accidents today are due to pilot error."

"The pilots are usually the ones who fuck up?" Provenzano asked.

"In most cases," Fontanello spoke, accusatory. "The training for pilots have become more technologically-advanced and extensive."

"Where are you going with this?" Provenzano deliberated, yearning to learn more.

"Flight simulators enable pilots to fly in adverse conditions that could be dangerous."

"Come a little clearer, Tuffy."

Fontanello moved the mouse across the large screen. "Everyone, take a look at the outlined diagram of this jumbo jet."

"Figuring out Chinese arithmetic or Japanese geometry would be easier," Provenzano chided, moving more towards his own understanding. He tried avoiding a migraine headache from thinking too hard.

"Once that plane crashes somewhere around New Orleans, and once the FAA and the NTSB do their investigations, they'll assume that it was pilot error."

"NTSB? FAA?" Randazzo asked.

"The National Transportation Safety Board. The Federal Aviation Administration."

"How will they assume that it was a fuckup on the pilot's part?" Gagliano asked.

"Observe closely, men," Fontanello said.

Fontanello circled the mouse around the engine's diagram. "Air that enters a turbo-jet engine is compressed and passed into a chamber."

"You're a fucking genuis, Tuffy!" Provenzano cheered.

Literally, Stefano "Tuffy" Fontanello was an *evil genius*.

"Once it goes into that chamber it is oxidized, and the energy produced by the burning fuel spins the turbine that drives the compressor. This, in turn, creates an effective power cycle."

"But what will eventually bring the plane down?" Calabrese asked.

"I've arranged for the ground crew out at the airport to place the oxidized combustible components in the cargo section of the plane," Fontanello had plotted with preparation.

"How are we going to arrange for that to happen?" Randazzo asked.

"Remember, my New Orleans family controls the unions that handle cargo out at the airport."

"What will this oxidized material do to bring down the plane once it's in the sky?" Provenzano asked.

"It'll cause an overheating of the plane, which will ignite a fire and make that jumbo jet drop out of the sky like a wounded duck," Fontanello explained in wicked details.

"Brilliant!" Provenzano yielded. "The witness and the detective will be out of the way soon enough."

"My men are watching the witness and the detective around-the-clock," Fontanello spoke assuredly. "They'll be keeping them under close tabs all the way up until they step on that plane leaving New Orleans."

"Shit, Tuffy, this is more sophisticated than the *River Quay Wars*."

"Tommy, Carmine, and Mikey, we once talked about the wars that went on in the River Quay back in the 70s. Compared to those days, something like this is non-inflammatory, definitely not as costly. Just like Angelo protected the Teamsters back then, we're protecting the Teamsters here in the present."

"And like Tommy always told us, the Teamsters is our very bloodline," Randazzo confirmed.

Fontanello didn't feel the need to launch a tirade about the other innocent people who'd lose their lives. Unfortunately, Sheila and Brittany had no clue they'd become serious problems for the Galluccio, Bernazzoli, and Fontanello crime families. The four crime bosses didn't excel in the area of sympathy. Their viciously cold Italian and Sicilian blood ran rapid through their veins of greed. Fontanello reminded the men that they were saving billions of dollars involved with the International Brotherhood of Teamsters Unions.

"Men, let me mention this," Fontanello paused, firing up a fat Cuban cigar. "The Teamsters Union is the most powerful force in the United States. The government in this country call themselves more powerful. We provide the transportation that gets people back and forth to work. We get the food to the stores so people can eat. We get the clothes to the stores so people will have clothes on their backs. We get the medicines to the hospitals so people can be healthy. We get the soap and toilet paper to the stores so people can wash and wipe their asses. So, if the politicians wanna shut us down, then they're shutting all of America down. Therefore, no matter what the fucking government has to say about the Teamsters Union, this goddamn country couldn't function without it."

There became an immediate chanting of *"I agree"* and *"Most definitely"* and *"No question about it"* among the trusted members and associates of the three crime families. Thank God somebody stood up for the common working man. People who busted their asses in trying to make a decent living for their families were the same people who were intolerable with the shabby work conditions.

Thank God somebody possessed some bravery when it involved uniform wage and benefit conditions for the working class. Still, the United States Government wanted to embarrass the Teamsters officials who created phony local unions, putting in office the "paper union" officials who were connected with notorious Mafia figures.

"You're absolutely right, Tuffy," Provenzano appeased Fontanello. "Tommy has always drilled it into our heads that the same motherfucking politicians who lobby against corruption within the Teamsters, are the same pukebags who've taken dope and hooker money under the table from people like us. Those sonofabitch-cocksucking politicians have got more skeletons in their closets than every cemetery in the United States. They've got more dirty laundry than every washhouse across America."

Fontanello strongly blinked both eyes. "The government tried sending my old man to jail because they said he'd gotten a couple'a million dollars in illegal payments from a merchant fleet company that he had set up in my mother's name."

"In the end, the Teamsters is bigger than the government," Randazzo said.

"We call a nationwide Teamsters strike, this goddamn country would come to their knees," Fontanello bluffed. "We'd paralyze every working man and every working woman in America."

"No question about it," Provenzano said.

"We own the goddamn the Teamsters," Randazzo boasted.

"Every single dime that fills its coffers."

Provenzano, Randazzo, Calabrese, and Gagliano were to remain in New Orleans until the plans had fallen through.

Fontanello thoroughly explained his treacherous plans. Now, they had to wait and hope those plans would fall through. Angelo "The Animal" Galluccio and Nicodemo "Rough Ends" Fontanello would've been proud of their nephew and son after knowing they did everything in their power to keep the legacy of the Teamsters Union alive.

Chapter 42

RANDY AND TRACEY sampled some of the finest cuisine New Orleans had to offer. The eclectic crowds at one of the lively jazz clubs in the city sent electricity through their bodies. Tracey left the club with a soaking wet dress clinging to her lucious body parts. She and Randy strolled along the French Quarter, taking a quick peek inside some of the other bars and raunchy strip clubs which showcased fully naked women. Randy knew to be on his best behavior. He made sure his eyes didn't wander for too long.

"This so romantic," Tracey crooned, Randy right by her side.

"What?" Randy asked, a hopeless romantic himself.

"Walking hand-in-hand along Bourbon Street."

"The French Quarter is an exciting place."

"Can't believe we're down here in New Orleans," Tracey fantasized, loving the sights.

"We're here, babe."

"Coming here seems so much different than Kansas City."

"The difference between the south and the midwest is like the difference between night and day."

"People down here seem friendlier."

"I'd say."

Throughout most of the day, the loving couple made unforgettable trips around New Orleans. They made stops to Jackson Square, the Napoleon House, The Voodoo Museum, St. Louis Cathedral, Preservation Hall, and the cemeteries where coffins sat above the ground. Most telling of all, the distinct auras of mystery surrounding the swamps and bayous captivated them. Randy and Tracey had been advised about the serious crime problems in the French Quarter. Coming in from a somewhat big city, they were smart enough to leave before the parasites came out to feed on their hosts, spotting weary tourists from their dark sanctums and invisible alleyways.

After a long day of sightseeing, they returned to their hotel and decided to stay put until Mardi Gras festivities made its debut the following day. Tracey just loved foot massages. No one gave them better than Randy. He sat at the edge of their plush bed holding a warm bottle of strawberry flavored body oil. Her feet were tortured after hitting the concrete grindstone around the city. Randy squeezed a tiny drop on each toe and spread the oil evenly around her feet. Giving special attention to the sole and the precious little pinky, his fingers went to work. Men knew they were highly-valued by women when they could caress a woman's body parts so tenderly.

"Yes! Yes!" Tracey crooned twice, eroticism filling the air.

The soothing effects of the oil, along with Randy's talented hands, sent her into a world of sensual pleasures.

Acting on impulse, he inserted the big toe of her right foot into his mouth. "Want me to suck all of your toes?"

"God, yes!" Tracey shivered. "Suck every one of them!"

"Nothing like gourmet toe souffle."

"Your warm tongue feels good."

"Want more, babe?"

"Yes, I do."

"I feel like sucking the meat off all your toes. It's like sucking the meat off a juicy neckbone."

"You're silly!" Tracey giggled.

With her eyes shut tight, she enjoyed her toes inside his warm mouth. Randy pulled her toes out of his mouth and allowed her body to drop across the bed. Clean feet or not, he went into the restroom and gargled with a tall bottle of Scope.

"Why did you stop?" Tracey asked, having valued his strong foot fetish.

Randy threw both hands over the shoulders of Tracey. "Remember when that FBI agent was killed that night in the *Westport District*?"

"Can't forget it," Tracey recalled.

"Who do you think killed him?" Randy asked, the memories still haunting him.

"It's hard to say. Didn't we already talk about that?"

"Why is it hard to say?"

"The newspaper and the news said a couple of men were trying to rob him."

"Do you really believe that?"

"I'm only going on what they've been telling everybody back in Kansas City."

"Question."

"What?"

"Do you still think there's still a Mafia around?"

"Of course there is."

"Why?"

"Because you'll never be able to get rid of them," Tracey strongly speculated.

"And why's that?"

"Money and power, Randy," she concluded. "The Mafia loves making money, and having power means everything to them."

"Another question."

"What now?"

"Do you think the Mafia is still in Kansas City?"

"Why wouldn't they be?"

"I don't know. That's why I asked you the question."

"My mom tells me that there are still Italians running crime in Kansas City."

"Do you know what that FBI agent was doing in Kansas City?"

"Investigating the Teamsters and the Mafia?"

"Exactly."

"What's your point, Randy?"

Randy slipped into a brief daze. From memory serving him right, he heard gunshots and people screaming. He visualized Agent Feliciano being gunned down and crowds of people running from the murder scene in the *Westport District*.

"Randy!" Tracey shouted, wanting his full attention. "Why would you bring up the FBI agent and the Mafia?"

"No particular reason."

Tracey shot Randy a stare of excruciating curiosity. "Did you see something that night down in Westport?"

"No."

"Do you know something about him being killed?"

"Of course not."

"You'd tell me if you did?"

"Of course I would."

"After all, we were down there the night he was killed."

"Let's forget about it."

"Are you sure?"

"Let's forget about what went on in Kansas City. Let's enjoy our time down here in New Orleans."

"Now you're talking what I wanna hear."

"I've filled my gut, now I wanna fill your gut."

"With what?"

"With that coconut crème stuffed in my nutsack."

Randy graduated from the smooth and creamy feet of Tracey. His freakish talents earned him higher places towards her athletic thighs. Having a specially talented tongue secured him special favors. Gliding his tongue along both thighs became unspeakable pleasure for her. Romantically, Tracey slid off the spaghetti straps to her pink silk nightgown.

A set of ripe homegrown breasts stared into the lustful eyes of Randy. His moist warm tongue arose from his mouth like a cunning serpent on the prowl for its next prey. The tip of his tongue met her seasoned nipples with gratitude. He gyrated his tongue in circular motions while it created erotic pleasures for Tracey. Gently, she pushed him away as she gasped to catch her breath.

"Something wrong, babe?" Randy asked, just getting warmed up.

"I just had to stop before I—," Tracey huffed, light sweat across her face.

"Come?"

"Very funny."

"I haven't even got started."

"This hot pussy's not going anywhere," Tracey joked in a teasing way.

"I hope not."

"You've got me hotter than a stove."

"The fun's only beginning."

Tracey slid against the wooden bedpost and parted her legs. Randy explored new territory with his gifted erect tongue. The fine pliable hairs along her trimmed bush gave him enough incentive to grant her oral ecstasy. The tip of his tongue found a delectable flap of pink meat. Tangy juices from her moist pussy coated his explorative mouth.

"Wooooooooh!" Tracey trembled, her body taken over by uninhibited pleasure.

To top off their lovemaking, Tracey wanted some hot steamy sex. Her invitations were enchanting. Randy moved in for the kill.

"I want something hard in me," Tracey commanded, her desires shifted into overdrive.

"Say the word, and it's done," Randy smiled, ready to fulfill her every desire.

"I want something fat in me," she chanted, playing with herself.

"Give the command, and it will be granted."

"I want something long in me," she dreamed, getting herself quite moist.

"Let me be your love slave."

"I want something warm in me."

"Tracey, my dick can't get any harder," Randy said, his patience getting short.

"Show me what you mean."

"Alright, have it your way."

"Yes, I want it my way."

"Okay, here goes, babe."

Within an instant, Randy entered her moistness with authority. Their bodies met with invitation. A few strokes later, he unleashed an explosive load inside of her. The lovemaking drained their energy to the point of sending them to sleep. Going to Mardi Gras would be so much sweeter.

Chapter 43

GETTING PAST THE FACT that Scotty was still a married man who had prior engagements with another woman, defected the secretive relationship he'd cultivated with Brittany. Falling in love too soon with him might've been the biggest mistake she'd ever made. Gossipers in her circles warned her there were many men throughout history who promised their mistresses and girlfriends they'd leave their wives for them. Many men came up with piss poor excuses as to why they wanted a divorce. Many married men cited reasons of their love dying and happiness not being there anymore.

Scotty didn't know how to step up and admit to Brittany that his wife Nancy was still attached to his heart. To give her more self-assurance, he promised to divorce Nancy as soon as they got back to Kansas City. Was he bluffing or trying to make Brittany feel special? Was he going to marry her after dumping his wife? Scotty drifted into a brief daze. He stood at the edge of their hotel balcony staring at the glistening lights which lit up part of New Orleans.

"Something on your mind, Scotty?" Brittany asked, wanting to pick away at his brain.

The reflection of the moonlight shone straight into her blue-green eyes.

"New Orleans is the most exciting city in the world," Scotty confessed.

The mild night breeze formed a blanket around his face.

"Mardi Gras should be exciting," Brittany pictured.

"Wild people having a wild time."

"We're really down here to see all the hoopla."

Brittany moved closer to Scotty. She locked her arms around his waist. They'd been trying to keep the lines of communication open ever since they arrived in New Orleans. Many questions went unanswered. The future remained uncertain for both of them.

"For some strange reason, New Orleans has given me the creeps," Scotty had attested.

He turned away to view another section of the vast city.

"Afraid of the dark?" Brittany teased. "Afraid of ghosts? Afraid of the boogie man?"

"I've read many of Anne Rice's novels, and I've watched movies about the voodoo legends down here."

"Those things are just made-up stories."

"Maybe so."

Their moment on the balcony together shifted over to a dead silence. Brittany twitched her fingers nervously. A desire to quench her thirst for answers were not fulfilled. Handing her heart over to Scotty on a silver platter frightened her. Falling in love with a married man sent most women into a disarray of fright. Brittany held the hand of Scotty with concern. She caressed his fingers with care.

"Your wife and I are still waiting on an answer," Brittany cleverly emancipated.

"Answer?" Scotty shrugged.

He played dumb with her, but only this time around, it wasn't working.

"Where's that coming from, Britt?"

"Either you make your mind up before we leave New Orleans, or it'll be over for us by the time we both get back to Kansas City."

"It's like you're putting me between a tight vice grip."

"Your choice, Scotty."

Brittany grew tired of all the games. She'd given him the chance to make a sound decision once again. The line had to be drawn somewhere. Brittany sketched the line plain enough for Scotty to see.

"Get off this ultimatum kick, okay!" Scotty blasted, her nagging having gotten to him.

"You can't straddle the fence forever."

"Didn't we talk about this back in Kansas City?"

"We'll keep talking about your divorce until you give me a definite answer."

"You're driving me nuts, Britt."

"Who do you really love, Scotty?" Brittany grilled Scotty. "You heard me tell you back in Kansas City that I was tired of this crazy triangle game. I have every reason to believe that you're still in love with your wife and just don't know which way to turn."

"Filing for a divorce isn't as easy as it looks," Scotty spoke defensively. "You wouldn't know since you've never been married."

"Easy going in, but hard coming out, huh?"

"You're catching on, Britt."

Brittany stepped to the other side of the balcony. She turned away to view the awesome lights which had speckled bits of the New Orleans nightlife. "Scotty, the killing of an FBI special agent hangs in the balances back in Kansas City. I'm still assigned to that homicide case, and I owe it to that agent to find out who the two killers are."

The thin red lips of Scotty had pressed together. Not a muscle or nerve in his body moved. "Which comes first, me or your law enforcement career?"

Brittany averted her eyes over to where Scotty stood against the protective railing. She exchanged fierce eye contact with him. "Who comes first, me or your wife?"

"I asked you first."

"If I had a husband who supported me, then there'd be a balance between the two."

"There goes that same problem with you women of the 90s."

"Women of the nineties?" Brittany shrugged as she leaned back.

"Women of the new age put their careers before their family."

"And you believe that?"

"Statistics show that more women are staying single."

"That's their choice. That's their God-given right."

"Statistics also show that more women are independent and career-driven."

"If there'd be more available men, maybe there wouldn't be as many career-driven single women."

"I don't buy that."

"When I decided to become a homicide detective, I knew it required hard work, discipline, and lots of hours at the Headquarters."

"You care more about that FBI agent being killed than anything else."

"It's my job to care."

"If you want to wrestle with a bunch of Teamsters goons and Mafia hoodlums, then be my guest, sweetheart," Scotty rudely blurted out.

Brittany rushed right up to Scotty. She pointed her finger straight to the middle of his face. "How can you say something like that?"

"Mobsters killed that FBI agent!"

"You know my job better than I do?"

"It looks that way."

"The KCPD and the FBI are getting close to cracking the case."

"I'm still getting eery feelings about the agent being shot to death."

"You know, Scotty," Brittany politely paused. "With the selection that's available in the men's department, it's a wonder that there aren't more lesbians in the world today."

"The same can be said about the poor selection of women these days."

Brittany exited the balcony one angry soul. Eyes of vehemence watched Brittany and Scotty from down on the street. Their orders were to keep them within plain eyesight.

Chapter 44

AT THE SUFFERANCE OF Galluccio, Fontanello, and the Bernazzoli Brothers, Calabrese and Gagliano were ordered to keep close watch on Sheila. Faithfully, they surveilled her around-the-clock. The Chicago executioners kept a closer watch on her during her trips to and from the hotel. Using high-powered binoculars, Calabrese observed Shelia's trips to the bathroom while she took showers and got dressed. Having no special man in her life, or even someone to travel with for companionship, meant there'd been a void waiting to be filled. Calabrese and Gagliano waited across the street from the Sheraton Hotel of New Orleans holding pairs of binoculars up to their eyes.

"Can't wait until this broad gets on that plane leaving New Orleans," Calabrese had only wished.

"We'll all be happy when she's gone," Gagliano affirmed to his partner.

"Tuffy usually whacks his enemies another way."

"What, butchering them up and dumping them around the bayous?" asked Gagliano.

"That's how he does it."

"Hey, Louie, remember those stories about those bums that Tuffy whacked?"

"Yeah, bums he whacked across the head with those baseball bats."

"Tuffy would give them a good working over before dumping their bodies in bathtubs filled with lye."

"Boy, and that lye ate straight through their skin inside that tub."

"The only thing left of those bums were their bones."

"And then Tuffy would throw their bodies in the swamps for the snakes and gators to finish off whatever was left."

Calabrese bumped Gagliano with his arm to signal that Sheila stood in the window wearing her sexy nightware. Tilting their focused binoculars, they got the clearest view possible.

"Hey, Bart, that broad's got a nice body," Calabrese commented, his mind wandering.

"Didn't know they bred chicks like her in Kansas City," Gagliano said.

"I'd like to go up in that room and put a stiff one in her."

"Control your hormones, Louie."

"Try telling my libido that."

"I'm sure you've got a ton of ass back in Chicago."

Calabrese and Gagliano remained at their post until further notice.

Chapter 45

INSIDE SHEILA'S SPACIOUS HOTEL room designed with flavors of electric chic, the phone shot off a loud ring. She rushed to the other side of the room and snatched it up.

"Sheila speaking!" Sheila answered, breathing in heavy spurts.

"Everything okay?" her sister Sherry asked, pausing momentarily.

Sherry had called her sister directly from Kansas City, Missouri. In the comfort of her North Kansas City townhome, she sensed a strange tone in her sister's voice.

"Everything's fine," Sheila assured her sister. "This whole Mardi Gras thing has got me very excited."

"Having a good time so far down in New Orleans?"

"Wonderful time."

"Seeing any of the sights there in *The Big Easy*?"

"The restaurants and museums are terrific."

"I'll bet the Cajun and Creole food are great."

"The gumbo soups are out of this world."

"Good."

"I'll probably come back to Kansas City ten pounds heavier."

"Gold's Gym and Jenny Craig will probably do you good."

"Very funny, big sis."

"Got some news for you," Sherry said, her voice lowered with caution. "Don't know if you'll take it as good or bad news."

"You won the powerball and neither one of us have to work again?"

"Wishful thinking," Sherry hoped. "The FBI and the KCPD believe they might be close to finding the two men who killed the FBI agent."

"The night we were in Westport?"

"Right."

"How?" Sheila asked, her voice trained for secrecy.

"They're still working on those FBI sketches since the last time you and I went downtown to Police Headquarters. They've been going around to bonding companies here in Kansas City asking lots of questions to bondsmen."

"Any names?"

"Not a one."

"That's strange."

"But, they've been posting FBI sketches on telephone poles, and in post offices all over Kansas City."

"Both Missouri and Kansas?"

"Yes, both sides of the river."

"Did it ever occur to the FBI, or did it ever occur to the KCPD, that those two men skippped town after they killed that FBI agent?"

Logical thinking on the behalf of Sheila made her a lot more intellectual than what most people realized.

"Don't think so."

"Sherry, I beg to differ."

"Hopefully, they'll catch the killers and lock them up for life."

"What more do the cops want from us?"

"Glad you asked that question."

"Well?"

"The FBI wants us to come to their office in the federal building in downtown."

"Thought they were through asking us questions."

Sheila felt they'd performed their civic duties by fully cooperating with the FBI and the KCPD.

"Well, you know how it is when they're putting together those sketches. They have to add this and they have to add that. Then, they have to take away this and they have to take away that. Why do they spend so much time trying to get things perfect?"

"We only caught a glimpse of their faces. Plus, they were wearing black skullcaps with all-black clothing on."

"They ran up on that FBI agent, shot him a few times, and then they ran like hell."

"Like I said before, how do they know those two maniac killers are still in Kansas City? As far as anyone knows, they could've jumped on a plane or bus and went thousands of miles away."

"True," Sherry agreed. "Whether we go to the FBI's office or KCPD headquarters, they're going to come looking for us. They're determined to catch the men who killed one of their own."

"What, that never give up attitude?"

"Yeah, I guess."

"Some people just don't know when to quit."

Sheila pulled the phone away from her ear. She sat at the edge of the bed with "suspense" scribbled all over her face. An omen of danger created strange sensations all around her. Back to logical thinking she went.

The pieces missing to the puzzle had fallen in place.

"Damn, Sherry!" Sheila gristled, her mouth twisted sideways. "Do you even know why the FBI agent was killed that night in the *Westport District*?"

"Never gave it a second thought."

"From what I read in the paper, and from what I saw on the news, in which the police at headquarters never mentioned, was that that agent came to Kansas City to investigate the Teamsters and the Mafia."

"Teamsters? The Mafia?" Sherry wavered.

"Yes, that's exactly why he came to Kansas City."

"Can't be, Sheila," Sherry couldn't believe.

Gradually, the phone slid away from her ear. She felt the creeps coming over her.

"Sounds unreal, but Mafia guys who've got a hand in the Teamsters were being investigated by that very FBI agent."

"Come straight out and say what's on your mind."

"The two men who killed him are probably connected to the Mafia," Sheila strongly suspected.

"The newspaper and the police said that it was just a random street robbery. That's what I thought it might've been all along."

"Don't be ridiculous, Sherry," Sheila objected. "Nothing was taken from that guy."

"Which is saying?"

"Not his wallet, nor his watch, nor his other jewelry, or anything of value was taken from off his body."

"I thought the news only reported true stories."

"Sherry, the media is no different than any other venue in America."

"Which is saying?"

"The media is controlled by a bunch of rich and powerful propagandizing idiots who thrive on poisoning millions of people's minds."

"That, I'd have to agree with you totally."

"People believe what they wanna believe."

A moment of silence occurred between Sheila and Sherry. "Hey, Sherry, remember the *River Quay Wars* that happened back in the middle and late 70s?"

"Who could ever forget the wars that went on in River Quay?"

"Remember those Italians using dynamite to blast away one another's businesses?"

"Of course I remember. Everytime you turned on the news, that's all you saw."

"Alright, do you remember those black people being on the news telling the police about the explosions they heard?"

"The black people from over there in those housing projects?"

"Yes."

"They talked about being scared shitless after feeling the trembles from those explosions."

"Now, do you remember what those *River Quay Wars* were really about?"

"Not really."

"It was about the Mafia and the Teamsters."

"No kidding?"

Sheila inhaled strongly. She exhaled even stronger. "It's been said that history repeats itself."

"And you're saying what?"

"What happened back in the days of River Quay is still going on today."

"I'd hope not."

"Some things seem to never die."

"Hope we're not doing the wrong thing by telling the FBI and the KCPD what we saw that night in Westport."

"None of this occurred to me until recently. Maybe if we were in danger, the police would give us some type of protection."

"We should be alright."

"We can only hope so."

"Don't worry."

Sheila humped her shoulders and grinded her teeth. "Sherry, I'm feeling something bad is going to happen."

"Don't say that, Sheila."

"I'm feeling that I'm being watched."

"By who?"

"I don't know."

"There are other witnesses who are still talking to the FBI and the police."

"Look, I want to end this conversation. Who knows, somebody might be listening in on us."

"Give me a call the minute you get out to KCI airport," Sherry said. "I'll come and pick you up so we can finish talking about this."

"See you when I get back to Kansas City."

"Love you, Sheila."

"Love you, too, Sherry."

The plot orchestrated by Galluccio, Fontanello, and the Bernazzoli Brothers went as planned. Sheila had every reason to believe that she'd been marked for death. The specter of death lurked within her shadows.

Chapter 46

THE LAST DAY OF the week-long Mardi Gras festivities arrived. Wild revelers jammed the streets of the French Quarter. The drunk euphoria and general abandon created an electricity of loose women and men running wild along the quarters slinging beer and hard liquor every which direction. New Orleans residents decorated their city with steamers and flags to compliment the traditional Mardi Gras colors of green, gold, and purple. Now came the day for most people to symbolically recognize the last opportunity for indulgence. Party animals roamed fancy free without a care in the world. Most of their minds were soaked with hard alcohol and filled with perverted thoughts.

Randy and Tracey joined in on the lavish parties and masked balls held earlier during the day. Being a far cry from Kansas City, they found it difficult getting used to the wild nature of New Orleans. Most of the Mardi Gras festivities took them on a crazy rollercoaster ride. Conservatism became a way of life for most Kansas Citians, but when they ventured down to Louisiana, they had to let loose by letting it all hang out. Tracey found it hard getting used to lesbian and bi-sexual women making passes at her. Women had invited her up to their hotel rooms for wild sex parties and lesbian orgies.

People continually crowded the French Quarter indulging in food and drink and lots of wild partying. The spectacular floats graced Mardi Gras with the arousal of freedom. Men and women danced crazily through the streets. Together, they held one another and slammed food and liquor down one another's mouths.

Costumed krewe members rode the highly-decorated floats with extreme pride. They tossed strings of assorted colored beads and glittering trinkets into the crowds of spectators who lined the streets. Some of the everyday, ordinary people designed their own costumes and paraded through the streets. Randy stretched his arms high and one of the set of beads landed in his left hand.

"Look! Look!" Randy shouted twice to Tracey.

He clutched the beads like they were rolls of high bills.

"They came right over to me and fell in my hands."

"Let's see," Tracey requested, feeling the smoothness of the beads.

"They're supposed to bring you good luck."

"Just some superstition."

"Maybe I'll win that lottery powerball."

"You and 200 million more people in America."

"This parade is really a sight to see."

"Haven't seen this many drunk people since going to a football game."

"Or some wild bar or nightclub back home."

"Didn't expect to see a bunch of women pulling their pants down and showing their bare asses to everybody here."

"They're raising up their shirts and showing their breasts to everyone, too."

"This is one wild parade."

"You remember me telling you about the wild reputation of Mardi Gras?"

"Should've given me more details," Tracey said disdainfully, the parade growing wilder.

"The show *COPS* gave a lot of footage about Mardi Gras."

An inferno of intoxicated bodies streamed along the French Quarter trying to find restrooms to release their consumed alcohol and food. Turbulence rumbled inside their stomachs. Very hard, they tried keeping the digested food from throwing up. Randy happened to be one of the unfortunate ones. Two men, one standing in front of him, the other standing behind him, unleashed big globs of vomit onto his shirt and pants. Disgusting colors of green, yellow, and brown digested food oozed down his clothing. The noxious odor of *Cajun* and *Creole* food, mixed with hard liquor and beer, created an explosion of cocktail and culinary hell.

"Muthafuck!" Randy exploded, his face painted with anger.

Badly, he wanted the gross food removed from his clothes. No way was he willing to touch a drop of the vomit.

"You two sonofabitches did this shit on purpose!" Randy confronted the two drunk idiots.

"Hey buddy, sorry about that," apologized the first highly-intoxicated man.

He reached forward to try and shake Randy's hand.

"Sorry, but I couldn't hold it," said the second extremely-intoxicated man.

"I'll just bet you're sorry!" Randy boiled over. "You could've puked that bullshit somewhere on the ground."

The drunk man standing behind Randy appeared to be younger than the alkie standing in the front. He offered more apologies for the gross catastrophe. "I tried running to the bathroom, but it just forced itself out of my stomach."

"Bathroom or not, you could've let that shit loose somewhere else!"

"Here's twenty bucks for your troubles," the second drunk offered.

A strong Southern accent indicated he was from somewhere in the south.

"Keep your fucking money!" Randy dejected. "You two have got me looking like I've fallen in piles of raw food. You've got me smelling like somebody's rotten gut."

"Forgive me, sir," said the first drunk man.

"There's no excuse for you two puking all over somebody!" Randy exploded. "How would you like it if somebody dumped a bunch of fresh cowshit all over you?"

"Let me go before I puke some more," snoozed the second intoxicated idiot.

He rushed away from the grotesque scene he'd created.

"Yeah, get the hell out of here before you throw up on my girlfriend!"

Tracey saw the fury which burned through the eyes of Randy. This totally ruined their trip to New Orleans.

"And just as we were having a good time," Randy complained further.

It's been said how shit usually happens. This was the most embarrassment that Randy had ever experienced.

"What time does our plane leave tomorrow?" Randy asked Tracey.

Lethal hostility burned him inside and out.

Tourists and New Orleans residents walked past him. Abruptly, some walked around him as though he was a freak in the circus.

"Our flight leaves New Orleans for Chicago at one o'clock," Tracey informed Randy.

Tracey had her own reasons to stand aside. She avoided the smell and sudden swarm of flies.

"After this shit, I'm ready to go back home."

"Don't let this ruin our trip," Tracey tried pampering Randy. "Don't let it take away from the fun we've already had."

"I'll be happy when one o'clock tomorrow comes."

"We'll go back to the hotel so you can shower real good. Then, you can put on some fresh clothes with a big splash of cologne."

"A big splash of cologne?" Randy rectified. "After being drenched in somebody else's vomit, I'll need some of your perfume, your deodorant, your scented lotion, my after-shave spray, and just about anything else that'll kill this digusting raw food smell."

"Let's end our trip in style."

"Fucking bastards!" Randy fractured. "These clothes are going in the trash."

Randy and Tracey disappeared from the Mardi Gras scene to return to their hotel room.

Chapter 47

BRITTANY AND SCOTTY enjoyed the Mardi Gras celebrations quite well. Brittany finally withdrew from her plans of nagging him about getting a divorce and becoming her husband. The lovemaking between the two lovebirds the night before became a pleasant experience. Love remained one of the greatest mysteries throughout the course of history. Love sent men and women over the edge. Love caused them to engage in unexplainable activities.

"Look at that float right there, Britt!" Scotty shouted to Brittany.

He pointed to the huge float coming down the crowded street.

"Where, Scotty, where?" Brittany shouted back.

She scanned the floats which made their way along the jam-pack street.

"The one man with the white beard like Santa Claus, and the golden crown on top of his head," Scotty described in full details, his eyes fixed on the brilliant array of colors.

"Oh, the float of *King Cotton*."

"How'd you know the name?" Scotty asked, Mardi Gras having fascinated him.

"Did my homework," Brittany smiled at him.

"Neat, huh?"

"Real cool, babe."

"There's no more exciting place in the whole world."

"This parade is charged with electricity."

"I've never seen so many people in one place having such a good time."

"New Orleans is pumped."

"Raw energy."

"We've got to come back again."

"Sure do."

Brittany and Scotty grabbed at some of the beads and trinkets. Scotty reached over the heads of people in front of them. Mardi Gras had drawn three million people from all around the world. An atmosphere of multi-national euphoria was born. The revelry created among the people featured a reminiscent of elaborate showcasing.

An Indian tribe which incorporated colorful feathers and intricate beadwork covering their bodies, marched down the street in full stride. Like Randy and Tracey, Brittany and Scotty were shocked to see the wild women bearing it all. They witnessed women drunk and naked running from one alleyway to the next one.

"Look at those women flashing their breasts for everyone," Brittany noticed, sort of turning her head the other direction.

"Nice set of tits, huh?" Scotty joked, his eyes planted on their flopping breasts.

"Very funny, Scotty," Brittany objected. "Keep it up and you won't be going back to Kansas City alive."

"Was only kidding, Britt."

"Bet you were."

"No woman has tits as nice as your's," Scotty teased.

"Not even your wife?" Brittany asked in comparison.

"Not even Nancy."

"So, you only like me for my tits?"

"You've got a nice ass to go with those babies."

"Oh, do I?"

"Yes, you do. But you also have brains and personality to top it all off."

"Scotty, that's so sweet."

"Now, flash some ass and tits for me."

"Keep it up, and you'll be dead even before you get on that plane tomorrow."

"We'll both be dead."

"Oh really?"

"I'm only kidding, Britt."

"I've got a homicide case that I'm still assigned to."

"Let's not talk about that FBI agent again."

"Why not?"

"It gives me the creeps to think about it."

More women pulled their pants down and raised their dresses up. Some showed their young tender asses to everyone nearby. Some had tanned skin smoother than woven silk. Others flashed pale asses cursed with cellulite and dents. Scotty sure got his peeks and thrills in when he didn't think Brittany was looking.

Men were whores just like women. The female species got paid for the sacred gift locked between their legs. Brittany couldn't take her eyes off the elaborate costumes worn by the participants in the gala parade. The merrymaking came non-stop from the crowds who were controlled by the police on foot and those on horses.

"My Lord!" Scotty bolted, using his strong sense of smell.

"Something wrong, babe?" Brittany asked.

"You don't smell it?" Scotty whisked with his arm.

He fanned the disgusting odor out of his face.

"Guess I don't."

"Did somebody around here die?"

"What does it smell like?"

"Like something spoiled or like something rotten."

Scotty tilted his head to the ground. One of the most grotesque sights was spread out everywhere.

"That'll ruin your appetite for good," Brittany wooed.

"You bet it will."

Piles of raw vomit were spread out in large and small puddles. Other thrillseekers avoided stepping in it. The rice, sausage, chicken, shrimp, peppers and onions indicated that whoever spilled their digested food out on the ground, they'd been dining on some cuisine *Cajun* food earlier during day. Hard liquor and beer didn't mix too well with the varieties of food.

"This is totally disgusting!" Brittany frowned upon.

"Vendors should wash this crap away," Scotty suggested, closely watching his step.

"Let's get the hell away from this section."

Scotty wanted to spectate more women flashing their lucious body parts. Brittany already knew she had an eye-catching posterior, one Scotty worshipped when she walked in front of him.

Sets of dark cunning eyes, ones which casted death, watched Brittany and Scotty as they moved through the dense crowd of Mardi Gras. Calabrese and Gagliano blended in cleverly with the crowd along the streets of the French Quarter.

"Where's the detective and her boyfriend going?" Calabrese questioned Gagliano.

"Probably back to their hotel," Gagliano had only guessed.

"Tomorrow's the big day, Bart."

"Louie, we're supposed to touch basis with Tuffy and his men when they're leaving for the airport."

"Our work will be done once they get on that plane."

"That'll be a relief."

"We've got some unfinished business back in Chicago."

"That we do."

Sheila moved along the crowded streets of the French Quarter carrying an array of beads that she'd caught from the krewes standing on the many floats. The scopeful eyes of Calabrese and Gagliano watched her closely. She wasn't to leave their jurisdiction for long. New Orleans turned out to be a bit wild for Sheila. Mardi Gras presented a ferociousness which'd been a far cry from the conservatism of Kansas City, Missouri. She'd seen enough of the week-long festivities and was ready to head back home.

A man riding on horseback wearing a colorful costume designed to make him look like a peacock asked, "Would you like a bowl of gumbo?"

"Sure, why not?" Sheila accepted, taking the warm bowl and cradling it in her arms.

"You'll love this thick flavored gumbo soup," the parade participant appraised.

"What are the ingredients?"

"Can't tell you that, my dear," he smiled.

"Why not?" she smiled back.

"Ahhhhhh, that's a part of legendary New Orleans secret."

"Smells good."

"Tastes better."

Generously, he rode off to be a part of the continuing Mardi Gras festivities.

"Thanks."

"Enjoy."

Sheila removed the aluminum foil from the top and took a strong sniff of the gumbo. The aroma pleased her sense of smell. Her tastebuds did a tap dance inside her mouth. Calabrese and Gagliano studied her every move. They'd grown tired of keeping tabs on Sheila.

"Tomorrow's not coming soon enough," Calabrese griped, ready to get it over with.

"Isn't that the truth," Gagliano agreed.

"Once her and that detective step into that airport, they'll be in the hands of Frankie and Bobby."

"Then, they can deal with the headaches."

"And headaches it has been."

"Tuffy is probably pulling his hairs out by now."

"You got that right."

Sheila had disappeared to her destination. Calabrese and Gagliano had disappeared to their destination.

Chapter 48

BRITTANY AND SCOTTY escaped the madness of the Mardi Gras celebrations to enjoy some last minute time together in New Orleans. Their door was locked. Their window blinds were closed. Their television had been turned off. Only a radio playing enchanting love music from one of the premiere soft rock stations there in New Orleans dominated the atmosphere. Scotty locked his arms around the gentle, yet fragile back of Brittany. He leaned forward and their softs lips met with invitation. A magnetic charge of sensuality shot through their bodies.

"Scotty, I want to be your wife," Brittany pleaded, seriousness coating her eyes.

"Do you know what that means?" Scotty asked, his heart racing wild.

"I don't care what it means," she replied. "All I know is that I'm in love with you."

"And I'm in love with you, too."

"Then let's make it official when we get back to Kansas City."

"Are you ready to put up with somebody like me?"

"Yes, I am."

"Are you ready to put up with my bad habits?"

"Yes, I am."

"Can you put up with my burping, farting, and snoring around the house?"

"Yes, I can."

"Can you put up with me throwing dirty clothes around the house? Can you put up with me leaving dirty dishes in the kitchen sink for days at a time?"

"I sure can."

"Can you put up with me leaving hair in the bathroom sink after I shave? Can you put up with me leaving the toilet seat up after I take a piss?"

"It's all a part of being a man."

"Are you sure about that, Britt?"

"If your wife Nancy can put up with all those things, then I know I'll be able to put up with the same things."

Scotty pulled Brittany closer. He threw his tongue down her throat. "Now, what all do I have to put up from you?"

Brittany prepared an outline of her shortcomings. "Well, if you can put up with me working long hours as a homicide detective, then we wouldn't have too many p7roblems."

"I'd have a problem with you being assigned to cases involving the Mafia."

"Why?"

"I wouldn't want no wife of mine's being put in dangerous situations."

"Everyday I walk into work is dangerous."

"As long as you're happy, then that's all that counts."

Brittany sensually clamped both of her hands to the side of Scotty's face. "Scotty, to show you that I love you, I insurgently left an important homicide case to come down here to New Orleans with you."

"And I appreciate that greatly, Britt."

"Do you really?"

"Yes, I do."

Brittany glanced into the boyish eyes of Scotty and asked, "Will you ask Nancy for a divorce when we get home?"

"It won't be easy, but I'll ask her."

"You'll make me the happiest woman on Earth."

"She'll want to know why."

"Be truthful with her."

"That'll be the hardest part."

Scotty and Brittany wore matching terry towel robes. Simultaneously, they peeled off one another's robes. Pleasing raw flesh opened up for display. Lovemaking opened up for business for the hopeless lovebirds. Scotty lifted Brittany off the ground and placed her at the head of the bed. Her legs were parted for purposes of oral exploration. Blessed with a long tongue like a slithery serpent, he entered her fleshy pink moistness. Juices of ecstasy sprouted around his riveting tongue. Brittany moaned and groaned from unspeakable pleasure.

"Oh, Scotty!" Brittany shivered. "Feels oh too good!"

Scotty explored open territories along her svelte body. The needle-sharp nipples on Brittany's breasts were ripe. They begged for affection. He clamped her nipples with his talented mouth. He circled his tongue around the tips and borders.

Brittany possessed some special talents of her own. She positioned Scotty on his back so she could travel between his legs. For her, giving was better than receiving. In order for him to receive maximum pleasure, she glided her tongue along the sensitivity of his hardness. She teased the swollen head. She aroused the puffy balls underneath. Scotty slipped into *pleasure paradise*.

"Damn, Britt!" Scotty squirmed. "You give the best head!"

Brittany accomplished her goal by giving Scotty a rock hard erection. She dropped on her back and he entered her pink moistness with his fleshy hardness. His strokes were short and slow, yet so very effective. Their bodies were joined by boundless pleasure.

He exploded with a hot load inside of her. Pleasurably, they held one another with a tight grip. The lovemaking they had experienced satisfied them enough to roll over and fall asleep.

Chapter 49

THE LEGENDARY FONTANELLO crime family of New Orleans grabbed control of the unions which handled cargo coming into and out of the busy New Orleans International Airport. Their men were placed into immediate positions of having access to the Boeing 747 jumbo jet departing New Orleans at one o'clock p.m. A stopover in Chicago for a 45 minute layover was part of the schedule. Passengers on the flight to Chicago were destined to fly into Kansas City. TWA Flight number 2309 rested on the tarmac near the west entrance of the airport.

The usual ground crew responsible for handling cargo being loaded and unloaded from the plane were given the next two days off. Front office personnel, the people responsible for scheduling hours for the crews, were instructed by corrupt airport officials on Tuffy Fontanello's payroll to give the men time off. None of the men had much vacation time or sick leave built up. At the request of a corrupt union leader, a whole new crew of men were scheduled to work the ground cargo. Four men dressed in dark gray jumpsuits drove up in one of the airport vehicles with a small load of boxes. Who were these four men?

They were Provenzano, Randazzo, Calabrese, and Gagliano. They came dressed for their murderous assignment. The boxes were filled with flammable goods which were supposed to be stored at room temperature. A loyal group of Fontanello's men who posed as aircraft mechanics gained access to the engine compartment of the plane. Utility belts hung around their waists. The group of executioners jumped inside and altered the compressor blades, turbines, and the gearbox.

Provenzano and Randazzo represented the Galluccio family with great pride. Calabrese and Gagliano represented the Bernazzoli family with an even higher esteem. The Chicago and Kansas City crime families counted fully on their men following through with their plans. The TWA flight crashing somewhere before arriving in Chicago was a definite must. Provenzano and Randazzo served as the overseers right down to the job being finished.

"You get to the compressor blades?" Provenzano asked a Fontanello unionized crime member.

Provenzano had gone over all the details of the disastrous plans.

"Absolutely," replied the loyal Fontanello Mafioso. "Did exactly as Tuffy ordered."

"How about the engine turbines?" Provenzano asked, his authority ironclad.

"Slightly altered some of the wiring near the turbines."

"And the gearbox?"

"Same there."

"Get your crew and get the hell out of here."

"Right away, Frankie."

The made Mafioso from the Fontanello faction faded away from the airport. Left behind were the men who'd been recruited to serve as the cargo crew.

"Are the boxes loaded like you were told?" Provenzano asked of Calabrese.

"Yes, Frankie, just like we were told," Calabrese answered with due respect.

"Flammable materials inside?" Provenzano asked of Gagliano.

"The best for the money's worth," Gagliano replied back.

"So, what are we working with?"

"Bottles of acetylene and acetone are placed dead in the center of the cargo section."

"Perfect!" Provenzano fizzed. "Let's hope things go as planned."

"The plane should burst into flames once the engine reaches a certain temperature."

"Tuffy said at about 95 degrees celcius."

"Once this plane is up and running, it'll get ten times hotter than 95 degrees celcius."

"Between the plane catching on fire, and between mechanical failure, they don't have a chance in hell. Am I correct?"

Provenzano made sure that he went over last minute details.

"Absolutely," Gagliano spoke assuredly. "Everything's right on schedule, Frankie."

"Alright, round up the men and disappear from this airport."

"Okay," Gagliano acknowledged. "Anything else?"

"That'll be it for now."

The crew who stored the boxes of acetylene and acetone into the middle of the cargo section of the plane jumped into a waiting car and disappeared. The switch would pay off in the biggest way. The names of the usual cargo crew workers and aircraft mechanics were brilliantly left on the list of those scheduled to work. Once the heat started coming down, they'd be the first ones who had to answer to higher authorities. Provenzano, Randazzo, Gagliano and Calabrese were anxious to see the fruit of their evil labors.

Chapter 50

RANDY AND TRACEY stepped inside New Orleans International Airport at exactly twelve noon. Logically speaking, it would've been wise to arrive early to avoid being at the end of a long and frustrating line. People flying back to Midwestern destinations like Chicago and Kansas City waited by the gate for their place in line. Carefree travelers waited with their duffel bags and guitars and multi-piece luggage sets. From the look on their tired faces, there were those people who'd had an overdose of Mardi Gras. Still, their exhausted bodies swung back and forth as they walked around or waited in line. Alcohol odors seeped from their mouths. The smell of potent marijuana faltered in their clothing.

Brittany and Scotty walked into the airport wearing bursting smiles. Their gleaming smiles indicated their night of passionate lovemaking brought about immeasurable excitement. The attractive couple held hands as they stepped up to the board for scheduled departures and arrivals. Travelers from around the country poured into the busy airport swinging and dragging their luggage. Many rushed to and from bathrooms and restaurants and gift shops. Scotty promised Brittany during the early morning hours he'd ask his wife Nancy for a divorce. She cried to hear him speak those magical words.

From the opposite end of the airport, Randy's memory had once again kicked into full gear. Witnessing the two killers who pumped fiery bullets into FBI Special Agent Wilfredo Feliciano, shot into his psych clearer than ever. The sounds of the loud gunshots. People running and screaming through the streets. The two killers fleeing the scene afterwards. Those excruciating memories were just as audible and visible as though it had just happened. The haunting memories frightened him into the strongest daze.

"Randy! Randy!" Tracey belted out twice. "Earth calling Randy Rivera. Please come in, Randy Rivera."

"Sorry about that, baby," Randy apologized once again to Tracey.

Abruptly, he came back to the present.

"You left me there for a minute."

"Got a lot on my mind."

"Like what?"

"Just a few things that I have to take care of when we get home."

"Let's go and get something to eat."

"Good idea, honey. I'm starved."

Sheila became a late arrival when she stepped into the airport with her travel belongings. She raced to the arrival and departure board to make sure she would gain her spot in line. Luckily for her, other passengers hadn't arrived. This gave her the opportunity to board the plane before others. Minutes following her arrival, Provenzano and Randazzo followed her in hot pursuit.

Provenzano and Randazzo stood near a pay phone while following strict orders of not letting Sheila nor Brittany out of their sight. She took a seat inside the terminal. She pulled out a recent Danielle Steele novel inside her white burlap travel bag. Reading not only became therapeutic for her, but she found it quite relaxing during long trips and during lunch and breaks at her job. Randazzo studied Sheila as her head swung back and forth while reading the lengthy novel.

From out on the busy and noisy tarmac, the crew of union workers who normally handled cargo at New Orleans International Airport, were called in to work at the last minute. Some were outraged to learn that it became mandatory to report to work. When their supervisor informed them that they'd be paid time and a half, plus the luxury of a juicy bonus, they jumped up and reported to work. Clever move on the part of the Galluccio, Bernazzoli, and Fontanello crime families. Their plans fell right into place.

"I really didn't wanna come to work today," said the first cargo handler.

"But time and a half sounded so sweet," said the second cargo handler.

"Personnel need to make up their fucking minds," complained a third cargo handler. "First, they tell us we have the next two days off. Second, they tell us to bring our rusty asses to work."

"But that bonus will look good when we get our paychecks," chirped the second handler. "I'm sure all of us can use the money."

"Why do you think they called us in on such short notice?" asked the first handler.

"Look at all the people who flew in for Mardi Gras," replied the second handler. "Betcha they left millions of dollars behind for our city."

"Mardi Gras ending equates to a lot of work for us," said the third handler. "And lots of work equates into lots of money."

"Can't argue with that," said the first handler.

The trio of cargo handlers had their hands full. Several planes waited on the airport tarmac to be loaded. The imposters had come and gone. Little did the handlers know that a tragedy was waiting to happen. Back inside the busy airport, Brittany and Scotty rushed to gain their places in line. Sheila found a place towards the end of the line.

A ticket agent at the TWA counter announced, "Flight number 2309 will be departing from Gate Seven to Chicago, with connecting flights to St. Louis, Kansas City, Milwaukee, Minneapolis, Cincinnati, and Cleveland."

Ticket agents sent passengers through the line while tearing apart their ticket stubs. Brittany followed Scotty to the first class section of the cabin. Scotty stuffed their small carry-on bags in overhead compartments as they dropped down into their seats. How romantic it had become for them to join hands and gaze hopelessly into the eyes of one another.

An elderly woman sitting across from them looked over and said, "My, my, you two make the cutest couple."

"We're getting married when we get home," Brittany happily announced to the elderly woman.

She cuddled up with Scotty like there'd be no tomorrow.

"How nice," the elderly woman cheered, a big crease lining her old face.

"We're so excited!"

"Where's home, dear?"

"Kansas City, Missouri."

"I'm on my way back to Chicago."

"Must be a gang of people on this plane from Chicago."

"There are plenty of people on here from K.C., too. How'd you enjoy Mardi Gras?"

"Had a blast."

"So did I."

Sheila stood in front of three other people before claiming her place in line. She stepped up to the agent and handed over her ticket.

Provenzano turned his body away from the congested airport crowd. He dropped five dollars worth of quarters into the pay phone.

"The witness and the detective are on the plane, Tuffy," Provenzano informed Stefano Fontanello.

"Perfect!" Fontanello buzzed. "Now, let me call Tommy in Kansas City."

"Tommy will call Carmine and Mikey in Chicago once he gets the news."

"Great."

"Look, Tuffy, I'll see you when we all meet up in Kansas City."

"I'll see ya in Kansas City."

"Later."

Provenzano hung up and disappeared with Randazzo from the airport. The last passenger boarded the plane. Almost the last passenger. Randy and Tracey were still at the opposite end of the airport. Strangely, Randy developed a serious case of diarrhea after eating a greasy hamburger with a pile of greasy cheddar fries. The ticket agent announced the final call for TWA Flight number 2309. Tracey waited with impatience outside the men's restroom. Their carry-on luggage were shoved against the wall. Restless couldn't hardly describe how Tracey felt after waiting for Randy to discharge his body waste.

"Randy!" Tracey yelled. "What are you doing inside the bathroom?"

"Taking a dump," Randy responded from behind an echoing restroom stall.

"We're going to miss our plane!" Tracey yelled once again, her face up to the door. She refused to be left behind in New Orleans.

"Give me another minute or two," Randy pleaded, trying to finish up.

"We don't have another minute or two."

"I'm sorry, Tracey, but—."

"I don't want to be stranded here in New Orleans!" Tracey clearly defied. "I have to get back to work tomorrow morning."

"So do I."

The hatch to the TWA jumbo jet was closed. The huge aircraft moved away from the airport. Pilots prepared to make their race down the runway. Randy stormed out of the bathroom and sprinted down the aisle towards gate seven. Angrily, Tracey followed in pursuit with her small duffel bag slinging against her leg. The ticket agent for TWA sadly told them that they'd missed their plane.

"Shit, Randy!" Tracey exploded. "See what you made us do!"

Anger popped through the pores of Tracey like mortal sweat. The glare of fury burned through her shifting eyes.

"Forgive me, Tracey," Randy graciously apologized. "But, what was I to do?"

"I'll tell you!" Tracey fumed, pointing her wavering finger in Randy's face. "You could've easily used the bathroom on the fucking plane."

"But, I couldn't hold it any longer."

"But my ass!"

"Why don't you just shoot me and get it over with?"

"Please, don't tempt me, Randy."

"You're acting as though no one can't make a mistake."

Belligerently, Tracey stepped around Randy to move up to the TWA ticket counter. "What time does the next flight leave for Kansas City, Missouri?"

"Two o'clock tomorrow afternoon," the agent told Tracey.

"Are you sure?"

The ticket agent thoroughly checked her list of scheduled flights. "There're no flights leaving New Orleans for Kansas City any sooner."

"Could you check again?"

"Sorry ma'am, but unfortunately, there aren't any flights departing from here any sooner."

Tracey rushed up to Randy with her finger pointed at the center of his face. "Look at what you've done!"

"I can't believe that you're acting like this," Randy responded defensively.

"We're going to have to sleep in the airport tonight."

"Something good will turn out of this," Randy expressed with optimism.

He shot a big smile over to Tracey.

"What!" Tracey ruffled. "What good can come out of being left in New Orleans?"

"Don't know, but something."

Given her choice, Tracey wouldn't have had anything to do with Randy.

Chapter 51

FIVE MINUTES AFTER pilots informed flight attendants to prepare for takeoff, the TWA Boeing 747 zoomed down the runway at record speed, lifting off the ground and on its way to Chicago. Passengers looked out their windows to view the sights below. The traffic down on Highways 510 and 610 were backed up for blocks. Spectators could see the Louisiana Superdome, Southern University of Louisiana, The Yacht Club, and the swampy mucks of the bayous. The plane had reached an altitude of 12,000 feet. The weather remained sunny after traveling more than 60 miles north of New Orleans.

Inside the center cargo hold, the boxes of acetone and acetylene were heating up. The fiendish plots of Galluccio, the Bernazzoli Brothers, and Fontanello were happening just as planned. The flammable chemicals burned with a raging fire sure to take place. The center cargo section instantly burst into flames. One of the first passengers to notice the virgin roaring blazes was Sheila. During the first few seconds, she sat in her seat frozen as though her eyes had deceived her. No way could this be happening! Inside the cockpit, the pilot and co-pilot noticed their controls going haywire. Unexpectedly, the plane rocked from side-to-side.

The electronic and computerized equipment inside the cockpit weren't giving the correct readings or weren't giving readings at all.

"Did you hear something strange?" the distraught pilot asked.

A rush of heavy fumes crept into the cockpit.

"Sure did," the co-pilot said. "What's happening with the plane?"

"We've lost readings on our navigation and speed!" the pilot panicked.

"And our altitude and engine performance!" the co-pilot confirmed.

"There's nothing showing for our exhaust-gas temperatures and oil pressures."

"My goodness!" the co-pilot worried. "The rotating blades in the turbines must be having strange difficulties."

"Did the mechanics check the gearbox for any electrical problems before we left the airport?" the pilot asked.

"Heavens, we can only hope so."

"We must return to the airport immediately."

"We're all in danger!"

By now, passengers in the cabin were screaming from the very top of their lungs. TWA Flight number 2309 had caught fire. The bellowing flames consumed most of the plane.

"The plane's on fire!" Sheila screamed, a sheet of fright across her face.

Hysterically, she bounced up and down in her seat. One of her worst nightmares took place right before her very eyes.

"We're all going to be burned up!" Sheila cried out.

"Please, try and calm down!" shouted one of the flight attendants. "Everything's going to be okay."

The huge jumbo jet rocked back and forth. The aircraft lost great amounts of momentum. More passengers screamed louder and louder. Watching the hungry flames eat away at the wings of the plane sent them into a wild stir.

Brittany curled up into a fetal position. She watched the rising blazes consume everything in its path. She'd never seen anything like it before. Tears swelled in her eyes while she cowardly stared death right in the face.

"Scotty!" Brittany cried out, jerking him closer to her. "We're going to die, Scotty!"

More wells of tears burst from her gorgeous blue-green eyes.

"We're not going to die, Britt," Scotty encouraged Brittany. "We'll get back on the ground before the fire burns this plane up."

"Scotty! Scotty!" Brittany screamed out twice. "The fire's going to make this plane crash!"

"Please, please, calm down, Britt."

"Hold me, Scotty!"

"We'll get back to the airport safely."

From one end of the cabin to the next, people choked and gasped for air. The toxic fumes were sucked into their mouths and shot straight into their lungs.

"We're trying to get to some oxygen!" a flight attendant yelled to her colleague.

"I can't get to any of the oxygen in the overhead compartments!" her fellow flight attendant yelled back.

"People are choking to death!"

"I'm sorry, but—."

"But what?"

The angry flames made its way into the cabin. A thunderous pop caused the plane to swerve way out of control. Passengers unbuckled their seatbelts and ran wildly around the seats and along the aisles. There was no escaping the roaring blazes which sought to consume anything in its path. Brittany and Scotty held one another rather tight. Their very lives, from all the memories they'd recounted, flashed right before them. A montague of their wrongdoings painted confrontational frames in their minds. Scotty had a wife back in Kansas City that he'd been lying to for quite some time.

Brittany, being the nasty co-conspirator she was, someone who believed that she could brainwash Scotty into leaving his wife to marry her, would never face Nancy Borthwick alive and ask for her forgiveness. An *Angel of Death* appeared before several people aboard the burning TWA flight. The time to depart from their lives had come. Demons sent up from the fiery furnaces of hell came to take those away who hadn't lived a life of righteousness in the eyes of *God*.

Angels sent down from the pearly gates of Heaven came to claim the souls of those who lived lives of purity in the eyes of God. How unfortunate for some to leave destructive flames on Earth, just to be placed in the destructive flames of hell. Four scary looking demons surrounded Brittany and Scotty. The dark ugly figures formed a tight circle around them. Being adulterers, liars, idolators, and fornicators were the sins they would wallow in for much too long.

"Scotty, they've come to get us!" Brittany screamed in excruciating pain.

The demons of hell were ready to take them to their final burning place.

"We deserve another chance!" Scotty pleaded, having already passed over into the next life.

"Don't take us!" Brittany also pleaded.

"Give us a chance to repent!"

The pilot and co-pilot made a final attempt to return to New Orleans International Airport. Tragically, over 80 percent of the giant Boeing 747 burst into flames.

"Fire! Fire! Fire! Fire!" a passenger yelled four times from near the center aisle.

"We're going to die! We're going to die!" yelled another passenger at the end of the aisle.

The plane's electrical, hydraulic, and fuel systems were totally out of the control of the pilot and co-pilot. Passengers could only accept their fate by watching the fire take other passenger's lives or their own lives. The lead flight data controller back at New Orleans International Airport noticed strange occurrences on his radar.

NETWORK OF KILLERS 225

Other controllers at the TRACON facility observed the radar which showed no signs of the plane which had taken off less than 20 minutes ago.

"We've lost Flight 2309," the controller told his group of attentive colleagues.

"Disappeared off the radar?" asked one of the other controllers who stood to the side of the radar monitor.

"Find that to be quite strange," commented a longtime veteran of air traffic controlling.

"Never been any problems with landings or takeoffs here at New Orleans International."

"Think we better radio for help?"

"Yes, I think so."

To radio for help might've been too late. The only thing the pilots and passengers of TWA Flight number 2309 could do was accept their tragic demise. The entire plane burst into huge roaring blazes. More than half died from burns and smoke inhalation. The wide-bodied commercial jumbo jet made a nosedive for the swampy bayous around New Orleans.

By chance, a private pilot had returned from a trip to visit relatives in Baton Rogue. He couldn't believe his eyes. He watched the TWA plane pointing down at an 80 degree angle burst into full flames. Doing aerial manuevers was the furthest from his mind. With his much smaller twin-engine plane, he flew within close distance.

TWA flight number 2309 crashed into the shallow waterways of the world-famous New Orleans bayous. Commandingly, the plane leveled off the rows of cypress trees in its path. Residents nearby heard the explosion and frightfully ran from their bayou residences. Water and dirt splashed every which direction. Most of the plane got swallowed up as a result of the trajectory impact. The hungry scavengers were afforded the opportunity to sink their teeth into some appetizing human flesh.

The muskrats, alligators, snakes, and lizards, they all made their bid to consume the body parts of the victims in the crash. The alligators snatched up human legs and arms, then rushed back to their swampy bayou sanctum to feast. The snakes, lizards, and muskrats, they all nibbled on human intestines, eyeballs, and upper-torsos, scavenging for anything they found delectable. Blood from most of the crash victims made messy red spills across the thick muck and mud in the bayou area. Not one passenger survived the horrific crash. Several more body parts floated around the water, giving wildlife creatures more opportunity to enjoy a meal. Flies, mosquitoes, and fleas, they all swarmed in on open body part wounds to hatch eggs or to suck blood.

Back inside New Orleans International Airport, Tracey felt better about cursing at Randy and pointing her finger in his face. He tried telling her to sit down and calm herself, but she refused to hear a word he spoke. Her belligerency became a supreme annoyance to airport personnel.

Randy somewhat understood her anger. "We're going to get thrown out of this airport and have to catch a Greyhound bus back to Kansas City."

"We're both going to be fired from the IRS," Tracey charged, her nerves shot.

She circled around the chair where Randy sat.

Still, she pointed her finger in his face.

"The IRS will be there when we get back home," Randy explained, calm-voiced. "I don't understand why you're going and getting sore over some piss-ass job."

"Didn't you go to the rules of conduct meeting?" Tracey asked, still worrying herself.

"Sure I did."

"Did you pay attention to the part about attendance?"

"Yes."

"Someone misses too many days, then they're automatically fired."

"But you and I haven't missed too many days."

"We've used up all of our time coming down here to Mardi Gras."

"So."

"We need to be back to work by Monday morning."

"Everything will be alright, Tracey."

A mild hysteria was created among some of the airport personnel and passengers waiting for flights to other destinations. Flight attendants and ticket agents rushed to other sections of the airport.

Randy politely went over to one of the ticket agents for some information about the instant hoopla. "Excuse me, why is everyone losing control here in the airport?"

"TWA flight number 2309 just crashed into the bayous around New Orleans," she answered, lethal doses of fright in her voice.

"The flight going to Chicago, and then on to other cities?" Randy asked.

"Yes sir."

"My girlfriend and I were supposed to be on that plane."

"Good that you weren't."

"And she thought that this was the worst day of our lives."

"Consider yourselves two of the luckiest people in the world."

"As of now, we have a lot to thank *God* for."

Tracey hadn't heard a word they spoke. She stepped up and asked, "Hey, what's going on around this airport? These people are running around here like a bunch of wild beast savages."

Technically, someone would've thought the New Orleans Saints won the Superbowl. The ticket agent had lots of work to do; therefore, strutted the opposite direction.

Randy pulled Tracey closer. Lovingly, he threw his arms around her waist. "Remember me telling you that something good would become of us missing that plane?"

"Yes?" Tracey chanted with sarcasm. "And?"

"And that plane just crashed into the bayous around New Orleans," Randy explained to Tracey, his voice laced with relief.

"Here in New Orleans?"

"Not very far from this airport."

"Seriously, Randy?" Tracey brisked.

"The ticket agent for TWA just told me."

"But—."

"Now you see why I told you that something good would come out of this?"

"Our lives being saved," Tracey strongly exhaled.

"We have a lot to be thankful for."

"We were meant to miss that plane."

"Sure we were."

"Hold me, Randy."

Tears of joy welled up in her eyes. Grunts of relief echoed from inside. Tracey embraced Randy with her arms locked around his waist. Both were happy to have existed in the land of the living. They could've easily perished on the plane along with the others. They fell to their knees to pray to *God* above.

"Heavenly Father, I thank you for causing me and Tracey to miss that TWA flight," Randy prayed as he thanked the supreme being.

"Dear Lord, thank you for stepping in and saving me and Randy from that plane crash," Tracey said, also being worshipful in prayer.

Randy and Tracey took a seat next to one another and held hands. Until they were able to catch a flight to get them back to Kansas City safely, they continued giving praise to *God Almighty*.

Chapter 52

GRAY SKIES WERE LITERALLY cast over the Midwestern cities of Chicago and Kansas City. After family, friends, and associates learned about the devastating crash of TWA flight number 2309, making a nosedive straight into the swampy mucks around the New Orleans' bayous, many were stunned to receive the bad news. Native Kansas Citians and Chicagoans traveled to New Orleans as soon as they received the news. Galluccio, the Bernazzoli Brothers, and a heartless Fontanello, were the chief beneficiaries of the horrific air disaster. Sheila and Brittany were now out of their way. For the time being, their three Mafia families operated in secrecy and with efficiency.

The Teamsters Union meant everything to them. Their grip on the powerful unions remained ironclad. Billions of dollars were at stake. Anyone who stood in their way, they were subject to meet up with a tragic demise. Galluccio and the Bernazzoli Brothers held firm with both women turning up dead in a plane accident. It deflect all suspicions away from their criminal organizations. Fontanello reasoned how the Teamsters Union kept their powerbase absolute for many decades. The goal of Sheila and Brittany having perish from mysterious deaths was accomplished.

The *President of the United States* learned about the tragedy only hours after it happened. Professionally, the Commander-In-Chief asked Transportation Secretary Norman Stakley, and Federal Aviation Administrator, Anthony Caton, to personally inspect the crash site with some of their top personnel staff. Investigators with the National Transportation Safety Board arrived at the scene before nightfall crept upon the steamy and muggy confines of the New Orleans bayous. Airboaters, froggers, and fishermen assisted in efforts to recover visible parts of the TWA aircraft.

"Seems like most of the airplane went under this muck," commented Secretary Norman Stakley, eager to get the investigation underway.

Everyone wore protective clothing while standing in one of the airboats.

"The mud, too," added FAA Administrator Caton.

"This crash site reminds me of a bunch of confetti strewn across a swampy area."

"Or a bunch of garbage that someone just dumped on the ground."

"Gotta be one of the worst air disasters that I've ever seen in my whole years working in transportation."

"Doubt if there are any survivors."

"Have to agree with you, Anthony."

"This was just an absolute, unfortunate tragedy," Secretary Stakley expressed sympathetically.

While in awe, he looked around at the massive bits of airplane parts.

"Hey, Norm, the air traffic controllers said that the plane went off radar ten minutes after takeoff."

"This crash here explains where they were headed."

"Pilot error, you think?" Caton asked his esteemed colleague.

Both experts played the guessing game for the time being.

"Good question."

"Outright mechanical failure?"

"Hard to say right now."

"We probably won't know until the investigation gets underway."

"God rest all of their souls."

"Amen."

The froggers and fishermen stood by to keep the alligators and snakes away until everyone left the scene. They held bayonet-type poles in their hands to poke at the potential scavengers who came close enough to devour remaining human body parts. Camera crews with *ABC*, *CBS*, *NBC*, and *CNN* stood from afar with their equipment in an effort to tape a story for their headquarters in Los Angeles, New York, and Atlanta.

"Okay, I want some of our men to start collecting pieces of the aircraft," Norman Stakley had mandated.

Disgustingly, he and his staff viewed bits and pieces of the wreckage. How disheartingly for the Transportation Secretary to handle such a tragedy.

"Getting to the voicebox might be impossible," Caton said, his eyes attached to human arms and legs. The body parts floated around parts of the site.

"Willing to bet it's buried under all this swamp water."

"The remaining body parts?" asked Caton, someone also left in suspense.

He pointed to an arm with a sparkling diamond ring on the middle finger. A host of legs bobbled nearby.

"The medical examiner's office should take care of that."

A large alligator dove near part of the wingspan to snatch an arm into his powerful jaws. The vicious reptile submerged itself back into the swamps with a human body part to feast on.

One of the fisherman shouted, "Yaaaahhhh! Yaaaahhhh!"

The fisherman poked and poked until the ferocious creatures were driven away. Copperheads and lizards swarmed around the airboats and wreckage in search of a meal.

The same fisherman shouted a second time. "Shewwwwwww! Shewwwwwww!"

The long poles with the razor sharp knives at the tip pierced at the reptiles until they fled.

"How much work can be done before it gets dark?" Caton inquired, the muggy hot weather causing his shirt to soak with sweat.

"Can't do too much with this aviation fuel everywhere," Stakley answered with uncertainty, having grown tired of being at the ugly crash scene.

"Alligators and snakes and lizards are popping up everywhere."

"Whatever's left of any of these bodies under this swamp, they'll finish them off before we find them."

"You're right, Norm."

"Listen, I want all authorized personnel to pick up everything and get it to the lab for investigation. Sometime before the following week ends, I want a report on my desk with details about this crash."

"Bring any equipment here to the site that can pull the other part of this wreckage from the swamp," Caton directed his team of rescuers and investigators. "We'll also need a report from the medical examiner's office concerning any remaining body parts."

The potent aviation fuel sent head rushes to the men closest to the direct site. This indicated that everyone needed to wear protective masks and keep their distance. Published transcripts and records from New Orleans International Airport would reveal there were many passengers aboard TWA Flight number 2309.

Chapter 53

FROM THE SECLUDED confines of the exclusive *Pendergast Mansion*, one of the most important Mafia meetings in the history of the Teamsters Union was due to take place. International Brotherhood of Teamsters Union President, Mason Shellenberger, prepared himself for one of the biggest moves of his illustrious career. Representing interest for the New Orleans family's piece of the mighty Teamsters Union was Stefano "Tuffy" Fontanello, and his top union official, Carl *"The Brains"* Bernstein. To put things in proper perspective, Bernstein was a handsome, sharp-dressed, smooth-talking, and quite intellectual man with extraordinary business skills.

Often compared to one another by their bosses, Shellenberger and Bernstein possessed phenomenal business skills. Fontanello and Bernstein caught the first available flight out of New Orleans to Kansas City to attend the meeting they'd yearned to be a big part of. Galluccio and the Bernazzoli Brothers were ecstatic to have them on their side. An engulfment of sheer power was created in the conference room. What did the cunning Mafia bosses of Chicago, Kansas City, and New Orleans all have in common? The Teamsters Union. Their motto remained: *The bigger the enterprise, the bigger the payoff.*

The dignitaries invited to the elaborate *Pendergast Mansion* were made to feel right at home.

"Men, your presence at this meeting is greatly appreciated," Galluccio spoke, gravel-voiced. "As always, I thank Carmine and Mikey Bernazzoli of the Chicago Outfit for helping me to arrange this crucial meeting. I thank Tuffy Fontanello and his Teamsters representative, Carl Bernstein, for coming in from New Orleans to be a big part of our future plans. It goes without saying, that it is an honor, as well as a privilege, to have Mason Shellenberger present, with him being the man who holds the strings together when it comes to our strength over the Teamsters. We're proud to have had Eddie

Gargotta fly in from Chicago on short moment's notice. When I think of the political muscle that we have access to here in Kansas City and other parts of Missouri, it's a pleasure, once again, to have Joey Weinberg present at this meeting."

Galluccio fired up a fat cigar. He sucked off a couple of strong drags and continued. "And last, we are grateful to Frankie Bonecutter, Bobby Crusher, Louie Calabrese, Bart Gagliano, and some of Tuffy's men down there in New Orleans, for the beautiful piece of work that they did in helping us get rid of the witness and the homicide detective. Men, welcome to the *Pendergast Mansion*."

Carmine Bernazzoli rotated his eyes around the huge conference table. "Men, we are grateful to Tommy for helping to arrange this meeting here at the *Pendergast Mansion*. We all agree, that Tommy remains a man's man. His fierce loyalty and dedication to our families are to be treasured for all times."

Michael Bernazzoli came in to speak behind his brother. "It is through our vision and dedication that we move into the future. We are a united blood brotherhood, and no one will come along and tear down what we've built up. With the FBI agent clipped, and with the witness and the homicide detective gone, we're now ready to move forward."

"Before we get deep into this meeting, I still maintain that we own the Teamsters," Galluccio bolstered, puffing away at his cigar.

"Always have and always will," Michael affirmed, speaking with bold assurance.

"Alright, what do we have first on the table?" Carmine questioned his criminal constituents.

Fontanello, the evil genius of organized crime in New Orleans, spoke with stability. "In my city, we've got the Teamsters under control. We're looking at pulling off one of the biggest deals ever. Right now, my family controls the Farmers International Life Insurance of New Orleans, Baton Rogue, and Shreveport. We also control the Central States and Southeast and Southwest Teamsters Health and Welfare Fund. I have a man posted up in Baton Rogue who's overseeing the International American Life Insurance Company. We're looking to get all the Building Trade Union insurance business in Louisiana."

"To accomplish all of this, Tuffy, aren't we gonna have'ta pass along some hush money?" Galluccio asked, seeing more of the business side.

"I know we're gonna have'ta grease some palms along the way," Carmine insisted.

"We're constantly on the lookout for public officials who'll take the money under the table," Michael returned.

NETWORK OF KILLERS

Carl Bernstein, being Tuffy Fontanello's money man and Teamsters powerhouse, motioned into the ingenuous business discussion. "With the power consolidated between Chicago, Kansas City, and New Orleans, we can exercise considerable influence in both the Teamsters and Longshoremen's Unions. Everyone sitting here in this meeting knows that in order to do this, we must contribute funds to political figureheads here in Kansas City, as well as Chicago and New Orleans. Yes, it's going to take hush money and the greasing of some palms for us to yield this power that we're seeking."

Shellenberger gestured with his arm and spoke with relevancy. "In order for this plan of our's to work in gaining control over the Teamsters Southeast and Southwest Health and Welfare Fund Life Insurance contracts, we'll have to slip the money under the table to the fund's trustees."

"Shell's gotta good point," Galluccio interjected.

"I've been involved with the Teamsters for over 30 years," Shellenberger continued. "In order for us to garner more labor insurance business contracts, we'll have to offer union officials big kickbacks."

"Union officials don't care if we dip our fingers into that bottomless cookie jar," Galluccio drawled. "We're all on the same team when it comes to the Teamsters."

Bernstein thrusted his hand into his briefcase for a stack of papers. "Tuffy suggested that I submit a bid to the New Orleans City Council. With this bid, we're trying to change health insurance coverage for 50,000 thousand employees from Health South to another carrier. The same can be done for Chicago and Kansas City."

"Does that translate into more money going into the pension fund?" Carmine asked.

"Absolutely," Bernstein answered with much assurance. "Here's where we stand. If we can get these major Teamsters funds insurance contracts switched to Mutual Fidelity, I figure it'd be worth three million dollars a month in commissions."

Shellenberger signaled with a grunt over to Bernstein. "For the Teamsters officials in your state, the ones who'd make it possible for the unions to award the contracts to Mutual Fidelity, how much money in kickbacks would have to go into the hands of the officials who'd make it possible?"

"At least a half-a-million dollars a month in kickbacks."

"That's fair, I guess," Shellenberger calculated. "Tommy, Carmine, and Mikey, do you all agree with that?"

"Half-a-million a month is within reasonable boundaries," Carmine said.

"I'd have no problem with a half-a-million a month," Michael said.

"Five-hundred grand a month is fair," Galluccio said.

"This is the big one!" Bernstein applauded. "If we can gain control and keep'a hold on something like this, we're looking to swell our coffers."

"Men, this is going to be the biggest fucking deal ever!" Fontanello cheered. "Two-and-a-half million bucks a month. You can't beat that any day of the week."

"It's a sweetheart of a deal," said Galluccio.

Putting two brilliant Jewish minds together created unspeakable wealth and power.

Carmine stared into the eyes of Bernstein and saw great dollar signs. "With a half-a-million siphoned off to grease the palms of union officials, that leaves two-point-five million. I've always been a man of reason, a man of strong business principles. That two-point-five million left for the Chicago, Kansas City, and New Orleans families, it can be split fairly three separate ways. I figure that the Bernazzoli, Galluccio, and Fontanello families can take eight-hundred grand and some change a piece every month."

"Eight-hundred grand a month is some nice pocket change," Galluccio praised.

"Tuffy, we know that you've got a lot of juice down there in New Orleans," Michael mentioned to his criminal brother. "Our weak brothers from the past in the Chicago and Kansas City families, they've allowed others to reap the harvest from a field where we've planted our seeds of hard work. Now, when I say weak brothers, I'm speaking of the incompetent pukebags who fucked up our operations in Las Vegas. Tommy's Uncle Angie, and our old man, they convinced the Teamsters to turn over big loans to guys to build one casino after another in that fucking desert town."

Michael slammed down a shot of brandy and continued. "They were the men who made the Teamsters what it is today. They were the men who made Las Vegas what it is today. Working class men and women have opportunities they've never dreamed of because of the Teamsters. On his deathbed, our old man promised Tommy's Uncle Angie, that he'd keep the Chicago and Kansas City families tight-knit. We promised that we'd support Tommy every step of the way. Tuffy, every man sitting at this table knows how important the Teamsters is to us. What I'm saying to you, is to make sure you know the people that you're dealing with. There are goddamn stoolies all over the place. Always have been and always will be."

"My brother's right, Tuffy," Carmine concluded. "Be absolutely, 100 percent confident about the men that you're dealing with down there in New Orleans. We have made this *infamia*, these bargaining agreements with these little unknowns in the unions willing to do business with our families. A lot of these scumbags that we're dealing with today are spineless jellyfish, and their blood is about as diluted as watered-down Kool-aid. Tommy's Uncle Angie, and our old man, they were men of honor, men of respect, men of loyalty, and certainly men of vision. If this deals goes smoothly, then we're looking to walk away with our prizes."

Delivering his unique southern Sicilian accent, Fontanello broke in and said, "Before I establish liaisons with anybody in my state, I check out their backgrounds real thoroughly. I pay my men good money to check out their backgrounds, I mean right down to the bare bone. I've never dealt with people who had the potential to become stoolies later on. I can smell those hard asses who become soft asses later on a country mile away. The people in New Orleans, Baton Rogue, Shreveport, and Tunisia, I've dealt with them since the early days."

Fontanello felt exhilarated knowing that Louisiana remained outside the mainstream of American life. To his advantage, he used the separate culture of peculiar traditions and customs and codes of ethics where political corruption was a way of life. He learned what exploiting fear and greed could get him.

"And from the famous words of my old man," Tuffy recited partially. "Three can keep a secret, if two are dead."

Displaying an exuberant ego, Shellenberger turned to ask Fontanello, "Tuffy, don't you control all of Jefferson Parish?"

Using his characteristic impetuosity, Fontanello responded by saying, "I control Jefferson Parish and all of New Orleans."

"What are your means of control?" Galluccio asked.

"I've been with the president of the Jefferson Parish Council for many years. Once these contracts go through, we wouldn't have to grease him too heavy."

"Sometimes, those politicians present us with the biggest problems," Carmine said.

Fontanello grinned as he took a puff from his cigar. "In my state, I'd know better than anyone about them dirty politicians. If you're not careful, they'll take your fucking money, and then they'll tell you good-bye without a kiss. One time, I put ten grand in a guy's pocket who was running for the Louisiana Senate. I ended up hating the motherfucker, because he ended up taking my money and did nothing for me. I believed in him when he was a nobody in my state."

"Your heart's softer than our's, Tuffy," Carmine said. "Had some politician taken our money and then screwed us later, then that would've been grounds for him to be hit."

"We don't play take the money now and fuck us later," Michael asserted. "We're used to dealing with standup type of guys with a solid pair of *cajones* on him."

Galluccio, the Bernazzoli Brothers, and Fontanello all fed off politics. In return, politics fed off them. Either side of the fence aided and abetted one another's growth.

"Politicians want money, just like everybody wants money," Fontanello screeched with contempt. "Anytime a politician goes into office, he's going in there for money. They've got a racket just like we've got a racket."

Talking about dirty politicians only caused Galluccio to get hot under his breath. The dirt they'd done to the citizens, he'd known about it all the time. To his gain, he corrupted his share of Missouri politicians.

"After this operation is up and running, what type of advance share commissions are we looking at?" Shellenberger asked, going deeper into the business aspect.

"At least 50 grand for each family," Bernstein calculated.

"Fifty-grand is not bad for advanced commissions," Carmine gestured.

"Fifty G's is a nice cut," Galluccio said.

"We'd all like to fatten our pockets with an extra 50 grand," Michael broke in.

"Here's our initial plan," Bernstein continued. "We front the money to purchase the insurance companies, slip the payoff money to the union and government officials in order to gain health insurance contracts for the insurance companies, let the money accumulate in the company's accounts, and then siphon off the money."

Shellenberger cut back in. "Now, after siphoning off this three-million bucks every month in commissions, aren't these companies going to be left high and dry?"

"Absolutely not," Bernstein objected. "We'll collect the monthly commissions and move on to more prosperous pastures."

"Wouldn't be wise to invest in these companies and then milk them dry," Carmine said.

Galluccio moved his attention over to Senator Weinberg. As a veteran Missouri Senator, Weinberg possessed a formidable stable of political connections. "Joey, I know that as a senator, you're not involved with *'coonass politics'*. I know that you've got a vast network of powerful acquaintances up there in Washington. You know the secrets and inside stories better than anyone up there in Washington. With this deal about to take flight with Tuffy and his man Bernstein, the deal with the government employee insurance contracts through the Teamsters down there in New Orleans, we'll need you to convince your friends in politics to cooperate with union officials. We don't need the FBI sending anymore of their watchdogs to Kansas City to investigate us. We definitely don't need the U. S. Attorney's Office trying to build anymore cases against us."

Senator Weinberg cast a perpetual grin at Galluccio. "Tommy, when it comes to politics here in Missouri, or politics in Illinois or Louisiana, we're all cut from the same cloth. There's a vast collection of useful, powerful, and potentially dangerous colleagues of mine in Washington who exercise considerable influence in every aspect of government. These colleagues of mine have arms of influence that reaches all over America. But, in order for their arms to stretch to the max, there's a need for campaign contributions and special favors."

"In other words, if we wash their backs, they'll wash our backs?" Galluccio asked.

"Sure."

"We can't leave behind a trail for the government to pick up a scent," Galluccio feared.

"None of my colleagues in politics leave dirty trails behind."

"Good."

"Either way, we're all playing a high-stakes game."

Galluccio gestured with a nod over to the Bernazzoli Brothers. "Carmine and Mikey, with your permission and blessings, we're ready to get this operation up and running."

Fontanello exchanged grim eye contact with the Bernazzoli Brothers. "Under your guidance and stewardship, Carmine and Mikey, we'd like to get started with our plans. We're looking at peeling off some really big money here."

Shellenberger and Bernstein barely kept their composure. The brilliant Jewish financial wizards were dying to catapult their plans into action.

Since Carmine's words were absolute among the top echelon of Teamsters leadership throughout America, he spoke with words of satisfactory agreement. "Three-million bucks a month is a sweetheart deal. You're right, Tuffy, this might turn out to be one of the biggest fucking deals ever. I give my blessings and my permission."

Michael sealed the agreement by saying, "Tuffy, I couldn't have thought of a more clever plan to peel off three-million bucks a month. Like my brother, you have my permission and my blessings."

The meeting ended with a momentum of optimism.

Chapter 54

DON AND HELEN GOLDBERG fell apart after discovering that their only daughter was a victim in the air tragedy down in New Orleans. Much disappointment pumped from their hearts when they learned Brittany had been having an affair with a married man. As a strict Jewish family, they banned extramarital affairs. Finding out Brittany had snuck away from Kansas City to follow Scotty down to Mardi Gras put them in a state of shock. The wealthy couple summoned Nancy Borthwick, now the official widow of Scotty Borthwick, to their palatial home in the exclusive section of Mission Hills, Kansas. Helen showed her hospitality by offering Nancy coffee or juice or soda.

"Nancy, dear," Don mildly purred. "My wife and I invited you to our home to give you some heartbreaking news."

"What news?" Nancy asked, still left in suspense.

Anxiously, she wanted to hear whatever Don had to say.

"Sweetheart, it's not easy telling you this."

"What is it, sir?"

"Our daughter and your husband were having an affair," Don unleashed with civility.

Nancy jumped back on the sofa. She whisked her hand in the air. "Say what!"

"We wanted you to come here to offer you a formal apology."

"Apology my ass!" Nancy dejected. "My husband's dead now because of your freaking daughter."

Helen wormed around Don. She abruptly interjected by saying, "Back your horses up, young lady. You can't necessarily go blaming Brittany for your husband's death."

"Yes, I can!" Nancy blasted.

"No, you can't!" Helen blasted back.

Nancy belted out a strong hiss as she grinded her teeth together. "Your daughter was nothing but a whore, a slut, a bitch, and a lowlife. She probably seduced my husband into taking her to Mardi Gras down in New Orleans!"

Don moved around Helen to bombard his way back into the fiery debate. "How dare you use such obscenities to describe our daughter! She was no saint, but for chrissake, she deserves more respect than that."

"Scotty and I planned on having kids one day," Nancy dreamed, still crying overtime as a result of the air tragedy. "My whole life is going to be miserable without him."

Helen handed several tissues over to Nancy. She dried up the quick rush of tears.

"At this point, we're not sure who invited who to the Mardi Gras festivities," Don said. "All we know, is that you're without a husband, and we're without a daughter. Let's not go throwing stones at one another during trying times like these."

"Scotty never gave me any reason to believe that he was cheating."

"Honey, we're sorry," Helen apologized, trying her hardest to console Nancy.

"Brittany's been known for doing scandalous things," Nancy accused their daughter.

"Such as?" Don asked, not happy with her abrupt accusation.

"Such as seducing all kinds of police officers and detectives on the force."

"That's not true!" Helen charged, rising from the sofa to stand over Nancy.

"She was nothing but trouble to anyone whoever came into contact with her."

"Not true!" Don gravely rejected.

"My husband would still be alive had it not been for your daughter," Nancy blamed.

"Nobody's in a position to point the finger at the other party," Helen reasoned.

"Maybe that explains why he never answered his cell phone."

"We do know that they carried on an affair for quite some time," Don acknowledged.

"You know, I must've called Scotty a thousand times," Nancy recalled. "After awhile, I started getting worried and believing that something bad had happened to him."

"Did you know that your husband was going down to New Orleans?" Helen asked.

"Had no clue," Nancy commented. "Scotty told me that he had to leave for New York for a few days to take care of some business."

Don stood aside long enough to hear Nancy rant and rave about how Brittany was to blame for the tragic death of her husband. She approached the tragedy thinking selfishly.

"The only man that I ever loved is gone," Nancy wept, still drying away her tears.

Helen added to her statement by saying, "The only daughter that we had is gone, too."

"Scotty was my world."

"Brittany was our world, too," Don added.

"My life is gonna be so empty without him."

"Honey, we understand," Helen said.

"Do you?"

"Dear," Don said, his tone quite calm. "Let's put the past behind us now. I can understand you being upset and pointing the finger at everyone. But you can't go around blaming people for what happened. My wife and I called you to our home to break the disheartening news to you. We must admit, it wasn't easy telling you that your husband and our daughter were having an affair. We are here today to apologize for the actions of our daughter. And, yes, there was no excuse in the world for Brittany sneaking away on vacation to have a secret rendezvous with a married man. Also, there was no excuse for your husband sneaking away to have a weekend escapade with our daughter."

Helen rested her hand on the lap of Nancy and said, "Now is the time for us to pull together and hope the investigators can find out why the plane crashed in the first place."

"You have to understand, Mr. and Mrs. Goldberg," Nancy chimed in, sounding weary-voiced. "Even if they do find out why the plane crashed, they're still saying that none of the bodies are going to be found. I won't even be able to have a decent burial for my husband."

"And we won't be able to have a decent burial for our daughter," Don reciprocated.

"Scotty's only a memory," Nancy said.

"They're still pulling a lot of that wreckage out of the bayous around New Orleans," Helen said.

"The *Kansas City Times* said that most of that plane is still buried under all that swampy mud and muck stuff."

"True," Don confirmed. "But, we trust that they will be able to dig deep enough to pull the rest of the plane out."

"Again, Mr. Goldberg," Nancy intervened. "The *Kansas City Times* stated that there were many alligators, snakes, muskrats and lizards living in those swamps. These are the animals that actually eat human beings."

"To my knowledge, they don't eat human beings," Don investigated.

"I studied biology and microbiology during my four years in pre-med at KU," Nancy explained to the Goldbergs. "I know that these are scavengers who feed on human flesh."

"State your point, young lady," Don insisted.

"By the time they find anything, the scavengers would've devoured them."

"Can't you be optimistic for once in your life?" Helen said with coercion.

"Not when I know my husband's never coming back."

"Neither is our daughter," Don replied.

Nancy had gotten an overdose of watching *CNN* on cable television. She watched one journalist after another from *ABC*, *NBC*, and *CBS* speak out about the air tragedy. News stations in New Orleans flooded the airwaves.

Nancy took a deep breath. Her emotions were tangled into tight knots. "Mr. And Mrs. Goldberg, did you know that your daughter was assigned to that homicide case involving the killing of that FBI agent?"

"FBI agent?" Don shrugged. "What are you talking about?"

"The KCPD assigned her as a lead homicide detective in that case," Nancy disclosed.

"The agent killed in the *Westport District*?" Helen asked.

"So, you know what I'm talking about?" Nancy cued to familiarize the Goldbergs.

"Of course," Don nodded. "That's all Brittany ever talked about."

"Do you know why that FBI agent was in Kansas City?"

"Were we supposed to know?" Don inquired, trying to unravel the mystique of it all.

A sheet of incisiveness coated the eyes of Nancy. "Mr. Goldberg, the FBI agent killed that night down in the *Westport District* had been sent down from Washington, D.C. to investigate the Teamsters Union and the Mafia. The government's been putting pressure on the Mafia here in Kansas City and in other cities around America."

"Where'd you get your information from?" Don asked.

"After finding out about my husband being killed in that plane crash, I decided to do some investigating of my own. Besides, I do read the newspaper and watch the news. Your daughter might've been in danger and didn't know it."

"You've crossed the line, young lady," Helen imposed, speaking confrontational.

"Not hardly, Mrs. Goldberg."

"Certain things are confidential," Don said. "People are entitled to their privacy."

"Here's the conclusion that I've drawn," Nancy returned. "The same people who killed the FBI agent that night down in Westport, might've been the same people who sabotaged that plane leaving New Orleans."

"Heavens!" Don splintered. "What makes you think someone sabotaged that plane? The FAA and the NTSB haven't even done their full investigations."

"Planes don't fall out of the sky for nothing," Nancy resolved, being quite bullheaded.

"Accidents happen all the time."

Nancy grunted and locked intense eye contact with Don. "Mr. Goldberg, the paper said that the FBI agent was killed as a result of a random street robbery. None of his valuables were taken from him. When the police got to the crime scene, his watch, rings, and wallet were still on him. Why would two men kill an FBI agent in the *Westport District* on a Saturday night in the midst of hundreds of other people?"

"Why?" Don questioned her.

"To keep the agent from finishing his investigation."

"Where'd you obtain all of this information?"

"Using common sense. Plus, at KU, I majored in biology, and I minored in law."

"What's this got to do with our daughter?" Helen asked.

"The same thing that it has to do with one of the witnesses."

"Where's this going?" Don wondered.

"There was a witness who got a close look at the two men who killed the agent," Nancy cleverly imparted. "Coincidentally, that witness was on the same plane with Scotty and your daughter Brittany."

"How'd you acquire that information?" Don examined.

"I saw the roster of names printed in the *Kansas City Times*."

"And that very witnesses' name was printed along with the others?"

"Yes, it was."

"What point are you driving at?"

"Someone sabotaged that plane, Mr. Goldberg," Nancy theorized. "Someone went inside and altered some things around the engine. Also, I believe that someone placed hazardous components under that plane to make it catch on fire. Mr. Goldberg, I have a master's in biology and microbiology, with a minor in law. I'm not a stupid woman in any sense of the word. Somebody, people we'll probably never find out about, wanted your daughter and that witness out of the way."

"Are you speaking out of anger, or are you speaking from straight facts?"

"My belief is that powerful people connected with Mafia characters did something to bring down that plane."

Helen motioned back into the inconclusive debate. "Understand something, young lady, that there's no more Mafia left here in Kansas City. I'm old enough to know that when the government sent all of those Mafia guys to jail from Chicago, Kansas City, Cleveland, and Milwaukee, those same men from around the midwest who'd been skimming all that money from those Las Vegas casinos, that signaled the demise of the Mafia. You don't even hear about those men anymore."

"Mrs. Goldberg, you're so naïve," Nancy clucked. "The Mafia is alive and well and operating in most cities around this country. If you think they don't exist anymore, then you must not have access to substantial information."

Don signaled over to Nancy. "I used to hear stories about Angelo Galluccio all the time. I'd read stories about him and other Mafiosos going to war down in the River Quay section of Kansas City for control of turf and businesses. I'd read stories about how the Chicago Mafiosos would send Kansas City Mafiosos out to Las Vegas to bring back money skimmed from those hotel casinos. My associates would tell me stories about the Italian hoods who used to torture men and throw them into the trunks of their cars. Stories about gangsters putting cement blocks around the feet of other gangsters, and then dumping them into the *Missouri River*, got around town real fast."

"Let's look at this thing deeper, Mr. Goldberg," Nancy asserted. "The FBI agent sent to Kansas City to investigate the Teamsters was taken out by the mob. The Teamsters is billions of dollars, a goldmine with a guardianship of vicious watchdogs. The agent was a threat and had to be taken out. Your daughter and that witness were threats and had to be taken out. If anybody else becomes a threat, they, too, can be taken out just like the rest."

"Can you back up any of these allegations with facts?" Don wanted to know.

"Not necessarily."

"You've allowed your emotions to override your logical thinking."

"I've added the missing pieces to the puzzle," Nancy assured Don.

"The Galluccio Mafia family ceases to exist."

"Says who?" Nancy opposed.

"Says news sources."

"Believe what you want."

"The former mob boss of Kansas City, Angelo Galluccio, he died some years ago after leaving the Federal Penitentiary in Springfield, Missouri," Don outlined for Nancy.

"But his criminal legacy didn't die," Nancy pressed on. "Mr. Goldberg, the truth is yet to come out. Maybe I can't go blaming your daughter for the death of my husband. One thing's for sure, is that the government will find that that TWA flight didn't catch on fire while in mid-air and just fall out of the sky."

"And you're pointing the finger at the Mafia?"

"Not directly."

"Let's say we do find out the plane was sabotaged. Will any names start surfacing?"

"It's possible through governmental investigations."

"Pointing the finger in the wrong direction, is not going to bring Brittany back to us, nor is it going to bring Scotty back to you."

"It wouldn't hurt to do some inquiring on our own."

"True."

"Ask yourself this question, Mr. Goldberg. Did the *River Quay Wars* of the 1970s really ever end?"

"With that agent investigating the Mafia and the Teamsters here in Kansas City, it makes you wonder, did the *River Quay Wars* ever end?"

Nancy ended her visit at the Goldberg estate with cups of hot chocolate and a good television program.

Chapter 55

THE *NEW YORK TIMES* AND the *Los Angeles Times* both ran lengthy articles in special sections of their newspapers about the New Orleans air tragedy. The President of the United States held a brief news conference offering his condolences to the victims' families and friends. The President assured every one of them efforts would be made to bring forth findings as to why the TWA Boeing 747 plunged into the bayous around New Orleans. Kansas City and Chicago were the two main cities which joined together after the air tragedy occurred two weeks prior in New Orleans.

Crowds of people from Cook County out of Chicago, and people from Jackson County out of Kansas City, met with counselors and federal authorities at an undisclosed location inside New Orleans International Airport. More than 400 men and women crowded into a large room designed for conference purposes. Open microphones and chairs were placed for everyone in attendance. Before a stunned and silent audience, Federal Aviation Administrator, Anthony Caton, posed at a refined stance with the microphone rested to the side of his mouth. *BAD NEWS!* Those two eery words seemed to echo through the minds of the crowd before Caton said one word.

"Thank you all for coming down here to New Orleans," Administrator Caton began. "The fatal plunge of TWA Flight 2309 was an unprecedented tragedy in America. We've literally spent two weeks examining every piece of the wreckage, and since we've launched this very intense investigation, our findings weren't that of an electrical fire. Top FAA and NTSB specialists found that the transportation of hazardous materials caused the flight to go down into the bayous around New Orleans."

The room filled itself with chants of "oooooohs" and "aaaaaahs". Disappointment, heartbreak, anger, retaliation, those were the immediate emotional responses of the victims' relatives and friends. Don Goldberg made his presence known by springing out of his seat.

"My daughter died on that flight!" Don implicated, his voice coarse. "You mean to tell me that some jackasses, some incompetent nitwits, weren't doing their jobs right?"

"Not exactly, sir," Caton defended. "Our investigators and authorities are viewing this tragedy as an honest mistake."

"Exactly what were these hazardous materials?"

"Containers of acetone and acetylene."

"You don't transport dangerous chemicals like that on an airplane!" Don thundered. "I'm no expert here, but acetone and acetylene can easily catch fire from the slightest overheating or spark."

"I agree, sir."

"Where did these chemicals come from?"

"A defunct aircraft maintenance company."

"Could you please explain the exact nature of the crash?"

Caton spoke in the calmest voice. "FAA and NTSB experts learned that the crash was caused by a fire that started in the aircraft's center cargo compartment, thereby igniting the containers of acetone and acetylene."

"Stupid jerks!" Don fired off.

"Sir, our apologies go out to you and everyone here who lost their loved ones."

"Didn't personnel here at the airport know that they were transporting hazardous materials?"

"Honestly, no one claimed to have known the containers were aboard."

"Why is that?" Don asked authoritatively.

Angry and in disarray, he wanted to get to the core of the two-week-old air tragedy.

"The containers of acetone and acetylene were improperly secured, labeled, and packaged before they were loaded aboard the TWA flight," Caton explained.

"Who's going to jail for the deaths of all these innocent people, including my daughter?" Don instigated, wanting immediate justice.

Anthony Caton pointed over to Transportation Secretary Norman Stakley. He moved aside to allow him air time up at the podium.

Secretary Stakley explained everything in full details. "Sir, Louisiana State Prosecutors have already charged this aircraft maintenance company with a 135 counts of second and third-degree manslaughter, in addition to 20 counts of the unlawful transportation of hazardous materials. We assure you that these people will be punished for their crimes, and the proper authorities will continue to work towards future safety precautions."

"Well, you don't say," Don smarted off.

"Our condolences go out to the family and friends of the victims," Stakley apologized.

"Your condolences aren't going to bring any of them back."

"Sir, we're terribly sorry."

"The goddamn crash was completely, absolutely, positively, and most assuringly preventable!" Don roared, his voice crackled from much anger. "This was not an accident like many other crashes in flight history. This was simply a lowdown dirty crime!"

Don had associated with flight experts over the years. He had every reason to be upset. The only daughter he'd fathered wasn't coming back to him.

"Sir, I'm going to ask you to watch your language," Stakley atoned. "We couldn't agree with you more. In fact, Orleans Parish State Attorney, Marilyn Steinberg, calls this tragedy totally careless on the part of the aircraft maintenance company."

"Who exactly will be doing jail time?" Don boldly asked. "Hell, if I was given my choice, I'd give everyone involved the death penalty."

By now, the conference room came alive. People got more involved. Relatives and friends nodded their heads and chanted words of absolute agreement with Don.

Stakley pushed the mircophone closer to his mouth. His voice was heard clearer. "Once again, state charges were filed only against the company, and not necessarily against the executives on the board."

"What are you telling me and everyone else here?" Don blurted out.

"No certain individuals will be facing jail time on any of those counts."

"We want justice!" Don felt the need to shout out once again.

He shot a pointed finger up at Stakley and Caton and other government authorities.

"And justice will prevail," Stakley pledged to the attendees.

"Some people working here at this airport committed a crime, and they should be punished severely for those very crimes."

Stakley cleared his throat, straightened his tie, tilted his head to the microphone, and then told everyone, "We hereby inform you that the U.S. Attorney's Office announced a 30 count federal indictment against this aircraft maintenance company and five former employees of New Orleans International Airport."

"Were those workers FAA licensed mechanics? Were the ground crew qualified to transport proper cargo onto planes?" Don wanted to know.

"Yes, they were."

Don also heard about the mechanical failure the plane had experienced minutes after takeoff. "Were these men contracted through TWA, or were they contracted through a private sector?"

"To our knowledge, they were contracted through the private sector," Caton said.

"What do these federal charges include?"

"First, conspiring to make false statements to the FAA," Caton rendered. "Second, using falsified documents related to the removal of acetone and acetylene from TWA planes. We mentioned earlier that they are also being charged with violations of federal regulations regarding the transportation of hazardous materials, for mishandling, mislabeling, and mispacking the containers of acetone and acetylene."

Nancy Borthwick sprung from her seat out of nowhere. Furiously, she shouted, "How much time are those bastards looking at?"

Caton spoke into the microphone. "Each count is punishable by ten years of prison and a one-million dollar fine."

"Is that all?" Nancy snoozed. "They should die in the gas chamber or the electric chair or before a firing squad. You should kill all of them with lethal injection or hang them."

"Calm down, ma'am," Caton spoke, trying to console a distraught Nancy. "This company is facing approximately 20 million dollars in fines and restitution. These individuals are looking at at least up to 60 years in prison, with more than three million dollars in fines and penalties if convicted as a result of the federal charges."

"I also lost my husband in that crash," Nancy explained, quite obtrusively. "These bullshit indictments will never bring a sense of justice to any of us. You're just trying to pacify us with a bunch of crap that the government fed to you. We're not leaving New Orleans until you all give us some straight answers."

Nancy didn't have the courage to tell everyone that Scotty was a liar, a cheater, a manipulator, a womanizer, and a man who let his dick get him into trouble.

"I'd like to know more about the mechanical failure of the plane," Nancy demanded.

"No one was aware of mechanical failure," Caton openly denied.

"The investigative reports from the FAA and the NTSB said that there were some faulty wiring in the engine and turbines."

"Miss, you've been reading the wrong reports."

"C'mon, Mr. Caton, these reports are a matter of public information. That TWA flight had experienced mechanical problems before it caught fire."

"What are you implying?"

"I'm implying that pilot error had nothing to do with the plane's engine failure. Someone sabotaged that plane, Mr. Caton."

"Those are words of absolute absurdity," Caton rejected.

"Really?" Nancy pressed on. "The faulty wiring of the plane's engine system, along with the placing of the hazardous chemicals, were the work of hijackers or terrorists."

"There's no hard proof to back up any of those allegations."

"Terrorists wanted that plane to drop out of the sky."

"The crashing of TWA Flight number 2309 wasn't the work of hijackers or terrorists," Caton steadfastly denied.

"Did your staff retrieve the voicebox?" Nancy asked, still thrusting forward.

"They did."

"And their discoveries?"

"Definitely not the work of hijackers or terrorists."

"Air traffic controllers from the New Orleans airport reported that the plane went off radar ten minutes after takeoff."

"We're aware of that."

"Were you also aware that a witness to the killing of an FBI special agent back in Kansas City was on that plane?"

"No, my staff and myself weren't aware of that."

"Were you also aware that a homicide detective with the KCPD was assigned to that case, someone who investigated the killing of the same FBI special agent?"

"No, we weren't."

"Well, now you're aware of this valuable information."

Don took command of the meeting once more. "The death of my daughter and the others was murder. Seems like they were forced against a wall with guns put to their heads. We'll never have any sense of closure knowing that none of our people will be coming back to us."

"Our sympathy and heartfelt apologies go out to each and everyone of you," Caton repented, his blood tainted with remorse.

Don stared around the conference room with eyes of sole vengeance. "Whether these people are indicted, whether they are convicted, or if they spend the rest of their lives in jail, even if they receive the death penalty, none of us will find any true closure."

"We assure you that justice will prevail," Caton said as his way to pacify everyone.

"This process is ongoing and we'll just have to learn to live with it."

Stakley moved up to speak into the microphone. "FAA and NTSB specialists are working around-the-clock to make sure tragedies like these won't happen again."

"How?" Nancy asked, her level of fury rising to unhealthy levels.

"By requiring all commercial airlines to have fire detection and suppression equipment in their cargo holds."

"You're only millions of dollars short and hundreds of lives late," Nancy accused.

"Hey, we're not the bad guys here," Caton said, wanting to defend his party.

"Airlines should've already had fire detection and suppression equipment in their cargo holds," Don exposed, using his own accusatory tactics.

"I agree, sir," Stakley said.

"There were babies and children on that plane," Don recalled too well.

Having lost his only daughter, a stream of disappointment pumped straight to his heart.

"We are aware of that," Caton replied.

"Their futures are now washed down the drain."

"Sad, but true," Stakley said.

"Our government needs to pay closer attention to who they hire inside and outside of these airports around the country," Nancy hurdled back in. "You're dealing with human lives here, and we all know that you can't give a life back just like that."

"New federal regulations will propose a rule that will ban the transporting of hazardous flammable chemicals in its cargo holds," Stakley cited to everyone.

Stakley cleverly devised ways to come back with comments, suggestions, or critical innuendos brought on by Don or Nancy or any of the other attendees.

"Mr. Caton, could you explain published information about the gear box on the plane?" Don asked.

"Sure can, sir," Caton replied. "There's no concern at this time that the engine played a part in the crash."

"My wife and I were handed reports that the gear box had malfunctioned and electrical faults may have occurred after the plane had taken off."

"NTSB spent over a week examining the wreckage and there's no real proof of this."

The meeting suddenly came to an abrupt end. Further questions had to be taken up later with FAA and NTSB officials.

While standing at the muddy banks of the New Orleans bayous, FAA administrator Anthony Caton walked over to Don and Nancy and the others to offer more words of assurance. A mind-boggling and choking stratum of grief closed in on the people standing around the humid swamp, a place where fleas and mosquitoes became rather bothersome.

"A special fire and explosion team is part of an ongoing investigation at our headquarters in Washington, D.C.," Caton explained to the grieving crowd. "We have several hazardous material specialists interviewing the men who handled the containers of acetone and acetylene before they were loaded onto the plane here in New Orleans. Other than that, there's not much more we can do at the present time."

"My wife and I, along with others, trust that justice will fall into the hands of the proper jurisdiction," Don spoke with reason. "We trust that we will all go on with our lives and not let bitterness consume us."

"Our President of the United States will be sending all of you letters to offer his condolences during your times of grief."

Nancy stepped up to Caton smashing her tears. "Mr. Caton, once your investigation is complete, your staff will find that this crash was the work of a bunch of felonious thugs. You'll understand why I've become this conspiracy-driven enthusiast. You'll understand why I'm so fanatical about finding out who was really behind this plane crashing."

"Yes, we're hoping to bring the truth forward."

"We thank our beloved President for his thoughts and prayers," Don said.

Officers with the New Orleans Police Department escorted everyone to a levee near the precise location where the TWA Boeing 747 plunged deep into the bayous. Many cried endless tears. Many sobbed terribly for the flesh and blood who were now part of their distant memories. Others interlocked their hands in prayer as they watched their reflections off the wavering water.

"We're never going to see our Brittany again!" Helen wept uncontrollably.

She fell into the arms of Don and planted her head into his chest.

"Honey, she's in a better place now," Don assured his wife. "She's in Heaven smiling down on us with the angels."

"Our only baby girl is gone now!"

"We'll have to honor her since she was our only daughter."

"God, I'm going to miss her so much."

"We're all going to miss her."

Everyone left the crash site grieving in the arms of their loved ones. Stakley and Caton followed behind them feeling their pain. Kansas City and Chicago and other surrounding areas were the destinations they returned to before the end of the day.

Chapter 56

CHEMI-TECH AIRCRAFT Maintenance Company Attorney Ernest Fletcher blew off enough steam to put an overheated boiler room to shame. In a soundproof room, he and the five grounds crewmen held responsible for loading the boxes of acetone and acetylene into the cargo section of the plane, all met with Special Prosecutor Matthew Silverstein from the Southern District of Louisiana. Bringing all of these men together in a small office, conveniently located in the heart of downtown New Orleans, only created a hostile environment. Proving guilt or innocent was the core of their discussion.

"We understand that these families desire to seek vengeance and retribution," Ernest said to Prosecutor Silverstein. He paced around the office wearing a cheap tight suit. "But I have to question, why are you guys pointing the finger directly at these five men? Why is the news media and newspapers here in New Orleans slinging mud all over them?"

"It's simple," Matthew Silverstein started. "These five groundsmen here in this office are guilty of a crime. They violated federal regulations by transporting the boxes of hazardous materials."

"Why aren't you all looking at TWA or the FAA?" Ernest began to wonder.

"Neither of them put the flammable chemicals aboard the plane," Matthew explained in his own plain terms. "That's the issue that we're dealing with here."

"Bullshit!" Ernest blustered. "C'mon, Matt, there's absolutely no evidence, whatsoever, of any willful or criminal intent to violate the law or cause this terrible tragedy. We're not going to stand by idled like a bunch of patsies and be made into some criminal scapegoats."

"Criminal scapegoats who didn't follow federal regulations," Matthew boldly accused.

"You're making things difficult, Matt."

"Many people are dead because of these men's carelessness."

"These men here are well-intentioned individuals," Ernest spoke up, pointing candidly at the five ground crew workers. "They made honest mistakes that actually pale in comparison with the failures of the FAA, NTSB, and TWA in this crash. The families can clearly see that, Matt, and a jury will also agree with what I'm saying."

"TWA and airport personnel properly supervised the maintenance contractors and the contractor's procedures."

"We're aware of that."

"These five men did not properly prepare and package the boxes of acetone and acetylene," Matthew closely examined. "You can't lag behind in your jobs when it comes to dealing with human lives."

At this point in the hostile debate, everyone present, other than Matthew himself, detected that he had breath bad enough to knock someone into next week.

"Yes, but the FAA failed to adequately regulate airlines like TWA," Ernest rebounded with professional technicalities. "Also, TWA failed to require smoke detection and suppression systems in their Boeing cargo compartments."

"Yes, Boeing's responsible for smoke detection and suppression."

"Damn right they are!" Ernest brisked.

"Ernie, there must be some type of accountability for this unimaginable huge loss of human life," Matthew indicted. "These men acted irresponsible, and now they have to be held responsible."

Carl Morrison was one of the five men who set back and analyzed the dramatization between Matthew and Ernie. He felt compelled to bombard into their discussion. As a tall, skinny, and balding man, he had conservatively average looks. Carl was a 24 year airport veteran who worked his hands raw as a groundsman to do a good job for New Orleans International Airport. Was this how they showed their appreciation with these accusations?

"Have you ever thought that this might be the work of some terrorist?" Carl had imposed. "Nobody ever took that into consideration."

"That's absurd!" Matthew quickly rejected. "People of that calibre operate in more occupied terrorist ways."

A low-key hazardous material specialist gestured with his hand and said, "Also, a terrorist would never load boxes of acetone and acetylene in the cargo section of a plane. Explosives have always been their tools when it comes to bringing a plane out of the air."

"Did you all consider the theft of the uniform truck?" Carl was eager to ask.

Carl felt he and his four co-workers were victims of a conspiracy. All five had good reason to believe they'd been set up.

"What uniform truck?" Matthew asked. "You're opening up the gate to a herd of raging bulls."

"I read the paper, too," Carl sprung back. "The truck that carried a shitload of airline employee uniforms that were meant for the ground crew like us was hijacked. Uniforms for people who handle cargo, aircraft maintenance, airline ramp employees, and baggage handlers, they were all stolen off that truck."

"You're dreaming, Carl."

"Am I?"

"Sorry, but stolen uniforms have nothing to do with the genocidal death of over a hundred people," Matthew incriminated.

Eagerly, he'd been ready to step into court and mount a vigorous prosecution against the five men.

"We weren't even scheduled to work that day," Carl exposed. "We were called to work at the last minute. In fact, when myself and the rest of the crew arrived at work, there were already boxes stored into the cargo section on that TWA flight."

"Your names were on the list of scheduled workers for that day," Matthew proved.

"Says who?" Carl rejected.

"Says your supervisor."

"At what time?"

"Starting at eight o'clock a.m."

"Bullshit!" Carl scoffed. "We didn't get to work until two o'clock that afternoon."

"Time-in sheets don't lie, Mr. Morrison."

"Something fishy is going on here."

"The proof's on record, sir," Matthew said, grinning at everyone in the room.

"We weren't even timed in until two p.m."

Carl's four other co-workers shook their heads in absolute agreement. The five cargo handlers refused to set aside and be made into scapegoats. Matthew failed to realize the entire ordeal was a setup.

"I'm taking this matter up with the union," Carl threatened.

"Union?" Matthew questioned, a crook who was in one the conspiracy.

"That's right, I'm a full member of Teamsters Local 1519."

"Given the circumstances and the severity of this crash, Mr. Morrison, the union wouldn't be able to help you."

"You must don't know the juice that Local 1519 has with New Orleans International Airport. We're a strong union and we stand united as one."

"Are you saying that union officials are willing to go to bat for you?" Matthew asked.

"Damn straight!" Carl verified. "A ground crew had handled the cargo for that TWA flight before we arrived at the airport by two o'clock. We were pawn offs by some scumbags who wanted us to take the blame for that plane crashing. Read between the lines, Prosecutor Silverstein, someone set us up. There are some shitty-dirty politics going on with the people at the front offices there inside New Orleans International."

"Why do you think the union will help you?" Matthew had to know.

"For the same reason they'd help anyone who's a part of their union."

"The TWA plane crashing from the mishandling and the mispackaging of hazardous chemicals is out of the jurisdiction of the union."

"Do you know how powerful the Teamsters Union is?"

"It doesn't matter at this point."

"If I have to, I'll take this matter up with the Teamsters Headquarters in Washington," Carl bolstered. "I'll take it all the way up to the top dogs with the FAA and the NTSB?"

"Good luck," Matthew said in an arrogant fashion.

Being flagrantly distorted with his input, Carl pointed at Ernest and shouted, "Goddammit, impostors were hired in our place! When those boxes were stored onto that plane, we weren't nowhere in sight. I'll bet impostors were hired to kill somebody on that plane."

"Impostors?" Matthew laughed. "Where did you dream up such a fantasy?"

"Did you even check the roster for the list of passengers who were on that plane?"

"With a fine-tooth comb."

"Do you even know if a group of killers wanted somebody dead on that plane?"

Matthew whisked his hand towards Carl. "The thought never occurred to me. Someone deliberately planting an incriminating trail of evidence against your crew of groundworkers is absurd."

"Sir, we're being framed."

The Fontanello Mafia family had long since grabbed control of the unions which handled cargo going in and out of New Orleans International Airport. Virtually, his family gained tight access to security personnel who kept close ties on everyone moving to and from the airport.

"Your crimes are both dispicable and monstrous!" Matthew stormed at Carl.

With no second-guessing, he rested assured that a jury and judge would agree with him.

"Horseshit, Matt!" Ernest recoiled. "Your upcoming prosecuting tactics are a bunch of ridiculed baloney and psychobabble bullshit!"

The soundproof room had faltered to silence. The innocence of five men were at stake.

"Myself and my co-workers were told to take the day off, and that we would be paid for time and a half," Carl explained to Matthew. "Had either of us known that those boxes contained any flammable chemicals, they would've never been put into that cargo hold. To the best of my knowledge, the boxes were unmarked, which says that none of us knew what was inside."

The hazardous materials specialist spoke once again. "During our investigation, we intensely examined parts of the wreckage. We examined parts of the cockpit and a ceiling circuit breaker panel, and possibly the boxes holding the containers of acetone and acetylene. And you're correct, the boxes were not labeled and packaged properly."

"Think a jury will buy that?" Matthew said, still speaking unconvincing.

"It's possible," Ernest intervened, still very much convinced.

Carl propositioned with his arm held high. "Whoever stole those uniforms from that hijacked truck, probably had something to do with that plane bursting into flames. Like I said, Prosecutor Silverstein, I read the *Louisiana Piscayne-Times* like other people here in New Orleans. They stole that truck, cleaned it out, and then dumped it somewhere way over by the Louisiana Superdome."

"I'm still not convinced," Matthew held firm.

"And why not?" Carl inquired, trying his best to win Matthew over.

"The theft of that truck was nothing more than a conventional commercial theft," Matthew reasoned. "Those uniforms will most likely be resold or provided to the black market."

"Someone might've wanted to gain full access around the airport," Ernest assumed.

"FBI agents and the New Orleans Police Department immediately notified airport and airline officials," Mattew pressed on. "The theft prompted additional security measures at New Orleans International Airport. Besides, employees already in uniforms must produce valid security passes to enter sensitive areas around the airport."

Carl barged back into the fiery debate. "I still have every reason to believe that we're being set up. Don't downplay the fact that some clever terrorist, or terrorists, as far as that matters, wanted someone dead on that plane."

Fontanello was the mastermind behind the hijacking of the uniform truck in order for his legion of thugs to be a part of the ground crew. How they were issued identification badges remained a mystery.

"I mentioned to you before, terrorists are people who operate more skillfully."

"Can't you also blame engine problems on the crash?" Carl hypothesized.

Bringing up matters to deter Matthew away from the ground crew was clever on his part.

The hazardous materials specialist stepped in once again. "The FAA and the NTSB have assumed that there were problems with the gearbox and mechanical problems with the engine."

"Prosecutor Silverstein, I think you need to speak with the grounds crew supervisor at the airport," Carl prompted, wanting justice right away.

"We'll be speaking with him and Chemi-Tech Aircraft Maintenance Company."

"And representatives from Local 1519," Carl requested.

"Yes, your Teamsters Union tied in with New Orleans International, too."

"Can we leave now?" Carl asked in a proper fashion.

It frustrated everyone to be in the constant company of a determined, yet bull-headed, Matthew Silverstein.

"Yes, you can leave now. Do you understand that you all have been placed on administrative leave without pay?"

"Unfortunately, but we should've been put on leave with pay," Carl defended.

"We'll be in touch with you men, Mr. Morrison."

Carl and his co-workers left the office in a single file formation. The disgruntled ground crewmen interpreted their leave without pay status as possibly facing jail time if Matthew Silverstein could convince a jury that they knowingly and willingly cost over a hundred people their lives.

Chapter 57

CARL MORRISON USUALLY carpooled with his crew back and forth out to the airport to conserve time and energy. Since all five men had shown up at the federal courthouse together, they crowded into a small mini-van about 20 yards away from the downtown office building. Three men climbed into the back while Carl and another co-worker got inside the front. An unmarked car sat across the street with Calabrese and Gagliano inside. Their faces were concealed by the wide dashboard and large circular steering wheel.

The skilled Chicago executioners sat discreetly with their sinister eyes attached to two New Orleans Mafiosos who stood across the street. All four men served in capacities best suited for their roles as killers from the Galluccio, Bernazzoli, and Fontanello crime families. Silencing those who knew too much. It was their only way of life.

"Time for all five of them to go bye-bye," Calabrese said to Gagliano.

"Five birds who never learned how to fly straight," Gagliano returned to Calabrese.

"The bosses wanted us to do the hit right in front of that office building."

"They're all in the car now," Gagliano said, everything set up to commit the murder.

"We better make our move right now."

"No better time than the present."

"Or the future."

The two Fontanello Mafiosos stood several yards away from the spacious downtown office building. One served in the capacity of the *"lookout man."* The other served in the capacity of the *"button man."* While the five grounds crew workers were meeting with Ernest and Matthew, an explosives expert snuck under their mini-van and planted a bomb to the center fuel tank. Carl turned the key to the ignition. He noticed problems with starting the van.

"I just had this fucking van fixed!" Carl griped before his four other constituents.

"Sounds like the carburetor," said his co-worker sitting in the front seat.

"Could be the starter," replied one of the co-workers from the backseat.

"Should've bought a Toyota or Nissan," Carl said, still irritated from the meeting.

"Why?" asked another co-worker from the backseat.

"Foreign cars are built better."

From 20 yards away, the lookout man signaled to the button man. The button man, being another 20 yards away from the van, smashed down on the remote control detonator with authority. Seconds later, a tremendous explosion erupted. Four of the five men were blasted through the front and back windshields, and through the doors on both sides. Carl, being the true unlucky one, was shot straight through the steel roof and down onto the hard concrete. Shards of metal and glass ripped through the air. Body parts shot across the street like bloody boomerangs.

People raced out of nearby office buildings in downtown New Orleans to spectate the catastrophic explosion. A bloodbath had ensued. Though badly wounded, only one of the five men remained alive. Screams of sympathy were heard from all around. Women and children who'd never seen such graphic violence were in awe.

People yelled out from every direction. "Somebody call the police! Somebody call an ambulance!"

"What in Heaven's name happened?" asked a woman from across the street.

"Everybody better stand back!" shouted a man who worked up the street.

"Why?" another woman asked.

"With that van on fire, it might blow up again."

A man who'd recently drove up, looked around and yelled, "My God, somebody blew these guys to bits and pieces!"

"For Heaven's sake!" howled some distraught woman. "I heard the explosion from inside that bar over there. Sounded like this entire block was blown up."

People could've puked after watching legs and arms and even a pair of scrotum all scattered across the ground. The streets and sidewalks were drenched with pools of blood.

People continued yelling and screaming, "Somebody call the police! Somebody call an ambulance!"

Long after the explosion erupted, Calabrese and Gagliano had drifted off. The button man and the lookout man were nowhere insight. Matthew Silverstein and Ernest Fletcher were afforded the comfort of not having to prove innocence or guilt with the five men they'd just met with inside the federal building office in downtown New Orleans. Carl Morrison and his four co-workers had to be silenced. Potential sources would've been snuffed out. Silencing those who knew too much. Traditionally, it became a code of violence for the Galluccio, Bernazzoli, and Fontanello crime families. For Carl and his fellow ground crew workers, they'd been silenced at the opportune time.

Chapter 58

THE AVOIDANCE OF THE air tragedy created quite a stir in the somewhat troubled life of Randy Rivera. Visions of the unfortunate catastrophe flashed often through his mind. He held a recent copy of the *Kansas City Times* to his face, which explained the full details about the New Orleans plane crash.

"The paper said flammable chemicals were stored in the cargo section of the plane," Randy made reference to Tracey. "But, I believe that something else happened to that plane."

"Like what?" Tracey asked, still trying to get Randy to open up.

"Remember the FBI agent killed several weeks ago in the *Westport District?*"

"Who can forget," Tracey confided. "That's all the news and the newspaper kept talking about here in Kansas City."

Randy swung his head sideways and nodded. "One of the witnesses who saw that FBI agent killed, and one of the detectives with the KCPD, a young woman assigned to that same homicide case, they were both on that plane."

"Where's all this leading to, Randy?"

"Do you know why that FBI agent was in Kansas City?"

"Yes, we've only talked about it a billion times!" Tracey huffed in exasperation.

"Investigating the Teamsters Union and the Mafia."

"Are you saying that they're behind that plane crashing down in New Orleans?"

"Not necessarily."

"Then, what are you saying?"

"Do you realize how powerful the Teamsters Union and the Mafia really are?"

"Sort of."

"Do you realize how powerful our U.S. Government is?"

"Very powerful, to say the least."

"Do you remember an old Kansas City gangster named Angelo Galluccio?"

"The name sort of rings a bell. Isn't he the same Mafia guy who'd been skimming all that money from those casinos out in Las Vegas? I believe he was nicknamed *The Animal.*"

"Him and some other Mafia guys from the midwest."

"Galluccio is an Italian name that sparks fear in everybody."

"Exactly!" Randy thumped. "I think after that investigation is done, they'll find that somebody sabotaged that plane."

"But why?"

"Possibly to get rid of somebody on that very plane."

"Are you saying a possible conspiracy?" Tracey asked, growing wearier by the minute.

"Of course."

"I can't say either way."

"Something strange happened to that TWA flight and I hope they find out."

"Thank God we came back to Kansas City all in one piece."

"It's been said that the Mafia and the U.S. Government can find clever ways to silence people who know too much," Randy said, himself almost the victim of a conspiracy.

"Are you saying that they probably wanted to silence someone on that plane?"

"You never know, Tracey."

"Maybe the truth will eventually come out."

"Maybe it will."

Once again, episodes from the gunning down of FBI Special Agent Wilfredo Feliciano in the *Westport District*, raced through the deranged mind of Randy. Gunshots and blood! People running and screaming! Cars swerving everywhere! All of this would weigh heavily on his mind.

"Randy?" Tracey called out, studying his blank face.

Randy wouldn't snap out of his daze.

"Tracey calling Randy!" Tracey shouted once more. "Please come in, Randy."

Randy snapped out of his trance and said, "Sorry about that, Tracey."

"I sure hope I can figure out what's got you acting so weird."

"Yeah, me too."

In the meantime, he dealt with the demons which haunted him about the shooting death of FBI Special Agent Feliciano.

Chapter 59

A POLICE MEMORIAL SERVICE for Brittany Suzanne Goldberg had been set aside by the Kansas City, Missouri Police Department. For those who wanted to come and pay their final respects to Brittany, Police Chief Meyer Kirkpatrick invited the public to the Kansas City Police Department's 1994 Law Enforcement Memorial Service. Not having a body inside of a casket for the public to view gave them a distorted sense of what the services were all about. In front of the Police Headquarters, in the heart of downtown Kansas City, Missouri, the name of the very first officer ever killed in the line of duty was read before a massive crowd.

Several of those waiting in the midst of the crowd knew Brittany was not killed in the line of duty. They knew she'd been having an affair with a married man. Some also knew she'd been killed on a TWA flight destined to return to Kansas City with the same married man. She died in the wrong fashion, but was honored in the correct fashion. Scotty's estranged wife, Nancy Borthwick, stood off in the far background with her blood boiling at levels steamier than a hotwater heater. Questions arose in her mind as to how the KCPD had the audacity to honor a liar, a manipulator, a schemer, and an adulterer.

Though Scotty had cheated on her with Brittany, Nancy wanted her husband honored as well. Scotty's parents, the distraught Borthwick couple, were flanked around Nancy with deep scowls stamped across their faces. They hadn't met the Goldberg couple, but were eager to do so during or after the honorary ceremony. Veteran dispatchers with the Police Department read subsequent names of fallen officers from up at a podium near the front steps to the downtown Police Headquarters.

Rows of colorfully-dressed honor guard members marched along the crowded street. Motorcycle officers followed behind wearing honorary colors. St. Michael's Pipe and Drum Corps pumped the adrenaline of the crowd by blowing into their pipes and beating on their drums. Chief Meyer Kirkpatrick moved up to the podium wearing a tailor-made gray suit designed by Miguel's Clothiers. Eyes and ears tuned in tightly to hear what he had to say.

"Citizens of Kansas City," Kirkpatrick spoke, his voice rather resourceful. "Citizens of Missouri and citizens of America. We are here today to pay our final respects to a very special officer, an officer who performed her duties with honesty, integrity, discipline, and respect. We are here to say a final farewell to Brittany Suzanne Goldberg, a humanitarian with a purpose, a philanthropist with a vision, and above all, a dear friend to those with no one to turn to."

Nancy Borthwick became fidgety as she listened to the speech Kirkpatrick gave. To her, his words were a mere collection of false innuendos. Red-faced, gritting teeth, and steam rushing out of her nostrils, indicated that it was hard for Nancy to listen to the Police Chief say things that he knew he didn't mean.

"The Police Chief is full of himself," Nancy professed, whispering among other attendees. "Why don't he just tell all these nice people the truth about their beloved homicide detective?"

More citizens poured into the streets around the Police Headquarters to pay farewell to Brittany.

"There's enough brainwashing of people around here to fill up an insane asylum," Nancy said, growing angrier by the second.

"Brittany was a friend to us all," Kirkpatrick continued. "She was our Brittany and we're going to miss her dearly. She gave freely to those in need and didn't ask for anything in return. Brittany made our streets safer while she served as a police officer, being a smart and fair officer to all the citizens of Kansas City. Not having her as a Kansas City police officer is a great loss to all other officers on the police force. As dispatchers, clerks, desk sergeants, and captains, we're truly sad about this terrible loss."

Don and Helen Goldberg were all smiles as they listened to the nice words being spoke about their only daughter. Nancy and the Borthwick couple were all frowns as they witnessed the phony Police Chief playing the role of an ass kissing puppet while he stood at the podium.

"We mourn the loss of Brittany Suzanne Goldberg," Kirkpatrick said with full allegiance. "In the wake of our mourning, we must honor one of the KCPD's finest officers to ever come on the force. Ladies and gentlemen, I present to you something which will remind us of the legacy of Brittany Suzanne Goldberg."

Kirkpatrick stepped over to a square-shaped figurine covered with a pure white sheet. He reached forward to snatch it off. A beautiful canvas painting of Brittany all decked out in her blue police uniform was unveiled before hundreds of attendees. To glance up at the mortal beauty showcased on a canvas masterpiece, only augmented the fury which burned deep inside of Nancy Borthwick. During the applaud phase, Nancy made aggressive moves towards the podium with her finger pointed right up at Chief Kirkpatrick.

"You're honoring a murderer!" Nancy shouted, breathing in heavy intervals. "My husband is dead because of that bitch!"

"Silence!" Kirkpatrick demanded. "Either you move away from this stage quietly, or I'm going to have you arrested immediately."

"You're honoring a liar, a fornicator, a schemer, an adulterer, and a manipulator."

"Zip up your lips!" Kirkpatrick shouted in fury.

"She doesn't deserve this fucking honor!" Nancy rumbled back.

"Are you on some type of medication?" Kirkpatrick asked an emotional Nancy.

"Listen to me, everybody!" Nancy yelled before the crowd. She refused to submit to Chief Kirkpatrick's orders. She knew she had rights as a taxpaying citizen. "She seduced my husband into going on a vacation trip down to Mardi Gras in New Orleans. Both of them were killed on that TWA plane coming back to Kansas City. Brittany only seduced married men, and she was also a crooked cop."

The crowd stood around in awe. Some found it entertaining listening to tirades dished out by Nancy. Talk about airing out people's dirty laundry in public. She aired out the laundry of a former detective buried deep in the depths of the New Orleans bayous.

"I'm warning you, young lady!" Kirkpatrick fizzled, coarse-voiced. "We're not going to let you ruin this special ceremony with your militant outbursts."

"Did you people know that Brittany was investigating the case which involved the killing of that FBI agent in the *Westport District*?" Nancy shouted, now really stirred up.

"You're way out of line!" Kirkpatrick shouted down at her.

"Did you people also know that one of the witnesses that Brittany and the FBI worked with was on that same plane which crashed around New Orleans?"

"Button up your lips!" Kirkpatrick insisted, moving away from the podium.

By now, Nancy was fired up. "Since the KCPD won't tell you all the truth, it's my civic duty to come forward with the facts. The plane that my husband was killed on was sabotaged. Brittany is responsible for everyone being killed on that plane."

Nancy slowly backed away from the stage. A sea of curious eyes watched her every step.

Chief Kirkpatrick growled and pointed down at Nancy. "One more word out of you, young lady, and I'm going to have one of these officers slap some handcuffs on you!"

Don Goldberg came forward and shouted before the crowd, "This woman is insane! She's on medication and she needs special psychiatric help."

Helen Goldberg moved right in front of her husband and declared, "Please excuse this young lady, everyone. She has deceived herself with nothing but false accusations."

People condensed into the crowd talked amongst themselves. Some didn't know what to believe or what not to believe.

"Nancy's not deceived," Joseph Borthwick spoke up, his voice a high falsetto. "She's my daughter-in-law and she knows what she's talking about. Yes, it's true that Brittany seduced my son Scotty and sweet-talked him into going on that trip to the Mardi Gras festivities down in New Orleans. Going on that trip cost my son his life, and my wife and I are still looking for some straight answers."

"My husband's right," Jane Borthwick said in her chirpy voice. "This young lady, this Brittany Goldberg, she lured our son out of town and tricked him into having an affair on our daughter-in-law. I have to ask the same question as Nancy. Why are you people here honoring a liar, a schemer, an adulterer, and a fornicator?"

Not a single muscle or nerve in the body of Kirkpatrick moved. He never could've imagined that the ceremony would switch gears over to a heated debate. Police officers and other law enforcement officials, along with members of the honor guard and the drum corps, had their jaws twisted and mouths wide open.

"Enough!" Don grumbled, shoving his way through the crowd of curious bystanders. "I refuse to stand here and allow you to humiliate our daughter in such a degrading fashion. Your son was no goddamn angel himself! In fact, he had been having multiple, extra-marital affairs on his wife."

"My husband's right," Helen blatantly imposed. "We can't blame one person no more than the next person. Both Scotty and Brittany were having an affair with one another. We all know that it takes two for that to happen. So, let's stop throwing stones at one another and cut through all this red tape."

Jane locked eyes with Helen and said, "It was told to my husband and I that your daughter was known as a master seducer."

Joseph locked eyes with Don and said, "From my understanding, your daughter tried manipulating my son into divorcing his wife."

"Brittany and Scotty being involved with one another was a mutual agreement," Don stressed, speaking very candidly. "Like my wife mentioned, both were guilty and we're still acknowledging that. When we were down in New Orleans, we offered our apologies to Scotty's wife, Nancy Borthwick, who just wants to fly off the handle at this ceremony for our daughter."

"We're apologizing to you, Mr. and Mrs. Borthwick," Helen appeased. "We're especially apologizing to you, Nancy, once again, for what happened between your husband and our daughter. We both have suffered great losses and now we must go on with our lives."

"All this bickering and badgering and arguing isn't going to bring either one of them back," Don rationed. "We can only pray for their souls to be taken into the care of the *Good Lord* above."

The honorary ceremony might've been the catalyst for the Goldberg's and the Borthwick's to make a truce between both families. Spitting out harsh words at one another brought forth confidential information which should've been exposed behind closed doors.

Chapter 60

KANSAS CITY, MISSOURI elected its first black mayor. African-American citizens celebrated jubilantly throughout the city. After nearly 150 years of Kansas City's existence, the midwestern city brought about innovations never before seen. Bernard Yarbrough was the new mayor's name. Tall and muscularly-built, he sported a thick mustache with sideburns trimmed to perfection. He always wore the finest tailor-made suits. Bernard owned several dry cleaners and barbeque joints he'd inherited from prior family generations. He promised his deceased father he'd make his way into politics, adding just a spark of prestige to the upscale Yarbrough name.

He received his education from Howard University, returning home after his master's degree to oversee the family businesses. His rise to local political prominence was hardly something Galluccio or Shellenberger feared. If given their choices, they'd annihilate every opportunity given to politicians like Yarbrough, despite the very walk of life they'd come from. No achievement he'd ever accomplished impressed them. Galluccio and Shellenberger could've cared less about trying to buy friendship inside city hall. They already had most of the city councilmen from every district in their hip pockets.

"Look at the smile on this nigger," Galluccio said as a spiteful commentary. He pointed to the new mayor standing near the polls after his landslide victory. "He's happier than a fat rat in an open cheese factory."

"Yarbrough's got a lot of history here," Shellenberger said. "Never thought they'd put him at the top of city hall."

"What history?" Galluccio asked.

"He quit the United Way several years back because he charged them with covert and institutionalized racism."

"That's his fucking problem."

"He called the K.C. School Board racist," Shellenberger brought forward. "He called Kansas City, Missouri more racist than Birmingham, Alabama, and Jackson, Mississippi."

"Just another ungrateful nigger trying to make waves," Galluccio said, his speech laced with strong racial overtones. "Can't satisfy those black coons for nothing in the fucking world. A nigger's going to be a nigger in the end."

"Worst of all, he called for some stupid investigation into the Kansas City Police Department."

"What investigation?"

"Like handling crime in black areas, brutality of blacks by white cops, the hiring of minorities, and the response times of white cops into inner-city neighborhoods. You name it, this nigger went through and tried to clean it up."

"Now, this uppity coon is stepping on the wrong toes," Galluccio said, his breath steamy. "You know, Shell, he may be the new mayor of Kansas City, but this nigger is going to play ball, or we'll get his country black ass booted right out of city hall."

"I agree, Tommy," Shellenberger said in conformity. "He'll be a puppet like all the rest of them that came before him. We can't afford to have a loose cannon running around up at city hall."

"Especially no nigger."

"No how, no way."

"A nigger like him should be glad that a bunch of honky tonk rednecks decided to let him slip through the cracks."

Shellenberger grunted as a gesture to gain the attention of Galluccio. "This Yarbrough character, he's the first mayor elected president of the Kansas City Board of Police Commissioners."

"Where'd you get this information from?" Galluccio questioned Shellenberger.

"Same place where I get all my other information from."

"Kirkpatrick has no power over this guy?"

"You need not worry, Tommy," Shellenberger said. "Kirkpatrick will meet with Yarbrough from time-to-time, but our coppers out on the streets know what role they have to play."

"Anything else I need to know?"

"Yarbrough plans to have the city audit the books," Shellenberger unveiled.

Galluccio's old fears of city hall taking complete control over policemen were rekindled.

"Shell, what can we do to stop this ambitious coon?" Galluccio asked Shellenberger.

"If Yarbrough gets too cocky with his position, city workers and city councilmen will start protesting, and then our backs will be against the wall."

"Why can't this jerkoff just be smart and run those cleaning businesses and barbeque joints that his old man left him?" Galluccio scourged. "We'll do whatever we have to do to stop him right in his tracks."

"Rumors are circulating that he's trying to indict some of our city union workers," Shellenberger demonstrated to his superior. "He'll do massive damage if he opposes the half-cent sales tax that's coming up on the next election ballot."

"Half-cent sales tax?" Galluccio asked.

"For the infrastructure throughout the city."

"Really, now?"

"Claims it will punish the poor."

"The poor have always been punished," Galluccio reasoned. "The poor don't count and they never will. I know that from not having two nickels to rub together. The way the government sees it, bless the *haves* and curse the *have nots*. Politicians feel that poor people deserve to be crushed into the grindstone."

"People who don't stand for something, they usually fall for anything."

Galluccio had sent Angela out to purchase a copy of the *New Orleans Times-Piscayne*. The bombing deaths of Carl Morrison and the other four airport groundsmen stirred up much controversy. Threatening to run to local Teamsters officials there in New Orleans had spurred Fontanello into the acceleration of their demise.

Ernest Fletcher ran around New Orleans like a wild man. He demanded answers from the Police Department. He wanted to know why the five men were blown to pieces shortly after their meeting inside Silverstein's office.

Headlining a fresh copy of the *New Orleans Times-Piscayne* was: **Mystery Surrounds Car Bombing Deaths of Airport Groundsmen**.

Suspicions arose among FBI agents, ATF agents, Federal Prosecutors, the FAA, and even the NTSB. After an extensive investigation, law enforcement didn't have a clue as to who could've planted the bomb under the car. Plotting the killings of rivals became an expertise of Fontanello and many of his New Orleans colleagues. Their thirst for power was never quenchable. Their hunger to grab control of the rackets closest to their disposal could never be satisfied.

"This New Orleans paper says that one of the groundsmen got his balls blown off," Galluccio said, followed by a quirky smile. "Some woman down there in New Orleans claims to have seen a pair of testicles lying in a puddle of blood."

"Some number that explosive did on those five groundsmen," Shellenberger whimsically added. "Wasn't nothing left of them nor that fucking van they were in."

"Guess the New Orleans cops won't have use for full body bags. That's just one less problem we'll have to deal with."

"Body parts were scattered all over the street."

Shellenberger developed stronger concerns about the newly-elected Mayor, Bernard Yarbrough. Since he functioned in major union capacities at the sufferance of Galluccio and the Bernazzoli Brothers, he felt obligated to safeguard the unions. With Kansas City, Chicago, and New Orleans having major connections, the Mafia bosses met sporadically to settle minor disputes which dealt with the unions. What went on down in New Orleans didn't spark too much of an interest with Shellenberger. Galluccio and Fontanello owed one another favors, promising wholeheartedly to rush to one another's rescue.

"Are you really worried about this Yarbrough coon, Shell?" Galluccio asked, one of his fat cigars meeting up with a bright match.

"Granted that he reforms city contracting, the unions will be hurt badly," Shellenberger thoroughly outlined. He took mini sips of his bourbon on the rocks.

"Either this nigger plays ball, or he'll never be heard from again," Galluccio threatened.

"Hold up a second, Tommy," Shellenberger signaled with his stiff arm. "We can't go after this guy no matter what happens."

"Says who?"

"He's got heightened police protection."

"For what?"

"He's been getting death threats every since the day he got elected. Some local Klansmen have burned crosses in his front yard."

"Kirkpatrick's on our payroll, and whatever needs to be done, it'll definitely get done."

"Kirkpatrick's under his jurisdiction."

"We'll figure out something."

Galluccio adjourned the meeting between he and Shellenberger.

Chapter 61

SHERRY WELCH GRIEVED night and day from the time she learned that her beloved sister perished as a passenger on TWA Flight number 2309. Both women served as valuable witnesses to the shooting death of FBI Special Agent Wilfredo Feliciano. The sisters came close to helping the FBI solve the mysterious murder. Sherry couldn't attend the special ceremony down in New Orleans for the over 100 victims due to the lack of funds and time off from her job.

Pulling out old photo albums and framed pictures were the lasting memories she had of her sister. The legacy of Sheila Bridgestone, though only recognized within the immediate family, would endure for generations to come. Sherry and their heartbroken mother, Beatrice Bridgestone, sat on the sofa flipping through old crinkly pages of a thick photo album.

"Look, Mom," Sherry said to Beatrice. She pointed to a large color photo. "This is Sheila and I when we were teenagers at Six Flaggs down in St. Louis."

"You two were having the time of your lives," Beatrice cherished, a flow of tears to follow.

"Remember this photo, Mom?"

"You and Sheila were at Silver Dollar City."

"We were having barrels of fun."

"You two did everything together."

"Laughed and cried together," Sherry relished. "Fought and played together."

"My darling little girl's gone now!" Beatrice wept, falling into the open arms of Sherry.

"It's going to be alright, Mom," Sherry said, speaking rather encouraging to her grieving mother. "Sheila called me when she was getting ready to leave for New Orleans. She told me that she felt she was being followed."

"By whom?"

"No one in particular," Sherry remembered. "She talked a little bit about that FBI agent being killed here in Kansas City."

"The one who was killed in the *Westport District*?"

"Yes, the Puerto Rican guy that the FBI sent to K.C. to investigate the Mafia."

"Investigate the Mafia?" Beatrice shrugged. "Investigate them for what?"

"Something that had to do with the Teamsters Union. Sheila told me she felt that the Mafia had something to do with him being killed."

"How?"

"Who knows, Mom? Sheila and I, along with other people, actually witnessed that FBI agent being killed. He walked out of Kelly's along with the rest of us."

"Aren't you still helping the FBI make sketches of the men who shot that agent?" Beatrice feared. She slammed the photo album shut and pulled Sherry closer.

"Only because they asked Sheila and I for our help."

"Be careful, Sherry," Beatrice warned. "The Mafia is still alive and well in Kansas City and everywhere else. There are still Mafiosos lingering around everywhere, milking us for every other dime that they can."

"Milking us? How?"

"The dope, the liquor, the gambling, the prostitution, not to mention all the people they've killed over the years."

"Bring this a little more into focus, Mom."

"I can't paint a clearer picture for you."

"You've still got me in the dark."

"Those Mafia men," Beatrice pointed out to Sherry. "Those bastards, those rotten sonofabitches, they've got a hand in everything legitimate and illegitimate. Whether it's right here in Kansas City, or whether it's in another city somewhere in America, they've frightened people into giving them whatever they want."

"Take whatever they want from whoever they want it from?"

"That's right."

"They're no worse or different than the government. They take whatever they want from the masses of people. I mean, look at all the taxes that we pay."

"Those people have control over car lots, garbage collection, bars, restaurants, insurance and real estate companies, the unions, and shopping centers."

"How do you know so much about the Mafia?" Sherry asked her mother.

"Who doesn't know who they are? Who doesn't know what they're about?"

Beatrice realized how the method of operation for organized crime and their strength depended upon the maintenance of monopolies through extortion or imposing the fear of violence. Their advantages over the competition were gained from undisclosed ownership of businesses.

"Remember the *River Quay Wars* that happened back in the 70s?" Sherry asked.

"Who could forget the *River Quay Wars*?" Beatrice recalled so well. "That part of town looked like a junkyard of wood and plaster and steel after those crazy Italians were done blowing up one another's businesses."

"It's makes you wonder if the *River Quay Wars* ever ended."

"That was the 70s, this is the 90s."

"Mom, the FBI and the KCPD aren't for sure if the Mafia had anything to do with that agent being killed down in the *Westport District*. They're saying that it was just a random street robbery."

"Let's say for instance if they did. Let's say for instance that the two men who shot him are connected with the Mafia."

"And, if they are?"

"Sweetheart, you and others might be in serious danger."

"I can't back out now, Mom," Sherry spoke out of bravery. "Those two men might go around killing more innocent people."

"Have you ever thought that you might be putting your own life on the line?"

"The men responsible for killing the FBI agent will be caught soon enough."

"Don't be so sure."

"The FBI and the KCPD only want to ask me and some other people a few more questions and we'll be done."

Sherry kept a diligent, yet determined attitude in helping solve the bizarre murder of FBI Special Agent Wilfredo Feliciano.

"Have you ever heard of Angelo Galluccio?" Beatrice asked, fear stirring up her nerves.

"The Mafioso who died in the Federal Penitentiary down in Springfield, Missouri?"

"Yes, the one they nicknamed *The Animal*."

"What about him?"

"Do you realize how dangerous of a man he was?" Beatrice questioned. "Do you realize that he could've snapped his finger and somebody was dead in Kansas City?"

"Why does any of that matter when he's dead?"

"I honestly believe that somebody is running the Galluccio Mafia family here in Kansas City. You don't hear about them like you did back in the 70s and 80s, but you can best believe that they're still around."

"Didn't the Galluccios skim lots of money from those casinos out in Las Vegas back in the day?"

"Robbed those Las Vegas casinos blind," Beatrice lectured to her daughter. "Kansas City became a secret goldmine here in the midwest."

"Mom, I'm not worried about a bunch of gangsters coming after me."

"We still don't know the truth about your sister dying in that plane crash down in New Orleans."

"As far as?"

"As far as why the plane really crashed."

"The flammable chemicals being stored underneath the plane is the reason why it caught fire and crashed into the New Orleans bayous."

"The air traffic controllers are saying that the pilot signaled for help because they were also experiencing mechanical problems."

"Now, people are saying that the plane might've been sabotaged."

"Something suspicious has been going on."

"Whaddaya mean?"

"You didn't hear about the men blamed for putting the boxes of flammable chemicals underneath the plane?"

"What happened to them?"

"All five of them were blown to pieces inside a mini-van in downtown New Orleans."

"Whoa!" Sherry squirmed. "Think it was someone related to one of the crash victims?"

"Possibly."

Sherry and Beatrice browsed through a series of newspapers to gain more knowledge about the TWA crash in a sister and daughter was lost.

Chapter 62

RANDY TURNED ON THE television to watch the immensely popular television crime show, *America's Most Wanted*. He only wished topics surrounding the notorious drug lords of Southern Florida, the kind of shows that *COPS* aired straight from Broward County in Fort Lauderdale, wouldn't dominate most of the program. John Walsh, the host of *America's Most Wanted*, congratulated the show's success on its 450th capture. The ugly mugs of infamous criminals moved across the center of the television screen. Randy was stretching across the plush leather sofa while nursing a sandwich and soft drink to keep him company.

Disgusting couldn't begin to describe the mass murderers, arsonists, extortionists, sexual predators, serial rapists, burglars, strong-armed robbers, child molesters and child abductors, con artists, thieves, and bank robbers. This raw puke earned their places in the criminal hall-of-fame. Many criminals were on the run and wanted by the law from all across America. Added to the show was a missing children's advisory, special alerts televised when pedophiles moved to certain areas, escapee alerts, and updates on criminals who were still at large. Bringing criminals to justice was their only task.

The sequence of stories showcased on *America's Most Wanted* went through its proper order.

John Walsh stepped closer to the camera and said, "On this particular broadcast, *America's Most Wanted* reaches back several months to help catch two men accused of one of the most senseless and gruesome crimes in Kansas City, Missouri history. FBI agents and the KCPD said that two men, suspected robbers from high-crime areas of Kansas City, systematically murdered FBI Special Agent Wilfredo Feliciano while he was leaving Kelly's in the historic *Westport District* of Kansas City."

"Tracey! Tracey!" Randy called out with urgency.

Nervous to the max, his heart could've blasted straight through his chest.

"I'm sleeping, Randy," Tracey moaned from inside the other room. "Besides, you need some television time to yourself."

"Come here, quickly!" Randy requested, still not able to contain himself.

"Tell me when I wake up."

"You won't believe what's on television."

"What?"

"The FBI agent who was killed in the *Westport District* the night that we were there."

Tracey threw the pillow away from her face. She came into the front room yawning. There, she saw Randy's eyes open wide and glued to the television set.

"The same night that we were in The Hurricane?" Tracey clearly reminisced.

"Yeah, the same night we got sweaty inside The Hurricane."

Randy watched the award-winning crime show in absolute fear. One secret he'd probably take to the grave was the actual witnessing of Agent Feliciano being murdered by the two gunmen who pumped several bullets into his slumbering body. The episode of the hotdog slipping from his hands and staining his clothes with mustard and ketchup, were forever etched into his memory. A crippling silence had created an engulfment around the room.

"Look Randy, they're showing the exact spot where the FBI agent was shot," Tracey pointed out, giving Randy a quick reminder of the horrific night.

Echoes of gunshots and people screaming rang out in his ears. Blood oozing from the bullet-riddled body of Agent Feliciano, with people running wildly through the streets of the *Westport District*, were flashed before his very eyes. The sounds of police squad cars, fire trucks, and ambulance sirens, they created a trembling through his body.

"Randy!" Tracey shouted, her voice quite squeaky.

She sprayed mists of saliva on the side of his face to get his attention.

Randy huddled over by the front door holding his chest. Sudden hotflashes caused beads of sweat to pop from his pores. Witnessing someone being shot repeatedly became unbearable for him.

"You okay?" Tracey asked, studying him up and down.

"Sure, sure, I'm okay," Randy responded in fright. He moved around Tracey and fell down on the sofa.

Tracey placed her soft hand across his lap. "Do you know something about that FBI agent getting killed?"

"No, I don't know anything about that," Randy denied.

"You're bullshitting me, Randy!" Tracey blabbed out, wanting him to just confess.

"No, no, Tracey, I'm not bullshitting with you."

"Then, why is it that everytime I mention something about him being killed, you act like you're getting chased by the *Boogey Man* or *King Kong* or *Godzilla*?"

"These murder stories, they scare the living donkeyshit out of me. They always have."

"If you saw something, then why don't you tell me about it?"

"Let's just forget about it."

"Thought we could talk about anything."

"Not people being killed," Randy objectified. "I've seen and heard about enough murders in one lifetime."

"When have you ever seen someone getting killed?" Tracey inquired, a young woman who possessed strong intrigue when it came to murder and mayhem.

"Growing up in Wayne Miner housing projects," Randy said inductively. "I was right there when guys got shot with .38 snub-nosed revolvers, .357 Magnums, .45 automatics, Nine Millimeters, and .22s. I watched guys being stabbed with hunting knives and butcher knives, some stabbed with screwdrivers and forks. I've stood aside and saw guys beat to death with baseball bats, boards, crowbars, pipes, and jackhammers."

The savages who terrorized the Wayne Miner neighborhood where Randy resided during his younger years, were the perpetrators of many killings, creating bloodbaths along the deadly streets in the north end of Kansas City.

"Thank God you didn't turn out to be no killer."

"Let's watch *America's Most Wanted*."

Randy and Tracey ceased their intense discussion. He turned up the volume to the television. Beyond unreasonable comprehension, Randy became a prisoner within his own heart and mind. John Walsh turned *America's Most Wanted* over to one of the show's main correspondents.

The correspondent stood live in the *Westport District*. The many patrons in the background had gone to and come from the restaurants and bars. As with any of their other shows, actors were hired to play out the actual dramatization of the crime which took place. *America's Most Wanted* were just as diligent about finding Feliciano's killers as the FBI and the KCPD.

The cameras rolled and the first actor to emerge onto the screen was a little known local Hispanic man with limited theatrical training. Some still considered Kansas City, Missouri, just some midwestern cowtown not known for much, with crime seeming to always make national headlines. Poverty remained a breeding ground for many of the inner-city neighborhoods which were disenfranchised. Generations of welfare, poor housing, poor education, and limited health care left an enduring legacy.

The correspondent, someone who'd narrated parts of the dramatization, sliced into the film clip by saying, "FBI Special Agent Wilfredo Feliciano worked out of the Organized Crime Section of the FBI's Criminal Investigative Division in Washington. Agent Feliciano came to Kansas City to gather documents for the ongoing federal investigations of links between organized crime and the midwestern Teamsters Union. Police have gotten lots of tips, but they have no great leads in the brutal slaying of Agent Feliciano."

The dramatization ran through its entirety. Now, the correspondent took the liberty of interviewing some of the people who were either investigating the case or those who witnessed the crime when it took place in the *Westport District*. The correspondent moved closer with his microphone and the camera crew for *America's Most Wanted*. Supervising Homicide Detective, Cyrus Manley, the tall, lanky, and bottle-necked veteran of the KCPD, agreed to an interview. Manley was a man who'd aged gracefully during his tenure in law enforcement.

"Detective Manley," the correspondent began. "Several months have passed since the shooting death of FBI Special Agent Wilfredo Feliciano. Do you have any leads, whatsoever, in this case?"

"Well, let's see," Manley politely hummed. "The FBI and the Kansas City Police Department's Homicide Unit have worked together by setting up command posts at the FBI's downtown office, and at the Police Headquarters building there in downtown."

"Any substantial evidence to help further along your investigation?"

"We've swarmed this area many times. We've interviewed hotel guests and business owners and residents in the *Westport District*. Evidence has been collected and our labs are busy around-the-clock to help piece things together."

"And what evidence would that be, Detective?"

"Cigarette butts, footprints, DNA, fingerprints, tire tracks, anything to link the two men to Agent Feliciano's murder."

"When you say tire tracks, could you be more specific?"

"Our homicide team believe that the two assailants fled on foot and rushed to a waiting car about 40 to 50 yards from where the shooting actually took place. We're still hoping to match those exact tracks with an automobile that is still in operation out on the streets of Kansas City."

"So, you're diligently pursuing all important leads?"

"Jointly, the FBI and the KCPD have a mutual interest in getting this murder solved."

"Now, *America's Most Wanted* has learned that law enforcement has rejected any notion that Agent Feliciano's murder was linked to his duties."

"First of all, killing Agent Feliciano isn't going to stop the government's investigation of the Teamsters Union alliance with organized crime," Manley made very clear. "Real organized crime members are aware that they don't want to get into a tight situation like that. U.S. Attorney's are fighting these men with every piece of arsenal they've got."

"Detective Manley, does organized crime still thrive in Kansas City?"

"Regardless of the name used, the fact remains that organized crime still exists in our Kansas City area. Local law enforcement is actively involved with the Citizen's Crime Commission, which is a privately-supported organization opposed to organized crime, racketeering, and corruption. We'd like to express our sincere gratitude to the law enforcement agencies and public officials who are supporting this effort."

"Sources have informed us that Agent Feliciano's killing could possibly be a throwback to the violent *River Quay Wars* here in Kansas City during the nineteen seventies. Detective, could you further elaborate on that?"

"When the *River Quay Wars* ended back in the late 1970s, that was the end of an era of unprecedented violence. There's been a changing of the guard when it comes to organized crime and the Teamsters. There's no hardboiled proof that Agent Feliciano's murder had anything to do with what happened during that time period."

"Thanks for your help, Detective Manley."

"My pleasure."

Randy and Tracey could barely move from the sofa. Both were live and present when the killing of Feliciano took place. Their eyes watched in amazement while the correspondent for *America's Most Wanted* continued to move around the *Westport District* and the city to interview others who were present.

"Know what I think, Randy?" Tracey said.

"What's on your mind, Tracey?" Randy said.

"The Mafia might've killed that FBI agent after all."

"No way, no how," Randy objected, his bony shoulders humped high.

"Do you know the power and influence they've got when it comes to taking people out?"

"I think a couple of thugs desperate for money killed him."

"He came here to Kansas City to investigate the Mafia."

"And?"

"Use your head," Tracey spoke with persistence. "I've heard stories about how they get other people to do their dirty work. They will kill people or make them disappear whenever they become a threat."

"My dear Tracey, everybody's in the Mafia, in some way or another," Randy clarified for his better half. "The President of the United States, governors, senators, congressmen, state representatives, city councilmen, they're all in the Mafia. Movie stars, movie directors, singers, dancers, football players, baseball players, basketball players, soccer players, and the boxers who climb into the ring to get their faces pounded into mush, they're all in the Mafia. Bigshot businessmen, flagrant businesswomen, pimps, whores, dope dealers, gamblers, extortioners, bank robbers, and porno pukebags, they're all in the Mafia. Let's face it, Tracey, everybody's a part of the Mafia, whether anyone admits it or not. Everybody's trying to get some piece of the pie, whether it be legal or illegal. That same pie is being sliced up and handed out all the time."

The room converted into an inquisitive silence.

"Wow!" Tracey exhaled, herself in awe. "How do you know all those things about the Mafia?"

"Reading books, looking at documentaries, watching news clippings, and listening to cops and sheriffs tell stories about those Mafia guys. Those Italians and Irish got off those boats during the immigration wave with one specific mission."

"What mission?"

"To fucking rob America blind!"

"With all the poor people out there, they've done a good job."

"If those mob guys can talk slick enough, and if they talk enough money, they usually get anything they want," Randy personified. "This whole system in the United States is far beyond being corrupt."

"I think we can all agree to that."

Randy and Tracey cuddled up to finish watching *America's Most Wanted*.

Chapter 63

FROM THE PRIVACY OF the exclusive *Pendergast Mansion*, Galluccio and Shellenberger had the volume on the widescreen television at a comfortable level. Both men listened closely to what the correspondent from *America's Most Wanted* had to say. It appeared he'd interviewed another witness who was present during the Feliciano killing. The witness was Sherry Welch. Sherry stood five-foot-four inches. She had clear, but milky-white skin painted with brown age spots. Her hair was sandy brown and flowed to the tip of her shoulders.

"Miss Welch, how well can you recall the shooting of FBI Agent Wilfredo Feliciano?" the correspondent asked.

"At first, my sister and I were coming out of Kelly's," Sherry briefly described. "The FBI agent was a few feet away from us. Then, all of a sudden, two men wearing dark clothing rushed up to him with guns in their hands and they started firing away."

"*America's Most Wanted* has learned that you got a good glimpse of these two men."

"Yes, my sister and I got a very good look at them."

A look of grimace outlined the face of Galluccio.

"We understand that you and your sister have helped the FBI and the KCPD add greater detail to the existing composite sketches."

"My sister died in a plane crash down in New Orleans," Sherry unexpectedly sobbed. An aura of sadness masked her bright pale face.

"We're very sorry to hear that, Miss Welch."

Had Sherry known that the same men responsible for bringing down the TWA flight which killed Sheila and Brittany, along with over a hundred others, she would've backed away from her efforts in helping police solve the mysterious murder.

"Your cooperation and honest citizenry is greatly appreciated, Miss Welch."

"Anything to help the police catch those men, sir."

"You're doing the right thing."

Was Sherry really doing the right thing? Was the correspondent trying to boost ratings for their popular crime show? Did Agent Feliciano mean anything to her personally? Sometimes it paid for people to keep their lips buttoned. During crises like these, keeping quiet meant a matter of life or death.

The correspondent now directed the attention of the millions of viewers who watched *America's Most Wanted* towards one more witness. This particular witness decided to come forward after watching countless local news stories and international headlines about the killing of Feliciano. Posing in front of the camera was a 22 year old college student who attended the University of Missouri-Kansas City. He majored in accounting and minored in marketing.

James Hines was his name. Medium in height and well-groomed, he was a young man who wore his hair champagne-tinted and parted to the side. Wild tattoos and body piercings gave him a distinctive look. Those who studied him knew he led an alternative type of lifestyle. Though James was gay, he still partied with notorious lesbians and a handful of straight women. Several of his gay lovers tagged along to make sure he didn't sway back into the straight lifestyle.

"Mr. Hines, what can you tell *America's Most Wanted* about that tragic night here in the *Westport District*?" the aggressive correspondent asked.

James cleared his throat in the gayest fashion and said, "Some of my friends from UMKC and I were going to and from the bars here in Westport. We decided to go inside Kelly's since a lot of other college students hang out in there."

"You and all of your friends?"

"Yes."

"Okay?"

James looked sicker than ever. Having full-blown AIDS, he ended up on the wrong side of eighty pounds and some small change. His face was sunk in with a skeletal appearance.

"Well, I was the first one to walk out of Kelly's," James continued. "Then, all of a sudden, I heard gunshots being fired off and looked around to see what was happening. Two men wearing all-black clothing with black skullcaps were running very fast across the street. I looked down the steps and saw the FBI agent holding his chest and stomach. My God, his blood made a big splatter all over the sidewalk!"

"Did you get a good look at the two assailants?"

"Very good look," James confidently verified. "Especially the man who took off running first."

"Knowing something is a lot better than knowing nothing at all," the correspondent reputed.

Eagerly, he wanted to bleed as much information out of James as possible. Journalists lived to heighten their blossoming careers.

"The next thing I knew, people were screaming, 'Call 911! Call the police! Call an ambulance!'"

"And, like Miss Welch, you've been working with FBI sketch artists in helping to put together composite sketches of Agent Feliciano's two killers?"

"Yes, I've been frequenting KCPD headquarters in downtown while police are asking questions about the men's identities. I won't stop working with the FBI and the KCPD until these men are caught."

"Thank you very much, Mr. Hines," the correspondent obliged. "Your efforts are greatly appreciated."

"Glad to have been of assistance."

James turned away displaying strong homosexual tendencies. A comical sight, indeed. A sweet woman's voice he had. He swurved with his hips set in motion. He gestured with feministic overtones. Millions of viewers who watched *America's Most Wanted* knew he was the "gayest of the gays."

Within the confines of the *Pendergast Mansion*, Galluccio and Shellenberger turned and stared at one another in disbelief. Galluccio pressed the mute button for open discussion purposes.

"Whaddaya think, Tommy?" Shellenberger asked Galluccio, sipping on a cocktail.

"That homo-faggot's got a voice sweeter than cotton candy drenched in melted sugar," Galluccio rallied, puffing on his favorite cigar.

"Another goddamn witness has come to the surface," Shellenberger had worried.

"Getting rid of that fruitcake shouldn't be a problem."

"What about the woman, the Sherry Welch chick?"

"We'll worry about her another time."

"There's no better time than the present."

"It's the punk-faggot that I'm concerned about," Galluccio said. "Shell, we both heard him tell the reporter that he wouldn't stop until somebody's caught. It's almost like he's taking this matter personally, like he wants to go out and arrest our men himself."

"What'd ya have in mind, Tommy?"

"It's time to call another meeting."

"Will we have to let Carmine and Mikey in on this meeting?"

"I think so."

Galluccio pressed the mute button to listen to the ending of the show.

In the final moments of his special assignment from Kansas City, Missouri, the veteran correspondent with *America's Most Wanted* reported back to the headquarters in Washington, D.C. "If anyone else who might have information in the shooting death of FBI Special Agent Wilfredo Feliciano, please contact us at: 1-800-CRIME-TV."

Silencing those who knew too much. It remained a part of their traditional spheres.

Chapter 64

ISOLATED FROM THE CRIME families of New York and other East Coast families, Galluccio and the Bernazzoli Brothers were used to playing by their own midwestern Mafia rules. The Bernazzoli Brothers and Eddie "The Elephant" Gargotta decided to pay Galluccio another visit at the *Pendergast Mansion* to discuss past and current business ventures. The trio flew in from Chicago on very short notice.

"The G-men are putting heat on the Teamsters guys back East," Galluccio virtuously spoke. "Carmine and Mikey, I respect you two men as the *capo di tutti capi* in this *thing of ours*. I respect you fully when it comes to the Teamsters, and your word is law when we're dealing with the unions."

"We've tried to restore loyalty to this *thing of ours*," Michael instituted. "It's been said that the bosses back East are catching all kinds'a hell. Shit, the government's throwing all of their top Teamsters dogs out of office."

"The rats do us in and we're left with the residue," Carmine attested. "Nowadays, you install some new guys in big Teamster's positions, you've gotta check them out real thoroughly."

Galluccio swallowed two strong drags from his juicy cigar. Before everyone's eyes, he flashed an old magazine. "Let me tell you men why I'm flashing this copy of *Time* magazine in front of you all. Part of an article talked about prison pay phones being legally tapped. The fucking feds blamed my Uncle Angie for directing killings from the prison in Springfield and trying to bribe the prison warden. Those nosy sonofabitches, they bugged the visitors room and indicted him for all kinds of different crimes. Everybody here knows about him going to the can for peeling off his share of profits from those casinos out in Las Vegas. My Uncle Angie, he'd roll over in his grave if he knew the trouble the unions tried giving us."

"Keep in mind, Tommy," Carmine broke in. "These aren't the old days anymore. Back in the 40s, 50s, 60s, and on into the late seventies, we could replenish ourselves with definable limits in terms of manpower."

"The government kicking us out of Vegas didn't stop no show," Galluccio boasted. "With old casinos coming down and new ones being built, we can still supply materials to the construction companies. Big union bucks come out of those building projects."

"Get this, Tommy," Gargotta said, his excessive body fat bouncing around the chair. "The G-men, those pricks are nothing but rats themselves. They claim that it's twilight for us, and they think that we don't know it's dark, and that the sun is slowly going down on us."

"Let's all stay true to the three rules from the oldtimers," Galluccio said, crushing out his cigar. Imperiously, he gazed around the table. "Our families have to take care of our territory. Let New York and the others take care of their territory."

Gargotta flipped his elephant neck forward and said, "Making money, exercising power, and minimizing bloodshed, that has kept us strong in this *thing of ours*."

"So, Eddie, I see you've remembered the three rules," Michael said.

"It's etched in my heart, Mikey."

"Good."

"It's how we've survived all these years."

"The unions are still our biggest concern," Carmine stated with impunity. "There are huge bucks still being made in bid rigs and contract allocations with the construction companies in our territory."

"We own the Teamsters," Michael bragged. "We always have, we always will."

"My ideals are still very close to that of my godfather," Galluccio elaborated.

"What ideals, Tommy?" Carmine asked.

"If any of these companies disobey the bidding rules, they'll find themselves with unexpected labor problems. Their construction supplies, especially the bulks of cement, will dry up quickly."

"We've already cornered drywall, sheet metal, lumber, and insulation," Michael added.

Galluccio appeared to have dominated the meeting. Still, his orders were handed down by the Bernazzoli Brothers. They were the unified strongarms and muscles of the midwest crime families. Carmine and Michael valued the expertise and input of Galluccio, certainly when it came to creating revenue for the powerful families.

"You're as ingenious as you look, Tommy," Carmine smiled. "This guy who's under our control in Chicago, Bobby Rampino, we put him in charge of the Cement and

Concrete Workers District Council. We made sure that he accepted big bucks in payoffs from a lot of those concrete firms in Chicago and Joliet and Oak Park."

The doorbell to the *Pendergast Mansion* sounded off with a loud ring. Galluccio and the Bernazzoli Brothers had expected Shellenberger, Provenzano, Randazzo, Calabrese, and Gagliano to be a part of their meeting.

"Angela!" Galluccio yelled with authority. "Could you please answer the door?"

"I'll get it, Mr. Galluccio!" Angela yelled back.

Angela appeared from the dim shadows of a private room Galluccio had picked out for her during his most private meetings. The room was designed to be soundproof. The windows were covered with black curtains. Privacy became an absolute must.

Galluccio had Angela under his complete control. Commands were given for her to come and go. Orders were enunciated for her to get up and to go to bed, to prepare his meals, wash and iron his clothes, and to make passionate love to him until fireworks shot straight from his ass. Conditionally, he rewarded her with generous sums of money and expensive gifts. The tradeoff couldn't have been sweeter for either party.

The men were received into the *Pendergast Mansion* by Angela with her usual warm smile and old world manners. Angela set up ice buckets and bottles of liquors on the table. She placed clean ashtrays before each of them. Within record time, platters of meats, crackers, fruits, and vegetables with assorted dips, were lined up at the center of the table. She disappeared back into the private room and closed the door.

"Tommy," Carmine said, positive connotations sure to follow. "You have one very beautiful housekeeper."

"Hired her over four years ago," Galluccio appeased. "Angela's a good girl. She keeps me feeling young and alive again. In case you don't know, Carmine, I love those young, blonde sweetie pies."

"Have you always trusted her working here in the Pendergast Mansion?" Mikey asked.

"Moreso than I trust those *black yard apes* and *greasy fence monkeys* working in my liquor stores. I wouldn't trust those niggers as far as I could see them. That's why I've got cameras and video recorders in all of my stores."

"Seems like you've always gotta keep your eyes on those dark people," Carmine attested.

"Shit, my godfather, Tom Pendergast, he had a colored maid working for him when he was still alive. She worked right here in this very mansion. His wife, Momma Pendergast, she loved that colored woman more than anything in the entire world. I trust colored women just a little more than I do those colored men."

Galluccio never wanted to venture off into issues about trusting black women or trusting black men inside the confines of his elaborate mansion. He arose from his seat and disappeared into the adjoining study room. He rolled out a 60 television with stereo sound. He slipped a videotape into the VCR while he reached for the remote. The same program, *America's Most Wanted*, which broadcasted the previous Saturday, was recorded on the very tape. Galluccio pressed the play button. The correspondent sent to Kansas City on special assignment shelled out information about the killing of FBI Special Agent Feliciano. James Hines, the valued witness who surfaced later in the investigation of Feliciano's murder, flashed his sunken face in front of a camera down in the *Westport District*.

Distinctively, Shellenberger studied the demographics of James as he made his own assessments. *James Hines. A white male. Gay. An honor student at the University of Missouri-Kansas City. Parties excessively in the Westport District. Has many gay lovers. Dying slowly of full-blown AIDS.*

While flashing across the bright television screen, Sherry Welch happened to be the first interview subject with the ambitious correspondent.

"Our problems with these goddamn witnesses just won't go away!" Galluccio barked out to his valued Mafia contemporaries. "We take this G-Man out, and the law's acting like the President of the United States got clipped."

"It's been the talk of Kansas City the last few months," Carmine had dreaded.

"We've worried ourselves up to our asses in trying to cover up the hit that we did on this G-Man," Michael edified, his concern greater than his brother's.

Carmine belted down a shot of straight bourbon and said, "We should've known that there were gonna be serious repercussions after we clipped Feliciano. We can't ignore the fact that the feds were gonna bite into everybody's ass looking for answers."

Shellenberger broke his silence. "I've got a plan that I think will help us get rid of the rest of our problems."

"Take out this Sherry Welch broad, just like we did her sister and the detective on that New Orleans plane?" Galluccio promptly suggested.

The plotting of fresh murders were always on their minds.

"No, no, Tommy," Shellenberger objected. "This Sherry chick, she turns up missing or dead, then we'll all be in hot shit. The government's really gonna come after us."

"Jesus, Shell!" Galluccio muzzled. "You're talking softer than medicated cotton. We should've gotten rid of this broad a long time ago."

"Suspicion's more like it, Tommy," Shellenberger respectfully corrected his boss. "The government will really start fucking with us if she just suddenly disappears or turns up dead. The heat will come down from all sides."

"Didn't we get rid of her sister without any suspicions coming back to bite us in the ass?" Galluccio asked, quite proud of their most recent murder.

"Sure we did."

"Don't we usually get rid of anybody who might open their mouths a little too wide?"

"Of course we do."

Provenzano and Randazzo turned to stare at one another. Discreetly, they nodded their heads. The atrocious crime in which they'd helped commit did enough to make Adolph Hitler or Napoleon have sympathy for all of mankind.

"Could you play that tape again?" Provenzano requested of Galluccio. His short memory span faded during the playing of the videotape.

"The whole hour long program?" Galluccio asked.

"Just the part where those news pricks showed the FBI composite sketches."

Galluccio reached for the remote and rewinded back to the closing of the *America's Most Wanted* program.

"Stop right there!" Provenzano commanded.

Thoroughly, he studied the sketches which depicted somewhat accurate descriptions of what the assailants who murdered Feliciano looked like.

"Those shithead FBI sketch artists need to go back to art school," Randazzo affixed. He giggled from all the defects added into the composites.

"Looks nothing like Bobby or me," Provenzano rejected.

"It's to all of our advantage," Galluccio said. "But, if those asslicking, good citizen motherfuckers keep coming out of the woodwork, those FBI artist pricks will eventually get those sketches right."

During a brief intermission of their meeting, every man present poured themselves fresh drinks. Everyone picked away at the meat and vegetable and cracker platters. Galluccio and the Bernazzoli Brothers fired up fresh cigars. The bosses gyrated in their seats in order to find a healthy comfort.

Shellenberger continued over to a more crucial part of the meeting. Being the shrewd Jewish gangster he was, his uncontrollable greed and lust for power was only second to his bosses. "I've got a plan on how we can get another one of those witnesses out of the way."

"Are you speaking of a certain witness that we just saw on *America's Most Wanted?*" Carmine questioned Shellenberger.

"Yes, I am."

"We're listening, Shell," Galluccio said.

"I've got a brilliant plan on how we can eliminate the faggot boy," Shellenberger assured his superiors.

"So, all the bases aren't covered like we thought?" Michael asked.

"For now, they aren't."

"How can we take out the 'queenie boy?'" Galluccio asked, his strongest concern still Sherry Welch. "The fairy-faggot whose voice is sweeter than any feminine woman."

"I have a very close friend who owns about 30 pharmacies throughout the tri-state area," Shellenberger disclosed, all ears very attentive.

"We don't understand, Shell," Carmine said.

"Yeah, we're totally lost here, Shell," Michael said.

"Let me finish," Shellenberger spoke, guzzling down a quick shot of chilled vodka.

"What does a pharmacist have to do with us getting rid of some faggot?" Galluccio asked.

Simultaneously, he took long drags off his cigar and swigs of his brandy on the rocks.

"The fruity-faggot, I found out some very vital information about him," Shellenberger made known.

"Anything that'll benefit us?" Provenzano cut in, firing up one of his fresh Newport 100's.

"The homosexual-gaylord has full-blown AIDS," Shellenberger released.

"From looking at the faggot on *America's Most Wanted*, he looks real sick, like he's ready to die any day now," Carmine noticed. "His face is sunk in like a skeleton, and his body looks like he's malnutritioned."

Galluccio spun his head around. He displayed his signature smile of absolute satisfaction. "Shell, you must be thinking what I'm thinking."

"I believe we are thinking the same thing," Shellenberger smiled back.

"How did this goddamn tinkerbell get full-blown AIDS in the first place?" Carmine asked.

"How else?" Michael giggled. "Getting butt-fucked by other tinkerbells."

"Never could understand how those homo-faggots would let other homo-faggots shove their hard cocks up their tender asses," Galluccio commented with harsh insensitivity. "AIDS is every bit of a curse on all those fruitcake-faggots out there."

"We can get rid of this sweetie peetie quickly," Shellenberger plotted.

"Give us the rundown on this pharmacy friend of your's," Carmine ordered.

Shellenberger explained himself in fine details. "My good friend, Nicholas Ballard, he owns 30 pharmacies throughout Missouri, Illinois, Kansas, Iowa and Nebraska. He's worth about 60 million in stocks, real estate, and unliquidated assets. Since this gay boy is on all types of medications for his AIDS, Nick is a master at misbranding, tampering, and adulterating those same medications."

"We wanna know his whole history," Michael demanded.

"James Hines is his name," Shellenberger abstractly disclosed. "He's a senior at UMKC majoring in accounting. He parties regularly down in Westport. He's on all types of medications for his AIDS. Three of his gay lovers have already died from having full-blown AIDS."

"From seeing him on *America's Most Wanted*, we can tell he's real sick," Galluccio examined. "But, we want to speed up his death process."

"He's due to go out of here any day now."

"The sooner, the better," Carmine had only wished. "We can see that his face is sunk in, and we can see his ribs poking out and meat falling off his bones."

Provenzano came back into the meeting. "Shell, how did you get access to all of this information?"

"Nick's pharmacies keep medical histories and records on all of their patients."

"How sweet of him to let you dip into those records," Michael said.

"Here's the plan," Shellenberger schemed. "Nick can provide doses that contain far less of the prescribed potency than what's needed for the faggot boy's AIDS treatment medications."

Gargotta cut into the discussion. "How does Nick plan on doing this?"

"This less potency stuff, will it get rid of our problem?" Michael asked.

"Nick can dilute the drugs rather thoroughly," Shellenberger continued to explain. "This will cause the AIDS to spread further through his body. His T-Cell count will be a total disaster. He'll be nothing but skin and bones, and before you know it, he'll be packed away in a pine box."

"Isn't someone supposed to check the work of the pharmacists?" Carmine wondered.

"The Food and Drug Administration is left with that job," Shellenberger said. "But, I wonder if they make sure that the manufacturers provide high-quality products?"

"Jesus, Shell!" Galluccio snoozed. "With all of this modern-day technology, these medical people have built-in checks to catch errors before they do all sorts of damage to sick people. I know that from my Uncle Angie dying at that federal hospital down in Springfield, all the medicine and how they monitored him around-the-clock."

"Didn't you have problems with those pricks neglecting Angelo?" Carmine asked.

"All sorts of problems, until we got on their asses."

"Lots of people who administer medical treatments don't have enough training to recognize when something goes wrong," Shellenberger continued. "The physicians prescribing the drugs don't have 100 percent assurances that they'll be filled correctly."

"Won't the gay boy ask questions about his AIDS treatments?" Michael asked. "Won't he notice crazy symptoms if the drugs aren't doing what they're supposed to be doing?"

"He'll be occupying a cooler inside the morgue before anyone can start asking questions," Shellenberger affirmed with confidence.

"Shell, we want more of a thorough outline of this drug-diluting plan," Galluccio insisted.

Not quite absorbed into the plan, which was considered unprecedented, unthinkable, and sheer simplicit, the bosses desired to proceed with caution.

"You have to trust me on this one, Tommy," Shellenberger said. "Nick has big clout with the Missouri State Board of Pharmacy and the American Pharmaceutical Association Foundation. His word is law with all the chief executives and researchers and other pharmacists."

"Keep breaking it down for us," Carmine found it interesting. He crushed out an old cigar and started a fresh one.

Shellenberger shot into the details with expertise. "From a medical standpoint, James is dying slowly by the day. If he doesn't get the potency out of those AIDS drugs, then he'll be checking out of here in a split heartbeat."

Michael rebounded by saying, "We want him to die quickly by the day."

Carmine jumped back in to say," We need time on our side, not on his side."

"And your pharmacy buddy, this Nick Ballard, he's confirmed all of this?" Galluccio needed to know.

Galluccio wondered if this unknown pharmaceutical expert exercised high honesty and ethical standards. If he didn't, it would've solely been to the advantage of their criminal organization.

"Nick Ballard's an expert at making things look like drug-dispensing errors."

"Must say, Shell, you've come up with an ingenious plan," Galluccio praised, reaching for a rolled turkey and cracker. "How soon do you plan on meeting with this guy?"

"Before the week is up."

"Another one of our problems seem to be out of the way. In time, we've got to do away with this Sherry Welch broad."

Provenzano gestured to his boss with a noticeable grunt. "Whaddaya have in mind, Tommy?"

"This broad's gotta be bumped off nice and easy," Galluccio thought.

The predator side of him, the animal side of him, the Mafioso side of him, was ready to put his plans into action.

"Anything specific?" Provenzano asked.

"Kill'er and make her body disappear."

"Bobby and I will do just that."

Shellenberger belted down the rest of his drink. He pushed his arm into the air. "Aren't we making our move a little too fast on this broad?"

"The longer she's alive, the more we've got to worry about," Galluccio greatly feared. "Next thing ya know, *Sixty Minutes*, *Geraldo Rivera*, *20/20*, *Oprah*, and *CNN*, along with the rest of those news people, they'll all be coming to Kansas City asking people more questions about Feliciano getting clipped."

"But, if their star witness ends up dead or disappearing, they'll really be coming after us," Shellenberger regarded.

"Not if her death looks accidental. Remember me telling you, Shell, no witnesses, no case, no problems to worry about."

"Let's hope not," Shellenberger said.

"After she's gone, we should be in the clear for sure," Galluccio said.

Carmine shot his erect arm into the air. "For the time being, let's worry about getting the fruitcake-faggot with full-blown AIDS out of the way."

"I agree with Carmine," Michael said.

"Don't worry, Shell, everything will fall in place."

At the request of Galluccio and the Bernazzoli Brothers, Provenzano and Randazzo remained lowkey. Lurking in the dark wings of the *Pendergast Mansion*, they plotted the fresh murder of James Hines. Once again, they had to silence those who knew too much.

Chapter 65

IMPORTANT MEDICAL INFORMATION on James Hines was taken out of the files by renowned pharmacist Nick Ballard. Nick had access to every patient's file and studied the history of their ailments. He possessed boyish good looks. He kept himself groomed and sharply-dressed. At the ripe age of 55, he had strands of gray hair with noticeable facial wrinkles. Secretly, he met with Shellenberger at one of his pharmaceutical offices in South Kansas City. There inside of a brown, brick building he worked in conjunction with the nearby Baptist Memorial Hospital. Already a self-made millionaire, Nick looked to make himself an even wealthier man.

As a crook with the skills to make money underhandedly, he never aroused suspicion among his pharmacist colleagues. No one, not even friends and family members, ever questioned how his sudden wealth had been accrued from being just a successful pharmacist. Shellenberger positioned himself in a leather recliner on the opposite side of Nick's desk. Inside the spacious office, the walls were covered with every award imaginable, from Presidential and Governor awards, and to those given by renowned pharmaceutical companies.

"Glad you could see me, Nick," Shellenberger said to Nick.

He moved around in the chair with those business-oriented eyes darting over to Nick.

"Always have time for you, Shell," Nick said, shuffling through a stack of important papers inside a large brown envelope.

"Again, run down the situation with the faggot boy to me."

"James Hines is a patient at a hospital where one of my pharmacy resides," Nick disclosed, drawing a thin stack of papers closer to his face.

"The same fruitcake student at UMKC with full-blown AIDS?" Shellenberger asked.

Nick explained James' medical history to Shellenberger in refined details. "James is currently on the AIDS drug AZT. He's currently dosing at 600 milligrams of this medication daily, right in conjunction with other antiretroviral agents. Doctors and researchers are now moving into injecting a naked DNA vaccine for HIV and AIDS. Once the naked DNA vaccine is injected, it's taken up by muscle tissues and by APCs. These APCs produce gag protein and it's then presented to the immune cells, communicating using chemicals called cytokines. These cytokines and the gag protein activate immune cells that kill infected cells and make antibodies."

"Urrrrrhhhhh!" Shellenberger gargled, his face wretched. "Nick, could you break it down a lot more clearer? You're sitting here trying to explain Chinese arithmetic or Japanese geometry to me."

"This very medication that I just explained to you, if the dose is significantly decreased, then this AIDS patient, James Hines, he'll be dying that much sooner."

"How do you plan on decreasing his dosage?"

"Simple," Nick smiled. "By altering the medication and tampering with the prescription."

"I'm no doctor," Shellenberger admitted. "But you're saying that with more infected cells and less AIDS fighting antibodies swimming around his body, he'll die that much sooner?"

"Precisely, my friend."

"Quite an ingenious plan."

"There'll be a significantly great decrease in his CD4 cells, which will contribute to a minimum suppression of viral replication, along with a minimum lowering of the amount of the virus in his body."

"Nick, you're a fucking genius! A two-bit Teamster boss like myself could've never thought of anything as brilliant as that."

There they were, two evil genuises devising a plan to accelerate the demise of an innocent gay man who'd been trying to obtain his bachelors degree in fine arts from the University of Missouri-Kansas City. Their insensitivity towards those infected with AIDS from all over the world was displayed immensely in their attitudes. Neither of the two cared how more than 40 million people worldwide were infected with either HIV or full-blown AIDS.

"Tell you what, Nick," Shellenberger said. "You're actually doing the world a favor."

"What favor?" Nick asked.

"This homosexual boy who attends UMKC needs to be taken out," Shellenberger spoke unfavorably, evil adrenaline having rushed through him. "Faggots like him don't need to be butt-fucking other faggots and spreading that goddamn disease to others. They're giving that nasty bullshit disease to heterosexual people who are innocent and don't indulge in that gay lifestyle."

"I'm with you 100 percent, Shell," Nick conformed. "If it was left up to me, I'd put all those sonofabitches on an island together and have it blown straight to hell."

"How long do you think it'll be before James checks out?"

"Give or take, a couple of weeks, maybe less time than that."

"Hopefully by then, the coppers and G-men will have ceased their investigations."

"They should."

"Nick, there are some things that concerns me."

"Go ahead, Shell, voice any of your concerns."

"I'm no doctor or pharmacist, but won't others start asking questions if they find out you're filling prescriptions for outpatient AIDS treatments?"

"Absolutely not!" Nick objected. "I've been out of pharmacy school for more than 30 years. At one time, outpatient treatments were restricted only to hospitals, but these services have now been entrusted to pharmacists like myself. The Missouri State Board of Pharmacy have given us liberties over the years."

"The state licensing boards," Shellenberger said.

"What about them?"

"Jesus, Nick, they're some nosy bastards. Remember, I deal with the unions that are connected with the pharmacies throughout the state."

"No need to worry, Shell," Nick spoke assuringly. "While I'm handling his AIDS medications inside the sterilized laboratories, I'll be inside a sanctum that only myself has access to."

"Like a one-person environment?"

"Exactly."

"Nick, we can't screw these plans up," Shellenberger warned his corrupt partner. "The sooner James checks out, the less worrying we'll have to do. The future of the Teamsters and all the unions are on the line. We're depending on you to help these plans not fall right through the cracks."

"Everything will stay on schedule."

Shellenberger never gave thought to how improperly filled prescriptions accounted for more than eight-thousand deaths a year, how there were too few pharmacists around to meet the growing demand for prescription medications. Nick Ballard was in the early stages of adding to those number of deaths.

"I told my bosses how you explained to me that tampering with his AIDS medications can be worse than him not getting the treatment at all," Shellenberger outlined. "Let's hope that I can prove to my bosses that you know what you're talking about."

"Most mistakes in pharmacies are systemic," Nick enlightened Shellenberger. "Lots of times phone-in prescriptions are greatly misunderstood, with a lot of those doctor's handwritings all screwed up. The resemblance of the names of the drugs cause a lot of confusion. The dim lights might cause someone working in the pharmacy to reach for the wrong bottle or vial on the shelf."

Shellenberger projected his mischevious eyes around the office. He slid his finger across his sealed lips.

Unprecedented thoughts of initiating more diabolical plans swam inside his head. "My bosses and I were talking things over before I decided to pay you a visit. We came up with a proposal that can make all of us very rich men."

Shellenberger was already rich. His bosses, notorious Chicago and Kansas City Mafia leaders, Carmine and Michael Bernazzoli and Tommy Galluccio, were richer beyond anyone's wildest dreams. Shellenberger interpreted to Nick that their criminal organization was made up of a bunch of greedy sonofabitches who wanted it all, men who refused to give their competitors a piece of the pie, maddog killers who'd win at all cost.

"Are you ready to do what it takes to go to the very top?" Shellenberger proposed to Nick.

"Whatever it takes, Shell, whatever it takes!" Nick answered, electricity having charged through his inner emotions.

"Well, my bosses and I outlined a plan that'll fill our coffers with mega-millions," Shellenberger illustrated. "What's the exact cost of the drugs they're using on the faggot boy?"

"The cost of the AZT or the ZDV drugs go for about 500 dollars for a full prescription."

"Wow, that's damn expensive!"

"Very expensive."

"I've always seen it as a license to steal."

"It doesn't take a brain surgeon to figure out that prescription drugs are sky high."

Shellenberger cleared his throat before words of trickery were discharged from his mouth. "Here's the exact plan that my bosses and I outlined that I think you'll tapdance over. We deal with the unions that handle the pharmaceutical supplies that go out to the pharmacists who are mainly here in the midwestern region. Now, aren't you buying those AIDS drugs in big bulks?"

"It's the only way to go since the supplies dry up quicker than evaporated water."

"Don't your pharmacies get it at a cheaper wholesale price?"

"Yes," Nick said. "Patients need those drugs more than ever before."

Shellenberger flashed a crafty smirk at Nick. "Like I asked you earlier, are you ready to become a much richer man?"

"Yes, I am!" Nick answered enthusiastically. "Whatever's required, Shell, I'm willing to go down the full stretch."

"About how much medicine are they giving the faggot boy?"

"James Hines is slamming down AZT and ZDV by the bottleful," Nick acquainted to Shellenberger, viewing the outlined medical chart of James Hines. "Due to his weight and the severity of his AIDS condition, he's taking enough to keep him alive."

"That's why you're going to make sure he'll be taking it by the handful, barely enough to not keep him alive. Isn't that right, Nick?"

"You're absolutely right, Shell."

"Alright, here's the proposal that my bosses and I came up with," Shellenberger said, his voice tainted with evil professionalism. "Let's say that you use four bottles of this AZT drug at 590 dollars a bottle. The total cost will run around 2400 bucks after taxes. You can turn around and use those same four bottles to give drugs to about six AIDS patients and bill each one of them for that solid 2400 bucks. This maxes out about six times as much money. In terms of dollars and cents, we're looking at maxing out some serious cash."

Nick jerked out the center drawer of his large oak desk. He brought out a solar panel calculator. He pressed a few numbers on the calculator and came up with a figure. "The total cost for six patients would run right at $14,400 dollars."

"Precisely!" Shellenberger acclaimed.

Nick pressed more numbers on the calculator. He came up with fresh figures. "This will produce at least six times as much money. We're looking at a $12,000 dollar profit. My God, Shell, we've stumbled upon a serious goldmine here."

"My bosses and I are willing to put up the initial investment for 30 percent of the split."

"Shell, you've got yourself a deal!" Nick cheered.

He grabbed Shellenberger by the hand and squeezed it tighter than any vice grip. It became just as much of a task for Shellenberger to protect the lifeline of the unions as it was for Galluccio and the Bernazzoli Brothers. Eliminating James Hines became the next challenge for the powerful crime families.

Nick Ballard wasted no time executing part of a plan which deepened his pockets with millions of more dollars, not caring about committing systematic genocide on thousands of innocent people. Silencing one man led to silencing thousands of others.

Chapter 66

THE WICKED PLAN DEVISED by Shellenberger and Nick worked out splendidly. The most devious medical pharmacist and Teamsters Union boss on the planet couldn't have dreamed up a plan such as theirs. Pharmaceutical salespersons sold AZT and ZDZ AIDS medications in huge quantities. The Galluccio and Bernazzoli crime families waited with patience for the accelerated demise of James Hines. With him eliminated, the only remainder who posed as a threat to their crime families was Sherry Welch. Thousands upon thousands of dollars lined the pockets of Galluccio and the Bernazzoli Brothers. A nice chunk of those thousands were peeled off to deepen the pockets of Nick Ballard.

The list of AIDS drugs that Nick misbranded, tampered with, and adulterated were endless. Innocent lives were lost as a result of sheer greed. Faultlessly, Shellenberger, Galluccio, and the Bernazzoli Brothers didn't care. As long as the unions were protected from potential bigmouths, with illegal earnings potential rolling in like boulders down a mountainside, the bosses were content. No one knew what hit them once patients started dying from unexplained complications. No one cared to keep track of the dosage those same patients were required to keep them alive.

James Hines showed up at the Harry S. Truman Medical Center with his blue card ready. He'd gone into the same blue clinic where the walls were covered with sky blue paint. Desperately, he'd been trying to get the federal government to pick up most of the tab for his AIDS treatment. He felt the government owed it to him since he was a full-time, seasonal employee with the Social Security Administration. The federal entity refused his request with impunity. Without crashing his feelings, they denied his claim as a patient, proving him to be an uninsured worker. One of the more familiar nurses pulled James' chart and reviewed his medical information since the last vist.

"How do you feel, Mr. Hines?" asked the courteous nurse.

She ran a ballpoint pen down the smooth paper.

"Been experiencing headaches, vomiting, dizziness, and drowsiness," James explained with drudgery in his voice.

He sat at the edge of the bed inside the examination room looking like a skeleton with pale, droopy skin.

"The other day I was vomiting and sweating more than I've ever done," James explained further to the nurse.

"Are you taking the medication as the doctor prescribed to you?" the nurse asked, reviewing his chart from the previous week.

"Ever since the doctor first prescribed it to me."

"So, you haven't missed any days?"

"Not a single one!" James replied with conviction.

"You surely haven't missed any of your appointments here at the clinic," the nurse said. Thoroughly, she scanned every important detail on his chart.

"Can't afford to."

"Any other possible adverse effects?" the nurse asked.

"Been waking up nauseated with my mouth feeling swollen."

"Alright, let's get your weight."

James stepped onto the scale. A frightening number gave his weight. The nurse nodded her head without him noticing.

"Have I gained or lost weight?" James asked the attentive nurse.

"Unfortunately, Mr. Hines, you've lost ten more pounds."

"Could you tell me what I'm down to now?"

"Seventy-five pounds."

"Isn't the medicine working at all?" James questioned, more worried than ever.

"The medicine the doctor's been prescribing to you is the most effective. Researchers have proven that patients live longer with the medicine you're taking."

Using the saddest expression possible, James looked at the nurse and said, "Nurse, I realize that I'm living every day with full-blown AIDS. Nobody with full-blown AIDS lives for too long. You don't have to tell me, but I know that I'll be checking out of here real soon."

"We're doing everything to keep you alive and healthy, Mr. Hines."

"I'm aware of that."

Standing over in a corner of the blue clinic with his face half-covered was Nick Ballard. Like a phantom lurking unnoticed, he tuned in tightly to the sensitive conversation between James and the nurse. Yes, James was dying quickly, and it was music to Nick's ears.

The nurse projected an optimistic smile at James and said, "I saw you on *America's Most Wanted* the other night."

"Cool!" James cheered.

"I recall them talking about the FBI agent killed in the *Westport District*."

"They interviewed me and another woman about the FBI agent being shot to death that night down in Westport."

"And you actually saw him being shot?"

"Sure did."

"What kind of experience was that for you?"

"Like seeing your worst nightmare being played out before your very eyes," James described, rather feminine voiced.

"Did they ever say why the two men shot him in the first place?"

"Police claimed it to be a random street robbery. Word on the street is that some people connected with the K.C. Mafia put a hit out on that FBI agent."

"A hit?" the nurse shrugged.

"That's the word out on the streets."

"The Mafia?"

"Yeah, like a contract to have somebody killed."

"But, I didn't think the Mafia was still around in Kansas City," the nurse begged to differ.

"The Mafia is still here, and they always will be."

"Didn't they get rid of the Galluccios after sending Angelo to jail for skimming all that money from those casinos out in Las Vegas?"

"Not hardly," James grunted. "They're still here, but they're a lot more lowkey nowadays."

"Question is, why would they put a hit out on an FBI agent?"

"From watching the news and reading the newspapers, supposedly the agent was here in Kansas City investigating the Teamsters Union's ties with the Mafia."

"You can't be serious!" the nurse crumbled.

"As serious as this AIDS that's eating away at my body," James bounced back.

"Then, aren't you afraid to have been seen on *America's Most Wanted?*"

"Afraid of what?"

"Helping the FBI catch the men who killed that agent. You never know who they're connected with."

"Not really. I figure that if they were gonna come after me, I'd be dead by now or would've disappeared."

"Didn't you say that that agent was here investigating the Teamsters and the Mafia?"

"Sure did."

"Remember the *River Quay Wars* back in the 1970s?"

"Vaguely. My parents often talked about the *River Quay Wars*."

"Well, the bombings in River Quay were about mobsters trying to see who was gonna control the Teamsters here in Kansas City. Those wars went on for a long time and they were quite destructive. The whole city was terrorized and people were afraid to travel to that part of town."

"Nurse, are you driving at something?"

"If that agent was here investigating the Teamsters and the Mafia, then the wars in River Quay probably never ended."

"Maybe not."

To Nick's advantage, the nurse nor James noticed him hidden over in the corner. Like a satellite picking up vital information, he construed every word they spoke.

"Alright, let's get your blood pressure and temperature."

James opened his sunken mouth and stretched out his arm. The nurse shoved a thermometer inside and wrapped a blood pressure cup around his arm.

She studied his arm and noticed how it looked almost like a broomstick. She studied his face and felt sympathy since he looked like a scarecrow. Both his temperature and blood pressure were high.

"Nurse, how's my blood pressure?" James asked.

She knew she dealt with a dying AIDS patient. "Way out of normal range."

"And my temperature?"

"Way too high, Mr. Hines."

"Can I tell you something, nurse?"

"Sure."

"Maybe it's true what they say about us homosexuals."

"Which is?"

"The wrath of God has come down on us."

"How's that?"

"Being gay has a price."

"What price?"

James shot a straightforward look at the nurse. "Catching HIV, then the disease turning into full-blown AIDS, was all in the name of butt-fucking another man."

"James, don't be so hard on yourself."

"It's true, nurse," James mumbled with bitterness. "God didn't mean for men to be butt-fucking other men. From what religious fanatics have told us, God meant for men and women to enjoy sex with one another. Popes, preachers, monks, and priests have said that a relationship should be between a man and a woman. But since the time I was ten years old, I've always liked other boys. When I became a man, it didn't stop there, because I started liking other men. I don't have much time left here on this Earth, but I'll die liking other men."

"One day, you're going on to a better place," the nurse said to pacify James.

"Do you think God's going to have homosexuals in Heaven?"

"That I can't answer."

The experienced registered nurse moved over to one of the bedside tables to pick up a sterile needle, a rubber tourniquet, and a rack filled with empty glass tubes. She ripped open a small packet of alcohol swabs. James rolled up his sleeve and she glided the swab across the vein which barely appeared at the middle of his right arm. The tourniquet was wrapped around his arm. Expertly, she punctured his vein with gentleness.

The nurse knew how AIDS patients were fragile and required tender loving care. The tubes were filled while labels were placed at the middle section. The lab technicians awaited the samples for testing. The nurse exited the room and one of the top physicians from the blue clinic closed the door. He observed James with eyes of sympathy. Clearly, he noticed his sunken face and thin body frame which scarcely held up his clothing. With his state of full-blown AIDS seeming to worsen, the physician offered optimism even in the midst of all hopelessness.

"Whaddaya say, Dr. Zimmerman?" James said, soft-spoken. He coughed and wiped moisture from the inner rims of his eyes.

Doctor David Zimmerman was his name, a 25 year veteran with the Harry S. Truman Medical Center. Dr. Zimmerman was tall, handsome, intelligent, and solid in body frame. He'd seen more AIDS patients before they made trips to the cemetery.

"Fine, James, doing just fine," Dr. Zimmerman obliged.

"Haven't been feeling all that great, Dr. Zimmerman. Like I told the nurse, seems like everything's striking me hard all at once."

"What type of discomforts have you been experiencing?"

"All type of things, doctor."

"Explain it to me."

"Those migrane headaches that make me wanna cry. Dizziness to the point where everything is blurry. Everytime I eat something, I vomit it right up. What's going on, doctor? I take the medication exactly as you prescribed."

"James, let me explain something to you, son," Dr. Zimmerman paused. "The medication and treatment that we prescribe to you isn't a cure for AIDS. They don't protect completely against other infections or complications."

"Sometimes, I feel as though I'm not taking any medication at all," James pleaded. "Really can't see any benefits from taking it."

Actually, James would've never seen any benefits from the AZT or the ZDV drugs if an evil genius like Nick Ballard had his way. Continuously, he tampered with and adulterated the medication. The wicked pharmacist made sure that the pharmacy where James went to get his prescriptions filled carried the medications he'd tampered with.

"I'll be checking with the clinical laboratory to specifically watch the level of your blood glucose, triglycerides, T-cells, and liver toxicity."

"Will they be able to tell you anything about my condition worsening?"

"Possibly," Dr. Zimmerman said. "There's something that I'm really concerned about, James."

"I'm listening, Dr. Zimmerman."

"Since you've been started on this therapy, there remains to be a detectable viral load and a CD4 cell decrease."

"What you're trying to tell me is that I'm about to catch that early morning train out of here real soon?"

"Don't count yourself out just yet, James. We're doing everything we can to keep you healthy."

Yes, James Hines was as good as dead somewhere in the near future. Dr. Zimmerman placed the stethoscope up to his chest. He placed a thermometer in his mouth and pulled out a blood pressure cup. Silencing those who knew too much. This was the primary goal of the Mafia. Galluccio and the Bernazzoli Brothers were closer to eliminating yet another witness. James' days on Earth were numbered.

Chapter 67

BOTTLE AFTER EVERY purposeful bottle, Nick Ballard continued to tamper with and misbrand medications which AIDS patients depended on to sustain their lives. A light tap sounded at the door of his laboratory. Nick knew who he'd been expecting and calmly said, "You may enter."

Shellenberger stepped into the lab wearing one of his favorite tailor-made suits. A refreshing glow wavered off his face, like he'd spent most of the day being pampered with a mesmerizing facial.

"You've made this place your second home," Shellenberger told Nick. "Bet your old lady and kids hardly even know who you are anymore."

"They'll be okay," Nick smiled at Shellenberger. "Business is business, and I'm sure they understand that by now. The boys are hardly ever at the house."

"Haven't you got that medication mixed up yet and ready to send out to those doctors?" Shellenberger asked with authority.

He came around the table to observe the tampering and misbranding process. Nothing more diabolical could've taken place inside one of Nick's laboratory.

"This shit takes time, Shell," Nick explained. "This substance is expensive, as you already know. I screw up one of these pills, and there goes a hundred bucks down the drain. You know we can't afford to let that happen, now can we?"

"You're right," Shellenberger agreed. "It's all about dollars and cents in this life."

"The good part, Shell, is that this process can be done in the same time that it takes to make a pitcher of Kool-aid."

Shellenberger unbuttoned his suitjacket and moved towards Nick. "Business looks as though it's steadily on the rise. Would you agree with that?"

"Soon, we'll be even richer men," Nick chuckled. "We're undercutting other pharmacist's costs by buying AIDS drugs in massive bulks."

"The faggot boy," Shellenberger said, his face in great suspense.

"What about him?"

"How much longer does he have?"

"He'll be fertilized under six feet of soil faster than we can blow a load of crusty boogers out of our noses."

"But Nick, the FBI and the KCPD are still showing up at his house asking questions," Shellenberger rectified. "I'm getting pressure from my bosses as to how I should handle this problem."

"Shell, everthing's under control. The gay boy was fucked up long before I started tampering with his AIDS medications. He's probably still butt-fucking or getting butt-fucked by his faggot-homo lovers. His CD4 cells are probably lower than the dirt under the Earth. When I was at the blue clinic, right there inside Truman Medical Center, I heard him tell the nurse and doctor that he's gotten much sicker. That's good news for all of us. Trust me, he'll be taking his last breath very, very soon."

"Let's hope you're right."

"There are thousands of consumer deaths every year," Nick enlightened Shellenberger, more corrupt dollar signs coating his eyes.

"Yes, I know."

"With him dying, it won't make any difference to other people with AIDS."

"Keep up the good work, Nick."

Shellenberger left the lab and Nick continued performing his evil acts. How many more people with AIDS had to die before he got caught? Money and greed ruled his world. Nothing stopped him and his associates from making lots more money. Collectively, they had easy access to enterprises that were off limits to others.

Chapter 68

WEEKS FOLLOWING HIS REGULAR AIDS treatments at the Harry S. Truman Medical Center, James suffered in agony at home. He gained the notion that his days left on Earth were short. Doctors did everything to preserve his health. Researchers dedicated weeks, months, and even years, in their effort to find a cure for the AIDS virus. They came up short every time. Was the AIDS virus truly this man-made disease that conspiracy-driven fanatics blamed the U.S. Government for? Was it about population control? Was it genocide? Some people were volatile. Others were logical. James blamed himself for the astronomical decline in his health, which seemed to have taken place at the speed of light. Questions about his medication caused him to develop excruciating migranes.

Have I been taking my medication every four to six hours by mouth?
Have I been taking my medicine with food to reduce stomach upset?
Have I been avoiding alcohol like the doctor told me?
Should I have notified the doctors when I missed the prescribed doses?
Why am I taking these fucking drugs? They're not helping me anyway!
Why am I having these weird side effects?
All this drowsiness and dizziness and constipation and vomiting is driving me up a fucking wall!

With James developing new and mysterious symptoms, the final hours of his life ticked away. Standing at a measly five-foot-eight inches, his weight dropped down to a frightening 70 pounds. He had become a walking skeleton. Everything which existed in his world was now lethargic. Tardily, he walked towards the phone inside his congested home on the west side of the Country Club Plaza.

His heart started beating faster than ever. His vision became blurred to the point of him not being able to identify objects. James pressed his bony face up to the number buttons on the phone in an attempt to call his mother. Janice Hines, who'd been worried sick about her only son, had no clue he'd been dying. James gained enough strength to dial her number and he waited for a response.

"Mother! Mother!" James scoffed twice, holding his chest, his breathing escalated.

"James, is that you?" Janice answered from the other end with fright.

"Need you to get here as soon as possible!" James pleaded, taking long and hard breaths.

"You're wheezing like you can't breathe."

"I'm seeing triple, mom, and my heart's beating like a crazy drum."

"Oh, no!"

"Mom, I think somebody tampered with my medicine."

"What makes you say that?"

"This time, I may have opened my mouth a little too wide."

"James, what're you talking about?"

"I can't explain it, but telling the FBI and the KCPD about the FBI Agent getting killed, might've gotten me into some serious trouble."

"Son, I don't know what you're talking about."

"Somebody, somewhere, they wanted to shut me up."

"Like who, son?"

"Like the people who had the agent killed."

"Stay right there, Jimmy. I'll get there as soon as I can."

"Mom, it'll probably be too late."

James stumbled backwards and crashed into an adjacent wall. His skeletal-like frame trembled across the hard floor. Thick yellow mucous was discharged from his thin nostrils. No oxygen got to his brain. His heart beat slower and slower. A light purplish coat spreaded across his face.

Janice yelled into phone. She cried and hoped James would respond. "Jimmy, what's wrong! Son, are you still there?"

The young, promising life of James Hines ended in his apartment. He was now stretched out across the floor with his yellow eyes wide open.

"Jimmy! Jimmy! Will you answer me, please!" Janice yelled again into the phone.

Little did Janice know that her son was no longer in the land of the living.

Chapter 69

INSIDE THE PLUSHLY DECORATED living room of the *Pendergast Mansion*, Galluccio and Shellenberger sat at opposite ends of an imported Italian leather sofa. Together, they read through the obituary section of the Sunday's edition of the *Kansas City Times*. Photos of James Hines were printed on the page. Galluccio fired up one of his favorite cigars. He swirled the melting ice cubes around the chilled glass of scotch. Shellenberger slammed down a mouthful of bourbon as he finished reading about the short-lived life of James Hines. What satisfaction it brought to both men knowing how another one of the FBI's most eager witnesses was now dead.

"The faggot boy, he was some kind of scholar," Shellenberger mentioned to Galluccio, reading about the many academic achievements of James Hines.

"What good would it do him now?" Galluccio said, whisking down the last shot of the scotch. "Let the homo-queenie butt-fuck somebody down in hell."

How cold could one person be? After all, Galluccio and his associates were indirectly responsible for James' murder.

"To think, Shell, we've come a long way since the 1977 *River Quay Wars*."

"I'd say that we've done damn good since the old River Quay days."

"Uncle Angie, he'd be proud of all of us."

"Yes, he would."

"The Teamsters is our baby. It'll be our baby for always."

Shellenberger shot an inquisitive stare over at Galluccio. "Tommy, what about this Sherry Welch broad? What're we gonna do about her?"

Galluccio knew their dirty work was far from being over.

"We'll have'ta find a way to take this broad out, too," Galluccio reasoned. "Just like we did with her sister and the detective, she'll never be heard from again."

The black hearts of Galluccio and Shellenberger could've cared less about killing Sherry Welch. In what fashion she would go, they weren't for certain at the moment.

Killing FBI Special Agent Wilfredo Feliciano wasn't enough. Killing Felix Harris and the Delaney Brothers weren't enough. Killing Sherry's sister, Sheila Bridgestone, and KCPD Homicide Detective, Brittany Goldberg, along with over a hundred others in the devastating TWA plane crash around New Orleans, weren't enough. Kill! Kill! Kill! For men of their calibre, killing became business as usual.

Galluccio turned to Shellenberger with his glass held up for a toast. With a mischevious grin, he said, "Shell, like my Uncle Angie once said, we own the Teamsters Union and all of Kansas City, Missouri."

"Yes we do, Tommy," Shellenberger agreed.

"River Quay, eat your fucking heart out."

It'd been nearly 20 years since his Uncle Angelo Galluccio made the very same comment. Galluccio shoved the obituary section to the side and retired to the den with Shellenberger. Silencing those who knew too much. It was a mainstay in their traditional spheres. The vicious network of Kansas City and Chicago killers were ready to plot their next killing.

About the Author

Dewey Reynolds was born in 1964 in an impoverished and crime-infested section of Kansas City, Missouri which came to be known as *"Devil's Playground"*. He spent several years reading books, reviewing magazines, researching newspaper articles, and studying countless video documentaries. After interviewing several FBI agents and U. S. Attorneys, and talking personally with two former made members of a Chicago and a Kansas City Mafia family, he became inspired to write a very powerful, provocative, controversial, chilling, and riveting novel that keeps readers on the edge of their seats. He also made a guest appearance on the former nationally-syndicated daytime talk show, *"The Sally Jessy Raphael Show"*, to speak about his horrific experiences in foster care. Kansas City, Missouri is where he currently makes his home.